SILVER and SALT

BY THE SAME AUTHOR

Every Contact Leaves A Trace

SILVER and SALT

ELANOR DYMOTT

W. W. NORTON & COMPANY
INDEPENDENT PUBLISHERS SINCE 1923
NEW YORK | LONDON

For information about permission to reproduce selections from this book,
write to Permissions, W. W. Norton & Company, Inc.,
500 Fifth Avenue, New York, NY 10110

For information about special discounts for bulk purchases, please contact
W. W. Norton Special Sales at specialsales@wwnorton.com or 800-233-4830

Manufacturing by LSC Communications Harrisonburg
Book design by Fearn Cutler de Vicq
Production manager: Louise Mattarelliano

ISBN 978-0-393-23976-8

W. W. Norton & Company, Inc.
500 Fifth Avenue, New York, N.Y. 10110
www.wwnorton.com

W. W. Norton & Company Ltd.
15 Carlisle Street, London W1D 3BS

1 2 3 4 5 6 7 8 9 0

CONTENTS

CONTENTS

And she is with me: years roll, I shall change,

But change can touch her not.

— ROBERT BROWNING

1 SUNDAY

Ruthie sits on the upper veranda of a villa, holding a pair of binoculars to her face. She is watching a little girl some way away, on the sun terrace of a smaller house.

The girl is wearing shorts and a T-shirt and lace-up trainers. Her hair falls in two plaits. She has pulled her chair up to the table and is swinging her legs. Bent over a book, she alternately chews on a pencil, or one of her plaits.

A man comes out of the house and hands the girl a red sun hat. She puts it on the table and he hands it to her again. She puts it down and he picks it up and tries to put it on her head. When she stops struggling, he goes in and she returns to her book.

The villa is on a promontory at the end of a series of olive groves. Beginning as far back as the foothills of the Taygetus, the groves straggle and slip through layers and terraces, giving way to clutches of pines and cypress trees and outcrops of rock falling steeply to the water. The veranda is wrapped around the first floor of the villa, which lies flat and almost hidden and is faded to an all-over ancient orangey-brown.

The boundary wall is punctuated by iron-bar gates. Inside, a path from the courtyard winds towards the sea. To the left are the steps to the villa's own cove; to the right is a small oval meadow, where the grass is yellow-white, and tall as a child.

After the meadow, the path drops further, twisting back and forth to a second cove.

Ruthie has come in from a swim and has nothing on under her dress. Cut from yellow cotton, the dress stops at the tops of her thighs. She is childishly thin. Her skin is the colour of mud, and her toenails a deep, dark red. Her hair is roughly cropped and boyish. Stiff with salt, it stands from her head or is slicked flat.

Once or twice she puts down her binoculars and sips a glass of water. Occasionally she turns and glances back into the villa. Otherwise, her gaze is trained on the girl.

The smaller house and its twin are halfway between the villa and the hills behind. A wooden post stands between the houses, so a laundry line can run from either terrace. They are otherwise separated by a newly laid footpath, an agave plant as wide as a car, and a fig tree, massive with fruit.

The violation of the grove, which is how Ruthie regards the construction of the stone houses, was something she agreed to only when her older sister, Vinny, explained they'd provide a steady income.

Still, she feels the intrusion as a physical pain.

In her childhood there was Eleni, the villa's housekeeper, and Eleni's brother, Ilías. There were her parents, and her aunt sometimes visited. Now, though, of her immediate family, only she and Vinny are left, and apart from Eleni and Ilías, no one else comes to the grove.

Eleni cleans the stone houses and tends the plants that grow around them. She's slightly stooped, and is often tired, but won't give up her work. How could she, she tells Vinny: it has been her life these forty years, since Ruthie was an infant and the villa first built.

Every evening, she walks to the tiny chapel in the grove. Closing the door behind her, she lights a candle for her husband. Because they had no children of their own, Eleni gave his tools and his ladders to her brother. Laying blankets under the trees for a fortnight in the autumn, Ilías combs down the olives with a three-pronged stick, and Eleni helps to gather them. Long summer days, sitting by the fountain in the courtyard, she unfolds the blankets and mends them.

When Ruthie was a child and had been stung by a jellyfish, or had hurt herself on the rocks at the water's edge or by running too fast in the Viros Gorge, or if there was a day when she and Vinny had misbehaved and been banned from swimming, she would listen to Eleni speaking softly and explaining that pain passes, and that although not everything is as she wants it to be, difficulties that seem insurmountable will soon be a distant memory.

These last months, Ruthie has wished Eleni would speak in the same way. But she is quieter than she was, and Ruthie no longer feels able to turn to her.

The girl and her family have been to the small supermarket in town. They have eaten lunch on their terrace. Now it is late afternoon and they have all gone inside.

All of them, that is, apart from one.

The little girl's plaits fall from under the red sun hat. She writes something in her book, then she sits back from the table and looks towards Ruthie, who, despite being quite hidden, takes the binoculars from her face. When the girl looks away, Ruthie puts them up again.

She reminds herself that this sense she has of the two of them being very close to one another is no more than a trick of the light.

A swallowtail drops out of the sky and dive-bombs the girl, almost touching her face so she flings herself back and her hat flies from her head. Jumping off the terrace, she chases the butterfly. Then she stands with both hands raised, tracing its path. When it disappears, she swings round to face the villa, and Ruthie feels stared at.

She knows, though, that the girl can't see her. She stood in the same place herself once, staying out of her father's way, and is sure that the angle of the sun at this hour means there's no sightline.

The girl lowers her hands. She goes to the stone house and calls out. When no one appears, she goes to the second stone house and stares at the shutters. Stepping onto the terrace she tries the door, then she rests her back against it and pushes. When she's done this again, she turns and kicks at it, then she leaves the terrace.

There is a raised-up trough in front of her, with a giant rosemary bush. She lies in the dust and snakes in front of it.

She stands up and takes a step backwards. She carries on doing this, walking away from the houses in reverse, until she turns and runs. Pausing behind trees, she flips her head back so her plaits jump and fall.

Ruthie takes the binoculars from her face, and frowns. When she puts them back, the girl is still tracing her patterns around the grove and Ruthie half hears an echo from the past.

The girl looks at her wristwatch and counts with her fingers, then there's a call from the house and the echo is silenced.

'Annie! Edward! Dinner!'

The girl darts behind a tree. A white kitten appears. The girl emerges and reaches out her hand and the kitten licks it. She tumbles with the kitten so the dust rises and hangs in the air, a golden aureole with a child and a kitten at its midpoint.

When a man's voice calls, the girl freezes. The kitten bites one of her plaits.

The name 'Edward' is called twice more and a boy appears. He is older than the girl, perhaps by three or four years, and Ruthie concludes that they must be brother and sister.

Edward stares at his sister, who does not appear to notice him, then he goes into the house.

Ruthie watches Annie.

The child is lying in the dust with her eyes shut. The kitten is draped on her stomach like a white silk handkerchief.

A half-minute passes, and the man who gave Annie her sun hat appears from the house. Annie jumps up, then they go in and the door bangs shut.

On the veranda, Ruthie's breathing is shallow.

She watches the kitten chase a butterfly. When it's over, she takes the binoculars from her face and goes into the villa.

The lamp on the veranda is out.

The water hardly shifts in the cove and the alarm of the cicadas is muffled. The earth creaks as it cools and once there is the soft thud of an olive falling, so that the kitten, curled under the terrace of the first stone house, twitches in its sleep.

Beyond the boundary wall, a path leads from the villa to the chapel, which is painted white and has the proportions of a large cupboard. Its wooden door gives out the day's warmth, but inside, the air is cool. An oil lamp flickers, lending a soft light. A packet of incense sticks is half open, and the scent lingers. On the altar is a bottle of wine, a glass not quite empty, and a new candle, burning.

Behind all these things, staring from the shadows, is a pair of human eyes.

The eyes are set in a face only just bigger than life-sized. The wall that the face is painted on is infirm, but the image itself has been reworked, sealing the cracks in the plaster and rendering the features clear. There are bright blues and ochre with bursts of burnt

5

gold. The face is tilted forwards, its eyelids heavy and its mouth falling open.

The door frame has strips of cloth tacked around it for the winter draughts, so that anyone wanting to shut the door properly would have to place both hands to it, and push.

Doing so, they would feel an indentation at the centre which would reveal itself, on closer probing, to be a tiny circular hole.

Outside the chapel, the moon is bright, and things in the grove are luminous.

The night-stillness is broken only once.

The incursion's sole witness is Ruthie, who is in the courtyard when she thinks she sees a child hurl herself at the boundary wall and, finding it too tall for scaling, slip between the bars of the gate.

There is the sound of footsteps further off in the grove, of someone running in circles, disoriented. The footsteps grow louder and a man goes past the gate, first one way then the other. When he stumbles, he draws his hand across the iron bars and Ruthie sees his fingers clearly.

The girl tiptoes to the fountain.

Ruthie wants to go to her and comfort her, but when she tries to take the first step, she can't. Instead, she moves back into the shadows and continues to watch.

The girl is trembling. She goes to the gate, and waits.

There is silence.

She waits a little longer then she steps through the bars, so easily it is as though she was never there.

Ruthie comes from the shadows. At the gate she sees the girl's nightdress, a blur of white disappearing through the trees, and she hears the footsteps again, faster and louder.

The courtyard is empty.

The villa, silent, is in darkness.

On the first floor, right at the end of a corridor, is a bedroom.

Slatted wooden doors open onto a veranda facing the sea, and the room is furnished sparely. A double bed stands just back from the veranda doors, so that anyone in it would be able to see the tips of the trees and, beyond them, the sea. Tonight the water is lit by the moon, as though someone has sprinkled shattered glass on its surface.

Vinny is in the middle of the bed. She is lying on her stomach under a sheet, her plump arms sprawled and her legs splayed. The room is still except for a gecko, flitting back and forth on the ceiling.

There is a knock on the door.

A moment later there's another.

'Do you really have to?' Vinny calls out. 'I was asleep. Actually I'm still asleep. I'm talking to you in my sleep.'

'Yes.' Ruthie opens the door. 'Yes. I really have to.' She sits on the bed. 'Vee,' she says. 'Vinny.' She places her hand on her sister's shoulder. 'Wake up. I want to tell you something.'

Finally Vinny holds the sheet up. 'Inside or out?'

'Inside,' Ruthie says, climbing under it.

'Front or back?' Vinny murmurs.

'Back.'

Ruthie turns her body away. Vinny nuzzles her face into her sister's neck, and wraps herself around her. 'What?' she whispers. 'What's the matter?'

When their breathing has synchronised and Ruthie can no longer distinguish between their heartbeats, she speaks.

'There was a child in our courtyard. I saw a child there, standing by the fountain.'

One summer night a long time ago, Ruthie ran through the grove from her father.

Now, in bed with Vinny, she believes she's told the truth: there was a child in the courtyard.

Instead, what she saw was a memory, as clear as though projected on a screen.

Since it would have been unbearable to have lived with it all this time, her mind had hidden it away.

But then Annie had traced her patterns and there was the memory's double, as though a mirror was held to the past.

Over the course of what remains of Annie's holiday, a number of such incidents will occur. Each time the mirror is held up, what's begun as a hairline crack will grow a little wider.

On the last evening, Eleni will go to the chapel to light her candle.

When she returns to the villa and tells Vinny what she has found there, Vinny doesn't understand, and makes her say it again. She still can't comprehend, not until she goes and sees it for herself.

In the oil lamp's half-light, with Eleni by her side, she will stand and stare.

When she is ready, she touches Ruthie's face, and lowers her own face to it.

'Oh my darling,' she whispers. 'Oh my beautiful girl, what have you done?'

For a long time Vinny will look for answers, and try to construct a sequence of events which could have led to what happened that night in the chapel.

Going further back, she will travel through the years, to her and Ruthie's childhood.

Once or twice she comes close but turns away, not wanting to know.

Through it all, there's a question she will ask herself more than any other: was it an accident, or had her sister intended it?

2 MAX AND SOPHIE

In March 1959, Max was sent by the editor of *Vogue* to Sadler's Wells for an afternoon shoot: the company rehearsing, and Joan Hammond in her dressing room as Rusalka, ahead of the evening performance. When he returned with a folder of prints of the 1st wood-sprite, his editor, Audrey Withers, rejected him.

'Look at them again,' Max said. 'She's incredibly beautiful.'

'Incredibly beautiful she may be, but she's sure as hell not Joan Hammond. I pulled a lot of strings to get you into that dressing room. Do you even know the girl's name?'

'Sophie.'

'Sophie who?'

'I'll find out. It's a detail.'

'Forget it.'

'Come on! The voice not yet heard? This gorgeous, undiscovered girl, waiting to be found?'

'The girl you want to get into bed this weekend, you mean? Poor little Sophie What's-her-name. Let's hope she's got the wherewithal to see through the Hollingbourne charm. You can't just come in here grinning like a schoolboy and expect everything to be alright. It's a cheap stunt, and I'm not paying. Cheerio, Max. Close the door behind you.'

'Hello,' Sophie had said in the rehearsal room. 'Are you here to do my photograph?'

'Miss Hammond, I presume?' He took her hand and kissed it. When she smiled at his joke, and loosened her hair so it tumbled to her waist, dark red and bright, he began to shoot. She was serious under his instruction and did what she was told. Turning to glance over her shoulder, letting him come in close and letting him touch her: once at the base of her neck to tilt her head; then her hand again, to place it on her hip.

'Are you always so obedient?' he asked.

'It's the first rule,' she smiled up at him. 'Don't you know anything?'

'The first rule of what?'

'Improvisation. Once it's started you can't say no.'

'And the second?'

'That's it,' she said, watching the orchestra take their places. 'That's the only rule I know.'

He developed the prints later that afternoon. After he'd been dropped by his editor, he kept the farewell promise he'd made, driving up Rosebery Avenue to find Sophie had kept hers also.

At the stage door he wound down his window.

'Dinner?'

'Yes,' she said. 'But hurry up, I'm famished.'

He parked on Camden Passage. Neither of them said another word until they were at their table at the Portofino.

The only thing he consulted her on was the wine. The waiter left, and Sophie raised her eyebrows.

'Something's wrong?' Max asked.

'People tend to assume I'm interested in what I eat, that's all. We French have views about our food.'

'Well, there it is. Didn't catch it in your accent. Wouldn't have chosen Italian, if you'd said. Where in France?'

'Don't be like that!' She smiled. 'Nice, which isn't so far away. Same sea, anyway. And I'm only half-French so I'll let you off. I'm an opera singer, remember. It's my job to slip between tongues.'

She objected only to the oysters.

'They made me sick the first time.'

'That's a myth, surely.'

'You think so?'

'Well, yes, since you ask. I do!'

'Shall I eat one and show you what happens?'

'No, no. No need. Sorry.'

There were several silences. He looked at her face or her hair, his eyes lingering on her neck. Then he asked again about her English, and whether all opera singers were so meticulous.

'My mother spoke only English with me. She said I had to sound like an Englishwoman in case I ever needed to. The French was up to my father. So it was easy to be either.'

'Never both at once?'

'Never. And you?' she said. 'Are you completely English?'

'As English as they come.'

He spoke a little of his childhood then, of him and his older sister, Beatrice, spending half their holidays in Hampstead with their mother in a tall red-brick house on Pilgrim's Lane, and the other half in Kent with their father, at Pennerton.

'They're divorced?'

'Yes. Were, rather. Couple of years before the end of the war. Then they died. It was later, though, when Bea and I were older.'

Sophie lowered her eyes then she said, 'Mine as well. I mean, apart from my father. I mean – they did divorce, but my father is – he's still alive. But they divorced, then – Oh dear.' She shook her head. 'Let's talk about something else.'

He told her about Pennerton, explaining it was a village, almost in the middle of nowhere. It had grown up around the house his family had always lived in, and was named after it. When their parents died, Beatrice had taken on the house at Pilgrim's Lane, while he'd settled for a much smaller flat at Wigmore Street, in return for complete control of Pennerton House.

He visited whenever he could, he said, and when Sophie asked him why, he told her it was beautiful, and quiet, and away from the world, and there was space to walk about in. Then he broke off. 'Questions, questions, all these questions!'

'You don't have to answer.'

'No, I like it! I'm just not used to the attention.'

'Nonsense! I saw the way you were mobbed after the shoot. I rather think I was the only person there who hadn't heard of you.'

'You have now?'

'Oh! Don't be— Of course I had! Management came to the green room and told us, Max "The Face" Hollingbourne was coming in to take Miss Hammond's pictures. There was a slate, first one to get your attention! You're taller than I expected. And your hair, it's sandier than it is in the photo I saw.'

He was easier with her questions then, telling her he hadn't always done the kind of work he'd done that afternoon, but had put in a stint shooting what he called 'real life'.

'Conflict pornography,' he said, half laughing, when she asked him what kind of real life. 'I was a photojournalist, though, not a war photographer. I just happened to take pictures of people fighting.'

There was a silence. He poured himself another glass of wine. When she asked why he had stopped with the real life, he frowned.

'Sorry,' she said. 'You don't want to—'

'It's fine. I'm perfectly happy—'

'No, really. It's none of my business.'

'It's fine,' he said again. 'I'm just working out how to start.' Then he told her he'd been sent to Leopoldville at the beginning of the year, and something had happened which meant he couldn't carry on. When it was over, he'd stayed on to clear a few things up, then he'd gone home to Pennerton. 'A few weeks later, Bea told me to pull myself together. Get back to parties, portraits, she said. Her kind of real life.'

'And you came?'

'Seemed like a good idea.'

'Do you always do what your sister says?'

The waiter brought the menus for dessert.

'Has it ever occurred to you,' Max said when he'd gone, 'that a tendency to cross-examination isn't especially attractive? Something you might like to think about.'

She flushed.

'I understand why you're doing it.'

'Why?'

'It's defensiveness. I was like that when I was your age. What are you, twenty, twenty-one?'

'I'm twenty-two.'

'Don't you see how it breaks the flow of our conversation?'

Her eyes held his.

'Well,' he said, 'it doesn't matter. You can relax. There's nothing you can say or do to stop me wanting you.'

She was quiet then, just watching him.

He called the waiter, to ask about the wine. There was a pause, and he said, 'Look. You wanted to know why I go to Pennerton so much. It's because there's nothing complicated about being there. Do you see?'

She shook her head.

'I went down as soon as I got back from Leopoldville. I put a kettle on and made some tea. I poured it into a white china mug, and
I took it to the meadow. It was a perfectly ordinary winter morning and there were cobwebs, covered in hoarfrost. I'm just trying to
say –. In the hedgerows, there were such –'

'Max,' she said softly, 'we don't have to talk about it.'

'But I want to explain.' He had raised his voice a little. 'You asked
me why I stopped. You have to understand, the things that happened
out there were so –. People do other things as well. In those kind of
situations, I mean. They sleep. They wash. They pray, share food. Do
you follow?'

'Yes.'

'I saw men sleeping, with their guns next to them. Some days
they danced, for no reason. They were kind to each other, in small
ways. Nobody wants to pay for those pictures. What you end up
with is – The spaces in between the big things, they disappear. And
then – I don't know.'

She touched his arm, and he spoke more quietly.

'There is a way people have of asking for a beating to stop. They
put out their hands with their palms facing up. As if they're holding something very precious. Something that'll break if they drop
it. It's like they're showing this invisible thing to the other person.
Like they're saying, so bloody politely, "Excuse me. Can you take this
thing I am holding? Can you take it from me?" They all look the same
at that moment, their faces always look the same.'

'And now? What about now?'

'Now?' He smiled. 'Now I only photograph beautiful things. And
I make no apology for that.'

When they'd finished, she thanked him for dinner. Then, taking a
piece of thyme from her plate, she reached across and pressed it to
his mouth. 'Please don't be too quick with me.'

In the street he tried to kiss her but she turned away. In the car, though, when he asked where she wanted to be dropped off, she said, 'Take me with you, Max. Take me to Pennerton.'

At the Long Avenue later, he took the keys from the ignition.

It was a warm spring night. He slung his jacket over his shoulder, and carried her coat. They walked between two lines of trees. Ahead, the lines converged at a white house, with eaves standing tall in the sky.

'I hope you like it,' he said. 'It will mean a great deal to me if you do.'

The stars were high and bright, and all down the avenue there were new leaves, unfurling. It was ten minutes, at least, before they reached the fountain, and he led her up the steps to the house.

The door was ajar and a small black cat slipped out.

'You left it open?'

'Yes. I tend to.'

Inside, they stopped in the hall and he kissed her. She put her hand to her lips, and drew away.

'A front door should be always open,' he said. 'Don't you think?'

'I'm not sure. And now your cat has run off, so you'll be here all alone.'

He laughed. 'Beatrice will visit. There's always Peter, in his cottage, and Little Peter will come back when he's ready.'

'Who's Peter? And who's Little Peter? Don't you worry that someone will walk in, when you're not here?'

'Questions, Sophie,' he said. He moved closer, and placed his hand on her lower back. When she stepped to one side, he exhaled. 'Little Peter is the cat we surprised on the steps. Who, incidentally, knows damn well he shouldn't be in here. Enemy to the darkroom. Hair everywhere, total chaos. He's an outlaw. A hard-boiled cold-blooded felon.'

Sophie raised her eyebrows. 'And Peter?

He told her about Peter then, that he had lived in the cottage behind the kitchen garden since Max was a child, and that he did things about the place, cleaning the windows, cutting the lawn, pruning the apple trees.

She smiled. 'Anything else?'

'As a matter of fact, yes. He grows the vegetables, and sees that the woods are in order.'

'Woods?' She laughed. 'You have woods?'

'Yes. Why do you laugh?'

'I just – I don't know. I didn't have woods, where I grew up. Well, not ones to call my own. There were woods in Nice that I played in. If you were an adult you'd have said they were hills with trees on, but for a child, they were big enough to get lost in. And they had streams running through them. Do yours have streams?'

'One, yes. Bea claims we swam in it, when we were children. But it's only really good for splashing about in, and when it gets to the meadow it's more a trickle. And yes, before you ask, we do have a meadow. It's triangle-shaped and it grows as tall as a child. In the summer, it's full of butterflies. Time you stopped asking questions and saw the place for yourself.' He held her hand. 'We'll start with the Long Library, I think.'

The following Christmas, walking with her father in the woods at Nice, Sophie would find it hard to remember the house with any precision. So that, for example, when Emile asked her to describe the hall where Max first kissed her, she could tell him only that it was dark, and that its walls, which were painted so deep a red as to be almost another colour, were hung with animals' heads and swords. There was a flag with a coat of arms, and she thought she might have seen some sort of a cage, the size of a man and the shape of one.

She'd retrieve snippets of Max's stories for her father, or glimpses of particular things. The stair carpets were more matting than wool, with holes in places and edges that curled away; she'd followed Max up and watched his feet fall and press off, and the frayed matting had caught on his socks. The kitchen table spanned the room, and the stove, which Max had said was put in when his mother was first there, was huge and black, with copper pans hung from a bar. Little Peter was curled on top and Max tickled him under his chin. He purred at first but when he was tickled some more, he showed his claws, and Max threw him from the back door into a yard, lined with stables.

From the hall, Max had taken her into a room the width of the house. It was full of books, right to the ceiling, with ladders against the bookcases and an enormous fireplace at one end. There was a map chest and Max was pulling open the drawers, quickly, before saying, 'No, wait, I've got a better idea.'

He picked up a small mahogany box that stood on top of the chest.

He flicked the key and flipped up the lid to show her a mess of coins in different shapes and sizes.

'Are they real?'

'Of course. A real King George V Sovereign. Bite.' He held it to her mouth.

'No.' She pushed him away. 'I believe you.'

'So you should. I'd never lie to you.'

In the eaves of the house there was a line of little rooms full of boxes, and furniture wrapped in sheets. Opposite was Max's darkroom, where he told her not to touch anything. An internal door opened into an adjoining room, in which the garden-facing wall consisted entirely of glass panels, set in white wooden struts.

'The Lightroom,' he said.

Everything was aligned so perfectly, she would tell her father it was more like a diagram of a room than one that someone used.

The desk was in front of the glass wall, and things were placed on it in neat groups. She picked up a shell but Max said, 'Not now, please. I'll show you it all tomorrow.'

When she put it back, he repositioned it. He took her to the glass wall, and said, 'The kitchen garden.'

The moon was bright, and there were soft trees and long walls. Beyond one of the walls, there was a small glasshouse, and further still, there was a cottage. A lamp glowed in the upstairs window, and a skein of smoke spooled from the chimney.

'Peter?' Sophie asked. And, when Max nodded, 'He's still awake?'

'The stove. It's how he heats his water. He always leaves it on.'

'Will I meet him?'

'If you want to. I'll take you over tomorrow.'

He didn't, though, nor did he say much more about this man who had always lived there. It would be years before she learned, and it would be his sister, Beatrice, who told her, that whenever Max was home from school for the holidays, he and Peter had been almost inseparable. Just out of his teens, Peter was taller and stronger than their father, who had very little time for his children. Peter's only weakness was in his eyes, so that he wore tiny brass-rimmed glasses tied on with a red velvet ribbon, and, instead of being sent to fight in the war, worked kitchen shifts at RAF Headcorn.

Peter was a hero for Max, and he made him his Son-of-the-Woods and called him Little Man and they mowed the lawn together and chopped wood, when it was needed. On his afternoons off, they set traps and coppiced trees and collected birds' eggs and butterflies. Sometimes, when a path had been laid or the cut bracken cleared and their jobs were done for the day, they'd make a campfire and sleep out under the stars. Beatrice was never invited. Once, when she asked her brother why he spent so much time with him, he said only that Peter was gentle, where their own father wasn't, and that his hands were enormous and always warm, and his face was enormous too – his whole head a giant thing in Max's mind.

She'd been jealous, she'd tell Sophie, until the Christmas holidays when their father intervened in Max and Peter's friendship in such a way that a distance grew up between them which, as far as Beatrice knew, had yet to be bridged.

Max had come home from school that summer, anxious and unhappy. It was a few months on from their parents' divorce, and she'd assumed that was why, until he told her he was being bullied by some of the older boys in his dormitory. As soon as Peter found out, he said he would think of a plan. Early mornings before his shift, and sometimes before it was even quite light, he led his Little Man through the woods to a clearing. There, he tied the ribbon of his glasses more tightly, and showed Max the rudiments of boxing. Beatrice crept after them one day and watched: stripped to their waists, they danced around and jabbed each other, dodging and cutting for an hour, breaking to rest in the sun, then up again. At the last, as Beatrice was on the point of creeping away, she saw Peter kneel, and she saw her brother punch him on the jaw, hard, first on one side then on the other, over and over until there was blood on Peter's chin and on his chest.

Beatrice said that Max returned to school in the autumn term 'older and bigger than he should have been'. Shortly before the Christmas holidays he'd employed his new-found skills and stood up to one of his bullies. He knocked the boy out cold, Beatrice heard her father tell their mother on the phone, calling to explain why Max had been sent home early. Instead of getting up when Max expected him to, the boy had just lain there. Blood came eventually from one of his ears and an ambulance was called.

He recovered, Beatrice told Sophie, but only after a week in hospital, and never fully.

That first night at Pennerton, Max told her none of this. Instead, he led her to the floor below.

'The upstairs sitting room,' Max said.

A series of objects stood in a row, tall and covered in white sheets, so they looked like winter haystacks. 'What are they?' she asked.

'Easels. My mother's easels. She left them to me. I fetched them from London when my father died. They're empty but I like the look of them. When the place is opened up I like them standing there.'

She reached to the first one and took a corner of the sheet.

'Don't,' he said.

Sophie let the sheet drop. 'When she left,' she said, 'after the divorce, you must have been glad there were two of you.'

'I'm sorry?'

'Your sister, Beatrice. You had someone your own age.'

'She's eight years older, as it happens. And I was already away at school. But she did look after me. Still tries to, actually. Drives me up the bloody wall.'

'Is she beautiful?'

'Apparently. Looks a bit like a chap, if you ask me. If it wasn't for the way she paints her face, you'd be forgiven for thinking so. Always has hordes of young men after her, of course. Glamorous war widow, husband a hero, left her a packet and everyone knows it.'

'And?'

'And what?'

'I want more than that!'

'Alright,' he smiled. 'She's as tall as I am. Athletic-looking. Lanky, broad across the shoulders. Hair's blonder than mine. Swears she doesn't curl it. Keeps it short, slicks it back if she's dressed for dinner, walks with her hands in her pockets. Bright red lipstick she never takes off, slacks not skirts, flats not heels, unless it's a proper party and there's someone she wants to take home with her. Will that do?'

'What sort of a person is she?'

'Christ! Why are you so interested in my sister? All I'll say is she's bloody gorgeous, and bloody difficult. We're friends,' he said. 'We always have been, and we always will be. Enough?'

'Enough,' Sophie said, then his hands were at her waist, steering her to the door.

The next room was his bedroom, he said. She crossed to a window and he stood next to her. Directly beneath them was a terrace which dropped to a lawn. In the moonlight, the turf was like a clean sheet, stretched on a bed.

'Is it part of the kitchen garden?' Sophie asked softly.

'No. It's just a lawn. Bea and I call it the Smart Lawn.'

She walked past each of the windows, him following, and asked why he kept them open.

'I like to be woken by the birds.'

'Even when you're not here?' She touched one of the curtains, running her hand down the heavy velvet, stopping when she met his. 'What if it rains? What if—'

'What if what? Actually, perhaps you've got a point.' Then he took her to the bed and knelt in front of her. He told her he'd once come back from a trip and found an unfinished nest on a shelf.

'What did you do?'

'I closed the window.'

'Then what?'

'A pigeon appeared on the sill.'

'What did it do?'

'It sat there, and it made a noise on the glass.'

'What did you do?'

'I opened the window and put the nest on the sill and closed the window again.'

'Did it go?'

'Yes.'

'Did you find anything else?'

'I did, as a matter of fact,' he said, then he kissed her.

'What?' she laughed, half kissing him back.

'An egg. On the floor, underneath the shelf with the nest.'

'You're making that up!'

'Yes, I'm making it up. Of course I am. I made the whole thing up.'

She pushed him away, and went to the door. On the stairs, he ran down after her. In the kitchen he scooped Little Peter up and threw him into the yard. 'And stay out this time or you'll regret it, I can tell you!' Slamming the door, he lifted Sophie onto the table. He undid the top button of her blouse, and she kissed him, loosening his tie.

'You must be starving,' he whispered. 'You didn't have a single oyster.' He pulled her blouse from her skirt and slid his hands onto her back. 'Not one.' He pressed his face into her neck and his voice was muffled. 'I'll take you to Whitstable tomorrow. I'll find you an oyster and I'll debunk your silly theory.'

'I won't eat it.'

'I'll make you.'

'You can't. I won't let you.'

When she slipped from his arms and ran to the back door, he followed.

She bathed in the morning, and there were scratches on her back. The deepest of them all was at the bottom of her spine, and there was an insect bite on her thigh that had swollen.

'No, I don't have anything for it,' Max said, when she found him downstairs. 'Ask Peter if you really can't manage, but we ought to get up to town.'

She would tell Emile that she'd wondered then why she'd believed him when he said he'd show her everything the next day, and why she'd let it happen in the way that it had. Her father had asked what they'd said to her at the theatre, about skipping morning rehearsal. And how she'd have felt if they'd wanted to call her to sing.

'I know, Papa,' she said. 'I didn't think.'

They'd gone through a low gate to the kitchen garden, then there was another gate and they were on the Smart Lawn. At its midpoint, with the eaves of the house behind them, he pulled her in and walked faster.

'Now?' he said. 'Now are you ready?'

'Yes,' and his hands were at her neck and they were kissing and he stooped to press an arm against the backs of her knees, at the same time as holding his other arm up and around her waist, and he was tipping her over, quite gently and suddenly so that her whole body was being lifted from the ground, and she flung out her arms to steady herself, and clasped them around his neck.

He stood to his full height and walked forward, kicking open the orchard gate and carrying her into the pitch-dark, then he stumbled on a root or a broken branch, and they were falling.

3 MONDAY

Ruthie wakes up alone. For a moment, she has no idea who she is or where she is. Then she knows she is Ruthie but has no sense of whether she's an adult or a child. A minute passes before a gecko appears on the ceiling and she knows she is in Greece. When she raises her head and sees the tips of the trees through the veranda doors and, beyond them, the sea, she realises she's in the villa, in the room that used to be her parents' bedroom. But when she lies back down and stretches out a hand, there's no one, and still she doesn't know whether the room is as it was when it was slept in by her parents together, or just Max on his own after Sophie left. Then she feels underneath the other pillow and finds a slip and holds it up. It is twice the size of anything her mother would have worn. Recognising it as Vinny's, she remembers that Vinny and Eleni are going to Athens on Wednesday and she will be on her own.

They had fallen asleep almost as soon as she'd got into Vinny's bed. Vinny had stroked Ruthie's head and told her not to worry, and Ruthie had heard her soft, low voice and let herself be comforted.

If Vinny was still in bed with her now, she thinks, she would tell her again about what she'd seen. This time she would describe how, after the child had slipped through the gate and away, the white of her nightdress and the speed at which she'd moved had made Ruthie think she was watching an owl flying low in the trees, rather than a child, running.

She places a hand on Vinny's pillow. With her eyes closed, she thinks of her sister, and remembers that the last time they'd shared a bed was the previous August, after Max died.

On the morning it had happened, Vinny was at the villa with her husband, Julian.

Max had gone for his swim before anyone else was up. His heart gave way on the shoreline, his body half in and half out of the sea. An hour after he normally came in for breakfast, Eleni went to clear the dishes from the courtyard. When she saw the food was still there, she put down her tray and ran.

He was lying on the pebbles with his legs lolling in the water, as though, she would tell Vinny later, he was simply resting.

Vinny and Julian were woken that morning by her cry. Julian pulled Vinny from the bed and down to the courtyard. The cry came again, louder, and they took the steps so fast Vinny slipped at the bottom and came to the cove on her knees, half crawling, half staggering to her father. Eleni was kneeling in the water by his side, shouting his name.

Vinny phoned but couldn't get an answer at Pilgrim's Lane. When, by the third day, Ruthie hadn't replied to her messages, nor any of her texts or emails, she flew to London.

Her sister was on a high ladder in the front garden, pruning the rose that grew over the door.

'Hello, Roo.'

'Ah,' Ruthie said, climbing down. 'So it *was* urgent.' She dropped the secateurs into her pocket, and held the front door open. She glanced at her sister. 'By the way, it's Ruthie, not Roo. I'm nearly forty, you know.'

Downstairs, they made tea. In the middle of the table was the gilded skull of a bird, tiny and rounded. Vinny moved it to a shelf. Ruthie put it back.

While the tea brewed, neither of them spoke. On the dresser was a black-and-white photograph of their mother as a young woman. Behind her was a bus, and behind that, St Paul's Cathedral.

'I've never seen this one before,' Vinny said, picking it up. 'Where did you – Is it one of Dad's?'

'Of course.' Ruthie took it.

When Vinny told her, Ruthie's mug slipped from her hands. She was a while sweeping up the pieces, down on her knees and swearing.

'No, no, it's fine,' she said, when Vinny asked if she'd burnt herself. 'I didn't feel it.'

She sat with the hem of her skirt in both hands, and saw that Vinny was crying.

'I'm sorry,' she said, letting her skirt go. 'I mean – I wondered if it was something like that. I'm sorry.'

On the question of a return to Greece, she wouldn't be drawn.

'I'll come, sometime. Of course I will. Just not yet.'

A phone rang upstairs and she disappeared. When she came back the skin around her eyes was red but she smiled at Vinny. 'Do say, won't you, if there's anything—'

'Anything what?'

'Anything I can do.' She pulled a lighter from her pocket. 'What do you think I mean?'

'Anything you can – Of course there bloody is.'

Vinny began to cry again, uncontrollably. Ruthie shouted at her, 'Stop, Vinny! Stop it!' She held her sister then, stroking her head and saying, 'It's OK, Vee. Vee-Vee. It's OK.'

When Vinny had finished, she pulled away. 'Are you seriously going to stay here and leave me and Julian to get on with it? Who are you, Ruthie? Who have you become?'

'I'm not sure.' Ruthie's voice was flat, and there was no movement in her face. 'But I'd like you to leave now. I'll be in touch, I promise.'

Clearing the tea things, Ruthie noticed that the photograph of Sophie was gone from the dresser. She looked for it that day and the next, then she stopped.

Afterwards, Ruthie had wanted to call.

When six weeks passed, and still she hadn't, Vinny and Julian went with Eleni, who'd begged them not to wait any longer.

In the late afternoon they took the path into the hills behind the grove.

After walking for an hour, they reached the place below Kata Chora where the olives stand in terraces and the air is like glitter. The grass there is long and golden and more like feathers than grass, so it catches the sunset and burns in it. Eleni said, 'This is where.' They waited for a time, then they scattered Max's ashes, their faces warm in the setting of the sun.

Vinny wrote to Ruthie, and by the end of the week there was an email.

You should have waited.

Another week went by, then she arrived. She wore a long black coat, and black jeans that made her legs like sticks. Her hair was in a plait, right down her back. Under her fringe her sunglasses were almost too big for her face.

The sisters were careful with each other at first, but after dinner they had the first of several arguments about Max's ashes. Ruthie had changed into shorts and left her coat inside, but was still wearing her sunglasses, so Vinny said, 'Are they ordinary sunglasses? They're really dark. When you talk it's like you're talking to someone else. Can't you –' but Ruthie said, 'Give me a break.' She was biting her nails, which were stubs already. 'And stop changing the fucking subject.'

She calmed down when Julian fetched a piece of paper and drew her a map. 'Yes,' Eleni said. 'That is where, looking out to the point where the sun falls into the water.' Then Vinny told Ruthie that Max had said it was the most beautiful place he'd ever been, and that he had always felt content there, and Julian said, 'I'll take you up in the morning, if you like. Show you where—'

'Right.'

'Really, I'm happy to, it's—'

'For God's sake, Julian, I have been here before, you know. I do know my way around.'

At about 3 a.m. Vinny stood by the bedroom door. Julian said why didn't she go and see if everything was OK, instead of eavesdropping?

'It's alright. I'm just—'

'Christ, she's been walking around for hours. She's only been here half a day and the whole place stinks of tobacco. She'll be like this all summer, you know she will. Go and talk to her. You can't spend the whole night standing there.'

'No. She'll just take a while to settle, that's all. Sorry,' and she lay back down. 'I'm sorry.'

By the time Ruthie ended up in Max's Lightroom, directly above their bedroom, Julian was asleep. Vinny was wide awake and staring at the ceiling. In the quiet of the night, with only the cicadas and the water in the cove, the sound of Ruthie moving Max's things around came through the floorboards. She was shifting his furniture, opening all of his drawers and his cupboards. She continued to do it for another two hours, then it was morning.

Eleni put their breakfast in the courtyard, beside the fountain. 'The way we used to, Vee. Ruthie will like it.' When she'd gone Ruthie stood at the table, her arms folded. She'd undone her plait and her hair was a mess, half tucked behind one ear and half over her face. Instead of her jeans, she wore a short white slip that was cut to show the hollow of her chest, and made her nipples tiny points in the silk.

'Where is it? What happened to it?'

'To what?' Vinny said.

'*The Road to Falicon.*'

'Hmmm? Aren't you going to sit with me?'

'The photograph. *The Road to Falicon.* Forget about the one you nicked off me at Pilgrim's Lane, the one of Maman. This one's important.' She pulled a chair next to Vinny and sat down.

'The road to where? Are you alright, darling? Are you going to get dressed? Are you going to eat? I keep looking at you thinking I'm seeing things. I'm sure you weren't that skinny when I saw you in London. How did you get so thin in six weeks? You must eat while you're here. You must.'

Julian ran in from the cove, water still streaming from his body.

'Ladies. It's ruddy gorgeous out there.'

'You know exactly what I'm talking about. Don't give me that shit. It was hanging in his lightroom, above the work surface. It always was.'

'Ah,' Julian said. 'Nice to have you back, Roo.'

'Don't call me that. And don't talk to me like that, either. This isn't your home. It's mine and it's Vinny's and you're a guest, right?'

'Of course, silly old me. Been a while since you came, that's all. Vinny and I—'

Vinny stood and kissed him on the mouth. 'Not now, sweetheart. Ruthie and I are talking. Take a shower. Ask Eleni for some eggs or something.'

They kissed again then Julian sat on the fountain wall, running his fingers through his hair. 'Welcome home, though. I mean it, Roo, really. It's good to see you.'

Ruthie stood up so fast her chair fell and things spilt: Vinny's coffee, the milk from the jug.

'Please,' she said. She was smiling but her voice was tight. 'I just want to know where it is.' She pulled her hair from her face. 'The picture. My picture.'

When Vinny told her their father had sold *The Road to Falicon* a long time ago, Ruthie turned away.

'How long?'

'A decade? More? I can't remember. He cleared a few things out. He signed some of his old pictures and sold them.'

'And the negatives? Where did he keep the negatives of the ones he sold? There are thousands of them up there – how the hell am I going to find it? Or are you telling me he sold that as well?'

'I said.' Vinny raised her voice. 'He sorted out some of his stuff. He told me it was hell organising Sophie's things at Pennerton after she went. He didn't want us to have to do the same. I don't know what he kept and what he didn't. He sold the pictures a long time ago and he started on everything else. Then, well—'

'Well what?'

'In the last year or so, I mean, when—'

'For fuck's sake. In the last year or so, what? Why is his stuff in such a mess? Why did you let him live like that? There's fifty films up there he never even developed. Why would he have left them? He never did that.'

'He gave up.' Vinny was shouting now, and she stood up. 'I told you in London. In the kitchen at Pilgrim's Lane, I told you.'

'No you did not!' Ruthie shouted louder. 'And who switched off the bloody freezer? It's full of films ready to go. We'll never be able to see—'

'I did tell you. We talked about it.'

'Well, it might surprise you to know I had other things on my mind that day. Like the fact my sister had just waltzed in unannounced and asked for a cup of tea and said, by the by, that my father had been dead for three days and no one had thought to tell me.'

'Jesus!' Vinny had lowered her voice. 'Will you stop shouting? I tried. I don't know how many times I called you. I emailed, I texted. You were ignoring my messages and you know damn well you were, and Jesus, I wrote to you about Max ages ago, when Pennerton was – You know I—'

'Alright. Alright. Will you just tell me again, now I'm here? Tell me everything.'

They sat together, at the table, and Vinny said that he'd just stopped looking after things.

'I don't know how else to describe it. He went up there one day to sort out some cameras to sell and he came back down crying.' Ruthie let Vinny take her hands. 'And that was it, he didn't go up again, not really. He said he was happier walking in the hills. Swimming. Sitting out here reading. Then he stopped letting anyone else go up there either. He said he'd box it all up another time and—'

'But why didn't you tell me he was actually selling stuff? Who did he sell them to? A gallery? A museum?'

'It was a private collector in London. The one-offs. He said he never looked at them any more. Nobody did—'

'Why not a museum? Or a university? Don't tell me none of them asked.'

'Two or three did.'

'Where? Here, or the US?'

'Both.'

'So why not? What did he get from the collector?'

'It wasn't about the cash. He said he didn't want people going through his stuff forever and ever. Deciding after he'd gone what was good, what was bad.'

'It was my picture.' She was speaking calmly but there were tears on her cheeks. 'He knew it was. He gave it to me. He'd written on the back of it. To my daughter. To my Ruthie. To my –'

Julian, who was lying on the fountain wall with his eyes closed, said, 'Hey, you two.' He scooped up some water and let it fall, drop by drop, on his stomach, which was tanned and rose in a gentle slope. 'It's the shock, Roo. It's the shock of coming back after so long. It's just a picture.'

'Come on, love,' Vinny said. 'There are other things of yours here. Jules is right, it's just a picture.'

Ruthie moved away. Julian got up and took a white shirt from the back of a chair, and a straw hat from another. He smiled at Vinny while he put on the hat, then Vinny told Ruthie they were going to spend the morning in town, and would probably stay on for lunch, since Eleni was going to see her brother. Ruthie was welcome to go with them, or she could stay at the villa and do what she liked.

Ruthie, who was untangling her hair, said she didn't need anyone to tell her what to do in her own home and could she please have the name of the collector, and an address.

'Fine,' Vinny said. 'They sent a card, I think. I'll look this afternoon.'

Ruthie waited until Eleni left as well, then she went to the cove. She put her clothes on the ground and wound her hair into a thick knot on top of her head. Then she swam right out, letting her body remember the feel of the water against it, like an old silk slip, and her tongue recall the salt.

She came in and stood in the sun, remembering a story her mother had told her in her childhood. A shipful of sailors were becalmed at sea. Lost, utterly, they ran down their supplies. After a period without food, they found they were starting to hallucinate. Strange hallucinations at first, so they knew the things they were seeing weren't real and should be disregarded. But then the sailors reached the point of starvation and began to lose their reason, rapidly and completely. Eventually, they woke one morning to see dry land stretching out before them. Believing they'd come to shore, they stepped from their ship and drowned, surprised by the water.

She sat for a long while on a rock at the sea's edge, her naked body the body of a boy.

Vinny and Julian came into the courtyard partway through the afternoon. There was the chest of drawers from their bedroom, upended by the fountain. Next to it was a small cupboard, with its door lifted from the hinges, and the contents strewn across the tiles. Clothes were draped on the fountain wall, and one of Vinny's German dictionaries was floating in the water. Inside the house, plates had been smashed and chunks of plaster knocked from the wall. Julian started to pick them up until Vinny said, 'Don't, please. I'll speak to her.'

Julian left for London the next day. Vinny had told him she and Ruthie needed to spend some time together, as sisters. When he asked her how long she'd stay, she said, 'As long as it takes.' When he said, 'But how long?' she said, 'At least a few weeks.' She'd come home as soon as possible.

After he'd gone, Ruthie shared her sister's bed for a week. Then, when Vinny had asked at breakfast if she would like to try sleeping on her own, she said she'd have gone days ago, but she hadn't wanted to hurt Vinny's feelings.

'Right. Well I'll ask Eleni to make up your old bedroom again.'

'Oh, but I'm moving rooms.'

'Where to?'

'I'm moving to the Lightroom.'

The top floor of the villa had always been reserved for Max, just as it was at Pennerton. The Lightroom formed the whole of one end, and provided the only way into the darkroom. Two of the Lightroom's walls were made of glass and gave views in almost every direction: to the one side, the sea, with Meropi Island perched on its surface like an almond; to the other, the grove and the mountains beyond.

'Why not one of the other bedrooms, if you really have to move?' Vinny had asked.

'It's where I want to be,' Ruthie had said. 'It's where I want to sleep. What's it to you?'

'Nothing.' Vinny had shielded her eyes from the sun. 'Bit bright up there, isn't it? The light comes in so early here. It's not like English light. And don't you want a proper bed?'

'Please, Vee.'

'Well, if you could see your way to sleeping on the same floor as me it'd save Eleni having to walk up so many stairs. She's old now, you know. She does so well but – Anyway, don't you want some privacy? You can look right in from the corridor with all that glass, and you'll have to get the fans fixed or you'll die of heat.'

'I'll be fine.'

In the Lightroom later that day, Vinny stood at the door while Ruthie knelt among Max's things. There were loose stacks of prints, and rolls of film, spooling from canisters. Six or seven cameras lay on the floor, and a telescope stood at the glass wall on the seaward side. Hanging from it was a pair of binoculars, their case still attached and falling open. On the wall above one of the work surfaces was a small gilded clock with feathers for hands.

'It'll take you ages,' Vinny said, craning her neck. 'There isn't really any room to do the sorting out, is there? You need some shelves, at least. If you're really going to sleep in here, ask Ilías to put up some shelves.'

'Where?'

'There, on the end wall. You've got a whole empty wall with nothing on it.'

'I need it to stay empty.'

'What for?'

'Something else. Doesn't matter.'

'Well, get him to make you some free-standing ones. Put them next to the telescope. And what's so great about sleeping on the floor? Why don't you want to sleep on a bed?'

'I'll fetch a mattress. And I'll do my own cleaning, so Eleni doesn't need to come up. I'll have the place to myself, which is just the way I like it. It's alright, Vee, please.'

'Come for a stroll before supper,' Vinny called up that evening. 'Quick, the sun's going down.'

Ruthie followed her through the meadow, where the fine yellow grass was to her waist.

'Look,' Vinny said, pointing. 'I thought they might be there, with this sun.'

They stood in the trees above the second cove. On the cliff opposite was a figure. Then two or three more. The figures hovered and their laughter came over the water, then suddenly they were running to the edge and diving in. The sun fell further, so these diving figures turned black against the gold sky and the sea was a flat bright disc. The sisters watched the bodies spin in the air like so many coins flipped for heads or tails. The figures climbed the rocks and dived in, round and round. When they began to flop instead of dive, like fledglings falling from a nest, Vinny said, 'Let's go.'

As they walked back, the sky was in flames behind them and the villa was umber, shot through with pink and gold. Please, Vinny asked, could they look through Max's things together, but Ruthie said she'd rather do it on her own: they'd only argue, and as Vinny said, there wasn't a great deal of room.

'That's unfair. I think it's a bit horrible of you, actually.'

'I'm sorry? Can you just say that again?'

'What do you mean?'

'I mean, can you just say that again? What you just said about unfairness.'

'Oh, come on. You know why we didn't wait.'

'Remind me.'

'Ruthie!' Vinny ducked under the vine and into the court-yard. 'Eleni and I lived with him all that time. I was here with him every minute I could be. You never came. We couldn't just hang on forever –'

'You knew I'd come.' Ruthie followed her. 'You knew! Well, it's too late now. All I want is to sort his stuff out on my own. You'll be able to see everything when I've finished, I promise. That's fair, isn't it? Anyway, I'm sure you've got plenty of other things to do. Aren't you supposed to be translating fifteen Schiller plays by September, or something? And if not, perhaps you could give Eleni a hand with something, seeing as she's so fucking high on your list of priorities.'

Eleni was there then, standing right in front of them. Her dark hair, with its streaks of white running through it, was held in a heavy plait, and she wore a shawl around her shoulders.

She'd lit the tea lights all around the courtyard: in a line beneath the pergola, and nestling in the pots of basil. More were placed in a ring around the fountain, and a cluster stood on the table with the food.

Looking at Vinny, Eleni dried her hands on her apron and said she would eat inside; she was tired. And, when Ruthie tried to apologise, 'It's nothing. You miss your father. You both do.'

When she went to the kitchen door, her bare feet made no sound on the courtyard tiles.

Vinny told Ruthie it was a while ago that someone had laid a path across the clifftop. She saw the figures quite often and didn't mind them. Max had watched them with her once, and when he'd waved, they'd waved back. 'Come on,' she said, putting a hand on Ruthie's arm. 'You're here now, and it's just the two of us. Why don't we settle down and do his things together?'

'I've already told you.'

'Yes, but—'

'But nothing. Just let me do this. You owe me that much, don't you?'

'Alright.' Vinny put her arms around her sister. 'Eat something, will you, while it's still warm? You've had nothing all day, you must be starving. Of course I'll let you. Not because I owe you, though. It's a gift, Roo. Think of it as a gift.'

Ruthie spent the month making the Lightroom habitable, and putting the darkroom in working order.

She'd begun with Max's records: arranging them alphabetically and taping her favourites to play downstairs on the reel-to-reel. She ran a cable to the courtyard so she could take the player out. Some of those evenings they chose Sarah Vaughan's 'September Song', which Ruthie wanted again and again, or Cannonball Adderley's 'Sack O' Woe', when she made Vinny dance until they were sweaty and Vinny was out of breath and her curls had come loose from their bright cloth band.

Once, Ruthie found one of Sophie's practice tapes among Max's reel-to-reels. The label was written in felt-tip pen: '*Lieder Master-class, 3rd January, 1959.*' She brought it down to show Vinny.

'I thought they were all at Pilgrim's Lane!' she said. 'I thought I'd heard every single one of them. This is new, Vee! Do you realise?'

When the sun had gone and tea lights flickered on the fountain's edge, they heard their mother's voice as though she had come back, and was there with them.

First, Sophie sang endless scales and arpeggios, flinging her voice higher until the sound rang back from the fountain. They heard her sing the same phrase over, then there was a man's voice. He sounded as though he was guiding her at first, or exhorting her. Then she flung the phrase up again and he was laughing and shouting, '*Oui! Ma belle, vas-y! Ça y est. Tu me coupes le souffle! Qu'est-ce-que c'est beau, Sophie! Oui! Oui! Oui!*' and Sophie stopped and laughed with him.

Ruthie played the tape several times that night, sitting hunched on the fountain wall. Rolling a cigarette and then another, she tried to recognise the man's voice. When Vinny asked, did she really have to smoke and shouldn't she at least use filters, Ruthie said, 'Don't you get it? It was just before she met Max, it must have been!' and, 'Who is that man? Listen!' until Vinny said how would she know and why did it matter, and, 'Don't flick your ash in the fountain, that's horrible.'

Ruthie put his negatives into chronological order, then she catalogued the ones that weren't already entered on his card index, and tidied the rest, marking those that were missing, or damaged. Vinny didn't ask whether she'd found *The Road to Falicon*, and for a long time, Ruthie didn't say. She chose which cameras to keep and which to discard, and the projector and slides were packed away, to be watched and indexed later. Individual photographs were collected into groups, and placed in cardboard folders. Tax and bank papers were sent to their lawyer in London, and she spent two days on the phone, cancelling subscriptions and memberships.

Telling Vinny she would begin an archive, since no one else had, she split his journals and correspondence into piles labelled Business, Personal and Miscellaneous, then she indexed all three and stored them in a wooden box she'd found in the darkroom. Long and squat and empty, the box was painted white. Its corners were capped in black metal, and Max's initials were inscribed across the top: M.M.H.

She took a paintbrush and added underneath, in smaller capitals of her own:

CORRESPONDENCE

(COLLECTED POSTHUMOUSLY BY HIS DAUGHTER, R.S.H.)

When all this was finished, she booked a firm from Kalamata to fix the ceiling fans, and to fit a system of blackout blinds. Apart from the mattress Ilías helped her to carry up, the only thing she added was the hanging mobile she'd found downstairs, stuffed at the back of a drawer.

It was a birthday gift from her father once, in her childhood.

Five white threads fell from a metal bar, and were strung with glass discs of varying sizes. When the room was swept clean, she unwrapped it from its tissue paper and fixed it to a long piece of flex. Climbing on a stepladder, she hung it from the ceiling. Afterwards, she polished the glass discs slowly, holding them to the light. Then she brought sheets from Eleni's laundry cupboard, and pushed the mattress into the middle of the room, directly beneath the mobile.

The darkroom was more straightforward. Having washed and sorted the equipment that was retrievable, Ruthie cleared the room of dust and scrubbed the floor and walls. When she'd sluiced them twice and let them dry, she reconnected the fridge freezer and filled it with fresh chemicals. While the ventilator unit was being repaired, she made lists and phoned for supplies.

Her first photograph was a failure. Assuming she'd lost the knack, she tried and tried again. None of the test strips made any sense; nothing emerged in the way she expected. It wasn't until the seventh or eighth attempt, breathing her Mississippis without meaning to, that she realised Max's timer was running either too fast or too slow. Turning it off, she counted as he'd taught her, naming the seconds, until she'd produced the print she wanted.

In the morning, she ordered a new timer.

Before it came, there was the sound about the villa, 'Two, Mississippi; Three Mississippi; Four.'

One morning at breakfast, Ruthie announced to Vinny and Eleni that her work was done. She told them she wouldn't go back to London for the autumn, though. When Vinny asked how long she'd stay for, she said she didn't know. Vinny told her she'd as good as finished the Wallenstein trilogy, and would email it that afternoon. She could ask the theatre to send the next batch of plays to the villa, rather than Cambridge, and stay on for a while herself. 'Yes,' Ruthie said. 'Why not.'

Vinny went in. Ruthie had brought Eleni's scissors from the kitchen. Sitting on the fountain wall, she cut off all her hair.

'Oh, Roo!' Vinny said, running back out. 'Why not a proper salon, if you have to?' But it was too late, so she knelt and picked up the dark red strands where they fell. 'At least let me help you. It's all jagged at the back.'

Ruthie nodded, and Vinny fetched a mirror.

But when it came to painting her nails, she said no thank you. 'I can do some things for myself.'

Vinny would find the broken bottle, left where it had fallen, and Eleni would clean the varnish from the tiles.

When Vinny was much older, and thought back to that summer of Ruthie's return, she remembered watching over her, like a mother might watch a child who had been unwell.

Sometimes while Ruthie swam, Vinny had sat on the cove with her hands to her face like a visor. She stayed the day through and saw Ruthie dive from the headland opposite, twisting and turning and coming up for air so the light was silvery on her face.

When it was too bright to make her out, Vinny followed the wake of her, a sharp white line across the surface.

Alone on the cove years later, when Ruthie was no longer there with her, Vinny would feel as though she'd been cut open, and a large stone placed where her heart was.

More than once, she looked to the island and fancied she saw her swimming in, and she imagined what she might say when her sister stepped onto the cove and shook the water from her body, throwing her head back and stretching her thin brown arms in the air.

In that imagining, Ruthie is pleased with her swim and is smiling. Vinny doesn't tell her she has been out too long and swum too far, nor does she ask if she'd eaten breakfast first, and would she be up at the villa for lunch, because she ought to, really, after all that exercise.

Instead, she says, 'Well done, Roo, you're getting your stroke back, aren't you? I'm sure you're faster than you ever were.' Then she steps forward and takes her in her arms, and tells her quite simply that she loves her, and is glad to be with her, after such a long time of missing her.

4 VINNY AND RUTHIE

By the following spring, Sophie was pregnant. She wrote to Sadler's Wells giving up her place in the company, and asked Max to go with her to France to meet her father. On the third day he took his cameras and drove to the hilltop villages above Nice: Tourrette-Levens, and Falicon. While he was gone, Emile asked Sophie to sit with him in his kitchen. He told her this was a man who would steal her soul and silence her, and she said, 'I know, Papa. But it's too late now.'

After Vinny was born, the family lived in Max's flat at Wigmore Street. She was named for his mother, Lavinia, and Sophie agreed to put her singing on hold while she was small.

Once, Max had a show at a gallery on Albemarle Street and Beatrice stayed with Vinny. Sophie told Max the crush of people was bothering her, and that she was anxious about the baby. At the party afterwards there was dancing, but Max was always with someone. There was a scene and she left early.

Showing her the press the next day, he talked her through the commissions that were coming in.

'Even Audrey Hepburn wants a portrait. Christ, what should I have done, said I didn't have time to speak to her?'

'Fine,' she said, 'but I won't go again.'

If he was out in the evening and took Beatrice, she told Sophie the next day who Max had talked to, who he'd danced with. If he went on his own, Sophie didn't ask.

Eventually, she said there was no point being in town if she was always with the baby, and why didn't they move to Pennerton?

Couldn't he see she was going out of her mind with nothing to do, knowing what was happening all around her, and who was going to whose recitals, and which of her friends' debuts she was missing? Mr Solti was the new man at the Opera House; everyone else had sung for him at least once; she hadn't even seen his *Iphigénie*.

The noise in the flat was bothering her, and she had to push the pram through a crowd to reach a park. There was soot, she said, everywhere, and had he any idea how many times she had to soak his shirts to get the collars white?

He refused on the grounds that she'd be unhappy: it was damp, and colder than she realised.

They argued, and they stayed.

Sometimes in the afternoons she took Vinny to Sadler's Wells. If there was a rehearsal and someone was saving their voice, she put Vinny in a cloth sling and stood on the stage to sing in for them. The cloth sling was cut from the sail of a boat at Nice, and had been made into a papoose by her father when Sophie was a baby, so that her mother, who had been an artist, could continue painting with her baby held to her.

Occasionally, Sophie booked a room at the Academy and tied

Vinny in this sail sling and practised for hours, or until Vinny cried too much. She'd have a lesson with her old teacher and the woman would say, 'Can't you hear this voice you have, don't you hear what we hear, don't you see what you could do with it?' but she knew that the time she was losing meant it was over for her in any serious way, and that the birth had so profoundly changed her voice it would be years before it settled.

Because her attempts to sustain it upset her more than they satisfied her, she told Max she'd rather not be around that world without being in it, and didn't he understand, there really was nothing to keep her in London?

Surely he could speak to Peter and make Pennerton warmer? Anyway, Emile's house was much damper, being beside the port and on top of a cave, at a place called Rauba-Capeù for the strength of the winds in the winter.

It wasn't just the state of Pennerton that was stopping him, he said. It was important he was in town. There was his studio for turning things round, and being on the scene meant people were used to him and hardly noticed his camera. Just last week, he told her, he'd been at the flat of an artist friend on the King's Road, and a group of boys played for them live.

'Played what?'

'They wrote a new song for us. Straight in from a show in Hamburg, so they had their kit. That's what I'm trying to say. It's a question of blending in, that's how I've always done it.'

'Who were they? Were they anyone?'

'They might be soon. From the North, apparently. Shot a whole roll of them writing that song. Went to my studio, printed them up. Couple of hours start to finish.'

'Fine. I'm happy for you. It sounds fun.'

'Don't be like that. They're just kids. Nice smiles. Nice suits. Nice haircuts. The prints are good. Could be gold dust, one day. If they make it, I'll take you backstage. I promise.'

A year later she showed him how her shape was changing, and told him she was sure it was a boy, and that their son should grow up running in the Triangle Meadow instead of Regent's Park.

'Enough,' he said. 'If it's what you want, I'll think about it.'

There was a miscarriage, though, late in the pregnancy. The family were at Pennerton when it happened, and afterwards Max asked the surgeon for the nearly-child's body.

'She won't want you to burn him,' he explained. 'I know she won't.' And, when the man advised against it, 'Don't you see? I would like – My wife and I would like to take our son to Pennerton House. We would like to put him in the ground there. We would like to know where he is, always.'

When the surgeon insisted, Sophie wanted to argue it, but Max told her, 'It's over now. Think of it like that.'

'Not it,' she said. 'Him. He was a boy not a thing.'

'I didn't mean – I meant the whole episode. The event. That's what I meant by "it". Think of Vinny. Think of Vinny and think of me, and come home.'

She closed her eyes and said she would stay until they gave her back her child.

'You can't change their minds just by being here,' he said.

As soon as she was well enough, she went with him to Pennerton. In the hall, she told him she'd come because she wanted to, not because he'd asked her, and that there was to be no more discussion: she wouldn't go back to town.

Sophie and Vinny lived at Pennerton in a makeshift way, and Max was mainly with them. By the spring of '63 she was pregnant again.

When he went each month to Wigmore Street, she complained but he told her it would be like that all summer: there was the season, and everyone was talking about the War Secretary and a call girl. There would be a trial, and people had asked about portraits. When his studio shots of Mandy Rice-Davies made the front pages, Beatrice told Sophie she could see his point.

'Pretty, isn't she?' Sophie said, handing back Beatrice's copy of *The Times*.

After the trial, Peter and Max did what they could to the roof, and the family moved in properly.

The first weekend, there were conkers from the horse chestnut by the stables. Max brought champagne from the cellar and much later, while Beatrice looked after Vinny, Sophie moved his record player into the Long Library so they could dance. Afterwards, the two of them lay on the Triangle Meadow to watch the dawn, choosing names for their new child.

The leaves turned. Peter swept them into piles on the Long Avenue, then he carried them to the oil-can burner in the orchard, so there were plumes of smoke.

If Max stayed in town for more than a night, Beatrice came to Pennerton. She said she liked being with Vinny, and slept better in the country: there were so many people to see in London, and there was always too much going on.

'Anyhow,' she said, 'I'm on my own, aren't I? You know I am.'

Before long, she sent Max a note: had he thought about a twin tub, and he knew jolly well the stove was put in by their mother and was awfully slow. He wrote back: the house was like it was for a reason, and in any case, he couldn't do it all at once.

In November he sold a print at auction, and put a copy in the upstairs sitting room on one of his mother's easels.

'Yank,' he said to Sophie when he found her staring at the image of high banks of snow on the lane into Pennerton, and she asked who had bought the original. In the picture, a car was half buried, and footprints led away. 'Took it in January, when you and Vee were stuck at Bea's and I got snowed in.'

'Where was the driver?'

'God knows. Found it like that. Abandoned. Hardly surprising. Peter and I had to dig our way out of the yard it was so deep. Took us a day. Two, even. You should've seen it.'

'I couldn't, could I?'

'What would you have had me do? Call the RAF to fetch my wife from London?'

'You shouldn't have left us there.'

'Didn't know it was coming. Took me completely by surprise. Give it a rest. You're seeing it now, aren't you? Do you like it?'

'Yes. Where was the auction?'

'Private do in Mayfair, one of Bea's millionaire Americans. Crazy for all things English, especially if there's snow. What'll I call it?'

Before she answered, he took a pen from his jacket. Adding his initials in the far left corner, he turned the print and wrote on the back: 'At Pennerton – Photographer's Proof – Nov '63.'

'How much did you get?'

'None of your business.' He reached in his jacket again and pulled out a tiny box. 'Don't worry, though. Spent half of it on you.'

It was a locket, in heavy, old gold. One side held a photograph of Vinny. The other was empty.

'For a picture of the little one.' He put both hands on Sophie's swollen belly. 'When she comes.'

'Max.' He tried to put the locket around her neck but she turned away. 'It's not time yet. We don't—'

He grabbed her wrists and held them in one hand.

'Stop,' she said. 'Please! You're hurting me.' When she gave in, he slipped the locket over her head and she said, 'Why "When *she* comes"? Why not "*he*"? What makes you think you know?'

The chain was caught on her hair. He pulled it free and she flinched.

'I just do. Trust me.'

Ruthie was born in December, shortly before Vinny's third Christmas. She was named for Max's grandmother. On the day they brought her home, her older sister stopped speaking. In the excitement, no one noticed the totality of Vinny's silence, so that almost forty-eight hours had passed by the time Beatrice asked her why she was so quiet.

It would be several weeks before she talked again, by which time Max and Sophie had run out of ideas, and so had the doctor in Headcorn. It was Beatrice who came to the rescue, saying she'd heard of a similar case from her neighbour in London, who had girls the same ages. Having found out the neighbour knew 'just the man' on Harley Street, she arranged for Vinny to see him straight away, and more than once if necessary.

A fortnight on, Vinny stood in the hall holding her aunt's hand and answering her parents' questions about the train home: where she'd sat; what she and Beatrice had eaten for their lunch in the restaurant carriage; that she'd wanted seconds of pudding, but Beatrice wouldn't let her.

Max, whispering, asked his sister who this doctor was, and where he should send the fee, but Beatrice told him she'd seen to it.

'At least a crate of wine then, Bea, or something. I'll have Peter take a hamper up, just give me the address.'

She said no, that wouldn't be quite the thing. Vinny said nothing very much about the doctor when Max and Sophie asked, and they didn't press it. Because Beatrice had told her so many times that they'd visited him, and because she'd been so entertained by her aunt's reminiscences about what the man looked like, and what he'd said to her, and how many stethoscopes were lined up on his desk, and the skeleton that stood by the window next to an umbrella plant that had grown so tall it was supported by a string running from a hook in the ceiling, Vinny had come to believe completely in his existence. If there had been the tiniest doubt in her mind, or if she'd felt at all confused by her parents' questions, the fact that Beatrice had said she could have treats every day if she kept them a secret, meant that Max and Sophie never discovered there had been no man in Harley Street and that, instead, Beatrice and Vinny had spent their time at the zoo in Regent's Park, or having tea and cake at Fortnum & Mason's before going to the ballet, or wrapping themselves in hats and gloves and scarves and walking up Parliament Hill, so that after ten days of her aunt's undivided attention and love and affection, Vinny said thank you and please could she go home to see her baby sister?

After that first separation, the girls were mainly together.

Max kept to a pattern of going to town every week, apart from a trip to shoot Machu Picchu, and Peru's coastal burial grounds, for *National Geographic*. Beatrice kept to hers, of staying if Sophie asked her to. Once, she found Sophie in the kitchen at midnight. She was on all fours, crying. Ruthie was on the table in her bassinet. Her face was red and she was screaming.

Beatrice held her hand to Ruthie's forehead. 'There, lovey. Hush.' Ruthie was quiet, and Beatrice turned to Sophie. 'What is it? For God's sake, what?'

She tried to pull her up but Sophie began to cough. 'Leave me alone.'

'Shall I call the doctor?'

'I'm alright.' She retched. 'Just leave.'

Ruthie screamed again, louder than before. Vinny appeared at the door.

'Maman. Ruthie is crying. Maman!'

'Up you go, poppet,' Beatrice said. 'I'll look after Ruthie. Back to bed, please. Maman's just having a little rest.'

When Vinny's footsteps had faded, Beatrice knelt down and stroked Sophie's head.

'What's going on? I need you to explain.'

The floor was covered in a fine white powder. A carton of formula was upended on the work surface. Beatrice righted it, then she knelt again and kissed Sophie's head.

Sophie flinched. 'Please go.'

Beatrice reached across Sophie's body and tried to pull her up. The two women struggled, then she sat back.

'I want to help you. But there's very little I can do unless you tell me what's wrong.'

Sophie sat with her knees drawn up. A minute passed. Then she said, very quietly, 'Max told me to count my Mississippis. Some stupid thing he does with the timer for his prints. I get to four and I think I've done five so I start again. I get to three and I think I've done four, or two. Or maybe – He doesn't understand. It's not how long, it's how many.' She put her hands on the floor, and moved them in the powder. 'It's no use. I can't feed her. I shouldn't be doing this.'

'Is she due one now?'

'An hour ago, I think. No, two.'

Beatrice fed the baby. She helped Sophie into bed and sat in the window seat, holding Ruthie to her chest. When Sophie woke, Beatrice put Ruthie down.

'It was a boy,' Sophie said. 'His body was blue.' She let out all her breath. 'Max won't talk about it.'

'He was there?'

'No.'

'Who—'

'I was alone. There was the baby, and there was me. I couldn't keep him in. I couldn't even do that. When they cut him there was so much – I wanted the baby. I wanted – There was so much –'

'Oh, love!'

'On the sheets. All over my skin. They told me it wasn't there but I could see it. It was like paint. It was even in my hair. I couldn't get it out of my hair. For weeks I could smell it.'

Beatrice lay beside her on the bed. 'I know.'

Later, she fetched Ruthie and placed her beside her mother. The child caught her breath and nudged closer, then Sophie held her. Beatrice watched them while they slept.

In the March of Ruthie's first year, Max went to Toronto for Richard Burton's *Hamlet*, then on to Montreal for the actor's marriage to Elizabeth Taylor. A week later he sent a telegram from New York: *Hamlet* was opening on Broadway. He would stay for the opening of the World's Fair, and to do Lyndon Johnson's portrait.

In the kitchen, Beatrice said to Sophie, 'Fetch the egg bowl from the pantry. Or a bag of apples. Anything. Take five of them out of the bowl and put them on the side. Then do your scoops. Every time you do a scoop, say the number aloud and put one of your eggs back. Then the next, and another egg. When all the eggs are in the bowl again, you know you've done enough. Alright?'

'Alright,' Sophie said. 'Thank you.'

'I shouldn't think it'll matter if you get it wrong every now and again.' She lifted Ruthie from her bassinet. 'In fact, let's do one now and get it wrong on purpose, hey? Six instead of five, see what happens.' She smiled, and Sophie smiled back at her.

When Max came home there was wild garlic in the woods, like splashes of white paint, and the swifts were high above the house.

He blew up a photograph of the Unisphere at Flushing Meadows.

The print was two foot by four foot, and Vinny watched him hang it on the wall above her bed. He worked in silence, then he left. Later, her aunt explained what it was, and where her papa had been.

In the morning, Beatrice walked with him in the woods.

'You need to spend time with your children.'

'Doing what?'

'Anything! Giving them a cuddle? I've never seen you read Vinny a story.'

'She's never asked!'

'She's three! She shouldn't have to. She's scared of you already. Have you seen the way she stares at you?'

'She's just being herself. That's how she is. She's quiet. She's serious.'

'Nonsense. And you hardly notice Ruthie.'

'What am I supposed to do? Discuss politics?'

'How about a feed?'

'Name me a man who does that. Anyone!'

'You're not "anyone". You're their father.'

'And our father fed us, did he?'

'And our mother left him. You can do things differently.'

'Wouldn't know where to start.'

'Oh, so you think I have the first bloody idea? Make it up! There's nothing complicated about it. Be gentle. Hold them. Cuddle them. Let them get to know you. Let them trust you. Christ, they're yours, Max. Have a go, at least. You might discover you're a natural! And you can stop smiling, right now. This isn't funny. I hope you've realised I'm talking about Sophie, too.'

'What about her?'

'She needs you.'

On Christmas Eve, Peter stood in the hall dressed in red, and stamping snow from his boots, with flour that Beatrice had combed through his beard, and a sack full of presents on his shoulder. After Emile arrived, the girls were put to bed and Beatrice stayed with them while the others walked to Pennerton for Midnight Mass. They all went back in the morning, to hear Peter sing matins with the choir. There was flour in his beard still, and when he took his solo, little clouds appeared around his face and Beatrice told Vinny off for pointing.

When all the presents were opened and it was dark outside, there were rockets and Catherine wheels on the Triangle Meadow. Vinny stood on a chair at her parents' bedroom window with Sophie, who held Ruthie in the sail sling, and kept her hands over the baby's ears.

Sophie caught a winter cold that settled on her chest and turned to flu, so that for weeks there was the sound of her coughing in the night. When she was half better, Max went to town for a portrait session with the Duchess of Devonshire, then in the evening, a party for the writer Norman Lewis. He'd be back first thing, he promised.

It was late afternoon when he parked by the fountain. Sophie had spent the day in bed, and when Max went up and said he had some news, she asked if it could wait until the morning.

He went on. He'd realised he needed to spend some money on Pennerton, so that she and the girls would be more comfortable. It would be a big project: there was the roof, and if the plumbing and heating were going to be seen to, the whole place might as well be repainted.

Thinking it through on the drive home, though, he'd come up with another plan altogether.

At the party, he'd bumped into an old acquaintance who told him about a journey he'd taken, walking the length of southern Greece. The country was unspoilt there, and the sea as still as polished stone. The house he'd been building was nearly ready, he'd told Max, and would be done within the month. It was as he heard his story that everything became clear, and Max's own idea had presented itself: he was going on a journey to find them some land.

Sophie looked away when he told her, then he said could she please hear him out. It would change their lives and make them happier, he was sure of it.

He couldn't afford a great deal of space, but it would be warm. Labour and materials were local and cheap, and he'd call in a favour from an architect friend.

He'd accepted some trips for the *Geographic* the following autumn, and had picture stories lined up for the *Observer*. A couple of American agencies were interested in his early prints, and French *Vogue* had been in touch about a cover.

With the new income, in addition to what came in from Bea's collector friends, he'd be able to settle the bills for the works at Pennerton. Taking into account the proceeds of Wigmore Street, there would be just enough for the new house as well.

He gave her proof of his promises in the form of contracts with roofers and plumbers. When she asked how long he was going for, he replied, 'As long as it takes.'

It would be worth it, he said: they could spend every summer there for weeks on end, and it would be an idyll for them all.

The piano that was delivered in the week of his departure was put in the upstairs sitting room, at the end of the line of easels. Sophie smiled and cried at the same time and asked how he had been able to afford it. Max told her the room would be called the Music Room now, and she should order what she needed and invite her old friends from the Academy to sing with her.

The morning he left, there were snowdrops on the Triangle Meadow. Sophie and the girls had said their goodbyes the night before, but Peter was up, coming back from matins at Pennerton Church.

At the top of the Long Avenue, he waved Max down and they spoke with the engine running.

'You should stay,' Peter told him.

'You already said.'

'I'm saying it again.'

'It's done.'

'So undo it. It's the worst idea you've ever had. She needs you, not some damn fool house in the bloody – You're running away.'

Max nodded, then he drove off slowly with his left hand raised, like a sunflower on its stem.

Beatrice and Sophie walked with the girls in the meadow most days. Once, when they did this, Beatrice and Vinny went ahead. They played in the grass and ran in circles to the lime tree border, so that birds rose up and banked hard above the trees. Sophie stopped the pram at the oak and sat on the ground, until they came back, laughing and out of breath.

'It's for blackbirds or magpies, Maman!'

'Teach me, ma chérie.'

'*One for sorrow. Two for –*' She stopped, and Beatrice had to say it with her.

'*Four for a boy, Five for a kiss –*'

Vinny was tired, then, and Beatrice carried her to the house on her shoulders. 'I am a giant, Maman!' she said. Sophie, pushing the pram, didn't answer, even when Vinny shouted it.

Sophie spent the next day in bed. Too hot or half frozen, with sweats and a fever, she coughed so much that Vinny came in at midnight to put her hands on her maman's head.

'Be quiet,' she said. 'Be quiet or Roo-roo will wake up.'

When Sophie was well again, Beatrice insisted on more walks, and whist or gin rummy while the girls had their naps.

Once, she found Sophie in the kitchen, staring at the wall.

'Sorry,' Sophie said, starting. 'I lost track of time. It's only soup, it'll be quick once I start. I never used to be like this,' and she frowned. 'He said that about me when we were first together. "You are the keeper of my clock,"' then she cried.

'You miss him.' Beatrice put a hand on her back. 'What is it now? – two months, nearly three? I was the same when Rupert was killed. Losing things, not knowing what day it was. My hair started falling out! I felt so sick I couldn't get up in the mornings. Oh, it was awful.'

'How did it stop? How did you—'

'Woke up one morning and decided I'd had enough. Went to a heap of parties. Drank lots of cocktails. Then I met a nice young man who took me to Paris, or I took him. Sex on a night train! My God, Soph, have you ever had sex on a train?'

Sophie smiled, then she cried some more. Beatrice held her and said, 'You're OK. Or you will be when he's home.'

Beatrice left her at the table with a board and a knife, and went back to Vinny. Sophie chopped an onion, then another, staring at the rain on the window. Slicing into the end of her finger, she carried on chopping, then Beatrice was there.

'How are you getting on? Vinny's upset and I – Oh God! Stop! Lovey, stop!'

At the sink, the blood ran freely. There were cuts to Sophie's palm and two of her fingers.

'What were you doing, Soph? Why didn't you—'

'Doesn't hurt.' Her breathing was quick. 'I didn't feel it.'

Beatrice wrapped Sophie's hand in a tea towel. She rang through to Peter and fetched the girls, then he drove them to the hospital at Ashford, and Beatrice held a cloth to staunch the blood.

One night in the spring, the two women crept into the library. Ducking under the tape, they ignored the WET PAINT signs and walked along bookcases shrouded in sheets. There were tools and pots and brushes which they skirted round, and scaffold towers. Beatrice told Sophie to hold a corner of the dust sheet, thrown over an armchair. They flicked it in the air and let it fall. Then, at last, they lit a fire and talked into the night, patterned in that shadowy light.

When Sophie asked her did she have a lover in London, Beatrice told her that sometimes there were a few and it was complicated, but not so as to be unmanageable. Sophie raised her eyebrows, and Beatrice explained that by keeping a few in rotation, she could avoid becoming too attached, which was essential: she wouldn't marry again, having promised herself once already.

'What about children?'

'I've left that a little late, haven't I?' She paused. 'Even if I could contemplate the idea of anyone other than Rupert being their father. I used to imagine them playing in the Triangle Meadow.' She half laughed. 'We made the great mistake of naming them.'

'Naming who?'

'Our future children. We were planning a brood. Houseful, you know. It'd be like treading on his grave, having them without him. When he went, everything went. My whole world, I mean. My world was there and then it wasn't.'

She wasn't particularly young when they married, and had begun to think she'd never settle down. But then there was a midsummer party and he declared himself. The day after the wedding, he returned to his crew. It was in part, she said, the impulsiveness of the whole situation that made her so certain he'd return: there was no time to doubt it. When his men came home without him, she knew she'd be always alone.

'Oh, Bea!'

'Oh Bea nothing. It was a long time ago. I was lucky to have known him at all, after growing up in a family like mine. He knew how to love, and how to express his feelings. I'd never experienced that in a man. He was easy about things. Even if he'd wanted to raise his voice, I'm not sure he'd have known how. And he was kind! Really kind, I mean. That was a novelty.' She reached in her bag for her cigarette case. 'My father was a bully, Soph. You may as well hear it from me.' She flicked her lighter shut, then she inhaled. 'Can't imagine Max has told you, not in so many words. A brute, even. My mother did the right thing by leaving him. Rupert was alien to all of that. Then he was killed.'

She looked at the fire, and neither of them spoke for some time.

'In any case,' she said. 'He left me well provided for, so whatever happens, you needn't worry about your girls.'

'What do you mean, whatever happens?'

'Don't be defensive.' She stubbed out her cigarette on the grate. 'You're in love with my brother, of course you are. But you're also very young, and very beautiful. Things might change.' She offered Sophie the silver case, withdrawing it twice as fast. 'Of course, your voice. I'm sorry. And for God's sake, don't tell Max I've been using his fireplace as an ashtray.'

On the last day of June Sophie went into the hall, caught in a decision: whether to wake the girls from their nap, or to play whist in the library with Beatrice.

Then he was there and she was hitting his chest with her fists and he was holding her, saying, 'Stop crying, will you, and let me kiss you,' and, 'Sophie-Sophie-Sophie! It was a birthday surprise!' and then he was laughing. 'I'm home, aren't I? I'm home.'

Beatrice said she'd listen for the girls.

They cut through the orchard to the Triangle Meadow and on

into the woods. Returning to the house, Sophie said, 'No, don't come in. Vinny will be up all night if she sees you.'

'Sophie!'

'Please. It's only for an hour or so. Go to Peter's. You should say hello anyway, tell him you're back.'

'I don't want to!'

'Well, have another walk, then! It's a gorgeous evening. Bea and I will give them supper and a bath and put them to bed. You can wake them up tomorrow and surprise them. Please.'

In the morning he fetched Vinny from her bed.

She was shy with him, so he persuaded her to talk. Then he wrapped her in her dressing gown and led her by the hand. She showed him where the picnic rug was and they put it on the lawn below the Long Library terrace. Later, they took a birthday breakfast out and left it covered with a cloth. In the kitchen garden there were poppies that were taller than her. They collected them with larkspur, and Vinny waited in the upstairs corridor while Max carried Ruthie from her cot.

He laid Ruthie on the pillow beside Sophie's head, then he fetched his camera. When Sophie woke up, Ruthie wriggled into her and Vinny held out the flowers.

'They are so beautiful,' Sophie said, then Vinny climbed onto the bed and Sophie shifted her position and folded both girls into her. They slept for a minute, until Max said her name and she opened her eyes.

In the second before the shutter closed, she smiled.

The family sat in the bright sun of the new month eating fruit and eggs and muffins and jam. When Peter came from the kitchen garden and said, 'You've come home, then,' Max only nodded, but Sophie asked him to sit with them.

Little Peter padded from the orchard with his tail in the air. When he saw them he ran across the grass then he climbed onto Max and off, slipping from his shoulders and curling into a ball on his lap.

Max showed them the drawings for the house that was being built, which would be called a villa not a house, and would be like Pennerton but smaller, standing lower from the ground and hidden in the trees so that a passing boat would have no idea it was there.

He told them about the sea they would swim in, which was deep and clear and warm. There were two coves to choose between, and when the girls were old enough they'd be able to swim from one to the other then climb out and run round and swim back again, all day long if they wanted.

Vinny said, 'Papa, where is Greece?' and he answered, 'Not so far from Africa,' but Beatrice told him not to be mean, so he went in for the atlas.

Taking Vinny's hand, he drew her finger down the page to the southernmost point of the mainland. That was where the villa would stand, he told her: at the tip of the middle claw of a three-toed dinosaur's footprint, overlooking the Mediterranean Sea.

A young woman called Eleni would look after the villa with her brother, Ilías. Eleni was already planting bougainvillea where the courtyard would be. It was hot enough for vines and lemons and every sort of herb, and Ilías was digging out a series of vegetable beds, for white aubergines, and mountain greens with purple tips, which Eleni would cook for them.

Stones were being brought from the mountains, some for the steps to the coves, others, for benches: an L-shaped one in the courtyard, to stand beside the fountain, and a C-shaped one on the promontory, so the family could take cushions and watch the setting sun.

The rest, he said, were being made into their home.

'Solid as a rock,' he laughed. 'It'll still be standing at the end of time.'

Then he fetched his camera and set the self-timer but Beatrice looked away and said, 'Wait, please! I want my sunglasses.'

'No,' Max told her. 'Stay exactly where you are,' but she was up from the rug and facing him. As tall as one another and as broad across the shoulders, they stood with their hands on their hips and their chins thrust out. Did he want her in the photograph or not, she said, and who was he to come back unannounced and tell people what to do? Of course she needed sunglasses: she hadn't done her face; the sun was too bright; and in any case, the girls should have their bonnets.

'The girls are fine,' Sophie said. 'And you look gorgeous enough. You always do.'

When he came home from his long journey, Ruthie was a baby and had never really known him. Vinny, though, was big enough to play by herself and to pick Ruthie up, or try to.

So when they sat on the rug and he told them the tale of the olive grove, Vinny was easy in her father's company. Ruthie, on the other hand, lay with her legs in the air. She was alternately rocked from side to side by Sophie, or tickled on her tummy by her aunt, simply registering his voice as that of a stranger and making nothing in particular of what he said, beyond a sense that it was emerging in the shape of a story.

When their light was out and it was just the two of them, Ruthie heard the tale again. In her sleepiness, she'd made no more sense of Vinny's version than of her father's. When Vinny reached the part where Max said, 'Where is the picnic blanket, Vee?' and Vinny answered, 'I know where it is, Papa!' she stopped listening altogether, and turned her attention to the series of images flickering across the inside of her mind as though they were spun in a zoetrope.

At the same time as watching these images, she was participant in them.

First, a man who was a stranger came into her room in the half-light and took her from her cot. As he carried her along the corridor there was his rough skin on her cheek and her heart began to flutter. Then they were in her mother's bedroom and this man she didn't know was putting her down on her mother's pillow and she could smell her mother's hair and feel her breath on her face. Her breathing was in sync with her mother's, and they were one person, not two, then they fell asleep like that with their faces right up close, until the sound of the camera woke her and the images started again.

They would play all night, and she would wake sometimes, and watch them.

After Sophie and the girls were in bed, Max developed his prints and wrote along their borders: '*My Girls, at Pennerton, July 1965*' and '*The Homecoming Breakfast*'.

At about two in the morning, he found Peter in the hall.

'What the hell are you doing?'

'And you?'

'I'm wide awake. It'll take me a few days to settle. It was a long drive home.'

'It was a long five months.'

Max opened the front door and gestured. 'We can talk tomorrow.'

'There's something I have to—'

'Tomorrow.'

'It won't wait.'

When Max made for the library, Peter said, 'No. Not in the house.'

At his cottage they sat face-to-face.

It had happened in April, when Beatrice was in London. Spring had been in for a couple of weeks, but there was a frost and he went back to lighting the fires. One morning, he was fetching more wood from the stables, at about 5 a.m. Trying his key, he found the kitchen door locked from the inside and another key left in. It was the same with the front door, so he went to the Long Library terrace. The curtains were closed but a light was shining. When he tried the French windows, they were locked as well.

Putting the episode down to Sophie being absent-minded, he left it. When he tried again in an hour, everything was the same. Trying once more at 8 a.m., he became concerned and telephoned from the cottage. When there was no answer, he peered through the kitchen window.

The lights were all on but the room was empty. He walked to the stable, meaning to find a log to smash the window.

Halfway there, he heard a sound.

He turned, but there was no one.

When it came again it was louder and he followed it. He put his ear to the coal shed door, and heard Sophie's voice.

'Two for joy. Two for joy. Two for joy. I must count. I must I must. She said I must count them out. Three for a girl.'

There was a bang, then, 'Three for a girl.'

Another bang, something being thrown against metal.

He tried the door but it was jammed, so he kicked it open.

She'd climbed over the wooden barrier and was squatting on the pile of coal, half in shadow, half in light. Her night slip was pulled up to her waist and her face and neck were streaked with black. There was a tin bucket in front of her into which she was dropping, or throwing, pieces of coal.

'But if it is one –' she threw a piece in – 'for –' then another – 'sorrow, then –' and another – 'she didn't say what to do. One for sorrow. One for One for One for.'

'Sophie,' he said. 'Sophie!'

The bucket was almost full now, but she continued as though in a trance: placing a piece of coal on top, counting and reaching for another.

'Sophie!' he said again, and she stopped. When she raised her head and looked straight past him, he jumped over the barrier. He reached for her, then she stood with her back against the wall.

'No!' she shouted. 'Oh oh oh no no no! Oh no! No you don't! Can't you see? It's alright for her. No babies, has she? No babies. I have to, absolutely have to get it right.'

Peter stepped back.

'Four for a boy.'

'She just emptied the bucket and started again.' Peter stared at Max.

'Did you make her stop?'

'Eventually.' He described how he'd put both arms around her, half grabbing, half embracing her, and asked her to let him help.

Only then did she look at him directly. Her shoulders dropped and she frowned.

'Alright,' she said. 'If you don't mind awfully. It's ever so hard on my own.'

He knelt beside her and they worked together: him passing pieces of coal, Sophie placing them in the bucket. When it was full, she put her hands to her face.

'Oh, Peter. I am so sorry.'

He smashed the kitchen window. Upstairs, he waited on the landing while she washed. When he'd helped her into bed, he stayed until she'd settled. Pausing at the girls' bedroom, he saw that their beds were empty.

He found them in the Long Library.

Vinny was asleep on the cream wool rug with Ruthie in her arms. The fire had gone out. Beyond them was a heap of coal, five or six buckets' worth, and on the wall to the right of the mantelpiece, in capitals a foot high, were drawn the words:

FOUR FOR A BOY

He turned to Vinny. Her face and her forearms were streaked with black and her mouth was half open in sleep.

Peter shook her gently. When she saw him, she said, 'Maman! Where is Maman?' then she started to cry.

He carried her to the sofa and listened while she told him everything: how Sophie had woken her in the middle of the night and brought her downstairs with Ruthie. How she'd passed Maman the coal for her letters, and stood on a chair to help her fill them in, and how, when Sophie said she had to go outside for a while, she did as she was asked and promised to lock the back door from the inside when Maman had gone, and to stay in the library with Ruthie until someone came.

Ruthie woke up. She looked at Peter, then she kicked her legs and scratched at her chest. There was a broad stripe of black across her face from one side to the other.

Peter carried Ruthie up, and Vinny followed. He bathed them both, then he put them to bed, telling Vinny their maman was asleep, so she wasn't to disturb her. He went to the library and washed the words from the wall and took the coal to the shed, and he telephoned for a glazier to replace the kitchen window.

In the afternoon, Sophie came to the cottage. She thanked him, then she asked him not to speak of it to the girls, nor to Beatrice, nor with Max when he came home. She was grateful for his kindness, but would rather the incident were forgotten.

'Did you tell Bea?'

'She was in town.'

'Should've bloody well been here, shouldn't she?'

'Your sister was away two days, maybe three, the whole time you were gone.'

'I'll have a word.'

'Sophie asked me not to. I wasn't going to tell you either, but when I saw you on the lawn yesterday, and her all wrapped around you—'

'What?'

'I just thought you should know. There's no point you saying anything now. I'd prefer Sophie to think I kept my promise.'

'She's hardly in a position to—'

'She was tired. And lonely. Beatrice came back and Sophie got on with things. It was forgotten.'

'And the girls?'

'They were fine. They won't remember it, or not so as to do any harm. I'm telling you for when you go away next time.'

'What difference will it make?'

'You might not go so long? Or if you do, you might let us know how to contact you.'

'Us? It's us now, is it?'

'Drop it. You were an idiot to go. You could at least try not to be one now you're back.'

Max started to leave. At the door, he turned. 'Thank you for looking after my wife.'

In July, he took them first to Italy, for the ferry from Brindisi, then they drove the length of Greece.

When they arrived at the villa, Sophie was silent.

She walked the grounds and stood on the cove and went to the high Lightroom, shading her eyes and turning to face Meropi Island.

It was an hour before she found him in the courtyard with the girls.

'Thank you, Max. I see now, why you wanted to be here.'

The villa's courtyard was bordered by a trellised walkway, which was hung with vines and bougainvillea and gave dappled views to the sea, and which Sophie named 'The Pergola'.

At Pennerton once, Max had given her a journal from the Long Library, kept by his grandmother, Ruthie: *On Building the Kitchen Garden at Pennerton House (with notes on its maintenance)*. She'd worked through it with Peter, attempting to return the place to something like it had been. Now, at the villa, she said she would do the same with Eleni, and try for an echo of that English garden.

The young woman showed Sophie how to tie a cloth scarf behind her head, and together they put pots between the arches, and planted them with basil and oregano.

Working side by side, they could have been sisters.

Afterwards, Eleni did a larger pot, with a basil plant taken from elsewhere in the grove that had grown as tall as Vinny. She put it by the kitchen door, and when Max moved it to the Pergola with the others, Ilías explained that by leaving it where his sister had put it, Max would be keeping his family safe.

Every evening, Eleni walked along the boundary wall to the chapel in the grove, to light her candle for Panagiotis.

From time to time throughout that summer, Max said to Sophie they should tell her to stop, and perhaps if she let the habit go, she'd find someone new, but Sophie said it wasn't their business to tell a woman how to mourn. Eleni was young, she said. She'd find someone when she was ready. And if she never was, that was for her to decide, surely.

In the afternoons, if Eleni had finished her housework, or if Sophie especially asked her to, she came with them to the cove. The girls had their hands held all the way, and Max was patient with Ruthie, who was so tiny and took so long on the steps.

There was the settling of the things on their rugs, and the building of pebble towers. The girls were shy but Eleni coaxed them, naming in Greek the birds they saw, or the breeze that was blowing. Testing the direction and the temperature, she declared it was the *voras* from the mountains in the north, or the *notos*, from the southern seas, or, from the side, the *meltémi*.

Vinny and Ruthie played at the shoreline before being lifted in their parents' arms and carried into the water. They cried the first time, but because they were held like that, feeling safe but also terrified, they grew used to the sea and its salt on their lips and, in the late afternoon when the meltémi came in, to its movement against their bodies.

When they were put to bed, Vinny told Max and Sophie that they would prefer to sleep out there, in the sea, and Eleni would sleep out there with them, and they never wanted to be on dry land again for the whole of the rest of their lives, and Ruthie said, 'Me too and Eleni! Me too and Eleni!'

5 MONDAY

Ruthie sat up in Vinny's bed, and called out lazily. Hearing nothing back, she went to the door.

'Vee!'

She listened for any movement. Wandering down the corridor, she looked in all the bedrooms. Then she looked in the book-lined room, with Vinny's desk, and her papers everywhere. When she reached the door to the veranda at the back of the villa, she stopped and retraced her steps. In Vinny's bedroom, she put on her sister's slip, then she went back to the veranda and took the binoculars from their case. The terrace in front of Annie and Edward's house was empty, the back door closed and the shutters as well.

Standing on one of the Lightroom work surfaces, she could see a way out to sea.

There was no sign of the family in the water. Swinging right round, she could see most of the grove as well. She looked until she was sure, then she climbed down.

On the work surface was an envelope containing two letters. The phrase, '*Sophie to Max*' was written on the front, together with the dates: 29 April 1965, and 28 October 1971.

Picking up the envelope, she remembered her promise to show her sister everything. Then she remembered Vinny's decision to go to Athens with Eleni, and to leave her all on her own. She pulled a lighter from her pocket and flicked it on. When just the corner of the envelope was singed, she let the flame go out, and read the first of the letters again.

Pennerton, 29 April 1965

Max my darling you haven't even told me where to write to you this month so I'll send this to the poste restante at Athens like the last one and hope that you will come back there after this town you were going to see but it hurts, it really hurts, that you didn't think of telling me. Have you found us a place yet, and are you coming home? I'm writing fast, and I'm tired, and I have a terrible cold on my chest again and a cough that will not go away. There is a widening of misery that you do not say where you are going. And you don't ever telephone and you know what it would mean if you did.

I cannot do this without you. There are days when I do not know who I am. In the afternoon, Beatrice takes them so I can sleep but I stay awake. I lie on your side of the bed and I think I have never met you and none of this is real.

There, I have begun badly now.

It is a cold spring. Next week the gas will go in, so poor old Peter can stop carrying in the coal. He's good to us, and makes the fires up. He brings in flowers from the meadow, and gives Vinny piggybacks. They are strong and well, your girls. It is only me who is poorly.

Beatrice sits with me in the evenings and we talk, and will you be cross if I say she has told me everything about you?

Everything! From when you were twelve years old and your mother left and she looked after you, and then from later, when you grew. So I know about Leopoldville and what happened there and I don't know why you wouldn't tell me. You did nothing wrong, you did your job and you took a photograph. You were not there to save that man's life and it is good that people saw that photograph and of course you couldn't know what would happen after you took it.

On Monday, before any of us had woken up properly, Bea came in to say she was going to London, and to give Ruthie and Vinny a kiss goodbye. She brought back presents for the girls and I think that is all she went for, to go to Hamleys and buy presents, and a new pair of gloves for Peter, and a pile of crossword puzzles for herself. She bought Vinny a wooden rocking horse that she says is being sent and will go in the Music Room next to the piano, and she bought a mobile to hang above Ruthie's cot and a soft little horse for Vinny while she waits for the wooden one.

I think of you at night and I pull back the curtains and I see the stars above the Triangle Meadow like an upside-down bowl full of stars, and I wonder which stars you can see from where you are.

The piano is beautiful, the sound is perfect. The keys are weighted just right, so they touch me back when I touch them and they can be heavy or they can be light and very quiet so I can play even at night. Vinny sits underneath sometimes and she holds onto my ankles. Ruthie sleeps on the floor beside her, with Little Peter curled up as well. (Yes! He comes in and I let him even though he's your sworn enemy!)

Beatrice says that when you come back you should take a photograph of your girls while they are sleeping because she has never seen anything so beautiful and they won't be like this forever.

When we walk with them in the Triangle Meadow, it is so quiet and there are only the rooks and Vinny runs ahead with Bea, and I push Ruthie in the pram and she falls fast asleep. She looks so serious when she sleeps. She has a face full of willpower but her eyelids are delicate enough for me to almost see through them if I look very close. Her lashes are so long they sit on her cheeks and her hair is the same colour red as mine. It is dark and straight and soft, not like Vinny's which curls into a bird's nest overnight. Then Vinny comes running back and shouts that she's seen something and wakes her sister, but really it is when they are both sleeping that you should see them and take a picture. In the morning darkness I feel some soft warm thing on my cheek and Vinny is climbing into my bed and she falls straight to sleep next to Ruthie and when it is growing light I watch the two of them and Vinny has one arm lying across her sister and their cheeks are touching and Vinny's hair is in a heap on Ruthie's face and there is only the sound of their quick hot breathing. Vinny looks so different from her sister when she is asleep. There is none of Ruthie's seriousness in her face and she is still, like a little girl who is thinking only of sleeping.

They do not seem real, they are so perfect, or they do not seem mine, but then I lie back down and we breathe together and we are not three people but one, and I am so happy then.

You should come home. When you do you will see we have a pocket paradise here, where everything is small, and quiet, and beautiful.

Sophie

Ruthie closed her eyes and heard her mother's voice, like bubbles rising through water.

When she left the room, the letter was still on the work surface, sealed back up in its envelope.

In the kitchen, she found Vinny's note with its generous, round handwriting.

Ruthie, sweetheart,

Eleni's left you breakfast in the courtyard. There's a peach so sweet you'll love it. Do eat, won't you, especially if you're going to swim. I'm off on Wednesday so you'll just have to put up with me fussing for one more day.

V xxx

PS That doesn't mean you can stop eating properly after that. It just means you won't have to put up with me fussing. But anyway, I'm not.

PPS Back in time for lunch, just going into town with Eleni so she doesn't have to carry it all on her own. (Ilías has borrowed the car today – AGAIN!)

PPPS If you do swim, wear something, won't you, now those people are here? Have one of my swimming costumes if you can't find yours. And remember to use our cove, not theirs.

PPPPS Obviously you know those things. Sorry. Love you lots xxx

Wandering into the courtyard, Ruthie dipped under the vine and picked up some grapes that had fallen. At the table she saw the peach, next to a bowl of yogurt. The honey had sunk and left its trace, a deep gold stripe against the white.

She bit into the peach. As she wiped the juice away from her chin she saw Vinny's bikini, dripping from a chair. She finished the peach, then she pulled off Vinny's night slip and used it to wipe the rest of the juice from her face. She picked up the bikini bottoms and held them to her naked hips; they stood out several inches on either side. Taking the bikini top as well, she wrapped them in a ball with the slip and put them on the kitchen floor by the machine, ready for Eleni.

In the courtyard, a swallow darted and brushed the top of her head. She heard Max: 'See that, Roo! They're dancing!' They were wheeling and playing in the air above the house, and he said it again: 'They're dancing for us.'

His voice was so loud she looked for him: under the Pergola, behind the fountain. There was no one, though, so she crossed the courtyard and went through the trees.

The villa's cove was in full sun and had baked hard, so the soles of her feet were burned. At the water's edge she found a place where the pebbles were smaller, on their way to being sand. She lay herself down on her stomach, adjacent to the water and right at its edge, then she wriggled her body, burrowing spaces for her ribcage and her hip bones, and for her knees and her feet. Lying with her left hand out, her arm was lapped by the water as far as her elbow.

The sea is gentle here, and until you swim outside the horseshoe and kick off into open water, clear and shallow and warm. After an hour, Ruthie woke and stepped in up to her thighs. It was so soft and so still it felt no different from the air, or a feather, brushed against her skin.

Then she pushed off and was swimming, unsure if she was half asleep or half awake. As soon as she was out far enough and could feel the water moving, she let the swell lift her up from the base of her spine. Taking her cue from this she flipped down and in, pulling her arms back, and again, shooting further down. Then she was on the bottom, tracking the sea floor as it lowered, rose, lowered. There were bright ovals of sand as big as meadows, then rocks in ridges then a sand-meadow again, whiter this time. Strips of weed floated past and a shoal of bass swam beneath her more like shadows than fish. She came up towards the surface and sudden clouds of tiny silver things burst apart and scattered, flicking against her stomach and in between her legs.

When she was six years old, Max had taught her to swim front crawl.

Vinny, who had only just learned, complained that she'd had to wait for ages, so Ruthie shouldn't be allowed.

'Don't be daft,' Beatrice said, coming in from the water and running her fingers through her hair, so it was slicked to her head. 'Why on earth would you want to go on proper swims without your little sister? Pass me my sunglasses, lovey. God, it's bright here. And the oil, please. Yes, that's it, I'm sure it's in that bag with my cigarettes.'

Ruthie took longer than Vinny had: she was small for her age and tired easily. When the girls had their first contest, though, she was faster by far, darting past Vinny in the water, under her and round her, while Max stood on the island's strip of sand and cheered her in. For the rest of that week and the next, Vinny got up early to practise, until they were each of a pace.

There was a wildness to that first summer of their seaworthiness, when whole days were spent swimming from cove to cove, and running up the path and round the headland to start again. Returning to the second cove they would pass through the oval meadow, which was full of butterflies. There were trees at the edge with limes that ripened through the summer, and because the grass was so tall, Ruthie sometimes disappeared in it, and Vinny was fooled into thinking she'd gone the other way, so that Ruthie doubled back unseen, waiting by the trees for what felt like forever until Vinny shouted, 'I see you, I see you, Roo!'

They went straight to the sea from their beds, tiptoeing across the courtyard so that Eleni wouldn't come from her apartment and make them have breakfast. If their father had gone ahead it would be a race to find out which cove he'd chosen, or to see whether he was already at Meropi Island, and to fight over who would get to him first.

When Vinny slept in, it was just Max and Ruthie. Until she was used to it, and for a long time afterwards, he struck out first and stayed just ahead, keeping watch for jellyfish. Sometimes he trod water to observe her stroke, and asked if she was tired. If she said yes, he said, 'Hop on, then,' and she came alongside and struggled up and lay on him with her face on his skin, just at the point where his neck met his back.

She clung to him and felt his muscles move while his shoulders worked the water. When he took her into shore, she crouched on the pebbles to hear what she'd done wrong, what to do differently next time.

This morning, catching her breath at the top, she was shocked to find herself alone.

Turning and turning, she realised she was looking for him, as though he had simply dropped back and would catch up any moment. Swimming on, her stroke was hesitant. It wasn't so much that she wanted him there, particularly; more that she'd assumed he was near and was about to take her by surprise, bursting from the water and calling her name and saying, 'Come on, Roo, hurry up!' so she'd tail him, chasing the wake of him and stretching out her crawl to touch the tips of his toes, or darting underneath him to rise and turn and say, 'Papa, I beat you, I'm here, hold me, I'm here.'

Then, suddenly, he *was* there.

Keeping stroke with her, he was a little too close so she lost her rhythm. She stopped, twisting in the water and looking, but there was no one. When she swam on, he was there again, too big and right beside her. This time she could see him clearly, and she wanted him there at the same time as not wanting him. Instead of breaking her stroke she veered left, but he stayed with her. The next time she turned to breathe, there was clear water.

Alone again, she slipped under.

The light fell on the sea in squares, separating its surface into thousands of small panels. Their frames were white-gold and moved in a regular way, as though a giant sieve had been laid there. She flipped up through a square and down through another and swam into a flock of little fish, one that went on so far ahead it confused her, thinking she'd reached the edge only to see it spreading out further in front, and further still.

She came up and breathed, then she held her face under again and lay on her front: a star suspended, her arms and legs out wide on either side. The water was so clear and the sun so bright and she was so far out she was a glider, and there was only air between her and the sea floor. She let her legs hang and they were tiny in that space, two pins, golden in the blue. She thrust her feet behind her and began to move, a steady crawl at first, each stroke long and even and seamless. She picked up speed and her arms felt no resistance, a careless movement not like swimming but more like sea-flying. Then she worked harder and moved across the surface as fast as she could, and the sea was so flat she was out of the water and could look down and see herself, a miniature swimmer on the flat blue sea.

She slowed to a stop and turned to face the shore. Because the route she'd followed had taken her further south than she'd intended, the view was only of her own cove, snug beneath the villa. There was more of the headland to clear before she'd be able to see the second cove, which the family would be using.

Switching to the west, she headed further out and held her course more carefully. When finally she turned, she could see the four of them strung in a line. Treading water, slow and low down, she wondered if they could see her too. She swam breaststroke, as smooth as possible so her head barely rose above the water. When she was square on, she stopped.

Tallish outcrops of rock rose up at the shoreline, to the left of the steps and some way away from them. The children had taken up their stations independently, one on either side of the cove. Edward was crouching, collecting pebbles in a mound. Annie, on the other side of the outcrop at the shoreline, was closer to the water than him, though not quite in it. She seemed to be doing nothing at all, squatting with her head in her hands. Their parents were on another part of the beach entirely, beyond the steps and lying down, holding books above their faces.

The mother got up and shook out her towel. She collected her things and walked forward to the water, gaining a sightline across the beach to the children. She called out and Edward and Annie looked up. She was only telling them she was going, though, not asking them to come. When she started up the steps, Ruthie dived. Thinking the woman might turn at the top and look out, she swam back and forth underwater. By the time she surfaced the woman had disappeared. On the beach, the man put down his book and came forward to the waterline, kneeling to splash his back. Saying nothing to the children, he returned to his reading.

Edward finished his mound of stones.

Annie stood and walked to the water.

Edward stood as well. He skimmed one stone first, hard and fast, and then two more in quick succession, straight across the sea to the right of where he was standing, away from Annie.

She stepped in up to her waist, scooping up a handful of water and tilting back her head, pouring it on her face, and rubbing it on her arms as well.

Edward carried on skimming, faster and harder, until the pile was almost gone. Annie waded on until she was completely in the water, then she began to swim a little towards Edward, who turned to her and, keeping the same hard fast rhythm, threw one of his stones so that it hit the top of her head.

She screamed.

Their father stood from his towel and stumbled forwards.

At that moment Edward turned away and flicked the last few stones so they bounced like swallows on the sea, and so fast Ruthie barely saw them. Annie was crawling from the water, falling onto the beach and crouching and holding her head and rocking back and forth, and the sound of her howls shot across the surface to Ruthie who put her hands to her ears and Annie's father was running through the water in front of the steps and was on the ground beside her. Edward sauntered over with his hands in his pockets. He watched his father kneel beside Annie and bring his face in close to her scalp. Then he picked Annie up and began to carry her towards the steps, saying something to Edward over his shoulder. Edward shook his head and followed.

Ruthie turned and swam. Pitching straight into a racing crawl, she calculated that she could be back at the villa before they arrived at the stone house.

She stumbled onto the villa's cove, taking the steps two at a time. With her breath heaving, she sprinted through the trees like a boy. Vinny looked up from her lunch as she passed. Shaking water from her hair, Ruthie grabbed the Pergola to steady herself, then she made for the kitchen door.

'Ruthie! You said you'd wear something! Those people!'

'Later. I'm busy,' and then she was inside.

'No, I'm sorry,' said Vinny, standing. 'That's just not fair.' She followed Ruthie in. 'It's ridiculous. They're here for a week and you can skinny-dip for the rest of the year if no one else comes. You're making an exhibition of yourself before we're even twenty-four hours in!'

Already on the stairs to the Lightroom, Ruthie ignored her. Grabbing her binoculars and throwing on a T-shirt, she ran to the veranda at the back of the villa.

'Ruthie,' Vinny called out, 'is this what you're going to be like whenever there's anyone here? Can you just grow up a bit, please? Eleni and I brought everything back on our own and you've barely touched your breakfast. I waited for you for ages for lunch. I said you could have one of my bikinis, I left you one. I've got enough to think about with my work—'

'Nobody saw me,' Ruthie said, coming in to stand at the top of the stairs. 'Of course I can't wear your bikini. It'd fall off as soon as I put it on.' She clapped both hands to her chest.

On the veranda she shut the door and turned the key. Then she sat, training the binoculars on the terrace of the stone house, scanning the grove and back again.

Annie's father appeared first. Marching rather than walking, he was still carrying Annie, who hung from his arms. Edward was trailing behind. Across the grove, the mother came out of the stone house with a laundry basket. She put the basket on the table and unravelled a line from beside the door. Holding the line in one hand and picking up a chair with the other, she stepped from the sun terrace and walked towards the wooden post. She climbed on the chair and fixed the line then she brought the basket. She climbed on the chair again and hung a white sheet. When she was fixing the last peg, the sheet slapped her legs, and she turned and saw them. In one movement she jumped down and ran across the grove. She took Annie from the girl's father, then they were back on the terrace and Annie was sitting at the table. Her mother was leaning over her, lifting one of her plaits, and the father was marching back towards

Edward who pushed past him and went into the house. The father followed him.

Annie's mother went in as well and came out with a glass of water and a towel. She gave the water to Annie and placed the towel around her shoulders. Then she left the terrace and fetched the hose. She called into the house. On the terrace again, she held the hose directly above Annie's head.

The water streamed red across the white tiles.

Annie's father came out of the house.

The two adults inspected Annie's scalp. Alternately they rinsed, and looked again, rinsing until the water ran clear on the tiles and the tap was turned off. Another towel was found and wrapped around her head.

Ruthie, on the veranda, heard someone trying to open the door behind her. She waited until they gave up, then she put the binoculars back in their case. She was slipping them under her chair when Vinny appeared at the other end of the veranda, having walked all the way round. She looked at Ruthie, then she looked over at the terrace of the stone house, which, apart from the table and chairs, was empty.

'Shall we have a chat?'

'About what?'

'About whether you're alright? About whether I should still go to Athens on Wednesday? About whether it mightn't be a bad idea for you to come with us?'

'I'm fine, Vee,' Ruthie said, 'Go and do your Brecht,' and she went inside.

In the aftermath of what happened in the chapel, this conversation haunted Vinny. When she returned to the idea that the whole thing might have been avoided, if Ruthie had only answered, 'Yes, alright then, I'll come,' Julian told her not to dwell on it.

Once, a year on, he lost patience, and said, 'It was just a matter of time. We both know that. It was a question of when, not if. And if not this, then something like it,' but she insisted, and told him he had no grounds, and would he please not speak to her about it again, if that was all he could say.

Up in the Lightroom that afternoon, Ruthie took the envelope with Sophie's letters, and held the lighter to it. Afterwards, she left the ash where it had fallen.

6 THE FEATHER-CLOCK

Sophie and Vinny lay on a rug in the kitchen garden. Sophie read Vinny a story, and Vinny read one back. Little Peter, who was almost asleep, flicked his paw at a butterfly.

Ruthie was on Max's lap, with a pod of broad beans in the palm of her hand. Together they teased the soft and pale green pellets from their hollows, which were downy and white inside. When the bucket was full, Max lay back and closed his eyes, and Ruthie slipped from his lap. Sophie tiptoed past him and fetched kitchen scissors for Vinny, so the girls could hunt for slugs. Vinny nipped the sleek-fat bodies in two while Ruthie watched the entrails ooze out, then they collected a penny from Sophie for each cut-carcass they presented, promising not to tell Max, and nodding when she said, did they understand: their work was essential if the cabbages were to grow.

Early in the morning, Peter stood under their window.

'The goosegogs are here! They're ready!'

At the gate to the kitchen garden, he told them they were lucky:

they'd be in Greece when the redcurrants cropped, but the weather had held, and the gooseberries were on time.

The two of them ran barefoot in the bushes with Little Peter, who in his old age had taken to following them everywhere. There were nooks of potatoes and runner beans, and Sophie held a colander on her hip, as if she were carrying a baby. She moved slowly, picking the gooseberries into it, and white butterflies settled on her hair. Max, standing on a stone bench, leaned his head back and watched.

'Girls!' he called. 'Your shoes, please,' and Sophie asked, 'Can't you leave them, it's only earth.' But their father answered, 'There are stones, and pieces of glass.'

Peter fetched their wellingtons and they turned them upside down to check for spiders. The lining cloth scratched Ruthie's calves. Without her socks the boots were too big and made her stumble. Her sister didn't say anything, so neither did she.

As soon as Max went in, they kicked off their boots and ran with Sophie and Peter to the Smart Lawn. Little Peter strolled ahead and back, brushing past Ruthie so she half tripped and righted herself. Quickly, before Max was in his lightroom, they crossed the lawn to the lavenders strung at the base of the slope like a line of cannonballs.

Walking between them, they scrambled up to the Long Library terrace, and sat with their shoulders touching, so that Ruthie's hair, straight as sheet metal and a red as deep as Sophie's, was half hidden by her sister's curls. Side by side and motionless, there was no sign that they were sisters: Vinny was pale and squat and Ruthie was tiny and dark. But when Sophie and Peter had pushed them off and they'd slid on their bottoms to the lawn, there was something in the way they stood and fell and picked each other up which made it very plain; something in the way they moved apart and came together and laughed one laugh and rolled on the grass and ran with their bare feet until Peter called, 'He's there, he's in the window,' and they raced down the Smart Lawn and into the orchard before their father looked out from his glass wall.

Peter kept watch until Max had gone, then Vinny went first and Ruthie followed, reaching for her big sister's hand when she stumbled, crying when she missed it and fell.

When it was time for them to go to bed, Max lifted them onto the stone slab by the kitchen sink and inspected their feet. Declaring them 'Too dirty for the stair carpet', he let the tap run until it steamed, then he scrubbed at them with coal tar soap and a wire brush.

When Little Peter curled up in the end stable and died, they held a funeral. Max said it was unnecessary but Sophie insisted.

'For the girls, Max, even if you don't want to. So they understand.'

'Understand what?'

'About death.'

'It's a cat. We're talking about a stable stray, not a pet.'

'They loved him. Vinny and Ruthie loved him. And Peter, you know he did.'

'Peter's an adult, isn't he?' Max said. 'Of course, though. If you want to.'

Sophie wrote a poem for Vinny to recite at the graveside, 'An Ode to Little Peter, Elder Statesman of the Stable'.

The day before the funeral, Max took a job. An oil well had blown during drilling, just off the coast of California. The slick was miles wide and growing, and the *Observer* wanted some shots.

'It's massive,' he told her, 'and it's happening now.'

'So is this,' she said, gesturing to Peter, who knelt on the Smart Lawn in a winter coat, measuring a space.

Just after sunrise, the air was thin and cold.

Vinny stood by the hole Peter had dug, beside the end cherry tree. She read the first line slowly, '*For he loved the sun and the sun loved him,*' and Ruthie began to cry. Peter and Sophie stood either side of her, holding her hands.

When Max's telegram came from Santa Barbara, Sophie dropped it on the fire.

'Give me your troubles,' she hummed that night as she tucked them in, and they told her their worries about Little Peter, and what would happen to him now, and wouldn't he be cold out there under the cherry tree? As the list of worries grew, she cupped her palms and told them to put them in, then she sang them the 'Sandman's Song' and threw their worries over her shoulder, one by one, sprinkling Magic Sleeping Dust on their eyes.

For a long time afterwards they would ask her to do it again. If their father was at home, and put them to bed, they would ask him instead. At first he said he didn't understand, so they explained their new game to him. Usually he'd say, 'No. Straight to sleep, the pair of you.' Once or twice, though, he let them show him their bruises where they'd fallen, or the scratches on their skin where they'd fought one another. He took the bruises and threw them in the air, then he kissed their wounds better and sprinkled Magic Sleeping Dust, whispering goodnight as he left.

He had come back from California with a book called *On How to Draw.* As well as the book, he gave Sophie a pile of sketch pads and pencils, with a box of watercolour paints.

'Just try it, Soph. Have some lessons if you want.'

In the Long Library, Ruthie found a piece of paper. On it were three spheres of varying sizes, with lines sweeping from their undersides. 'I don't know,' Max said when she showed him. 'Perhaps she's learning how to draw an upside-down *Sputnik.*'

'What's that?'

'A Russian spaceship. Not quite right, though, is it?'

When she showed it to Vinny, her sister turned the page and found three more spheres on the other side, with petals that were billowy, and stubby little thorns scored from the lines that swept from the undersides.

Apart from the half-finished sketches Ruthie continued to find, all of them scored too hard or scribbled too faint to see, Sophie's pictures were drawn with wax crayons borrowed from Vinny and Ruthie. There was a horse, scaled up and hung from an easel so they could play Pin the Tail on the Donkey. She stood in the Triangle Meadow with her easel, and attempted the oak from every perspective, using pieces of coal from the shed. Her face was streaked with black and Ruthie helped her clean it off with cold cream, smearing the white cream on the black coal. Sophie laughed, and let her cover the whole of her face in the cream and her own as well, so the two of them wiped it from each other's skin.

After a time, Sophie gave the unused sketch pads to the girls, and dropped the full ones in the oil-can burner.

'But I like them, Maman!' Vinny said in the orchard, watching the plume of smoke. 'Ruthie and I like them.'

Sophie said it was very sweet of Vinny but there was no need to fib. She shut the crayons in their case, and gave them to the girls with the paints and the brushes. Then she announced she'd had a different idea: she would take objects, and make them into other objects.

In the cupboards that stood in the hall, either side of the Old Library doors, Sophie found boxes of blue and yellow and speckled eggs that

Max had stolen from the hedgerows when he was a boy. 'They are so tiny,' she said to Max. 'This is where I'll begin.'

'Sophie, I'd rather you didn't. They're—'

'Of course,' she said. 'I'm going to use ordinary eggs, and make them as beautiful as these, that's all I meant.'

At the end of the week, Ruthie and Vinny woke to find a cluster of hollow shells hanging from their ceiling. Painted in pinks and pale blues and yellows, the shells shifted in the breeze.

Max brought two small pots of gold leaf from London and gave her a box from his lightroom.

'A gilding kit,' he said. 'It belonged to my mother. There's a book in there. It'll tell you what to do.'

She collected things from the garden and asked the girls to bring her whatever they found that was interesting. In an attic room, she made a wall of packing crates and set up a table behind them. Once, she fetched them from their beds. They stood in their nightdresses, rubbing their eyes, and looked at the brushes made of squirrel fur. She let them hold the tub of clear grease, and she let them try on her mask.

'Gold is like skin,' she explained. 'If you breathe on it, it'll disappear. Like old skin, I mean, dry skin. Or something lighter than skin.'

She put on the mask and held the brush and demonstrated the movements. Even with her nose and mouth covered, she turned away to breathe and back again, stroking the gold onto the surface.

Lined up for the morning was a tiny bird-skull Vinny had found in the garden, coated in grey paint.

'No,' she said when Ruthie reached out. 'Don't touch, it's drying. The book says it's the same paint that little boys use, for model aeroplanes. If you time it right, it's a tiny bit sticky at the last minute, then you take your squirrel brush and see if you can make it work.'

'Make what work?' Ruthie pulled the mask from Sophie's face.

'The finish. You'll get a sheen, I mean, if there's the right amount of stickiness, and you get the gold on quickly enough without breathing at the wrong moment and blowing it all away.'

'But how do you know when it's sticky enough?'

'I don't. I have no idea. Every time I begin, I've no idea if it'll work.'

'Can I have a go?' Ruthie asked. 'Maman? Can I?'

'No, darling.' She put her mask back on. 'I'm sorry, it's not for children.'

In July, Max was away again. Beatrice invited Sophie and the girls to Pilgrim's Lane, saying the rest of the Western world would be gluing themselves to their televisions, so she didn't see why they shouldn't.

'If he won't have one at Pennerton, you'd better come and watch it on mine. We shan't tell him,' she said. 'He'll only complain.'

It was a preoccupation for Ruthie that night, how she would avoid letting slip to her father that she'd seen a man walking on the moon. Vinny fell asleep three times, and when Beatrice said it was coming up, and this was it, Ruthie nudged her sister and said, it's about to happen, and how could they possibly not mention it, and what did Vinny think, but Vinny said which would she rather: keep a secret from Papa, or get Auntie Bea into trouble, and would she please stop fussing?

At the precise moment the first man stepped from the spaceship, Ruthie was biting her nails and focusing on which of Vinny's alternatives was worse, so that when it was over and Sophie took them up to bed, Ruthie said, 'Are you sure he did? Are you really?' even though, when the second man stepped down, she'd seen it with her very own eyes.

When Max got back, if he was nearby, they would whisper: 'The eagle has landed! The eagle has landed!' but say no more about it. And when he went to Buckingham Palace to photograph the astronauts with the Queen, Ruthie kept her questions to herself.

Before they left for Greece, Sophie and the girls made presents to take for Max's birthday. Vinny wrote him a story and painted pictures round the edge, and Sophie and Ruthie together made a small clock. Taking the moving parts of another clock and removing the hands, they found a plate for a face, which Sophie gilded. Then they attached feathers for hands in place of the old ones: a short stubby white one for the seconds, and two longer ones for the minutes and the hour. Vinny saw it, and said it wasn't fair: her story was boring, and why couldn't she have made the clock with them? Sophie said not to be a fusspot, and to come up and pack their cases for Greece. Max would be home any minute, and they were leaving as soon as he arrived.

At the villa, Eleni sat with the girls on the C-shaped bench and watched the water.

'It's blue today,' Vinny said.

'No!' Ruthie said. 'It's green.'

'Is not! It was green when we swam yesterday but today it's blue.'

When the colour changed the very next second, Vinny agreed with her sister and pointed, asking Eleni, 'What's the word for it in Greek?'

For an hour or more they sat there. Every time Eleni had a new word, the girls tried to copy her. There were more words still, and Vinny said, 'There can't be another one! In English it's blue, or light blue, or dark blue. You can't have hundreds of words for one colour. You're making it up.'

Vinny asked Ilías, who explained.

'The Greeks are sea people. If we're away from it too long we're unhappy. When we're not sailing it we're looking at it. Some days it's light blue, then one second later it's close to light blue but darker. Turn your head for a minute and it's somewhere between light blue and green. How would we talk about it without so many words?'

After lunch every day their parents went up to rest and Eleni drew chalk letters on the courtyard tiles, rubbing them away with her bare feet before Max came down.

If Ruthie couldn't make the sound, Eleni would tell her to smile, as though she was laughing. Or she would take Ruthie's hands in hers and press them to her own throat, so Ruthie heard the rasp and felt the young woman's hot breath on her skin, or to her stomach, to feel the muscles tighten.

At the second cove, where there were patches of sand among the pebbles, Vinny traced the letters out and Ruthie watched. In the evening they saw the water take them.

Then Max found out about the drawing of the letters on the tiles, and put a stop to it. In their bedroom that night, the sisters held each other's throats.

Eleni practised her English. There were some Greek words still, when it was just the three of them, and she lulled the girls into afternoon naps with stories of the noonday devil that roamed the Mani at the hottest hour of the day, and of summer ghosts haunting graveyards. When they asked for another, there was the cave in the mountains that fell from its mouth to the centre of the earth. Because it was so deep, if a man stood beside it and put out his hand, the air rushing up would be cold, even in midsummer. This, Eleni told them, was where criminals were thrown to their deaths in the days before prisons, and where they were thrown sometimes still if they'd done something so bad the prison wouldn't take them.

Every morning, she waited in the courtyard until they crept down. The three of them sat on the L-shaped bench by the fountain, which Sophie had named the Olive-Tree Bench. As wide and low as a bed, its corner leg was the stump of an olive tree, which Max had had felled for the purpose. When the stonemason had suggested placing the bench somewhere else, so the tree could stay, Max said no: the aspect was the one he wanted; wild thyme covered the ground around it; and in any case, he liked the idea that by being attached to the olive-tree stump, it could never be moved.

When the girls had eaten their yogurt with honey, Eleni took their hands and taught them how to catch the sun. Then she said, did they know the Olive-Tree Bench was actually a Dream Bench?

Swallows darted from their lintel nests and skitted in the fountain and Eleni asked to see their dreams. They performed little charades by the fountain, and she told them what they had really been dreaming about: a bowl of honey warned of future bitterness; a field of flowers, sorrow; eggs were a sign of a quarrel coming; and a roofless house was a grave. And if their dreams had been bad, she would ask had they been playing under the fig tree before they went to sleep, and what did they expect?

Most important of all, she said, was the ability to tell the difference between a dream-dream and a memory-dream. A dream-dream, she said, would make itself known by its having something fantastical about it. Something that would never happen in real life. Whereas a memory-dream would be the mind trying to tell them something they'd forgotten. Something they'd experienced for real but had buried away because they didn't like to think of it. In this kind of dream, she said, a cupboard will be opened and the memory you've put away will come back out to tell you it's still there, and you'll know it's for real because you will feel feelings you have had before, and you'll cry tears you've cried already, a very long time ago.

Those were the mornings when Max and Sophie were woken by their daughters climbing into their beds and whispering questions in their ears, questions about dreams and honey and hair and guns and cupboards with shut-away memories, so that Max groaned and took one of them under his arm and went straight to the cove and strode into the sea with whoever he'd chosen, and the other one running behind, squealing and protesting, 'Me, me, me! Pick me up! Papa, pick me up!'

On his birthday, they gave him his gifts. He asked Vinny to stand on the Olive-Tree Bench and to read out the story, then he asked her to read it out again, but he didn't say whether he liked it. When Ruthie gave him the gilded feather-clock, he asked her to help him hang it in his lightroom on the wall above his work surface, which was otherwise empty. Then he took a table down to the cove, and Eleni brought candles and a lantern, and they had his birthday supper there.

Evenings at Pennerton, Sophie was absorbed in her gilding.

Once, when Max came back from a trip, she stayed in the attic. He waited, then he went to bed.

Waking in the early hours, he went to look for her.

She was in the pool of a lamp, bent over her work table.

'Come to bed, Sophie.'

When he said it again, she told him to leave her alone and not to interrupt her while she was working.

The next night, he looked for her again but the attic was empty. He went from room to room, then he sat at the kitchen table. Some time later, she came from the yard with a bag over her shoulder. Her face was streaked with mud and her coat and trousers were covered in it. She jumped when she saw him.

'For God's sake, Max. What are you doing?'

'Me? What about you?'

At the sink, she turned up the bag. There was a thud, then a scattering of loose earth. She ran the water until it was steaming then she scrubbed at the thing in the bottom of the sink.

'I was looking for you,' Max said.

'In the kitchen?'

'I'd tried everywhere else. I was working out what to do next.'

'And?' She rinsed the sink and let the water run. Then she took a bottle of bleach from the cupboard and poured the whole of it into a pan, which she put on the hottest plate on the stove. 'What did you decide?'

'Where were you?' he said.

The clump she lifted from the sink was small and round. She carried it, dripping, across the kitchen. 'In the woods.'

'It's four in the morning. What were you—'

'I was looking for this.'

She dropped it into the bleach, which was simmering.

'What is it?'

'You'll see,' she said. 'It's a surprise.'

'The smell. Jesus, it's—'

'Only thing that works. Has to be properly clean before I can use it. It'll be done soon.' She brushed herself down. 'There's no need to look for me another time. I'll leave a note on my pillow if I'm running away. I was never a good sleeper. Not before I met you.' She turned to look at him. 'Emile used to say I kept baker's hours. "*Tu dois devenir la femme du boulanger.*" You'll just have to get used to it, now it's started again. Go to bed, Max. I'll have my bath then I'll tidy up. You won't even know I was here.'

When she went, he lifted the lid from the pan.

A tiny skull, already bright white in places, bounced and turned in the bubbles of the bleach. It was rounded, with no kind of snout. Because of the speed at which it moved, and the amount of steam rising, the precise shape was indeterminate and the teeth, if there were any, hidden from view.

At breakfast, the girls wrinkled their noses. Max opened the windows and the door, and the smell began to fade. The pan had been put away and the sink was clean. The loose earth had been swept from the floor, and there was just the empty bleach bottle in the bin.

'When will she come down?' Vinny said.

'Not for a while. What would you like? Toast, or muffins?'

'Is she poorly?' Ruthie said, and Vinny went to look.

'She's not poorly,' she reported afterwards. 'She's sleeping.'

Sophie gave Max a snail shell coated in gold, and they didn't speak about the night they'd met in the kitchen.

If he woke up alone he no longer looked for her. She slept in occasionally, and when she came down she'd behave distractedly, or stop halfway through a conversation. Max asked if he should take time off to be there, to help with the girls. He could pull out of the next trip, if that was what she wanted.

'Are you suggesting I'm not capable?'

'Absolutely not. I've just done my finances, that's all. I've made enough for a few months, a year. I thought if you—'

'If I what?' She folded her arms and looked away.

'If you're not happy here, on your own with the girls. I could—'

'What the hell is the problem?'

'Peter said he hears you in the woods sometimes, crying. He said he collects the girls from school most days.'

'Fine. So I was late to the gate, once, and he took over. Tell him to stop if he doesn't want to. Nobody's asking him to do it.'

'Why were you late?'

'I forgot, I should think.'

'Forgot?'

'I must have been having a rest! Lost track of time. They were perfectly fine! Anyhow, since when has it been against the law to take a walk in the woods and cry?'

'Howling, he said. Not crying, howling. And sometimes at night.'

'You've never done that? You've never walked in the woods and had a good cry? Thinking you were on your bloody own, I might add. If you really want to know, I sometimes cry for the child we lost. And I happen, occasionally, to get very, very bored. I didn't exactly plan this for a life, did I? If you want to take time off, take time off. But don't use a groundsman's gossip as a reason. I'm fine, the girls are fine. The only person who seems to be having any difficulty with the situation is you. Go on your trip, Max. Or don't pull out on my account.'

She had less time for gilding then, and did it only occasionally, when the girls brought her something and begged her to turn it into treasure. But then in December, at Vinny's ninth birthday party, a boy opened the pass the parcel and held a gilded skull in the palm of his hand. It was small, and shaped as a rounded oblong, with eye sockets that gaped and incisors that hung low on either side. Max took it back, and gave the boy an old spinning top instead, from one of the cupboards in the hall. Later, after Sophie had put the girls to bed, he asked her to the Long Library, 'for a talk'.

He said Peter had told him he'd found Sophie and Ruthie on the Smart Lawn, by the last of the cherry trees, on the point of starting to dig. When he'd asked what they were doing, she'd explained to him that they wanted Little Peter's skull. They were going to boil it clean, then rebury the rest of the skeleton.

'Ruthie wouldn't say a thing about it,' Max said. 'I asked her, before the party.'

'And?'

'She said it was a secret.'

'Well, so it would've been if Peter hadn't snitched! It was her own idea. I thought it was amazing. I asked her to think of something special to gild for Peter, for a Christmas present, and she came up with Little Peter. She'd seen me doing other bits and pieces from the woods, I suppose. And Vinny had brought me a bird's skull from the garden, so she'd seen me gilding that. I really did think it was wonderful of her. I don't want her to be scared of it, and I didn't want to stifle her. It's all around us. Why hide it?'

'What is? What?'

'Death, Max.'

'For God's sake. She's six years old. She had a child's idea which you should've laughed at. I don't know, changed the subject. Made a joke of it. Christ! She didn't think you'd actually do it. And what about Peter? Are you going to apologise to him?'

'For what? It's a cat, and it's a dead one.'

'He was Peter's—'

'We're talking about a stable stray here. You said it yourself, don't you remember? A lot of fuss over nothing, you called it. Ringing any bells? Your own daughters wanted that funeral for Little Peter, and you were perfectly happy to fuck off to California and leave them to it.'

'Jesus. I—'

'Jesus nothing. Peter's an adult. He should've been pleased. I was going to memorialise it. I thought he'd be quite taken with the idea, seeing as he'd gone to the trouble of burying it in the first place.'

'Not "it", Sophie. Little Peter was—'

'Little Peter was a cat. I stopped digging. Isn't that enough?'

'Are you alright? Have you been drinking?'

'Of course I haven't. I just happen to be disagreeing with you.'

'If you won't say sorry, you could at least explain to Ruthie that it was a joke.'

'But it wasn't, Max. It wasn't a joke.'

Sophie used up the rest of the gold leaf on six duck eggs that she gave to Max.

He went to St Ives, to photograph Barbara Hepworth in her studios, and brought back a china egg tray to keep his golden eggs in. He put the tray on his desk in his lightroom, beside the skull Sophie had found in the woods.

'We're alright now, aren't we?' he said to the girls one morning, while Sophie slept in and they ate breakfast just the three of them. Ruthie looked at Vinny, and Vinny nodded, so Ruthie nodded too.

One night the girls heard a fight.

When they were sure it had finished they stood in the kitchen corridor.

The door had been taken from its hinges and was resting against the wall. The whole of its glass panel was missing. Ruthie ran her fingers around the inside of the frame. She found a piece of glass, sticking from the wood. She pressed her palm flat and it pierced her skin and she showed Vinny and Vinny whispered to her to suck it.

Max was kneeling on the floor. His shirt was untucked and his hair was like marram grass blown about. He was picking something up, pieces of something shiny. Then they saw that they were coins, all of them different sizes, and he was laying them one by one on a newspaper, and Ruthie nudged Vinny and pointed at the table. There was the mahogany box from the Long Library, broken into pieces. Next to it was a hammer, and next to that, a dustpan and brush.

In the morning the door had gone. The hinges had been removed from the door frame and the holes filled in and painted over, and nothing was said about it. The girls went into the Long Library and found the mahogany box on top of the map chest, where it had always been. They turned the key and opened it and it was stiffer than before. Ruthie thought for a minute she'd imagined having seen it broken into pieces, but there was the plaster on her hand, and there was a small hole in the back of the box, just big enough for her to fit her finger through.

'They're my illuminations,' Sophie said, one day when Max called her to the kitchen. 'Can't you see?'

She took his hand and put it to the wall, where she'd painted lines of poetry, some in German, some in French. Drawing his fingers over the scrolls and patterns she'd placed around the words, she told him to think of them as emblems, or something baronial.

'I'm making our home into a castle.'

'It's not a castle, Sophie, it's my house.'

'Our house, don't you mean?' she said, half a smile coming.

'My house, actually. And Peter will—'

'Peter-Peter-Peter! Always Peter! You think he cares what I draw on the kitchen walls? Don't be like this.' She stepped forward and took him in her arms. She was still smiling, but when she tried to make him dance with her he wouldn't, so she leaned forward and put her face in close and sung the inscription in his ear. She tried to dance again, but he stood like a tree.

'Come on,' she whispered. 'Can't you see I'm making something beautiful?'

Finally he moved, and breathed back to her, 'I don't know what you're saying. I couldn't hear you, just now. And you might have asked me before you did it.'

They circled the kitchen and she sang again, softly, '*Du bist die Ruh*. You are longing and what stills it. That's what I'm saying. That's what it is in English.'

They held one another.

'I sung it for you once, in London, a long time ago. You liked it then. I'm sorry about your walls. I won't do it any more.' She kissed him. 'By the way, I do realise you're turning down jobs. I told you you needn't. I'm perfectly alright, and so are the girls. You should talk to them more, though. If you won't talk, then do something with them. And me. You should touch me, sometimes. You should let me touch you. All we do now is fight.'

He didn't reply, but when she went down in the morning, he'd got there before her, and painted something underneath it.

This morning the happiness,
While you stroked my back.
Those two or three words.

Later, she tacked pieces of paper to the wall, much lower down. She told the girls to bring their paints. An hour on, Max walked in. Vinny was in front of one of the pieces of paper, Ruthie in front of the other. The box of paints was on the floor between them, and there were tea towels tucked into their pinafores.

Ruthie saw him first.

'Maman said we could.'

'I know, darling,' he said. 'Carry on, don't stop because of me.'

Her hand was shaking, though, and her breathing was quick, so that her strokes went over the edges.

'Sorry, Papa,' she said, then she stopped again. Kneeling beside her, he told her to breathe properly. She couldn't, so he held her hand in his and raised the brush to the wall and they painted over the edges together, and there were oranges and reds in every direction.

7 MONDAY

After Ruthie watched Annie's parents inspect the girl's scalp, she washed her face in the darkroom sink. She dressed, then she stayed in the Lightroom, ignoring Vinny when she stood at the door and said she was sorry.

At around 2 p.m., the meltémi came in from the north-east. The wind was a dry one, and this was the first of the summer. It blew hard enough for Ruthie to know it would go on all day. As loud as an engine revving, it masked the cicadas, so they became the more distant sound. In the morning things would be calm, but for now, even the sea in the cove would be unsettled, and pushed across itself in lines.

Doors slammed and a shutter banged.

Her glass mobile moved about, and the pieces touched, making a sound like dice, shaken in a cup.

Downstairs, Vinny stood to pick up a book of vocabulary, blown from the kitchen table.

Ruthie left her room only once that afternoon, to stand on the veranda at the back of the villa.

She saw the father move the table to the side of the terrace. He left the chair where it was and Annie came out of the house.

She was wrapped in a sheet and she sat on the chair. Her plaits had been undone, and Ruthie was surprised to see that her hair was curly, like Vinny's had been when they were children.

In a minute, the mother came out with Edward.

He was carrying a plate, or a tray of some kind. He stood by Annie and held it in front of her face and the sun caught it, and Ruthie saw it was a mirror. Angling it this way and that, he adjusted his position while his mother leaned over to correct him.

Annie bowed her head. The father stood to one side with his arms folded, watching.

The mother took something from her pocket. It was made of metal, and was no bigger than a tin-opener. When she slipped her fingers and her thumb into one end and expanded her palm, the metal flashed in the light and Ruthie understood. The mother moved in towards Annie, and the father stepped forward and held up Annie's hair. As the mother began to cut, Ruthie brought her right hand to her mouth and bit down hard on her knuckles.

At first, Annie's hair fell to the floor in long and heavy shifts. The father let pieces of it drop from his hands, the mother took another section, and Edward tilted the mirror.

Annie's hair was as short as a boy's now, and softer and lighter.

What was left of it had dried to a dull gold, the colour of Vinny's hair. The mother moved in closer and the father put his hand on her arm and stopped her. Edward moved back, and when the adults had inspected Annie's scalp, the mother began to cut again. In the afternoon sun, the last of the hair fell in curls. The meltémi took them and they were carried on it, like gold leaf or wild-flower seeds, scattering.

Edward fetched a broom and swept the terrace. His mother inspected it, and his father moved the table back. He gave Annie her hat, and she sat with her head bent over her book.

Her pencil moved across the page, and she swung her legs beneath her chair. She reached under her hat, once, and then again. The white kitten appeared and ran between her feet, playing there until she picked it up. She stroked it with one hand and carried on writing with the other.

Beside the house, the washing line was weighed down by swimsuits and towels and broad white sheets. When Ruthie saw the way the sheets moved and slapped in the wind, twisting and untwisting, she became dizzy, and nauseous. She took the binoculars from her face, then she went to the Lightroom and closed the blind to the corridor.

The meltémi was constant but the sound had dropped. When Ruthie opened the window, it was gentle, so she held her head back and let it play about her neck.

In the evening there was a knock on her door. She opened it and was surprised to see Eleni, standing in the shadows. She was stooped, and Ruthie was unsettled by how much shorter she seemed than the Eleni she remembered. Her face had shrunk differently, so her cheeks were hollows and her eyes sat back in their sockets.

This new Eleni was quieter than she used to be. Now, instead of asking Ruthie for her dreams and telling her tales of the noonday devil, Eleni hardly spoke to her.

This evening, Ruthie asked, 'What is it?'

'I have something to show you.'

Ruthie saw her disappear for an instant. In her place there was her younger self, with fuller cheeks and brighter eyes, and the grey gone from her hair. She was reaching for Ruthie's hand and pressing it against her own throat and repeating a word in Greek that began as a rasp so that Ruthie felt her hot breath on her hand and was trying to make out the word. Then this younger Eleni was gone, and in her place were the dark eyes right back in their sockets and the old woman was saying, again, Ruthie, I have something to show you.

In Vinny's bedroom, they went onto the veranda.

'Your sister would like you to eat with her,' Eleni said.

Ruthie gazed down at Vinny, who was at the courtyard table with her head bowed. She was tapping her foot and Ruthie could hear it. Vinny laid her hand on the back of her neck. A bat swooped, almost touching her. Ruthie saw her shrug her shoulders, then the tea lights flickered and settled, and Ruthie felt the meltémi on her own face.

When Eleni took her arm, Ruthie went with her to Vinny, and the old woman said goodnight.

Later, holding a torch, Eleni walked back from the chapel.

She let herself in through the iron-bar gate, then she stood at the fountain, watching two tiny bats.

Vinny's room was in darkness, but the glow from the lightroom fell in a pool where she stood. She cleared the sisters' things from the table and went to the Olive-Tree Bench, to collect whatever else they'd left.

The night that she came back from the chapel after finding what Ruthie had done there, Eleni stood in the same place, looking up.

The glow from the Lightroom fell in just the same way, and when a shadow moved across it, Eleni switched off her torch and laid it on the table.

Vinny was at the window, and Eleni tried to think of what to say to her. The words wouldn't come, though, and she realised there was no right way.

All she could do, she decided, was tell her quietly and plainly.

She turned her mind to the small square object she'd taken from the chapel and carried to the water's edge. Crouching down, she'd struck a match, and waited. When the ash was cool, she'd ground it beneath her heel, telling herself she was performing an act of kindness: Vinny would have so much to bear, without seeing this.

She shivered, and told herself the same again. Pulling her shawl around her shoulders, she picked up her torch, and walked towards the house.

'Vinny,' she would begin. 'Vee, I have something to tell you.'

Ruthie lies awake in the Lightroom. There is a knock on her door. She waits a minute, then there are footsteps leaving.

The first thing she finds is the cardigan Vinny brought for her, when they'd finished eating and the heat had gone from the air, and Vinny said that just looking at Ruthie made her feel cold, the way she was sitting all hunched over and hugging herself.

The second is a silk bag, tied at the top with a ribbon. Feeling inside and wondering, Ruthie pulls them out: her teenage bikinis, stuffed at the back of some drawer and forgotten. As thin now as she was then, she undresses. Slipping one on, she hears her aunt's voice, as though she was right beside her.

'It's just not fair, not to Vinny or to me. We hate seeing you this skinny. If you want to stay slim, start dance classes, or athletics or something. It's terribly unsophisticated really, being faddy about your food. You realise, don't you, men will be far more likely to want to take you to bed if they think there's going to be something to hold on to when they get there?'

Standing in the corridor Ruthie smiles, thinking of the series of 'little talks' the two of them had, walking on the Heath, and her aunt's relief when she said, 'Oh, don't go on, Auntie Bea, I'm over it. And guess what, you were right! I've found myself a boyfriend!'

She stops smiling and scratches at her face, wishing Beatrice was coming to the villa. Then she reaches for the last of the things on the corridor floor.

It is the photograph, black and white and A4-sized, that Ruthie had fetched at the end of the evening.

'Wait,' she'd said, when they'd finished and were about to go to bed. 'Just a bit longer!' Then, softened by the wine and the tea lights and Vinny's warmth towards her, and wishing she hadn't burned Sophie's letter, 'Really, Vee. Wait. I have something for you.'

'I'm up early tomorrow. I'm completely stuck on the last scene, it's awful. Anyhow I'm not like you, I can't sleep in. I don't know how you do it with this light.'

'It's fine now. Total blackout.'

'Blinds or no blinds, the fire planes will be out tomorrow. Eleni told me there are forest fires at Itílo. They'll start early with the water.'

Vinny almost went in. Afterwards, she thanked Ruthie for insisting.

Ruthie pulls the cardigan on over her bikini. She lies on her mattress and holds the photograph above her face and wonders whether it was Eleni, or Vinny, who knocked on her door. Then she decides it doesn't matter, and that she's simply glad they left her alone.

One of the photograph's corners is slightly torn and there is a mark on the bottom right of the subject's face, but in all other respects the print is perfect. Discussing it over supper, the sisters agreed Max would have been straddling Sophie when he took it. That she was lying beneath him, staring straight into his lens.

Their mother fills the frame. Both her arms are flung back and folded above her head so that her left forearm falls down across it, covering her right eyebrow but leaving the other exposed. The tips of the fingers of her right hand can just be seen, clasping her left upper arm, and the light has caught the soft hair in her right armpit. She looks plump, with a roundness to her jaw, which had made Vinny say, 'Maybe she was pregnant.'

'With you?'

'Or you.'

'Can't see the date,' she'd said, holding the picture to her face. 'The writing's too tiny. I'll look in the light, later.'

Sophie's eyes are darker in this image than either of them had remembered. Max must have been looking down from above, they'd decided, her waist held between his kneeling legs, and he must have brought the camera in close, so that the tip of her left elbow is outside the shot and the border sits only a few inches below her clavicle. It's not possible to see, quite, but if even the smallest part of either nipple had been caught in the photograph, it would have been obscured by Max's note, written in ink that has faded.

Ruthie sits up on the mattress. In the light of that little room, so much brighter than the courtyard, she is just able to read his script and see there was no way of knowing when.

Sophie, at Pennerton. (Plat/pall print – 8 stops between – highlighted shadow detail – final.)

8 RED SKY

Sophie found a book in the library: *An English Country Cookbook for an English Country House, with Suggestions for the House-keeper on Economy and Household Management.*

On the shelf above the stove was a tiny china pie-cooler in the shape of a blackbird singing. The hollowed-out shell of a bird, with its head thrown back and its throat thrust forward, had a hole in its tummy and a beak that poked from the pastry. The girls asked what was in the pie their maman had made, and she said, 'Four and twenty blackbirds. Feathers and claws and everything.'

'Sophie!' Max said, but it was too late, and Ruthie, who wouldn't eat the pie, went without her supper. Putting her to bed, Sophie said sorry. She would make her some treats, how about that, and what would Ruthie especially like?

The next day she drove to Ashford for spices, telling Max that Ruthie had asked for gingerbread, 'Like the house in the story of the children and the witch.'

For a fortnight, Peter walked the girls to school. The air was sweet with sugar, and there were trays of gingerbread, and the girls came home to fudge setting.

In the evening, once, just as they thought supper was over, there were clouds of meringue: brittle swirls as big as toy boats, with damsons whorled through the white and baked to blood-red.

'What will you do now, Maman?' Ruthie said, when Sophie put the *English Country Cookbook* in the library, and parcelled up her baking trays.

'Oh, you needn't worry about me. I shall be your father's muse.'

Coming home from his long journey to the Peloponnese, Max had told Sophie he wanted her, or at least a part of her, to be in every photograph he took at Pennerton. She'd gone along with it up to a point, but only on and off. Now he had reminded her.

When he appeared with a camera, she would leave Ruthie at the table with her colouring books and ask Vinny to read in the Long Library. If Ruthie wouldn't settle, she'd take her with them. After the first few times, she said she didn't understand what the point was in having her there.

'I'll show you,' he said. 'I'll think of a way to show you.'

The next day, he woke before Sophie and stood at the window. It was November, and there were birds above the Triangle Meadow, maybe fifty or sixty of them, moving in a V that was steady and high. He said to Sophie, 'Wake up,' then he sat beside her on the bed. He ran his finger down the nape of her neck. 'They're leaving.'

'Who?' she murmured, still asleep. 'Who's leaving?'

'Come outside and see. Wrap up and come.'

At the meadow there was another V and he pointed. 'Almost winter.' She put her head back, then she followed their course until they'd disappeared.

He asked her to walk ahead of him, waiting until she was on the other side before he shot. When she saw the print she held her finger to the tiny figure at the image's edge. Hunched into a coat against the morning chill, it was dwarfed by the lime tree border.

'You can hardly see me,' she said. 'What difference does it make?'

'You give it scale,' he explained. 'You shape what I'm seeing,' and so she did with all of them: a fragment of her elbow on the sheet when he brought his camera into the bedroom in the morning and shot the girls sleeping, or in the summer, her foot, disappearing from a line of leeks in the kitchen garden. 'To provide movement. It would be too still, otherwise. Too flat, do you understand?'

Sometimes it was only her face, right up close and filling the frame completely. 'Don't smile, Sophie. Just look at me.' If she was reading the girls a story, or staring into the fire or concentrating at the piano, she would ignore him. He would take the picture anyway, and there were mornings when she had no idea it was happening until she woke to find him crouching over her, his lens in her face so she flung her arms up and back and he caught them and laid them down above her, part on her forehead, part on the pillow and folded, so her bare armpit was exposed, then he took his shot without her smiling.

Emile wrote that year that he wouldn't come for Christmas; the journey was hard, and he was worried about travelling in winter. Then Beatrice telephoned to say she was ill, and would stay at Pilgrim's Lane.

'We'll be alright,' Max said. 'We'll have the holidays just us.'

A week or so in, the girls complained to Sophie that it was boring being 'just us'. She telephoned Emile, and they piled the cases on top of Max's car.

On the way, Sophie told the girls that Emile wanted some time to get the house ready, so they would spend the first night at a place called Villefranche-sur-Mer.

'There's a sweet little hotel in a sweet little town and he's booked us a room on the very top floor. We'll be able to see the sea from our balcony and we can have the next day there, and it's where I used to go all the time, when I was a little girl, and I'll show you everything. Then your grandpère will be ready for us in time for our Christmas Eve supper. Don't sulk, Ruthie, it's only a day. And don't forget, it's presents on Christmas Eve this year. That's what people do in France.'

Early in the morning, Sophie stood with Ruthie and Vinny on their balcony at the Hotel Provençal. The sky was a solid red, cut through with orange and pink. The lights still shone from the night before, strung out on the opposite shore. On the Cap Ferrat with its dip in the middle, the houses became clearer.

'How does it go? Red sky at night –' Sophie began, then she stopped and held them to her. 'Oh, you do look miserable. We'll have an adventure today, exploring. I promise. We'll walk down the peninsula, to see the lighthouse. It's where your grandpère used to take me after supper sometimes, when it was as dark as dark can be. I'd hold the torch all the way until we got there, then we'd sit right down on the rocks and watch the signal on the water.'

The girls rubbed their eyes and didn't reply, then Max was behind them. 'Red sky in the morning,' he said. 'Shepherd's warning. Come on, let's get out before the storm.'

After breakfast Max said he wanted a proper walk, and set off to find the station. There was a clock, he said, that he wanted to photograph. Sophie and the girls found the beach, a thin strip of pebbly sand beyond the harbour. Halfway along they sat down, and listened to the sea: drawing in, falling out. She pointed at two rocks jutting from the water and said that Emile had taught her to swim there, in between the rocks. Ruthie said, 'Was it really there, actually right there?' and, 'When was it, Maman? When did he teach you?' and Sophie told them about the day Emile swam out with her on his back, and about how, when he'd reached a point midway between the rocks, he'd hoisted her onto his shoulders. He trod water for a half-minute then he lifted her up and hurled her in the air and went into shore on his own.

'What happened?' Ruthie asked, eyes wide.

'I swam, of course.'

Max came back, and from the beach they took a course through the town, slipping into a labyrinth of covered streets, and of passageways carved from stone. Porticos of wood guarded the entrances, and half-doors were suspended in the walls, with severed hands cast in bronze and fixed to them.

Turning from a tunnel, they found themselves suddenly in the open air, standing beside a fountain and blinking at the sun. When they became lost Sophie laughed and said it didn't matter, they were on holiday. Max picked up his pace, though, and Ruthie and Vinny stumbled in the darkness. Then he disappeared and it was only the three of them.

'Look,' Sophie said, after turning and walking, and turning and walking again. 'There's light up ahead.' They reached the sun and Ruthie stood with half her body in the tunnel's winter-dark, half of it out.

'I'm hot on this side, Maman! And I'm cold on this side!'

Sophie and Vinny did the same. They all three jumped and turned so their other sides were in the sun, over and over until they were laughing and falling and spinning in the hot and the cold and Ruthie said, 'It's just like at Pennerton! It's like when Papa and Peter have a bonfire and if you stand in front of it you're hot on your front and cold on your back and—' then they heard Max, calling to them to hurry.

Passing from house to house, they ran from a block of shade to a block of sun, with the sea appearing and disappearing, and sudden glimpses of little boats.

They left the restaurant after lunch, and saw the sea turn dark blue. A minute later it was churning and the rain came down in sheets and they were running to the hotel and the girls were squealing and all of them were soaked to the skin. In the room, Ruthie and Vinny shivered while Max stripped them and towelled them dry. They dressed, and he packed, and Sophie stood on the balcony in the full rain with her arms held wide and her head tilted back, letting the water run through her hair and down her chest and her legs.

On Christmas morning, Ruthie and Vinny agreed that opening their presents on Christmas Eve had been a good thing, but that Emile's house at Rauba-Capeù was quieter than they'd have liked. There was no Peter with a sackful of presents slung over his shoulder, or flour combed right through his beard. There were no carols at the piano, even, and for the rest of their visit, suppers would finish early, and the grown-ups went up to their rooms at the same time as the girls.

Heavy, warm rain fell until the third day. By the time it stopped, late in the afternoon, Vinny and Ruthie had explored every inch of the house, well enough to be able to recite an inventory of the contents of the kitchen cupboards; of the shelves in Emile's study; and of all of the drawers in all of the rooms as well, including Emile's bedroom. They could have described in detail the smell of the mould on the cellar walls, and the feel on their faces of the cobwebs in the attic. And so, when their grandpère appeared at their door and said the rain was over and he was going for a walk, they jumped up.

'Please can we come? Please, Pépé!'

Raising his eyebrows, he stood and listened. When there was no noise from downstairs, he came and put his face close to theirs.

'*Vos manteaux, mes petits-enfants, et du calme, du calme!*'

He crept along the corridor with one finger to his lips, frowning when a floorboard creaked. When Ruthie jumped down two stairs at once, he whispered, *'Une à la fois, une!'* While he wrapped himself in a coat so long it almost touched the ground, Ruthie cupped her hands around Vinny's ear and whispered, 'Are you sure? Don't you think we should tell Maman?'

'They won't even know,' Vinny whispered back, pulling on her gloves. 'You can stay if you like. I'm going.'

When Emile opened the front door and stepped into the dark, Vinny went with him. Ruthie waited, then she followed.

Because Emile was as tall as their father they had to run a little to keep up, just as they did when they walked with Max at Pennerton. He was silent until they were halfway along the Promenade des Anglais and then he asked them to choose a bench.

'Alors, mes enfants,' he said when he reached them. *'Allez, bougez!* Make room for me.'

He sat at one end, with Vinny next to him and Ruthie next to her. Emile asked them then if they realised they'd chosen their mother's favourite bench. Vinny said no, of course not, how would they have known?

Emile told them he would sit here in the evenings with Sophie, looking out to sea. She would answer his questions about what she'd done at school, or she might sing him a song she was learning.

A line of lamps was strung along the promenade and with the sea mist clearing, they glowed like fireflies. The girls wrapped their coats more tightly and moved in closer to Emile. He spoke mostly in English, pointing to the left and telling them that was the way to Villefranche, and then to the right, showing them the airport. When a plane came in it lit up the sky in two long triangles and they could see it was still raining on that side of the bay. Emile said the last time it had been this wet at Christmas was when Sophie was at the Academy. She'd sung enough Christmas concerts to be able to afford to fly on Christmas Eve, once she'd added to her earnings what Emile had sent her. But then, Emile told them, the rain set in and the runway was invaded by snails. There were thousands of them moving like a blanket, he said, so the airport was closed and Sophie's plane circled, and landed further down the coast. She'd stayed the night in a hotel and Emile had to drive to collect her, early on Christmas morning.

'There's no such thing,' Vinny said.

'What?'

'There's no such thing as an invasion of snails.'

'But there was! It's true! It was extraordinary.'

'You can't stop a plane just with snails.' She was tapping her foot now, and Ruthie knew she was cross.

'But you must understand this. It was thousands of snails. All the snails in Nice came out in the rain. It is true. Why, chérie? Why would I make it up?'

Vinny tapped her foot more quickly, didn't answer. She turned to Ruthie and raised her eyebrows. Ruthie only shook her head at her sister, then she pulled a face and ignored her.

When they walked on, Vinny whispered to Ruthie he'd probably made it up about it being Maman's favourite bench, and he'd definitely made it up about the snails, and Ruthie shouldn't believe everything people told her.

'Why not?' Ruthie said as Emile sped up and they began to run. 'Anyway he's not "people". He's Pépé.'

'Exactly. He's telling you a story. It's just a made-up story.'

'Alors,' Emile called back. 'Alors, mes enfants. Dépêchez-vous!'

They walked on for half an hour, until they saw the Paillon. It was full after the rain, and they stood on the bank looking down.

Emile called above the noise of the water. 'Did she tell you the story of Lou Païoun ven?'

'Of the what?' they called back.

'Loo. Pie. Yoo. Von!' he shouted.

'No!' Ruthie called. 'She didn't. The what? I can't say it, Pépé! Tell us! The story of the what?'

'I'm cold!' Vinny shouted then, her voice half taken by the breeze. 'I can't hear anything. Can we go home?'

When they were away from the noise of the river, Emile said it was much louder in the spring, when the snows melted and the water came rushing.

'That's when he appears, riding his horse.'

'Who?' Ruthie said. 'Who, Pépé?'

'Lou Païoun ven. I'll tell you in the morning. You can come with me to the baker's and we'll buy fresh bread and take it back for your maman, and that's when you'll hear it. Follow me now. One more place to stop, then home.'

As they wended through the old town, the shops were closed and most of the bars as well. Emile said hello to anyone who called out, and once, *'Mes petites-filles! Je suis leur gardien aujourd'hui!'* but he didn't stop to speak, and they jogged to keep up.

The bar he chose was the last in the line that ran the length of the Cours Saleya. He pointed to the building opposite, and told them some of the windows painted on the plaster were false, could they see? The face of a man at one of them that was so real even Vinny hesitated, but then she guessed it right. Ruthie said she didn't understand. Emile put her on his shoulders and they walked to the wall and she stretched her hands right up and placed them on the face and he said, there, now do you see?

'Yes,' she said a moment later, slipping from his shoulders and running back to her sister. 'I understand, Vee! Pépé showed me and I touched the face and I understand completely!'

They chose a window table. There was an archway opposite, and through it, they could see street lights shining on the sea.

The waiter brought orange juice for the girls, and Pernod for Emile, with a small jug of water. Emile filled his glass and stirred it, raising it to each of them in turn. When two men came in, Emile said, *'Un moment, excusez-moi.'*

Ruthie and Vinny finished their drinks. They watched Emile at the bar with the two men, laughing. Then Ruthie picked up Emile's bottle and poured what was left in it into her glass. She added some drops of water from the jug and touched Vinny on the arm.

'Look. This is what Pépé did. It goes cloudy when you put the water in. Shall I drink it?'

'Dunno,' said Vinny, looking at Emile. When Ruthie held the glass to her mouth and Vinny put out her hand to stop her, Ruthie pushed her away and drank it in one go.

'Ruthie!'

'I asked you and you said, "Dunno."'

'Did you finish it?'

'No.' She burped. 'I mean, yes.'

'Ruthie, he'll know.'

'My orange juice was fizzy. Was yours?' She hiccuped.

'Yes. But you shouldn't have –'

Emile was at the table then, putting on his coat. Without saying anything about the empty bottle in front of Ruthie, he opened the door. Calling goodbye to the men, he stepped into the night.

They rounded the corner, then there was the house in the distance and the port beyond. He asked them whether they knew how the promontory got its name.

'Yes,' Vinny said.

They recited it together, Ruthie shouting the words and running in circles around Emile, tripping and falling against his legs as he walked. 'It's called the Rauba-Capeù because it's so windy it'll steal your hat.'

Ruthie stopped running. She held on to her sister, placing one foot in front of the other so slowly that Vinny, trying to keep up with Emile, was half pulling her. A few steps further on, Ruthie stopped altogether and stood, swaying from side to side. Emile, who had turned back, laughed.

'Well,' he said. '*On y va*,' and he lifted her into his arms.

Ruthie let her head fall against his neck. Almost at the house, she vomited into the collar of his coat. Then, when he held her away from him, she vomited onto her own chest. She cried, loudly, and the front door opened and Max was there. He ran down the steps and Ruthie half fell and half jumped from Emile, stumbling towards her father in the dark.

In the hall she sobbed, and Max shouted. At her, at Vinny, at Emile. Sophie shouted back that it didn't matter, did it, they were here now, and could Max just stop being hysterical and let her take Ruthie upstairs and put her to bed so they could have dinner?

When Sophie came down later, they were in the kitchen. Max had stopped shouting but was arguing with Emile. She listened, then she put in, 'He's their grandfather. Of course he can take them for a walk if he wants to.'

'He could have bloody told us.'

'We're in his house. We're guests in his house and he probably thought he was doing us a favour, taking them out for a walk. They've been stuck inside for days with nothing to do.'

'So have we all. I'm just saying he could have told us where he was going. Or when he was thinking of coming back.'

'Yes. But he didn't, did he?'

Emile said he was sorry, then he said it again.

'There's nothing to say sorry for, Papa. Max should be saying sorry to you. To all of us.'

Max began to shout again and Emile held up his hands in front of his chest. When there was silence, he told them he was going straight to bed. He kissed Vinny and he kissed Sophie, then he went.

It was Sophie who found out what had happened. At two in the morning, when Ruthie sat at the end of her bed, her teeth chattering, Vinny brought their mother in and told her. Sophie smiled and said, 'He's naughty, isn't he, your pépé? I'm sure he didn't realise. I'm sure he wouldn't have let you, if he had.'

Ruthie asked her whether it was true about the invasion of snails, and Sophie said their grandpère would never lie to them, and of course it was true. She made Ruthie promise never, ever to drink someone else's drink, no matter who it belonged to. Then she held them both and said, 'You'd better not tell your father.'

In the morning, they woke to find Max in their room. He was packing their bags and laying out clothes. He told them to get dressed and hurry up. A minute later they looked from the window and saw him walking to the car, which was already loaded with their parents' cases.

They found Sophie in the kitchen. Her eyes were red. When she saw them she smiled, and asked if they wanted toast or brioche. No, she said when they asked, Emile had stayed in bed, and wasn't having breakfast.

Before they finished eating they heard the car start up. Sophie stood and cleared the things from the table. A glass slipped from her hand and shattered. Vinny fetched a brush and neither of the girls said anything.

In the car, Sophie sat in the back with Ruthie, Vinny in front with Max. As they pulled from the drive Ruthie said, 'Please can we stay, Maman?'

Sophie didn't answer.

'Pépé said we would go to the baker's with him, and he said he would tell us the story of the Pie-You-Von and—'

'I know, *ma pitchoune*. I know.' Sophie placed her arm around Ruthie and kissed the top of her head. 'He told me if he was too tired to get up in the morning, I had to make sure I told you the story instead. Here we are at the baker. Max. Stop, please.'

So it was that Ruthie and Vinny spent the first part of the journey from Nice eating fresh warm bread in the back of the car and listening to their maman, not their grandpère, tell the story of a riverbed so big and so bare that the washerwomen spread their sheets on its stones to dry in the summer heat. And about how they would do this every day, until the morning came when the watchman thundered down the valley on his horse, shouting at the women as he went.

And of how, when they gathered up their sheets and ran, they would glance over their shoulders to see the snowmelt rush from the high mountains and the river burst its banks and throw its stones in the air as the horseman hurtled on, calling out his warning.

'*Il est arrivé! Il est arrivé!*'

Max went to Canada in the new year, to photograph the loggers in the high camps for *National Geographic*. An hour after he left, Sophie emptied the kitchen bin and the bag split. Clearing up the rubbish she found a letter from a woman who sometimes worked as his assistant. Most of it was coffee grounds and orange peel and watery blots of ink, but the last two lines were as legible as the signature.

> *When can I see you again?*
> *I want you.*

When he came back, he laughed and said, how could she be angry for so long, about something so silly?

'They're all like that, those girls,' he told her. 'They're young and they're impressionable, how can I help it if they fall in love with me? They're not really, they just think they are, and it never lasts anyway.'

She kept it, though, and the one she found a month later, in the pocket of Max's walking jacket when she ran in the rain for the laundry.

It should never have happened, I see that now. Of course it's best we don't work together any more. I'll always think of you.

Beatrice came, and the two women walked on the Triangle Meadow.

The girls, watching from an upstairs window, saw them reach the oak at its midpoint.

Sophie sat on the ground with her head in her hands and Beatrice knelt beside her.

'It looks like she's stroking her back,' Ruthie said. 'Can you see? It looks like Auntie Bea's stroking Maman's back.'

After this, when Max travelled, Sophie would spend a few days at Pilgrim's Lane, on her own or with whoever she wanted. Beatrice would stay with the girls, and if they asked her why their maman had gone, and what she was doing, she would say Sophie had 'things to do', and it didn't matter what, and they shouldn't ask so many questions.

Max was home for the whole of October, and Peter said the first frosts would be early. The girls stood in the orchard and watched their father climb up until his head was hidden in the leaves. The ladder was a kind of tall, thin tricycle with a standing platform half-way up, and instead of a back wheel, a foot. Vinny helped him lift the foot, and wheel the ladder from tree to tree, while Ruthie collected windfalls.

On the third morning, the air was drifting with spiders' silk that floated in strands. Falling on the grass, it formed a mesh that couldn't be seen except at a certain angle. Ruthie stood by the orchard hedge, watching the last bees of the year. Then she sat with Vinny on the ladder's bottom rung until Peter came past, and they said, 'Please, Peter,' and he said, 'Jump on, then. One at a time, and don't strangle me.'

Ruthie went first. She waved goodbye to Vinny, and then they were on the meadow and the sun was so bright she squinted. Peter was running full pelt and she was being jostled up and down and his shoulders were hard against her thighs and she felt the spiderweb strands on her face: one, then another, until she closed her eyes. She cried out she didn't like it. He jogged back to the orchard and set her down on the ground beside the ladder. Picking up Vinny instead, he said she could only go round once; she was getting heavy, and he was getting older.

There was the soft thud of an apple into the bucket, then another. Ruthie was crying, and Max climbed down from the tree.

'What's the matter, misery-chops?'

When she told him, he sat with her on the grass. He took off his coat and put it around her shoulders so that she was almost hidden.

'Enough tears now.' He took out his handkerchief. 'You're a very lucky girl. Don't you know it's gossamer?'

'What's that?'

'Gossamer is –' He stopped and taught her how to say it properly, then, 'It's a very special thread, for making fairies' wings, and capes for fairy queens. They weave it with feathers and air, which is how they can fly. It's only been seen once before in the Triangle Meadow, as far as I know, and that was by my grandmother Ruthie, a long time ago.'

'Peter said it was spiders.'

'Well, Peter doesn't know about the gossamer.'

'Why not?'

'Because it's a family secret, that's why.'

Ruthie looked at him, blinking at the sun, and rubbing her eyes. He lifted her onto his lap and sung into her hair. *'It was just one of those nights, just one of those fabulous flights.'*

He stroked her back with one hand and cupped her head with the other and she hummed with him and copied the words and they were singing together about flying to the moon on gossamer wings, then she stopped and he picked her up in a piggyback.

Vinny was there again, and Peter said he'd finish off on his own. Vinny went in first and Max and Ruthie followed. Ruthie, her face buried in her father's neck, let her fingers play in his hair which was the colour of sand and thicker than straw, then she heard a noise and Sophie was at the kitchen window, knocking on the glass.

Inside, Max put Ruthie down, and Vinny stood with her arms around her. Sophie looked at him and said, 'So you do know.'

'Know what?'

'How to be with your daughters,' she whispered. He pushed past her, though, and went to the top floor.

Later, in Peter's shed, the sisters pulled out the apple-tray drawers. Peter lined the drawers with newspaper, and both girls helped to stack the apples in layers, then they pushed the drawers back in on their runners, and named the shed the Apple Store.

When Max next went away, Sophie wrote the second of the letters Ruthie would find in the villa after his death. As with the first, she would find her sadness on reading it unmanageable. Mistaking it for anger towards her sister, she would set fire to this letter also.

Pennerton, 28 October 1971

Max, since you are gone so long I will write to you.

We have had autumn in all its moods – golden (yesterday was so hot Ruthie came into my room in the morning in her bathing suit and asked to go to the stream and I said no which meant we argued before we'd even begun the day), stormy, or misty, or the damp which blends the colours of the fields into strips. Now, tonight, the wind howls in the big horse chestnut by the stables. It has kept its leaves but it will lose them in this storm.

I am much better than I was in May. Do you remember, when I was so ill? The doctor says my chest is clear, and my breathing is not difficult any more. The girls are well behaved but Ruthie will run away at mealtimes still and sometimes she is just not nice. She says she likes being at school but she is so restless when she comes home and will not settle to things. They say she needs more looking after than the other children, and that she changes every day from a monster to a poppet and is equally good at both. She has also become very affectionate, though, so I can't be cross with her for long.

Vinny has none of her sister's wildness, and is never naughty apart from that she has found some books in the library with your name in and she has read three of them already and takes them to bed at night and I tell her not to stay awake but she does and she is so tired in the morning. Ruthie has suddenly become jealous of her sister's books, which is good because she is very late starting. She won't concentrate for longer than five minutes and I have told her she should be able to, she's seven years old already.

They ask when you are coming home.

Yesterday I got to the school gate and I heard Ruthie saying to one of her friends, before she knew I was there, 'On Friday

*in three weeks' time my papa will pick me up and I will come
out of school and he will be standing exactly here on the pavement.' She knelt down and touched the ground and looked up
at her friend then she saw me. We waited for Vinny and we all
went home together and she didn't say anything about it.*

I cannot be father and mother to them.

S

There was a late-spring chill, and Peter had lit the fires. In the Long
Library after supper, Max wheeled the globe on its stand and showed
them the route he'd flown to photograph the Queen at Gan. He told
them about the people he'd sat next to on the plane, then he gave the
girls their presents.

This time, there were dresses made of tiny pieces of fabric, over-
lapped and stitched with thread so fine they couldn't see it. He told
them about the woman who'd made them, whose hands were so
small and moved so fast they were like hummingbirds.

They tried them on, then Max said they could stay up late, and
why didn't Sophie tell them all a story?

'What kind of a story?'

'What about *Rusalka*?' Vinny said.

'But you know that! All of you know it. And all of you know it was
the opera I was singing in when Papa took my photograph the first
time, and that was how we met.'

Vinny, curled on the floor with her head on a cushion, said,
'Again, Maman,' and when Ruthie said, 'Again, again,' Sophie began
to describe for them a woodland, then she said, 'In this woodland
was a clearing. And in this clearing was a lake, and on the shore of
the lake was a cottage.'

The girls half dozed while the wood-sprites sang and the Ancient
Spirit of the lake appeared from his watery home. As he listened to
their voices, wild and lilting and plaited in the air, his daughter rose

from the surface to ask her father's advice. Rusalka had seen a human prince, hunting by the lake. When the prince paused at the water to quench his thirst, she fell in love. Burning with longing, she wished she could be human herself, so she could be with her prince. Her father, filled with sadness, told her to visit the witch who lived nearby, and to follow her instructions. As he sunk back into the lake, his daughter Rusalka sung her 'Song to the Moon', confessing her desire.

Later, Sophie woke the girls to put them to bed. When Ruthie realised Max had gone without saying goodnight, she began to cry. Upstairs, they asked Sophie to sing them another song from the story of *Rusalka*.

'Only very quietly,' Sophie said. 'Or we'll wake Papa.'

Underneath the sheets they put their hands on her belly and she half sang, half whispered the story of the nymph who was made human, explaining the terms of her transformation: first, she is made mute, then she is told that if her prince should turn out to be fickle, the two of them will be forever damned.

When Sophie reached the part where the prince and the nymph lay dying in each other's arms, the prince having first stolen her voice, then abandoned her for another, Ruthie asked her maman what it felt like.

'What?'

'When you sing. What does it feel like inside?'

'I can't explain, *ma pitchoune*. Here, feel for yourself.'

She pulled back the sheets. Ruthie laid her head on her mother's midriff, and Sophie sang again. Her voice was fuller and Ruthie felt it right inside her face, behind her eyes and at the back of her mouth. Vinny said, 'What was it like to be in a concert? On a stage, I mean, in an actual concert?'

'It's hard to describe.'

'Please, Maman.'

'I'll try,' she said. 'But it won't really – It won't – I mean, I can't put it into words because it's inside me. It's an inside thing, not an outside thing, do you see?'

'No.' Ruthie touched Sophie's hair, then her face.

'I don't know how to tell you. It was different for different sorts of concerts. Sometimes there were only a few musicians and they would sit in a ring around me. A half-ring, like a horseshoe. I would stand in the middle and I would feel safe, as if they were holding me. The sounds they made were like someone's arms, I mean, and I was being held. Like this!' she said, pulling them into her. 'But when I sang with an orchestra, they were a fire burning and I was one of the flames.' She rocked the girls from side to side. 'I stopped being myself. I became my voice not my body. Once I began I never touched the ground and I never looked down and I was carried through the sky and I was free. That's what it was like: flying. The orchestra was the magic carpet, and I was Aladdin, and I could have flown around the whole world a hundred times and carried on forever.'

In the morning, their parents' bed was empty. They ran downstairs but there was no sign of them. In the Long Library, the embers had turned to powder and the curtains were closed. Slipping behind them, Vinny said, 'They're outside. Look.'

There was their mother, coming from the orchard, and there was their father coming after. Sophie was carrying his tripod. She walked partway across the lawn and Max stayed behind, framed in the orchard gate. Facing him, she set the tripod up and placed the camera on top. Max ran forward and helped her to adjust it. She raised her head for a half-minute and said something, then she put her face to the camera. Max moved around the lawn and she followed with the tripod. He stood in the same place again, leaning in profile against the gate, then turning to her. Afterwards, they walked towards the house.

The girls met them in the courtyard.

'Your mother is the Family Photographer now,' he laughed.

The girls saw the print on an easel in the Music Room: their father in the morning sun, shot from the waist up and smiling.

Sometimes, Ruthie went to his lightroom. If he was at his desk, she'd wait at the door for him to turn round and say, 'Well, don't just stand there like a ghost.'

If the sun was at the right height and something caught it at a particular angle, he would point out a reflection falling somewhere in the room. They'd look, the two of them, saying nothing, then he would ask her to find the source. One afternoon she saw a rectangle of light on the ceiling, small and striped with darker shadows that came and went. Then she saw the pattern had altered, and its straight edges dissolved. She walked around the room, stopping and turning, but still she couldn't see where it came from. The ripples disappeared and were replaced by circles oozing in and out: large then small then large again. Shot through by a sudden flutter, the rectangle was ripped into a million pieces before it settled back into the series of lines.

'Where is it coming from, Ruthie?'

'I don't know.'

He was staring at her. Her breathing was fast and she couldn't think what to say. He led her to the window. Placing his hands on her back, he pushed until she fell forward. Her forehead was pressed against the glass and she was beginning to feel sick, then she saw it.

A tiny pool of water had collected on the outside sill. Held between bubbles of paint, it moved in the breeze. The sun fell on it, casting it onto the ceiling.

'It's called the Angle of Incidence. Here.' He took a piece of paper and drew her a diagram, with dotted lines and numbers which he said explained the trick of it. 'You'll just have to try harder next time.'

Once, she was quick enough.

A glass vase Ruthie had never seen before appeared on Max's desk. Tapering to a tiny circular opening, it stood in the light and threw a double sphere across the room. When she pointed to the vase, he said, 'Well done,' and she asked where he'd got it from.

'It was a gift.'

'Who gave it to you?'

'Maman.'

'Why?'

'An appeasement.'

'A what?'

'An apology.'

'For what?'

'Never you mind.'

He gave her the glass mobile for her birthday that year, and she hung it directly above her bed. Woken by the sun, she would open her eyes to find the room a solar system, and the walls racing with its bright, small planets.

When Vinny and Eleni returned from Athens, they found the villa in darkness. Eleni made supper, while Vinny went from room to room. Then, in the kitchen, Eleni said not to worry: with the moon so bright, Ruthie was probably having a swim. Or she was walking in the grove, and wouldn't mind if they started without her. Vinny insisted they wait, though, so Eleni went to the chapel to light her candle for Panagiotis, saying that by the time she was back, Ruthie would be there and they could sit together the three of them, just as Vinny wanted.

Vinny jogged to the cove and flashed a torch on the water. Back at the courtyard, her unease growing, she called from the gate.

'Ruthie! Ruthie-Roo, we're home! Supper's ready!'

She listened to the cicadas, then she climbed the stairs to the villa's top floor.

In the Lightroom, there was a breeze. The glass mobile moved with it and the glass discs came together, making the sound of tiny bells.

Vinny watched them, then she reached up her hand to catch one, and to stop it turning.

Standing there, with her hand held high, she imagined Ruthie strolling into the kitchen and shrugging her nut-brown shoulders and saying, 'Well, if you will be so precise about timing,' and she thought of how they would lay the table the two of them, and Eleni would bring the food and Ruthie would light the tea lights and the wine would be golden in the glasses and her sister would be with her, and everything would be alright.

When the breeze dropped, Vinny let the glass disc fall.

9 WILD-FLOWER SEEDS

Max told the girls the villa had been let for the summer, and they would have their holiday at Pennerton.

He had been at home for three weeks and a pattern was in place of the sisters climbing into their parents' bed at first light. They'd fall asleep again, all of them together, and if it was a school day there would be a rush.

This particular morning was a Saturday. Surprised to find their parents' bed empty, they stood on the middle landing and listened until they heard Sophie's voice drift up from the kitchen. She was singing. They heard their father in his lightroom and they ran to the kitchen. Sophie, her slip falling from one shoulder and her hair swept up, said good morning, good morning, *mes pitchounes*. She folded them into her and the three of them held one another, the girls burrowing their faces in their mother's midriff until she said, 'Wait, stop, stop. I have an idea.'

She went to the laundry basket that stood by the back door, full of wet white sheets and towels and tablecloths. She asked them to take one end and help her carry it to the Smart Lawn.

As she reached for the basket, they glanced at one another.

'What?' she said. 'Come on, don't look so worried. He won't know until we've done it, then he'll see how beautiful it is, I promise.'

They crossed the courtyard with the basket between them and half walked, half stumbled through the kitchen garden. On the Smart Lawn they deposited the basket in the middle of the sweep of green, cut by Peter the day before. Ruthie and Vinny followed their mother back to the courtyard, running to keep up. Sophie climbed on a ladder and undid the length of rope looped against the stable wall. She slung it over her shoulder and collected another rope from inside the stable door, giving Ruthie the peg bag and asking Vinny to help with the ladder.

'Don't be such scaredy-cats. Come on, it'll be fun. It's boring, hanging it in the yard every time.'

She found a hook on the garden wall at about the same height as the cherry trees opposite, then she tied both ropes together and strung them right across the Smart Lawn. She brought stools from the kitchen, then she stood on one and told Vinny to stand on the other. Ruthie passed the things from the basket and Sophie got up and down and moved the stools along until, at last, there was a line of white fabric flapping wet in the breeze, like sails on a grass ocean. Vinny stayed on her stool and Ruthie ran among the sheets. They slapped her face and she twisted herself in one of them, turning round in it until Sophie said, 'Stop! Ruthie, stop! We'll have to do it again if you pull it down.'

Ruthie stood still, fastened in that blind dampness.

Then she unfurled herself and walked to her mother, feeling dizzy, and slightly nauseous. Sophie helped her onto the stool and the dizziness stopped. When the three of them looked back towards the house there was Max, watching from his lightroom.

They carried the stools and ran in. At the table, Ruthie put her hands on her cheeks and felt the moisture from the sheet. Her heart was thudding and she was just noticing the way her dress was wet from the sheets, and was sticking to her skin, when they heard Max's footsteps in the corridor.

He was there then, and he looked at Sophie. A half-minute passed before he said, 'It's beautiful.'

Ruthie and Vinny relaxed their shoulders.

'I know,' Sophie said, and she kissed him.

At the Long Library windows, the girls pressed their noses on the glass and saw the green, broken by the white.

In the dog days of August, they were told about the baby.

The girls helped their parents decide: if it was a girl it would be called Sarah, for Sophie's mother whom they'd never known, and if it was a boy, Emile, for their grandfather. Sophie spent an October afternoon planting bulbs directly into the Smart Lawn. When Max saw her, kneeling by the lavenders at the base of the slope from the Long Library terrace, he took a trowel and helped her.

'White narcissi,' he told the girls when they asked. 'For the baby's first spring.'

On Christmas Eve, when Beatrice brought the girls back from their week at Pilgrim's Lane, their parents had cleared out the box room opposite Max's lightroom. Max had painted sailing ships on the walls, and seagulls, and stars and the moon and the sun. Sophie had spent an afternoon at the kitchen table, painting hollow eggs in pinks and blues and yellows, for Max to hang in a cluster, above the baby Emile's cot.

'You know it's a boy!' the girls said when they heard their father say the name.

'Not exactly,' Sophie said, putting her hands on her belly. 'Papa has decided.'

'Why will he sleep up here?' the girls asked.

'So we can be boys together,' Max said. 'I've been surrounded by women all this time. Now I'll have a camerado.'

'What's a camerado?' Vinny said.

'A friend,' Max replied. 'A friend and a travelling companion. Someone who watches your back. Fights in your corner. Tells you jokes when you're low. A camerado,' he said, tousling Vinny's hair and kissing her, 'is someone who drops whatever they're doing and packs their bags and goes with you at a moment's notice.'

'But can we still come up here?' Ruthie said, taking Max's hand from Vinny's head and putting it on her own.

'Of course.' He knelt and embraced her too tightly, so she could hardly breathe. 'Only if you're invited, though.'

They agreed later that they'd have preferred their little brother to have a bedroom next to theirs, and for them all to sleep on the same floor of the house.

Christmas Day itself was bright and crisp. First thing, even before breakfast, Max fetched his camera and placed three chairs on the Smart Lawn. He wrapped Sophie in his winter coat and sat her in the middle with Ruthie on one side and Vinny on the other. He asked Sophie to open the coat as he shot, 'So my boy Emile will see one day, what he looked like before he was born.'

He went to the Long Library terrace. Looking down the lawn, he called out that he'd changed his mind, and that Ruthie and Vinny should stand, rather than sit; one either side of her. He took the chairs in, and came back to the library terrace. Then he started, coming closer and closer and shooting all the time. He took the final frame just of Sophie's face and neck, caught in a slant of light.

Sophie pulled his coat around herself and went to sit by the fire.

When Max had carried everything in, and left the girls helping Beatrice with breakfast, he went to his darkroom.

He missed the Christmas breakfast in the end, working and working on a print that showed the girls standing sentry to Sophie, their hands on her swollen shape. Just before lunch he came down to the Music Room. The girls were singing carols with Sophie at the piano, and Beatrice was turning the pages. He said he was sorry; he'd wanted the shadows just so. He listened to another carol, then he pinned the new picture on an easel: *'My Girls, before Emile, Christmas 1972.'*

Sophie began to bleed on Boxing Day morning. For the first time in a while the girls were woken by the sound of their parents arguing. The shouts came from the kitchen. Something broke, then something else. When the back door slammed Ruthie looked from the window. She told Vinny that Max had crossed the Smart Lawn and was in the orchard.

The bleeding continued for the rest of that day and all of the next. Max took Sophie to the hospital in Ashford and this new little Emile was cut, still, from his mother.

For two weeks Sophie lay in bed saying nothing. Her father arrived, and she became ill again, just as she'd been the first winter at Pennerton. The girls heard her coughing in the night. Ruthie went in and put her face against Sophie's, whose cheeks were burning. She opened the window and let the air in until her Pépé Emile came and closed it.

Sophie ate what she was given, but only if Emile insisted. Every few days he insisted as well that she let him sit beside the bath and wash her hair.

'No,' she said when Beatrice asked if she could do it. 'Only Emile.'

When it was done, Sophie sat on the floor by the Long Library fire with Emile on an armchair above her. Drawing a comb through the heavy length of it, he rubbed it gently with the towel. It took a half-hour, and afterwards, he made a single plait to the bottom of her back, as thick as a fox's foreleg. As he bound the last strands in, the fire shone from it.

Emile slept in his daughter's room. Max took a rug to the baby Emile's room, and lay on the floor beside the empty cot. Daytimes, he stayed outside, walking in the Triangle Meadow and the woods. That, or chopping firewood, even though the stack in the end stable was up to the roof.

It would be the only time the girls saw their father with a beard. In the evenings when he came from the yard and asked Beatrice why they were still awake, they began not to recognise him.

One night in the second week, hours after Beatrice had turned off their light, they heard their mother.

'Can't you speak to me? Can't you feel what I feel?'

'Can't you see I feel the same without me saying it?' Max shouted. 'He was my boy as well as yours.'

'But it was me he died inside. It was my body, his grave.'

Sophie got up the next day. For an hour or two the girls heard her walk around the house. Max was in the orchard, talking to Peter about whether it was too late in the season to move one of the apple trees. Beatrice had gone for a walk and Emile was reading in the Long Library. Hearing their mother hum to herself, the sisters agreed everything would probably be alright. They ran her a bath and chose some clothes from her wardrobe, then she came upstairs again. She stood by her window watching Max in the orchard. But when the girls went to her and asked her to come with them, she pushed them away, even when they told her about the bath.

They left her, and went to the kitchen. Looking in the pantry to see what there was for lunch, they found Max's gilded eggs that Sophie had made him for Christmas once, emptied from the white china tray and stamped on. The tray was next to the eggs on the floor, upside down and broken into pieces.

'It doesn't matter,' Vinny said, when Ruthie asked her if it was Sophie or Max who'd done it. 'It doesn't matter.' She brought the dustpan and brush and swept up the golden shells and put the pieces of tray right at the back of the shelf. That night, Max walked into their bedroom with the pieces in his hands. Half asleep and half awake, the girls only told him when he scared them into it.

When they went to Sophie in the morning to say sorry, she said she had no idea what they were talking about, and not to be silly, it really didn't matter.

She turned her face away but they'd seen already. It sat just under her right eye, purple darkening to black, and the girls agreed later it looked like crinkled silk: a pirate's eyepatch, slipped from its place.

It was late in the afternoon when Emile found Max in the orchard. The girls, with their mother, watched from their bedroom window. The two men stood apart from one another and Emile, arms folded, talked. Max held out his hands then, cupped into a bowl as though he was carrying something, something that would break if he dropped it. Emile shook his head. The girls saw their father look up at them, briefly, then he turned and walked through the gate in the hedge, making for the woods.

By the morning it had all been decided. Sophie would return with Emile to France. The girls would go with Beatrice to London. She would find schools for them immediately, or tutors if that wasn't possible. Vinny was old enough to go away to school in the autumn, and Ruthie would join her a year later. They would spend their Christmas and Easter holidays with Sophie and Emile in France, and their summers in Greece with their father.

Max kept away from the house, coming back at night to sleep in the baby Emile's room, or on the rug by the Long Library fire. Beatrice took the girls on walks in the daytime and helped them with their packing in the evenings, and Sophie and Emile got ready to leave on Friday.

On their mother's last morning at Pennerton, the girls went to their parents' bedroom and found her on her own. They climbed into her bed and clung to her. She spoke to them about their brother, and about what had happened. She explained she might be unwell for a long time, and that Beatrice would look after them a lot better than she could herself. She told them that when she was much, much stronger, they could visit her in the house at Rauba-Capeù, and they would see how they were getting on and what could be done about things. She didn't answer all of their questions, though, and she spoke too softly for them to hear everything she said.

Later, Sophie and Max said goodbye in the Long Library. The girls waited upstairs. When they heard the back door slam, they went to their parents' bedroom. From the window, they saw their father walking towards the orchard. They left the room and ran down the stairs and there was their mother, with Emile, her cases on the floor.

She opened her arms to them. When they reached her, she started to shake and they said, 'It's alright, Maman.' Then Emile separated them and said, 'C'est l'heure, Sophie. C'est l'heure,' and she became completely still.

'I'm sorry, my little ones,' she said. 'I'm so sorry.'

Ruthie opened her mouth and said nothing. Vinny said, 'Don't go. We love you,' but her voice was slow and heavy so that afterwards Ruthie told her she'd sounded like she was pretending.

In the bedroom that night, after Beatrice turned off the light, Ruthie said, 'Why didn't you think of something else?' and they stayed awake and argued.

On the Saturday morning, Max sat with Beatrice in his room at the top of the house. Vinny and Ruthie walked about, wondering what else to take with them. Each of them said to the other that they felt sick. Outside the Music Room, Ruthie said Vinny should ask about the rocking horse again, but Vinny said no.

'It's up to Auntie Bea, isn't it? She says we have to leave it here for when we visit Papa.'

They couldn't agree so they went to the kitchen instead, looking for something to eat.

Raising their eyes for Sophie and Max's inscriptions on the wall, they saw a blank space. Staring at this whiteness, Ruthie turned to Vinny and said, 'Where are they?'

Vinny, who was crying but only a little, took Ruthie's hands and moved them back and forth on the wall. The new nub of the fresh paint was sticky in places. Further down there were orange and yellow and red marks, where two strange, multicoloured anti-rectangles marked out the edges of the pictures that had been deleted, so that these ghosts of the girls' over-painting were all that remained.

Leaving the kitchen, Vinny said they should say goodbye to the rocking horse, before it was too late. Ruthie followed her sister to the Music Room.

There were the pictures on their easels, beside their mother's piano, and there was the wooden horse. On the easel closest to them was Sophie. Full-sized and naked, she was lying on her bed, facing away from the camera. The girls were lying just beyond her, so that their shoulders and their heads were visible.

This first print had been pierced with a series of small holes. Each of the little stabbings had been made quite carefully with a knife, or a pair of scissors, and their distribution was restricted to their mother's lower back and her calves. On another easel there was Sophie again, sitting in the middle of the Smart Lawn. Vinny and Ruthie stood to her right and her left, with their hands on her pregnant belly. This print had been stabbed as well but less carefully, so the cuts were randomly placed and more like slashes than piercings, which meant parts of the print curled away, and hung in ribbons.

On the last easel was Max. Leaning in to the orchard gate with his face turned to the camera, he smiled in the morning sun. A perfect circular hole punctured his forehead. Red paint was daubed beneath and fell from his eyes like tears. Ruthie held a finger up to the hole but Vinny stopped her, taking her hanky and trying to wipe away the red.

Within a week of Sophie's departure, the girls were at Pilgrim's Lane. Exactly a month later, Max took all the clocks from the house at Pennerton. He carried them to the woods, and placed them in the stream.

The following spring, when the white narcissi appeared between the lavenders, he wrote to tell Sophie, who sent a line in return.

'Do this one thing for me, Max: look after my girls.'

The May would be out in the hedgerows by the time Beatrice brought them for a visit. At the Triangle Meadow, he gave them both a handful of wild-flower seeds, 'For your baby brother,' and showed them how to let the seeds fall as they walked, so the breeze could scatter them.

Neither their father nor their aunt would answer their questions about the baby. Ruthie, who was still too young to understand properly, came to think of him not as a boy but as a kind of a sea-creature, drifting somewhere, unborn.

As they grew up, though, Vinny would remind her that he'd have been this old, or that old, and he'd have been smaller than them, and he might have looked like this, or like that, and they would have loved him.

Sometimes in Greece in the years that came after, when Ruthie lay on the villa's cove and fell asleep in the sun, she would be woken by the cry of a boy playing. With her eyes still closed she would see her brother Emile, blond and lithe and little. He was kneeling on the shoreline putting pebbles in a bucket for Sophie, who was kneeling next to him.

Then Ruthie would open her eyes. Sitting up, she would see the light on the water and know she was alone.

10 TUESDAY

The light in this part of Greece has a quality known nowhere else: the dryness of the air and the lack of any haze makes it impossible, at certain times of day, to estimate the proximity of a mountain range, or to distinguish between a pile of stones in the foreground and a hilltop tower, miles off.

Ruthie, waiting for the sun to hit each of the trees that stood between her and the sea, took some time to realise that the two lozenge-shaped things passing back and forth in front of her were giant wasps, right up close, rather than the fire planes tracking the bay.

She flinched, and trailed round the veranda to look into the grove.

Annie and Edward were already up. Standing by the steps to their terrace, they were dressed in shorts and hats and T-shirts. Both of them wore trainers. Their socks were pulled up, and they had little rucksacks strapped to their backs. The white kitten rolled in the dust beside them, stopping to lick itself, then rolling again. The children stood side by side, facing Ruthie. She lowered the binoculars to their trainers and up again, focusing in on their socks. Panning back out, she saw that Edward was clasping Annie's right wrist with his left hand. He had trapped her arm under his and was pulling her into him. The fingers of her right hand were splayed. She had her other hand on her hip, and was struggling. Edward took something from his pocket with his free hand and, keeping Annie's arm in place, turned them both around. They had their backs to Ruthie then, so she couldn't see what he did to make Annie jump, and try to pull away. He released her and said something. She looked at her hand, then she swung her arm slowly, sweeping it forwards and up until it stood above her head. Then, without breaking the movement, she let it fall back behind her and up again, tracing the shape of a circle in the air.

Annie stopped and looked at her hand. She shook her head and Edward said something and she traced out the same circle, faster this time. He spoke to her again and she increased her speed until she was almost falling over. Then she stopped and gave Edward her hand and he looked at it and laughed. She pulled her hand away, sharply, wiping her fingers on her shorts.

The parents came out of the house. The father handed them each a small bottle of water and they set off through the grove towards the road into town. Stopping once, they stood in a huddle and the father unfolded a map. He glanced at the hills and back at the map, then they were gone.

Ruthie knocked on her sister's door. When there was no answer, she went in and tiptoed to the bed. Vinny was curled in a ball at the wrong end.

'That's a funny position,' Ruthie whispered. 'Bad night? Thought you were going to start work at the crack of dawn?'

The pillows were on the floor and the sheet was pulled over her head. Ruthie lifted the sheet and kissed Vinny's neck.

'Hmmm,' Vinny murmured, turning over.

'I'm heading into town. I was going to just leave, but I decided to be nice and ask first.'

'Ask what?'

'Do you need anything, sleepyhead?'

'Travel pills. Tomatoes, maybe peaches. More feta. Thanks.' Vinny pulled the sheet over again. Ruthie sat beside her, placing her hands on the sheet and feeling for Vinny's ear, then coming in close and whispering.

'Travel pills?'

'Eleni. For Athens. Carsick. Pills. Chemist.'

'OK.'

'Thanks, Roo, you're lovely. Night.'

'It's morning, not night. And it's Ruthie, not Roo.' She stood and walked away. 'Get some more sleep. Oh, and if you swim, stay out as long as you like. I won't be back till lunchtime.'

Eleni had cleared the courtyard and put the chairs in their places. After Ruthie and Vinny had gone to bed, she'd swept the tiles and taken the tea lights from the fountain's edge. She'd missed one from under the Pergola, though, so Ruthie brought it in. Scraping the wax from the holder, she prised free the carcass of a moth.

From the villa she took a detour. On the path to the chapel there was the white kitten.

'Go away,' she said. 'I won't feed you, so there's no point following me.'

It rubbed itself against her legs until she nudged it from her and walked on faster than before. There it was again against the red-orange earth, shooting ahead of her just when she thought she'd lost it: a small white slip of a thing, more like a ghost than a cat. Standing there, she heard her mother's voice.

'Because of the noise they make at night, when they're fighting.'

This had been Sophie's final word as adjudicator, the summer Max found cat hairs in his darkroom and issued an edict against them, even in the courtyard.

The girls, though, who liked the sensation of something soft against their calves while they ate, begged indulgence for their habit of dropping food under the table.

Their mother was given the casting vote, and the ban was imposed immediately.

'End of discussion,' Max said when the girls still protested. 'They're public enemy number one in my book, and your mother doesn't like the sound. That goes for you too, Eleni. No more saucers of milk by the door.'

A butterfly had settled on his forearm. Creamy-white and petal-like, it quivered, then it was still. He lowered his head and blew on it, but it clung to his arm-hair and righted itself. Raising his other hand, he flicked it: a short, sharp flick that sent it across the courtyard. The sisters followed its trajectory to where it hit the wall and fell. Max ran his fingers through his hair.

'They're not fighting, though, Soph,' he said. 'That's not what they're doing when they make that noise at night.'

'What, then?' Sophie said, then she blushed and Max laughed.

Ruthie said, 'What? What, Papa? What are they doing?' but he wouldn't answer. Nor would Vinny, even when Max and Sophie had gone upstairs and Vinny and Ruthie went to the cove, and Ruthie swam behind her sister calling, 'What, Vinny? Tell me!'

'You're too sweet for that, aren't you?' she said now, crouching to the ground and tickling the white kitten, letting it wrap itself round her legs. Then it climbed up onto her front and laid its head on her neck. Feeling a low rumble from its chest, she scratched its back and rubbed its tummy in turn.

She slipped her hands around it, and held it to her face.

'You're sweet and lovely and soft and gentle, aren't you, my little one?'

It was still tiny, almost all-kitten. In the sunlight, the tips of its ears were as pink as its nose and its eyes were almond-shaped and yellow-green. She turned it and saw the bottom part of its hind legs were yellow as well, as though it had crouched in the dust of the grove.

'Apart from when you're killing mice and chasing lizards and – Stop! Stop scratching! – Alright alright alright! You can have another cuddle.'

She let it play in her hair and paw her neck, then it slipped from her arms. They walked together, the two of them, Ruthie in silence and the kitten making noises like a bird.

Then the kitten was gone, and Ruthie was on her own.

At the chapel, Eleni's packet of incense sticks were open on the shelf. Next to them was a fresh candle, ready for her evening talk with Panagiotis.

Ruthie closed the packet. She took the burner outside and shook it empty, so the ash hung in the air and caught the sun and looked like glitter. Inside again, she drank the dregs from the altar glass and wiped it with the hem of her skirt. When she left, closing the door behind her, she held a finger to the hole at its midpoint, just as she'd done when she was younger.

Eleni had shown her the chapel first, when she and Vinny were little and their fingers small enough to go right into the hole.

'Because it's a habit,' Eleni said at the chapel door, the first time they saw her doing it.

'What's a habit?'

'It means I do it every time I come here.'

'But why?'

'I don't know, I just do. Ilías showed me how when I was as small as you are, when we ran out from the town to play in the grove. As soon as I was tall enough I copied him.'

'Why?'

'Because he's my brother! Stop, stop, stop! Stop asking me so many questions.'

'It's like the mahogany box!' Ruthie whispered to Vinny, later, trailing behind her to the villa.

'What do you mean?'

'It's like when I put my finger in the hole in the back of the box, the one that Papa mended after the fight. Do you think it's exactly the same size hole?'

'I don't know. You shouldn't anyway. You might break it.'

Then one day Max came with Ruthie on her own, carrying her along the path and saying, 'I'm going to show you something very, very special.'

He'd lifted her in his arms, raising his knee up under her bottom and helping her to place her hands on either side of the hole to keep her steady. He brought his face in close and pressed his mouth to her ear.

'Hold your head away from the door, that's it. No, a bit further back, like that. Now look through the hole and tell me what you see.'

Because she liked the way he was holding her up against the door, with the hardness of his knee underneath her, and the tightness of his arms around her waist, she kept it to herself that Eleni had shown her already, and that she knew exactly what she'd see: the sun as a perfect circle on Christ's face, staring back at her from the wall above the altar.

She lowered her finger from the hole now, touching it to her ear and recalling the warmth of her father's mouth. Then just for a second she closed her eyes and was at Pennerton, watching from the kitchen doorway.

Her father was on all fours. Picking up the pieces of the mahogany box that had been taken from the Long Library and smashed, gathering the coins that had scattered, he was crying.

Then he disappeared and she was at the chapel again, on her own.

Further along the path, Ruthie turned off among the trees. Reaching the stone houses, she walked between them. She touched the laundry post as she passed and it gave back the heat of the sun. At the family's windows she stood on her tiptoes, but the inside shutters were closed.

Stepping onto the terrace, she saw a book lying face down on the table. There was a pencil sticking from underneath. When she turned the book up she saw a crossword puzzle.

Childish capitals spelled out three of the words. Flicking through the rest of the book, Ruthie saw there were other puzzles, most of them crosswords but some of them different kinds of word games. Here or there was a dot-to-dot, or a picture half coloured in. Some of the quizzes were begun, but none of them completed. The occasional page was scribbled over; one or two torn from the book altogether. Tentative half-words were written in the margins, with question marks and rubbings out.

She turned to the first crossword and found herself picking up the pencil. She flipped through the book and added a '*u*' to a word that Annie had found only an '*r*' for: '*4 Across: Broken; dirty; after a loss of fortune (6 letters).*'

When she'd done this, she left the book as it had been, and stepped down into the grove. As she walked away, the white kitten ran from under the terrace. She scooped it up and pressed her face into its neck, until it clawed her and scrambled from her arms.

She saw no one on her walk into town. At the taverna, she sat outside with her coffee. Annie and Edward were across the road, in front of the supermarket. Edward was clasping Annie's arm again. This time she was close enough to see that Edward was holding something in his other hand, and pressing it against the tips of Annie's fingers. Ruthie was trying to see what it was but it was too small and the sun flashed from it, so she closed her eyes. The parents came out of the shop. Annie moved away and Edward dropped whatever it was that he was holding. It glinted in the sun, but Edward left it there. Then their father was putting things in their backpacks: fruit, and biscuits, and extra little bottles of water, and their mother was reaching forwards and trying to rub suncream on Edward's cheeks.

'Edward! I have to, come here.'

'No! Stop it!'

His voice had broken, which surprised Ruthie, and she was just beginning to wonder whether he was much older than he looked, when his mother grasped his wrist and he looked like a boy again. She handed the suncream to the father, who started to daub some on Annie's face.

'I don't want to go on a walk,' Annie said, shutting her eyes and pulling her head away. 'I want to swim.'

'We'll swim later.' He pulled her sun hat down on her head. 'We'll walk now before it gets too hot. Come on, the pair of you, and no messing around.'

They went off towards the old town, and the start of the Viros Gorge. As soon as they were out of sight, Ruthie threw some coins on the table and stepped into the road. Halfway across, a moped took the corner too fast. Ruthie shouted something, then the driver swerved and hooted. As he sped away, her heart raced.

Standing where the family had just been, she felt sweat run down her back to her waistband.

She knelt on the ground, patting her hands in the dust. When she got up she was clasping a small metal comb. She felt its pointed teeth, and winced. Holding her fingers to her mouth and tasting blood, she stared into space for a whole minute, seeing without seeing.

Then, without knowing why she was doing it, she turned, following in Annie's footsteps and making for the old town.

The meltémi came in at two. When Ruthie heard it start, she was within sight of the grove, still trying to work out whether to tell her sister the reason she was so late was that she had followed the family up the gorge, and had tracked them.

By the time she reached the courtyard, the wind had dropped, slightly, but still it sounded, machine-like and grinding.

Vinny was by the fountain.

'Hello, Vee.'

'You're here!' Vinny looked at her, then looked away, but Ruthie had seen the redness around her eyes.

She sat beside her, trailing her fingers in the water.

She was on the point of telling her what she'd done, but then Vinny said, 'Would you think about coming with us tomorrow?' and Ruthie was angry, and decided against it.

'Why?'

'I don't know, you could potter around Athens for a bit while we're at the hospital?' She took Ruthie's hand from the water. 'Pick up some photo stuff instead of paying for delivery? Keep us company? I'm sure Eleni's cousin would put you up as well.'

'If you mean you don't want to be stuck on your own in a car with Eleni for hours then say so. But don't talk to me like I'm a child.'

'Of course I don't mind being with Eleni. I just don't want to leave you if you don't want me to. I mean, will you be alright here? Won't you be lonely?'

'What do you mean, will I be alright here?'

'I mean, you wake me up to tell me you're going into town and do I want anything then you disappear for hours, literally, and come back with absolutely nothing.'

'What? Jesus! Are you cross with me?'

'It doesn't matter. Some of us happen to have a functioning appetite, that's all.'

'I lost track of time,' Ruthie said, lying. 'I just forgot, about your tablets.'

'It would have been good to have something for lunch. Something nice.'

'How can you eat so much in this heat?'

'Don't be ridiculous. I'm talking about what, not how much. I just mean fresh tomatoes rather than tinned, and fruit for after.'

'I'm sorry. I got to the shop then I changed my mind. I thought I'd have a walk in the gorge first, while it was cool.'

'Why, though? You said you'd shop.'

'No particular reason,' Ruthie said, continuing to lie. 'I'm never awake that early, and I haven't been up there for ages. It's always too hot in the afternoons. And then—'

'And then what?'

'Nothing.'

'What, Roo? Did something happen?'

'No! I just forgot. The gorge was beautiful, there were butterflies everywhere like you've never seen, and I came back over the hills instead of through town and – I totally forgot to go back to the shop. And since you ask, no, I won't be lonely. I'm quite looking forward to a bit of peace and quiet. Anyway, why isn't Ilías taking her?' Ruthie asked, steering the conversation away. 'Why do you have to go?'

'He's working tomorrow. Don't you think it's right that it's one of us, after everything she's done?'

'Everything what? We pay her a wage, Vinny. We always have, or our family has. And what do you mean, one of us? Are you saying I should've offered to do it?'

'Hardly. You can't drive. Sorry, don't drive. And you're not exactly chums these days, are you? Roo, love, she is ill, you know.'

'Thought that's what you were going to find out. Looks pretty chipper to me.'

'You know she doesn't want to get the results on her own and you know what the symptoms have been and – Chipper? What kind of a word is that?'

'Same sort of a word as "chums", I should think. A Julian sort of a word. I told you this morning, please don't call me Roo. Anyhow, we haven't been chums for a long time now, Eleni and me.'

'Eleni and I, Ruthie,' Vinny said. 'Eleni and I.'

Eleni came from the kitchen with a tray of coffee. Ruthie, who was glad for the distraction, exhaled, slowly, and said nothing, but Vinny jumped up and took the tray.

'Sorry, Eleni. Sorry.'

They sat together, the three of them. The old woman told them to embrace, and not to fight any more. As Vinny leaned across to Ruthie, Ruthie shrugged, but she let her sister kiss her.

Eleni poured their coffee, then she said that she and Ilías used to argue as well.

'When?' Vinny asked.

'Every day, when we were little, then it stopped. It only happened again when I began to work for your father.'

'Was that what it was about? He didn't think you should have come to live here, at the villa?'

'About that, and about other things. My brother and I fought almost every day. He never wanted me to marry Panagiotis,' she said. 'He didn't want me to grow up. When Panagiotis died, he was sorry. And when I started to work for your family, he didn't want that either. He said I'd never find someone else, if I was wrapped up in you. But of course I never wanted anyone else. I loved Panagiotis, and I always had, since we were children. So I was glad that you were there, the four of you, and that you needed me.

'Ilías found it hard to understand, so we carried on fighting. But we loved one another, and when time had passed, we saw that none of those things mattered. So should you, now. You're old enough.'

They talked some more until it was settled: for now, Ruthie

would swim, and Vinny would go into town for Eleni's tablets, and to collect the car from Ilías. In the morning, Vinny would do as she'd promised and take Eleni to Athens. Ruthie would stay, and Vinny wouldn't worry about her. If they set off for home early enough the next day, they'd be back for a late supper, all of them together.

Some way out from the cove, Ruthie realises she is swimming like a child: scanning the water ahead, flinching at a piece of weed. The wind has churned the water up so it isn't as clear as usual but still, she flips onto her back and stares at the sky, annoyed with herself. She hasn't seen a single jellyfish all summer, and has nothing to be afraid of. She starts a steady backstroke, wondering whether she can swim as fast as she can on her front. She's pushing herself through the water, sweeping her arms under and up, under and up, finding a rhythm and increasing her pace. Just as she reaches full speed, and is beginning to think it might be feasible, she collides head-on with something hard.

She flips over but there's nothing.

Then it's beneath her, crashing against her stomach and clutching at her, and there are claws scrabbling her chest and there's a shape in front of her face, then it goes and comes back and it's clinging to her, pulling her down.

She's fighting it from her when it rises again, and she sees that it's a child, choking and gasping for air.

All at once it disappears under the water.

Slipping down her body fast, it grabs at her legs and slips further until it's only clutching at her toes.

Turning, she dives down and reaches after it. She finds only a head at first, then she's diving further and she's underneath it. She pushes this slippery child and pulls it, dragging and fighting it to rise to the surface.

They are tangled in each other and shouting, then they're gulping the air as if they're eating it. Then they are under again, and Ruthie is on her back again, and she turns the child and sees it is a girl. She pulls the girl up so she is stretched on top of her own body, then she hooks the girl's chin in the crook of her elbow and the child is coughing water, and crying and thrashing the sea with her arms, and Ruthie is shouting at her to breathe.

Then she is swimming into shore and the girl stops moving, and it's easier.

At the cove, the girl crouches on the pebbles. She coughs, several times, then she cries, quietly.

When she has stopped, and is breathing normally, Ruthie picks her up and carries her to the steps.

'It's alright, Annie. You are perfectly alright.'

In the courtyard, she puts her down.

'Thank you.'

'I'll get you a glass of water.'

'No, thank you.'

'You're scratched,' Ruthie says, pointing at the marks she made on Annie's arms, dragging her from the water. 'I'll get something for it. And you'd better have a drink.' Before Annie can reply, Ruthie is in the kitchen. She scrabbles through the cupboards, but she can't find the Savlon, so she grabs a clean cloth and dampens it.

Annie is stepping from one foot to another and looking over to the gate in the wall. Ruthie sees that she is shivering.

'You're freezing. Let me fetch you something.' She presses the cloth against the scratches on Annie's arm. Annie pulls away and looks at the gate again.

'I have to go back.'

'Alright. If you're sure you don't need to lie down?' Annie nods. 'Do you want to go back to your beach or to your house?'

'How do you know where my house is?'

'Because the house you're staying in belongs to me. Shall I take you there?'

'Yes,' Annie says. 'I mean, no.'

'You don't want to go?'

'I mean, please can I go back to the beach, not my house? How do you know my name?'

Ruthie doesn't answer. Annie frowns and turns her head, and Ruthie sees that she is shaking now, rather than shivering. Then she stops frowning and looks suddenly tired, as though someone was holding her up by pieces of string, and has cut them.

She squints up at Ruthie. 'Please can I have a drink, then? A hot one?'

Ruthie hesitates, but only for a moment.

'Alright. Follow me.'

When they come back out an hour or more later, they hear a woman's voice, faintly at first, from beyond the villa's boundary wall.

'Aaaa-neee! Aaaa-neee!'

There is a man's voice as well, 'Annie? Annie!'

They freeze, both of them, then the man's voice comes closer.

'I've looked this way already,' he says. 'I'm going back down to the beach one more time, then I'm phoning the police.'

'Don't be ridiculous!' the woman answers. 'She came back up with Edward, I'm sure she did.'

'She was in the water. Edward just told us, she wasn't with him.'

'She wasn't in the water.'

'You said you'd watch her. I was only gone for ten minutes. Can't you even –'

Ruthie looks at the door to the kitchen, wondering if Eleni will be woken by the noise. She beckons to Annie, who tiptoes towards her. 'Follow me,' she says. 'I'll show you another way.'

'Michael,' the woman says, 'stop panicking. It's perfectly safe.

They're probably playing some bloody silly game. I'm sure Edward knows exactly where she is. Back to the beach and we'll start again.'

Ruthie leads Annie to the path in front of the villa, then they jog through the trees. As they near the oval meadow, Ruthie can hear Annie panting. Then the girl shoots ahead into the tall grass and Ruthie, running to catch up, loses sight of her. Then she sees her head bobbing, like the head of a boy, and they are nearly at the start of the steps and Annie runs faster, tripping at the top and almost falling.

The voices on the other side of the boundary wall come closer.

'Aaaa-neee! Aaaa-neee!'

Ruthie grabs Annie's arm and says quietly, 'Tell them you climbed up the rocks from the corner and ran back down again. Tell them you scratched yourself on the bushes. And come back tomorrow, if you like. You know your way now.'

Annie runs further down the steps, slipping once and righting herself. Ruthie follows, stopping halfway down to stand watch.

When she turns to go back up, there is Max, leaning against a tree.

She looks away, disbelieving, but when she looks again he is there still, and closer: her father, one hand on his hip, staring right at her.

He is bare-chested, and older than he'd been when Ruthie saw him last. His skin is a deep shade of brown and hangs a little loose from his frame, and his hair is a thick shock of white. He is as tall as ever, and is just as broad across the shoulders. But with all this he is a little hunched, and he leans on a long stick. *'He's strong, but not as strong,'* Vinny had said in a letter once. *'Like an athlete past his best.'*

Because he is wearing sunglasses she can't make out his expression. She is trying to, when he speaks.

'Where have you been?'

'Papa?'

'Come on, Ruthie-Roo. I can't wait all day.'

'I've –'

'Why did you leave it so long? I –'

'I wanted –'

'You wanted what?'

'I couldn't –'

He moves towards her, hesitantly so she has time to turn and look for Annie.

The steps to the beach are empty.

When she looks back, Max has gone. There is only the sound of the water in the cove, and a turtle dove, calling.

11 THE ROAD TO FALICON

Before they left Pennerton, the girls helped Peter with their boxes. They'd talked about a gift, but because it was always Peter who'd taken them on secret visits to Headcorn for their parents' presents, they were stuck. When they asked Beatrice, she was distracted. As for Max, he'd become a stranger to them and, being unsure whether to interpret his behaviour as anger or sadness, they kept away.

On the final night, they fetched their paints and made a blanket-tent for a studio, holding the torch in turn.

They went at first light. Vinny said Peter would be asleep, and they should leave the pictures on the table, but Ruthie said they should wake him, to tell him they'd come back to visit, and they'd write.

'Write about what?' Vinny said.

'What it's like at Pilgrim's Lane. That the kitchen's in the basement but you can see up to the street because there are windows.

And there's a rose that grows over the front door that's white, and Auntie Bea has her own study and we're not allowed in it.'

'He wouldn't care.'

'He would! He's never been! We're going to live there and—'

'And what?'

His cottage was empty. There were dishes in the sink, and Vinny stood on a chair to wash them. She told Ruthie not to cry. He knew they were leaving that morning, he'd probably just gone for a walk. Either that, or he'd gone the other way to the house and missed them. When he realised, he'd come straight back.

'Here,' she said, passing Ruthie a plate. 'Dry this.'

They waited a quarter-hour, then Ruthie took the pictures from her satchel. She told Vinny they should leave a note. Looking in a drawer for a pencil, she found a brown-paper parcel, tied with string.

'Shall I open it?'

'Don't mind,' Vinny said.

'What do you think it is?'

Vinny felt it, and turned it upside down. 'Maybe it's love letters.'

'From who? Love letters from who?'

'How would I know? And it's "whom", not, "who". Go on then, open it.'

The stack of pages inside was crisp, and the colours still bright. There were twenty or thirty of them, the first uncertain and indeterminate shapes giving way to actual images, sketched lightly in pencil and watercoloured over.

Ruthie laid them on the table and Vinny read out the annotations. 'BY RUTHIE, AGED 6', or 'BY VINNY, AGED 9'. Further down the pile there was, 'LITTLE PETER, BY RUTHIE', the dash of black paint in the middle of the page no more or less precise than the almost-square of brown on the next one: 'THE WOODPILE, BY VINNY'.

The inscriptions were in Peter's pencilled hand, each of the letters careful and small and blocked into a capital.

Vinny turned the paintings over again, slowly. Then she took her new picture and wrote her name in the bottom corner. Ruthie did the same to hers, adding a line of kisses that ran to the edge and round, forming a criss-cross border.

Peter came from the woods to wave them off. Max kept the engine running while Peter held Vinny. When it was Ruthie's turn she jumped into his arms so he picked her up and cuddled her, then he knelt on the ground again, to hold them both together.

That first year at Pilgrim's Lane, Ruthie went to Little House School with the girls next door, whose mother was headmistress there, and Vinny was privately tutored. Every Saturday morning, Beatrice took them to the Heath for the bathing ponds, or to Bloomsbury for the British Museum, then on Sundays, they wrote to their maman, and their papa, or Max might telephone.

'We've got some time in hand now,' Max said to Ruthie at Easter.

They were at an inn in the hills above Nice. Beatrice and Vinny would join them the next day, then the girls would have a week with their maman.

'It's an evening to ourselves and we can do just what we like, you and me together. What'll it be?'

'Don't know.'

'Come on, we're on holiday! Anything you like!'

'Can I go to sleep?'

'No, you jolly well can't! Cheer up, we're having fun. How about this for a plan? We wait until it's dark. Really dark, I mean. It gets even darker here than at Pennerton, doesn't it?'

'S'pose so.'

'There's a long night ahead. We're in the middle of nowhere, with a car at our disposal. I'd have thought it was obvious. The conditions are ideal for some night photography.'

'But I'm tired. And it's snowing!'

'You know what your trouble is, Ruthie-Roo?'

'What?'

'You've got no stamina.'

'It's not supposed to snow at Easter.'

'Exactly. So we'd better make the most of it.'

'A passing car,' he said on the way. 'A passing car's the thing.'

They were huddled together up front. Ruthie was wrapped in several layers, with a hot-water bottle from the inn slipped under one of her jerseys. Max pulled over, and as the engine died, he pointed across the valley.

'See that little cluster of lights? It's a village called Falicon.'

'How do you know?'

'I went there once, a very long time ago, before you and Vinny were born.'

'What's it like?'

'Like a town from a fairy tale. It's tall and it's winding and there's a church with a tower, and a little house perched at the top of the town, with a garden full of geraniums, and an old lady who looks like a princess, who waters them every morning.'

'I'm cold, Papa. Why do we have to stay?'

'We're waiting.'

'What for?'

'A passing car. I told you. We're going to shoot a passing car.'

They put Max's tripod on the verge. The snow was to their ankles.

Kneeling to check his sightlines, Max said someone would have to be travelling at just the right speed for the photograph to work in the way that he wanted it to. He moved the tripod until he found his angle. A minute in, Ruthie began to shiver. She tried to tell him, but he whispered, 'Be quiet; I'm listening.' Her hat was pulled right down, but her ears had started to hurt. When the third car went past, her hands were sore.

'Damn,' Max said. 'Nearly had it.'

A pain was spreading across Ruthie's back as though she was being pinched, or scratched. By the time he attempted an actual shot, she was too cold to move.

When he finally turned, though, and said, 'Right. Job's done. Home time, Ruthie-Roo,' she was feeling quite warm all over. Waiting for him to pack his things, she pulled off her hat and rubbed her face.

It was completely numb.

When she told her father she was getting hot, and please could he unzip her coat because it was stuck and she was burning on the inside, he picked her up and carried her.

At the car, he laid her on the back seat and put his hand on her forehead.

'Nothing to worry about. We'll get you in the bath and straight into bed and you'll be absolutely fine.'

He drove so fast she was thrown into the gap between the back seat and the front. With one arm twisted and flung on the seat behind, and the other bent double beneath her, she stayed where she was for the whole of the journey: her right cheek jammed up against the door, her head as still as she could keep it.

In the bathroom she looked in the mirror. There was a stripe on her cheekbone, like warpaint. When Max sponged the cut and wiped it dry, she felt nothing. In the early hours, though, her temperature rose and the pain was enough to wake her. She listened to her father sleeping, then she was sick on the bedclothes, so they had to tell the concierge.

Vinny and Beatrice arrived at the inn the next evening.

When Beatrice saw the plaster that covered the whole of Ruthie's cheek, she put her hand to her mouth, and Max explained. At supper, Beatrice told Ruthie she should try to eat something, even just a little.

When their aunt went to the toilet and their father was talking to the innkeeper, Vinny let her swap her full plate for Vinny's empty one. Later that night, when Ruthie climbed into Vinny's bed and told her she hadn't really fallen on the stairs in the way that Max had described, Vinny said, 'Don't tell fibs. And don't make a fuss. You're always making a fuss and you should sleep in your own bed now. You're old enough.'

'Vee!'

'We're going to Pépé Emile's tomorrow and Maman will be worried if we're still sharing a bed. We shouldn't make her worried. Auntie Bea said it's not very good for her.'

Beatrice flew home in the morning. Max drove the girls to the Place Rossetti, where Emile had said he'd be waiting. When Max asked, 'What about the bags? Shall I bring them to the house?' Emile said it wasn't necessary, he would manage.

Their father's car disappeared, and Emile sat them on the fountain wall. He took his time, and coughed several times before he told them: because their maman was in hospital, he would be mainly with her, and they would spend the week with a neighbour instead.

In part because they were so shocked, and in part because Vinny said there was no point (their papa would be angry, and their aunt would only say it had been for the best), they decided to keep it to themselves.

A week later, Emile stood by the fountain again, a granddaughter on either side. It was early, and the girls blinked at the light. Max ran a finger down Ruthie's spine, said, 'Go on, you two. In the car, while I have a word with Emile. You'll be here again before you know it.'

The two men spoke, until Vinny rapped her knuckles on the windscreen.

On the drive to England, Ruthie closed her eyes, and Vinny read. A few hours in, Max said, 'Won't you even tell me about your holiday?'

'I'm tired,' Ruthie said.

'Vinny?'

'I'm reading. Nothing happened anyway.'

Ruthie opened her eyes. She met her father's gaze in the mirror and held it. Turning away, she waited until he'd stopped looking, then she watched him.

At their aunt's house, the girls went to their room.

Max said he had a morning flight, and couldn't stay.

Beatrice said he should go up and tell the girls himself; they shouldn't keep hearing it from her.

By lunchtime the following day, Ruthie stopped being able to keep it a secret. The girls next door reported it to their mother, and as soon as Beatrice found out, she telephoned Max.

'Didn't you think to ask Emile?'

'He said Sophie was ill. He made it perfectly clear she didn't want to see me.'

'So. You assumed it was all about you. It's a shoddy situation and you bloody well ought to be ashamed of yourself. Did you make any attempt to find out from Vinny and Ruthie what they'd done all week? Did you even ask?'

'I told you! Wouldn't say a word!'

'What do you expect? You never talk to them.'

'They're children!'

'They're people.'

'Maybe when they're older. I can—'

'No. Vinny's twelve. And Ruthie's nine. You need to talk to them properly. Not just instructions. Actual conversations. They have ideas, you know. Opinions. Give them a chance. Who they are when they're older will be because of how you treat them now, while they're growing. As it turned out, they rather enjoyed themselves. The neighbour sounds perfectly nice. Two daughters of her own, huge big barn to play about in, horses to rub down in the stable, ropes galore for coiling. Even Roo's almost chubby, they ate so much. Not that it's of any interest to you. Right, Whitsun Week. Have you checked your diary?'

In June, Vinny was awarded a full scholarship to the Grove, the boarding school her aunt had attended. Ruthie, however, had made little progress with the tutor in her after-school lessons: there were difficulties with concentration and she held back, always, even if she had an answer. It was decided that thoughts of one day joining Vinny should be put aside, and that she would complete her education at Little House.

The morning they were told, there was a summer storm and the rain was like gravel, thrown at the windows.

'Hats and wellies, please,' Beatrice said when they stood with their mouths open. 'Pryors Field, I think. It's torrential, but you've had a shock, and a walk's the best thing for it.'

Sheltering under the copper beech, she told them they'd understand when they were older, that everything had turned out for the best. Vinny could come home to Pilgrim's Lane twice a term, and they could write as many letters as they wanted. 'You'll be living with me, Roo. We'll have such a lot of fun together, really we will,' but by then her voice was singing and falling with the wind, so Ruthie couldn't tell if she was happy or sad.

At the house again, they cried.

'Oh, loveys! It's not so very awful, is it? It makes complete sense for you to go to different schools. You're different people, the two of you! Whyever would you be the same, just because you're sisters? Anyhow, you can't both push off to the Grove and leave me here on my own. Who would I do the crossword with? Take this, for example. "*Fake; a pudding.*" It's hopeless. Four letters, second letter, "*u*". Tell me some puddings. "*Puff*", I thought, like an apple puff, but it won't go. No point sending you somewhere you'd be miserable, Roo darling. It's the perfect place for you, though, Vee. You're only really happy when you're buried in a book. Or a tin of toffees, by the looks of it! Have you eaten all the red ones? What about your sister? Here, Roo, have one, quick. There, that's made you smile! Everything will be alright, I know it will. I can feel it in my bones.'

That summer holiday, the last before Vinny went away, Max was wild with his daughters at the villa, clinging to them then brushing them off. There was more drinking than there should have been, and while

Vinny stood her ground, Ruthie started to approach him as though he was a cat that scratched.

They came back, and Vinny spoke to Beatrice, who said, 'Of course I'll talk to him, and no, of course I won't say you asked me to. And for heaven's sake don't worry about telling me. You must always talk to me about anything you're worried about. Any little thing.'

Afterwards, Beatrice told Max that if he wanted to have them again, he mustn't drink when they were there and he had to be gentler with them both.

'I'm their guardian,' she said, 'if anyone is. I happen to think it's best for us all to keep things as they are, but I can't pretend I'm comfortable about them coming to you unless—'

'I've said, I'll try.'

'I need you to promise.'

'Alright. I promise.'

At her sister's farewell supper, Ruthie was perfectly well behaved. The next day, saying goodbye to Vinny in the driveway at the Grove, she cried no more than the other girls. But at her leave-taking with her father she wouldn't look at him, and it was a week before she said another word to her aunt.

The first time Vinny phoned from school, she told Ruthie she should think herself lucky: church was compulsory and lasted for hours, and she had to wear tights, even though it was a weekend!

On the subject of what it was like to sleep in a room with strangers, there was the story of someone pouring a glass of water on her face and waking her. When she asked in the darkness who'd done it, she was told to please be quiet, people were trying to sleep.

Ruthie asked about bathtime, and Vinny said there were seven baths side by side, separated by half-panels so things could be thrown over: a tennis ball, or a hairbrush. Or, once, Vinny's pocket dictionary so she went to her next lesson without it.

'What about your things?' Ruthie asked, and Vinny said she had her own cupboard next to her bed.

'What do you put in it? Your clothes?'

'No. My clothes go in the big cupboard with everyone else's.'

'What, then?'

'My picture of Maman and Papa that Auntie Bea gave me. Your letters, Papa's postcards. Parcels from Auntie Bea.'

'Did you get any letters from Maman?'

'No. Did you?'

'No. Auntie Bea said she was too poorly.'

'Tell me about you, Roo! Your handwriting's terrible and I couldn't read a word of your letter and I want to know everything. I have to talk to Auntie Bea as well, so hurry up.'

Ruthie said she was going to have a new bedroom at Pilgrim's Lane. She'd move from the room she'd always shared with Vinny, and would sleep all on her own at the top of the house. Vinny said Beatrice had already told her, and she'd explained that Ruthie was sad at first, but when she found out it was where their aunt had slept when she was little, she'd changed her mind.

'That's not why I like it,' Ruthie said. 'It's because it means I'll be the same as Papa! I'll have my very own floor at the very top of the house and you'll only be allowed to come up if you're invited! It's like Papa's room at Pennerton, and Auntie Bea says he's going to teach me photographs. Then we'll be exactly the same, Papa and me.'

'Papa and I, not Papa and me. Put Auntie Bea on.'

Their autumn half-term holiday was at Pennerton. Beatrice stayed three days, then they were on their own with their father.

The first time Ruthie asked, standing at the darkroom door with her hands behind her back, he said no.

'No to which?'

'No to both, little lady. You're not coming in, and I'm not teaching you. Never mind what your aunt's said. I haven't got time and that's that.'

The door closed. When the busy-light went on, Ruthie knew it would stay on for hours.

In the evening Beatrice telephoned, and Max left the girls by the Long Library fire.

'Alright, Ruthie-Roo,' he said afterwards. 'Only an hour, though, just to see what you make of it. Then it's bath and bed for both of you.'

In his lightroom, she made for the darkroom door.

'Not so fast.'

'But I—'

'There are some things you need to know.'

'Like what?'

'Like all sorts.'

'But—'

'And another thing.' He put a finger to her chin and pulled it up.

'What, Papa?'

'I'm in charge. No negotiation, no answering back. Yes?'

'Yes.'

'Sit down, then, what're you waiting for?'

She climbed on his chair and slipped her hands in the pockets of her pinafore. He opened a sketchbook so big it took up half the desk, then he brought a file and a tiny canister and an album of prints from the shelves. He went to the darkroom and came back with a thermometer, a white plastic bottle, a measuring cylinder, and a ring-bound book with a list of numbers on the front, which he placed beside the sketchbook.

He drew a plan of the room he'd kept her from. There was occasional commentary about his first ever teacher, the photographer he'd worked for on his national service: his extreme tallness, or the colour of his clipped moustache. Rubbing something out and redrawing, Max leaned back on his chair and said, 'I was nearly twice your age, Roo,' and, 'You're starting very early,' and, 'You might not take to it, you know. Not everyone does.'

He named things as he drew, showing her the work surface where films were developed and the canisters stacked behind, pointing out spaces set aside for jugs and funnels and sachets of crystals and bottles of chemicals and scissors and lightproof boxes with paper inside, wrapped in lightproof bags. He moved around his plan, letting his pencil hover over the trays, describing what she should expect from the smell and the colour of their contents before coming to land at a big ceramic trough, and a line for hanging prints. Then there were the things from his darkroom. Reciting their functions and explaining where they fitted in his diagram, he read out the whole of the hazard warning on the back of the plastic bottle and told her that the making of photographs wasn't a game.

In one of his pauses, she balled her hands into fists and pushed them deeper in her pockets.

'Why can't we go and look?'

'Because I said so.'

'Why?'

'You won't be able to see anything once you're in. Not properly.'

She clenched her fists, digging her fingernails into her palms. 'Will I be able to see you?'

'In total darkness? No. In the safelight? Yes, but not so as to recognise me. Not until you get used to it. And that's what you'll have to do! When you drop something, you need to know how to find it. If you're always stopping to work out where things are, you'll never

have any kind of rhythm. You need to understand, Roo. It's an altogether different way of looking. Best to learn in the abstract first.'

'What's "in the abstract"?'

'This,' he said, tapping his pencil on the finished drawing. 'First,
assimilate your environment. Then –'

'What's "assi-li-mate your –"'

'A-S-S-I-M-I-L-A-T-E. Ask Vinny to look it up with you
tomorrow.'

Then he drew a line down the centre of the drawing and pointed
to one side, 'The wet area,' and, to the other, 'The dry. Everything
has a place. Every chemical, every jug, every thermometer and
every plastic funnel. In any good darkroom these places will remain
invariant – Invariant. Keep a list, Ruthie-Roo.' He jumped up and got
a notebook, slim and grey and soft. 'Make a list of words and look
them up with Vee tomorrow.'

'Is it mine?'

'What?'

'This.' She touched the notebook. 'Can I have it?'

'Of course. I've got stacks.' He rolled a pencil across the desk.
'Write your name on the front if you like, so we know what's yours and
what's mine. Hurry up, though. We don't want to be here all night.'

Ruthie wrote her initials, 'R.S.H', in tiny block capitals at the cover's right-hand corner, cupping her hand around them.

'Finished?'

'Finished.'

'Next. There must be no cross-contamination.'

'Wait!' She opened the book and started to write, but when Max
took another pencil and spun it with two fingers, she tried to see how
and was distracted.

'No splashing from the sink or any of the trays, and your hands
must be kept completely dry.'

With her own pencil flat across her fingers, she tried to copy the
action.

'There must never be any dust. Not a single, solitary particle. Even the tiniest speck can destroy a negative.'

Max pulled a roll of film from his pocket, with a piece of black cloth. 'Talking of negatives –'

Ruthie slipped from her chair and crawled under the desk.

'Are you listening to a word I'm saying?'

'I dropped my pencil.' She stayed under the desk, moving her hands across the floor. 'What's a negative? Why do you have to –'

'Negatives are the beginning of the darkroom process.' When she emerged he was looking at his watch. 'Just a thought. Instead of asking me all these questions, write them down and save them up. Nearly bedtime. I'll make a start on the actual process, see how far we get.'

Later, Ruthie helped Vinny practise her French vocabulary, then she showed her the notebook Max had given her, and tried to explain what they'd done.

If he'd begun with the actual process, the plan of his darkroom might have made more sense. As it was, Ruthie climbed into bed with only a half-muddled upside-down notion of how you pressed a button on your camera and a shutter opened, so that light fell on the film inside, and how the film, which was made of plastic, stayed in the camera until it was all used up, then you put it in a bag with no light, and you shook it up and down in a liquid. After that, you dried it with a wipe and cut it into strips of miniature back-to-front pictures that were called negatives, then you chose one and put it in a flat tray in a big machine which she couldn't remember the name of and which, because it was in the darkroom, she hadn't yet seen. At some point you could turn the light on again, but she couldn't remember exactly when, and it wasn't the same light switch, and when you did it wasn't a normal light because the bulb was red and quite dim, and it was called a safelight. The big machine for the negative had its own light inside it. That was operated by another switch altogether and was like a torch, which shone through a sheet of coloured plastic called a filter, and then through the miniature back-to-front picture, for separate amounts of time called stops. You always had to count in case the big machine's timer, which was operated by a different switch again, M-A-L-F-U-N-C-T-I-O-N-E-D, which she'd written in her book.

You could count a second exactly by saying the word M-I-S-S-I-S-S-I-P-P-I in between each number, which was the name of a river in America where Max had photographed the river steamers, and the reason you knew you were counting a perfect second was because that was how long it took to say that word, which had four S's and two P's, but you had to just say the word instead of spelling it out, otherwise you'd be longer than a second.

When the lights were out, Ruthie shut her eyes and thought of the ringbound book of filters. He'd flipped the pages so fast, and spoken so quickly, she'd lost track immediately. Now, as she tried to recall it, the sheets of pink turned first yellow, then orange, then a deeper orange still and she puzzled over the question of why his photographs came out black and white, when they were made by shining a light through something pink-yellow-orange in a room that glowed too red for her to see him, or not so as to recognise him.

She went through the whole of the sequence again, moving her hands in the darkness or counting on her fingers. At the part where she dipped her still-blank paper in each of the liquids and switched the big light back on, she flinched and opened her eyes, remembering that if she did this too soon, the picture would disappear without her ever having seen it.

After lunch the next day she arrived in the Lightroom with her notebook in her pinafore pocket. Her pencil, sharpened by Vinny, was tucked in beside it. For every word on her list was a corresponding definition, written in Vinny's hand and extracted in exchange for a promise: Ruthie would make sure Max came down in time to help with supper.

'Why?'

Roo had asked this question in the Long Library, after breakfast.

'Because I'm not going to make it on my own.'

'But you don't need Papa! There's the list of meals from Mrs Green in the village. She filled up the freezer, Auntie Bea said, so you hardly have to do anything, you just have to—'

'It's not fair if you two stay up there.'

'Why not?'

'It just isn't! You didn't finish for ages last night. Papa didn't even come down to say goodnight and—'

'So?'

'Roo, that's horrible!'

'Well, you—'

'I what? Do you want me to help you or not?' She put the dictionary back on the shelf and flicked through Ruthie's notebook. 'Don't you even know what "incompatible" means?'

Ruthie did as her sister had asked and they left the Lightroom on time. Vinny had prepared the supper and was already at the kitchen table. Tapping her foot, she looked at the clock, then she looked away rather than at them, answering none of Ruthie's questions and hardly any of Max's.

Ruthie and Max would go only so far with the topic of light.

Her primary difficulty was the fact she couldn't see it, which meant she didn't understand when her father talked about a film being fast, or slow, or that he chose one over another depending on whether a day was gloomy or bright, so that he caught just enough of it but not too much. Why did he say caught enough of '*it*'? Light wasn't a thing, was it? All he would answer, though, was, 'Ah. Perhaps that's where you're going wrong.' Or, if she pressed him, 'It's to do with the size of the grains, and how much light they soak up,' which took her no further.

It proved so difficult that it ran on to the next day, when Vinny and Ruthie came in from playing tag with Peter in the Triangle Meadow, and Ruthie turned at the stairs and Vinny said, 'Are you going up again? Have you even done one yet?'

'No.'

'Why not?'

'We're doing it on the abstract.'

'On the what?'

'On the abstract.'

'"In", Roo. It's "In the abstract". What about lunch?'

'He said one o'clock. I can't be late.'

There were places where light had to go, and places where it mustn't. There was an object shaped like a teaspoon that could be waved about in this invisible light, above the blank piece of silver paper, which wasn't actually silver and had to be S-H-E-E-N-side-up, where the invisible image was being exposed. If the teaspoon object was waved about in the right place and for just the right amount of time, it would alter the I-N-T-E-R-P-L-A-Y between the blacks and the whites. This last was an action that had to be taken blind, Max explained, since the effect of it wouldn't be known until later when the picture had emerged, which he said was something that happened slowly, in much the same way as a bruise takes its time to appear.

When she could follow none of his attempts to explain the back-to-front-ness of what light did to film in your camera, he snatched her notebook and pressed it open and drew a diagram, with quick little arrows going both ways, and phrases like 'A-B-S-O-L-U-T-E R-E-V-E-R-S-A-L' and 'T-O-T-A-L I-N-V-E-R-S-I-O-N'. She still couldn't grasp it, so she turned up her pencil and started to rub out the diagram.

'Roo!' He reached out to stop her. 'Look at it tomorrow and it'll make sense, I promise you.'

'It's just for words, Papa.' She slipped the book in her pinafore pocket, noticing how it fitted exactly. 'Not pictures.'

She asked him whether things were still the same colour even though they looked different in different lights – for example, was a leaf still green at night, or was it only green in the daytime?

'That, young lady, is a question for another day. Or another night, rather. We'll wait for a full moon and go for a walk so you can see for yourself.'

He pressed a panel on the wall and the rectangular box in front of him lit up: two foot by one foot, it glowed a white cube and Ruthie leaned over it, trying to see what was inside.

'It's empty, Roo.'

'What is it?'

'A lightbox.'

'What's it for?'

'You'll find out tomorrow. Go and help Vinny with supper.'

'Are you coming downstairs?'

'Later. Don't wait for me, I'm not hungry.'

She arrived for her lesson in the morning to find him leaning over the lightbox. Standing as still as she could, she saw the light coming out of him and through him. Then she made a noise.

He stepped to one side and opened a file. Beckoning her over, he took what looked like a sheet of paper from the file. When he laid it on the lightbox, she saw that pieces of something darker had been slipped inside it, and showed through as bands falling in rows to the bottom.

He placed his hand on her back and tipped her forward over the box. She saw the darker bands were actually a series of strips of miniature pictures, made visible by the light from beneath. When her eyes adjusted to the scale of them, she became aware she was looking at row after row of versions of a picture of a woman, shot from the shoulders up.

Every single picture was the same or very similar. Most of them showed just the woman's head and her neck; others included parts of the top of her chest or her shoulders. All of them differed in some small way: her arms were held up in one but not the next; her face was turned to the right side or the left; her head thrown back or tipped forward.

Ruthie couldn't see them clearly, and was distracted by the way the blacks and the whites were back to front. She thought at first that she was looking at the head of a ghost which had had its eyes cut out, leaving white holes shining from the black.

Max nudged her away from the box. 'Watch.' He took what looked to Ruthie like a little Perspex egg cup from his pocket, and cupped it over one of the miniature pictures. Then he bent over and put his right eye onto it. Afterwards, he stood and passed her the egg cup. 'Now you have a go.'

Laying his hand on the back of her head, he pressed it down until her eye socket was resting on the egg cup and her face so close to the box she could feel the heat of the light on her cheeks. Then her mind adjusted to the effect of the egg cup, and her eye got used to this world of miniature, and she recognised her mother.

She held the egg cup with both hands, and clamped it to her face, raising herself up from the paper. Moving along each row, she paused over each image, going back a second time. The slither of space that remained between the Perspex and her eye filled up, and these tiny ghost-Sophies were drowning in her tears.

She handed the egg cup to her father.

'Paper's best for negatives,' he said, taking it without looking at her. 'Some people use plastic.' He leaned over the lightbox, wiping the egg cup on his shirt before holding it to his eye. 'Know what the problem is with a plastic sleeve?'

She didn't answer.

'Tiniest bit of moisture gets in and your negatives will rot, Ruthie-Roo, that's what. Leave them in plastic for a few years and you'll end up with a folderful of mould. Doesn't tend to happen with paper, not quite in the same way.' He turned to face her. 'And why do we have to look after our negatives so carefully?'

'I don't know.'

'Your negative is unique. If you take care of it, it'll last forever and you can make as many prints as you like. Take something like a hole, for example. Pinprick-sized, I mean. Look at this.'

He handed her the egg cup and pointed. She looked and couldn't see, then he pointed again and she found it: a bright white dot in the background, to the right of one of the miniature Sophies' heads.

'Plenty of tricks for that. Single-hair brush, dot of grey paint. Not my bag, I'm afraid. Anyone with half an eye will spot a print from a damaged negative. If it's ruined, it's ruined. Right.' He turned to the lightbox. 'We've only got a week, really, once we're through the theory. So we'll stick with one shot. See what happens when we mess around with things.'

'What things?' She rubbed her eyes.

'Anything you like! Change the timings, switch the filters. Mask the light, put the – Come on. Which do you want to spend the rest of your holiday looking at?'

But she gave him back the egg cup. 'You choose.'

He bent over the box. 'I like the line of her neck in this one, what do you think?' When she didn't answer, he pointed out a shadow between Sophie's neck and her hair, which she was holding just away from herself. 'Plenty to play around with. Nice and contrasty, no flaws.'

She watched him slide the line of Sophies out, then he gave her a pad of paper with a series of columns of varying widths.

'Slipped my mind at the time. May as well do it now, seeing as you're here.'

They recorded the Sophies together, discarding those that were damaged and keeping back the strip they'd chosen, then filing the rest away.

Throughout those hours of labelling and storing, he returned to the topic of the negative's mechanics: how the light passed through the negative to fall on paper made from grains of silver, and how the grains would catch the light and soak it up, so that the paper carried the image of the negative reversed, ready to be turned into a photograph.

She managed to follow his explanation more closely this time, but then she was suddenly and completely confused. When he asked her a question she couldn't answer, he grabbed her and turned her round and pushed her against the work surface and put his hand on her back and pressed it down with his fingers splayed.

'Stop grizzling and listen. If we were at the villa and we went to the cove and I kept my hand on your back for a whole day you'd have a suntan everywhere apart from here, wouldn't you?' He pressed his hand against her, harder than before.

'Yes.'

'Same as if you wear your swimming costume and you take it off for bed and you're half white and half brown, yes?'

'Yes.'

'Right. So we're in agreement that when we go to Greece your skin changes colour because of the sunlight?'

'Yes.'

She felt his hand fall away but she didn't turn round.

With his other hand he lifted her hair and stroked her neck.

'Well then. Your skin's the same as paper. When the sun shines on it and turns it brown, apart from where my hand is, it's doing exactly the same as the light from the enlarger. It shines through the bits of the negative that are white, but it can't get through the bits that are black. The black bits are the equivalent of my hand, which means that when the photograph shows up on the paper it's a back-to-front version of the negative. Black is white, and white is black. Do you see, Roo?'

'Sort of. But I'm not the same as photograph paper. I'm not made of silver so it's not the—'

'I didn't mean you were the same as the paper. It's an analogy.'

'A what?'

'Ask Vinny.'

'So you couldn't turn me into a photograph?'

'No, Ruthie. I couldn't.'

It had been such a long time coming.

At first she only watched. Or listened, rather, until her eyes were used to the half-light. In the middle of the afternoon he lifted her on his shoulders and stood at the enlarger. Her hands were resting on his head and her feet were crossed against his chest. He worked the dials and set the timer and changed the filters and the huge machine became a ship: he the captain and she the boy-lookout, high in the crow's nest.

Later she slipped down and rode him piggyback: inner thighs on his hip bones, stomach on his spine, face against his neck, eyelashes lapping his ear. Then he shrugged her away, and instead of clinging to him, she sat back and her hands were on his shoulders and the light shone through his head from the enlarger.

'Right,' he said. 'We can do the next bit together.'

She dropped to the floor. When he beckoned, she followed him to the rinsing sink. He lifted her on a stool and she put her hands on top of his. She moved as he moved: turning on the tap and turning it off; putting in the plug and taking it out.

At the work surface, though, he said, 'Better not,' so she kept her hands behind her back and when they finished he said, 'Well done, Roo. You've made more progress than I thought you would.'

In the days that came after, there was a mistake for every lesson.

Forgetting about processing the negatives, she pulled a roll of film from its canister. He was at the sink, rinsing out a tray.

'There's nothing on it, Papa.'

He turned and stared. 'What do you mean, nothing?'

'It's blank.' She was holding the strip of film to the light, straining her eyes. 'I can't see any pictures. There's nothing on it.'

She dropped it when he slapped her. Crouching on the floor she moved her hand around and felt for it. Then he was shouting and she was lying down and he was hitting her again but it was finished quickly.

She got into her own bed that night. When Vinny came in and said, 'How was it?' and, 'What did you do today?' she didn't answer. And when her sister stood beside her and whispered, 'Roo? Are you still awake?' she pretended to be asleep.

Once Vinny was in bed, and her breathing had settled to a rhythm, Ruthie cried properly.

She dreamed of her father. Light streamed from the whites of his holed-out eyes and his mouth was opened in anger. Caught from the shoulders up in an endless strip of negatives, he appeared and disappeared a thousand times.

In another lesson, she stood with a pair of tongs and realised she'd forgotten which tray they were from; which she should or shouldn't put them in.

The print they were working on was still in the first of them and he had his back turned.

Scratching her face and her neck, she recited the order of the trays to herself.

She was nearly sure when she felt something moving on her chest. She looked but there was nothing, only her heart jumping from her body and becoming a thing separate from herself: a snare drum played by a soldier on parade but louder so she thought he would hear it. Her heart went back inside her chest and the space around it was flooding with liquid that was cold and burning at the same time then it was streaming through her body then the drum roll stopped and her body had emptied out completely and there was nothing inside it.

She rehearsed the rule: it was alright to move the tongs between the trays in one direction but not the other. Again she might have worked it out but he turned and looked at her and he looked at the tongs and she knew that he knew what she'd done, and some part of her body that was shut away from her mind remembered how, when he'd hit her before (once on the head and then, when she'd fallen, two or three times more), he'd put his face close to hers and shouted: 'Get out of my sight,' and, 'I never want to see you in here again.'

Standing there now, she watched him raise his hand.

Time slowed down, and she wasn't in the room any more and this meant she couldn't hear and couldn't see and couldn't feel what he did to her.

Then it was over and she could hear his instruction and she handed him the tongs and everything became white and she felt her way to the door and stood by it with her chin to her chest.

'No, Ruthie.'

'Where then?'

'Anywhere you like, just not in here.'

She put her hand to the door and hesitated.

'Oh, you needn't worry about the light.' He switched off the safe-light and they stood in the pitch-dark. 'You've already spoilt your print. It's ruined, Ruthie.'

When the main light went on, she saw him at the sink, emptying out the trays.

It was one of the trays that tripped her up, and nearly brought the lessons to a close. Strictly speaking it was its contents that caused the problem, when Max told her to stand on a stool and take a corner with both her hands and lift it by 'an I-M-P-E-R-C-E-P-T-I-B-L-E amount' and shake it, gently, so that the developer could seep over the surface of the paper and back again until it was completely covered.

There were a number of things which made her falter, no one of them more significant than any other.

First there was the question of when, exactly, she should stop lifting the tray above the work surface for the height to meet the definition of 'an imperceptible amount'. Then there was the weight of the thing, which surprised her, and the heaviness of the liquid inside which moved sluggishly when she shook it, so that she lifted the tray a little higher and shook it a little harder and stopped trying to imagine what the word 'I-M-P-E-R-C-E-P-T-I-B-L-E' might mean and wondered instead whether it was correct to describe a liquid as 'heavy', and if not, how else she should tell Vinny about the strange loaded-down-ness of this fluid which, distracted as she was, took her completely by surprise and surged across the surface of the photograph and up the edges of the tray and slopped from the other end. When she lowered it too fast, the liquid surged again and rose in a miniature tidal wave and she flinched and the tray thudded to the work surface and slung the whole of its contents over her chest and her stomach and in between her legs and onto her feet so that Max shouted 'Jesus Christ!' and put both his hands inside the neck of her pinafore and ripped it from her body and pulled off her shoes and her socks and her knickers.

Shouting with his face up close, he lifted her and put her in the rinsing sink but she was too big so he held her legs in the air and shoved her in and the tap was jutting into her back and because of that, nothing came out of it. He turned it as far as it would go before he realised, then he swore and hauled her forwards and the water sprayed everywhere across the room and onto Ruthie and onto Max who swore again and turned off the tap and picked Ruthie up and put her over his shoulder and ran down the stairs and into the yard where he took the hose and sprayed it on her bare body and on her hair and on her face and on her bare bottom and her feet. The pressure was strong and the water was cold and hurt her skin so she said, 'Please, Papa! Stop!' but some of it went in her mouth so she closed it and didn't say anything else and he was still shouting and she was turning and turning in the water that was everywhere.

Her sister, who was lying under a blanket in the Long Library and next to the fire which Peter had piled so high it was crackling, heard none of it. Partly because Vinny's face was half buried in her book, and partly because she was facing away from the Long Library windows, nor did she see Max cross the Smart Lawn a minute later, holding Ruthie's clothes.

He took them to the orchard and dropped them in the oil-can burner on top of a heap of leaves and called over the kitchen-garden wall to Peter that there was more for burning, and that if he had nothing better to do, perhaps he could bloody well get round to it.

Ruthie, meanwhile, did as she was told and went stark naked into the house.

She waited until the bath was full, then she waited a little longer. When still he didn't come, she got in. Later, she took a clean pinafore from her holiday bag and stood at her bedroom window. A column of smoke was rising from the orchard. She watched until Peter appeared at the gate in the hedge, then she put on her pinafore and went to help Vinny with supper.

Much later, she felt in her pocket for her notebook.

In the bathroom, looking at the steam on the water, her mind had been only on Max. She'd tried to work out how angry he'd be if he came and she hadn't waited. Then she'd half wondered about her clothes, and whether they were still in the courtyard. When she started shivering, she got in and lay with her head under the water, holding her breath for as long as she could.

Afterwards, moving the towel over her skin in slow motion, she forgot about her clothes altogether. Instead she thought about Sophie, and about how, at midsummer once, she had helped Ruthie from the bath and let her run around the house until she was dry just from running, and how in the winter Sophie would ask Peter to light a fire in the bedroom and when Ruthie called, 'Maman!' she would come straight away and stand with a towel held wide and catch Ruthie as she climbed out and the towel was always crisp and warm and Sophie would wrap her up in it and carry her to her bedroom and put her down in front of the fire and rub her back and her arms and her legs with the crisp, warm towel.

She was surprised then, after supper, to reach for her notebook and find it wasn't there. She'd finished testing Vinny on her verb endings, and Vinny had taken down the dictionary and asked her for her words from her photography lesson. She reached in the other pocket, thinking she must have misplaced the little grey book.

Max was on the other side of the fire from them, holding a newspaper in front of his face.

Vinny was lying on the floor and Ruthie was sitting next to her. When Ruthie shook her head, Vinny asked again.

'It's alright, Vee,' Ruthie said. 'I don't have any.'

'You must have something.'

Ruthie flushed red and shook her head again and held a finger to her lips.

'Let me see, Roo!' Vinny made as if to put her hand in Ruthie's pinafore pocket. 'Give me your noteb—'

Ruthie whispered, 'Doesn't matter. Please, it doesn't.'

The following morning, the girls were walking through the kitchen garden when Peter appeared at his cottage door. He called to Vinny, 'Wait there. We won't be a minute,' then he beckoned Ruthie in.

At the kitchen table, she took the notebook with both hands. Believing and not believing, she looked at him and looked away.

'It's a bit creased up,' he said. 'I dried it on the stove then I ironed the pages, but the cover's still wrinkled. Sorry, love.'

She slid the book into her pocket.

'You'll be needing this,' he said, handing her the pencil. She tried to say thank you but it came out as a sigh.

'Alright,' he said. 'You'd better find your sister. Mind how you go, Roo.'

When Vinny asked her, she showed her the pencil only, and said Peter had found it in the meadow.

Apart from a pair of scales, positioned at its midpoint, Max had cleared his desk. There was a small piece of paper on the right-hand scale and on the base was a line of brass weights in varying sizes, each of them embossed with a number.

'Ready?' he said.

'Yes,' she answered, not knowing for what.

'Find me the five-gram weight.'

She picked it up but it slipped from her fingers. Crouching to the floor, she stood a minute later with it clutched in her fist.

'On the scales, please.'

She wavered between the two, then she placed it on the scale with the piece of paper.

'Not that one.'

When she'd moved it across, he adjusted the slide in the middle. 'Say stop when it's enough,' he said, taking a tiny plastic bag from his pocket and beginning to empty its contents on the other scale, directly onto the piece of paper.

'Stop,' she said, almost immediately

'Look at it, Roo. Tell me what you see.'

'Powder.'

'Really?'

'Crystals, I mean. Crystals.'

'Colour?'

'Black. No, purple. Dark purple.'

'So, tell me again. What do you see?'

'Dark purple crystals.'

'How many grams?'

She looked across at the weight she'd chosen, double-checking the number on the top. 'Five.'

'So. Tell me again, what do you see?'

'Five grams of dark purple crystals.'

'Thank you. The details are important, Roo. Now. Shall I tell you what I see?'

'Yes, Papa.'

He took the paper from the tray and slipped the crystals back in the bag. Then he wrote a short string of letters and numbers on another piece of paper.

'I see enough of this –' he pointed at the letters and numbers – 'to kill a child. Your five grams of dark purple crystals are an everyday ingredient for a photographer. What you did yesterday was very, very silly. We'll see how you get on, but for now, I want you standing back and watching. Understood? You touch nothing, and unless I tell you to, you do nothing.'

'Yes, Papa,' saying the words he wanted to hear instead of the ones she wanted to say, so they were stuck in her mind the afternoon through: 'You hurt me,' and, 'Why?' and, 'I love you.'

The first part of the lesson passed in near silence. Within an hour he'd relented, or forgotten, and they fell into a rhythm of sorts: him asking and her bringing a thermometer or a plastic jug; him opening a new packet and her sliding out a piece of paper and checking for the side with the sheen on; him pressing a timer and her counting aloud her Mississippis.

There was a moment of closeness: their hands touching in the light tight bag. The warmth of his skin on hers, feeling for the film and winding it onto the cylinder, kneading her knuckles so they clicked, but gently.

'Well done, Ruthie-Roo. Well done.'

It was easier like that, when the lights were out and they were in each other's company without him being able to see her. Max placed a stool at the corner of the enlarger and Ruthie climbed up. He took his time positioning the picture, then he placed the offcut paper on a diagonal, so it lay across the ghost-Sophie's head and neck and shoulders, catching as many different parts of her as possible: the soft section of her skull on the right of her face, just before her hairline began; the seashell-curve of her ear's inside; the shadow of her neck that had interested him; her eye, closed in a sharp dark stripe of lashes; a strand of her hair, swept back and held there; the underside of the wrist that kept it pressed to her head.

Looking down at her mother, Ruthie held the cardboard over the image so that only a segment of the paper strip was exposed to the light. She tried to stop her hands shaking by thinking about Pilgrim's Lane, and the fact she'd be there the following night, but when Max stood behind her it got worse. He started the timer and brought his hands to her hips. 'Steady, Roo. Steady.'

She listened to his breathing, then she listened to the ticks and counted her Mississippis. She moved the cardboard by an inch, keeping it as still as she could until the timer sounded. She did the same thing again so that, inch by inch and stop by stop, the exposures were repeated until she reached the edge of the paper strip. When Max switched off the enlarger, the ghost-Sophie disappeared altogether and the paper became completely white, as though the whole exercise was make-believe and her father was playing a game.

He took the paper strip. When he lowered it into the first tray, she moved her stool beside him.

As the image emerged in sharp segments going from dark to light, Sophie's head and neck became clearer and Ruthie's heart began to jump. While Max fixed the paper strip and washed it, switching the main light on, the jumping turned to thudding she could feel in between her eyes.

When he'd wiped the paper he laid it on the work surface and pointed to a segment of Sophie's neck. Because Ruthie's heart was jumping from her body and shoving itself back in again, she lost her balance and half sat, half fell onto the stool.

'Good work, Ruthie-Roo. Seven, I think, what do you say? Seven stops or eight? Can you see the difference it makes, just another six seconds?'

Ruthie had her eyes closed. She shrugged her shoulders and, while he decided, did her own calculations: counting the weeks that were left before she'd have to come back, wondering how to tell her aunt that she didn't like the darkroom, and if there was to be another half-term at Pennerton, that she'd prefer to spend her afternoons in the library with Vinny.

Then he was saying, 'Wake up, sleepyhead,' and they were going into the lightroom and he was standing behind her at the desk and dictating what to write on the back of the test strip, telling her to do this every time she made a print, as a record of how she'd done it.

On the final day, he said they just about had time for a contact sheet but that was the very last thing, so why not call Vinny as well and he'd shoot a whole film of the two of them?

She stood completely still. 'Why?'

'I thought it might be nice for her to see what we've been doing all this time. Hurry up, would you? We haven't got forever.'

In London that night, Beatrice went to the top of the house. Ruthie was fast asleep, curled in the chair by the window.

In her left hand was a tiny gilded bird's skull, which Beatrice eased from her grip and put on the windowsill. Falling from Ruthie's other hand was a paper strip, two inches wide and twelve or so long. When Beatrice took it, she saw an image of a woman's head and neck, or rather of a section of a woman's head and neck, as though a slice had been cut from a picture of the whole. The slice showed the left side of the face, the left ear, and the left side of the neck which, since the head was thrown back, was elongated.

The image was so light at one end it was almost white. Made up of a sequence of segments that varied in size and sat on a diagonal axis, each segment was darker than the one before so that the final one was an almost-black. The demarcations formed by the edges of the segments made lines, cutting right through the woman's neck and out the other side. Further up the paper strip, these lines severed the woman's face into pieces: just above her eye or right through the middle of her eyelid or just below her hairline. The broadest segment sat halfway down her neck, where the contrasts were most marked and the demarcations sharpest, so that her throat looked to have been slashed twice and then again.

Beatrice turned the strip of paper over and there were Ruthie's pencilled capitals:

MAMAN, BY PAPA, 8 X 4.5 SECENDS STOPS/FILLTER 1.5/APURRTIURE = 4/

Then underneath, in Vinny's firmer hand:

Seconds!   Filter!   Aperture!

On the floor beside the chair was an A4-sized piece of paper with a series of images in lines which ran across it. Beatrice picked it up and held it up close, then closer, then away and closer again. She glanced at Ruthie, then at the lines of images and back again. When she'd looked at the images one more time, she put the paper where she'd found it and carried her niece to bed.

The piece of paper would lie there all night. In the morning, not quite awake, Ruthie wandered across the room and stepped on it.

At the window, she held it in the light and opened her eyes wide, remembering.

There were six rows of images. Sitting on top of one another, the rows ran right to the edges and filled the whole of the page.

The top three comprised a series of images of Vinny, or rather, of parts of Vinny's face and head: her left eye in the first shot, and her right in the second, then both together and separately again, one shot after the other. Then a shot of just her ear, and afterwards her other ear. Her curls fell loosely around the first ear, but were held back and away in the second. Next was her nose, in three versions, each from a different angle. Her mouth followed: first open, then closed, then her lips pressed together and pushed into a pout. Last of all were her hands: her left and her right in turn, facing palms-front and held up close to the camera.

The bottom half of the sheet was made up of images of Ruthie, but the selection was slightly different. Her eyes were set out as Vinny's had been, and then there were her ears and the same three shots of her mouth; open or closed or pouting like her sister's. At the end, though, where her hands might have appeared, the final two shots were of her neck. In both of them, her head was out of shot but had been turned to one side and tilted back, or pushed there. Because of this, Ruthie's neck was exposed to the camera in such a way as to form a straight, sharp line. More limb than neck, it was pale against the dark sward of hair that was held away from it, making a shadow-pool.

Beatrice phoned Max and described what she'd found. He began to explain but she interrupted.

'For God's sake, I know what a contact sheet is.'

'What, then?'

'Oh, come on.'

'Come on, what?'

'You know bloody well. What the hell were you thinking? What did you put them through, to get those shots? You see my point?'

'No, I damn well don't. So? I took some pictures of my daughters.'

'They're not just "some pictures", though, are they? They're spooky and odd.'

'They're what? What did you just say?'

'You heard. They're more than a bit disturbing.'

'They loved it! We had fun shooting it. You're going to have to spell it out, I'm afraid. What exactly is the problem?'

'It's strange. That's what. It's more than strange, it's weird, chopping them up in bits.'

Ruthie was at the study door then, so Beatrice put her hand over the receiver and said, 'I won't be a min – why don't you pop down and choose what you want for breakfast? I'll come when I've finished talking to Papa,' and Ruthie ran away.

'Well, isn't it? Why on earth did you do it?'

'Isn't it what?'

'Weird.'

'Do you really want to know, or are you just phoning to give me a dressing-down?'

'Yes, Max, I really want to know. You've actually got them pouting! Vinny looks –'

He began to answer but Ruthie was at the door again, calling 'Hurry up, Auntie Bea!'

'I did it because I miss them.'

'But I still don't –'

'You told me to spend time with them and I did. I gave a copy to Ruthie because I promised. Actually, I did it for myself. I want to learn their faces. I'm beginning to forget. Do you know what that's like? I want to learn them, so I don't – I thought if I broke them down into parts I could – Can you even –? I don't want—'

'It's alright, Max. Stop. Yes, I understand now. Of course I do. Don't –' but Ruthie called a second time and Beatrice held the phone away and said, 'I'm coming! Really, give me a minute, please!'

When she held it to her ear again, she said she was sorry, and, 'Max? Are you alright, Max, are you still there?'

At the start of the holidays, they were told that their maman was too unwell to have them for Christmas. In answer to their questions, Beatrice would only say that it was complicated.

'Stop crying please, Ruthie. Your papa's only just found out himself, and he's going to such a lot of trouble to get things ready. Really! Don't look so glum. We'll have a wonderful time at Pennerton, won't we?'

'Yes,' Vinny said, and she nudged Ruthie, who nodded.

That night, Ruthie climbed into Vinny's bed.

'Front or back?' Vinny said.

'Back.' Ruthie turned away. Vinny brought her body up to Ruthie's. Lifting Ruthie's hair to one side and pressing her face into Ruthie's neck, she wrapped herself around her. A second later there were tears on Ruthie's cheeks and they ran onto her nightshirt.

'What?' Vinny whispered. 'Why are you shivering? You can't be cold, it's boiling in here. What's the matter?'

'I'm not cold.'

'Oh, Roo. Here, it's alright. I know.'

When Ruthie stopped crying, and when their breathing had synchronised, she said to Vinny did she realise it was forty-three days and forty-three nights since they'd seen each other last?

'Did you count?'

'Yes.'

'Why?'

'Because I missed you.'

Ruthie and Vinny had believed what their aunt and their father had told them, that the years would be divided in this way: Christmas and Easter in Nice with their mother and their grandfather; summers at the villa with their father.

This Christmas was marked as a milestone in Ruthie's mind. Whenever she'd imagined it, it had always involved a journey to France, to their maman. Instead, there was to be a train to Kent with Beatrice, and fourteen whole days at Pennerton.

The first morning, they climbed onto their windowsill. They put their foreheads against the glass and agreed the Smart Lawn looked like the top of the Christmas cake Beatrice had brought from London, it was so smooth and so white.

'Promise you won't tell Papa,' Vinny said.

'Promise I won't tell Papa what?'

'It's a secret.'

'What?'

'Promise first, then I'll tell you.'

'I promise.'

'I've started the curse.'

'What curse?'

'My period. I've started my period.'

'Why are you calling it your curse?'

'Not "my curse", silly! It's "the curse".'

'Why, though?'

'Because that's what it's called at school.'

'What's it like?'

'Horrible.'

'Why?'

'Because it hurts.'

'What do you do when it hurts?'

'Ask Matron for a tablet.'

'What kind of tablet?'

'Brufen.'

'Does it stop it hurting?'

'Sometimes. But if you can't get a tablet it really, really hurts. And it's annoying because if you don't know it's started it leaks and you can see it and sometimes it leaks anyway in your knickers, on the side of your ST and—'

'What's an ST?'

'A sanitary towel.'

'Is it a towel?'

'No, here, look.' She fetched one from her bag. 'It's like a brick.'

Ruthie asked if she could try it on and Vinny said, no, of course not, Auntie Bea had only given her one packet.

'Do you have it now? Do you have your curse now?' and Vinny said, 'Yes, but the bit where it hurts has finished so it's alright. And it's "the curse", Roo, not "my curse". I just told you.'

Wrapped in scarves and hats and coats, they did as Beatrice had told them, and went to Peter's cottage. He trudged with them across the Christmas-cake snow, dragging the toboggan. At the Triangle Meadow, Ruthie tugged Vinny's sleeve and whispered, 'Will you get blood on the snow? If it leaks?' Vinny pushed her away. 'What? I'm just asking!'

The meadow snow was so deep in places, Ruthie was up to her calves. When they climbed on the toboggan and Peter pushed them round the edge, he was out of breath straight away. Once or twice he came to a halt. After the third time round, he leaned against a tree and said, 'One more and that's your lot! I'm not as young as your papa, so go easy on me.'

He tied his glasses more tightly, then he waited. Ruthie sat in front, held in Vinny's arms, then Peter leaned in and ran, and snow sprayed into Ruthie's face and she opened her mouth and felt it on her tongue and the air was white and for a moment she could see nothing at all. At the orchard hedge, he said, 'I'm finished! Time for your breakfast,' but they cried out, 'One more go! Please, Peter, just one!'

Later, their father took them and they stayed out till dusk. When he gave up and sat on the toboggan himself, the two of them tried to push him but they couldn't, so they stopped in the middle of the meadow and built a snowman by the oak.

They were asleep before lights out. When they were kept as busy the next day, and the day after, they decided their aunt was trying to make them forget about Sophie, and had told their father and Peter to do the same.

Even if Beatrice had succeeded just a little in her attempts, her work would have been undone. Sent off for tea at other people's houses, they were told, more than once, that it must be terribly upsetting, but weren't they doing jolly well? They'd go to France for Christmas next time, wouldn't they? Or perhaps their maman could come to England?

'Oh, we're definitely going to France,' they replied in unison. 'She's just poorly at the moment, that's all.'

They meant it when they said it, and they carried on meaning it for a long time.

'Please!' Ruthie said on Christmas Eve. 'So it's like we're in France even though we're not!'

Max said no, but Beatrice insisted.

'For goodness' sake! It's the least we can—'

'Bloody hell!' Max said, and Ruthie thought there would be an argument but then he said, 'Alright, alright,' and they were allowed to open their presents early.

For the last of hers Vinny was given two leather-bound volumes of poetry. She opened them and looked at the first few pages and said, 'Yes I like them. Thank you, Papa. Thank you, Auntie Bea,' then she put them away. That night, though, she showed Ruthie the inside covers, each of them carrying an identical inscription: *Sophie Marie Louise, September 1959*.

Ruthie asked why their maman had been reading poems in German.

'She wasn't. She was singing them. She could sing in every single language. That's what singers do.'

'Did you hear her sing those ones?'

'Yes. So did you.'

'I don't remember.'

'You were still a baby, so you wouldn't.'

Ruthie had unwrapped her last present slowly: one of Max's cameras, loaded with a fresh roll of film. When she looked like she was about to cry he took it from her. He showed her how to hold it, then he tried to pass it back but her hands were shaking.

'It's nothing special,' he said. 'Think of it as birthday and Christmas together if you like. I never use the thing. It's just a bit of fun, Roo. Calm down.'

'What shall I do with it?'

'What do you think? No hurry. We haven't even started on how to shoot, so just experiment. When you've filled it up we'll look at what you've done and go from there. You'll have to work for it, though. Your shots won't come to you.'

'What do you mean?'

'You'll have to go after them. If you see something you want, do what it takes to get it. You'll know what I mean. Here, I'll show you the basics. Open this. Flick this. Press this. And for heaven's sake, don't look so worried.'

It was more than a toy to Ruthie. Tiny and solid and black, with a spare roll of film that Vinny had laughed at and said was the right size for the doll's house at Pilgrim's Lane, she thought of it as a treasure. As soon as she was given it she found her school satchel and emptied it of books. Later, when Vinny asked her why, she said it was the only thing she had that was big enough, and when Vinny said,

'But the camera's tiny!' she showed her the jumper she'd wrapped it in, and the woolly socks she'd placed on either side.

Several days would pass before she used it. Every night before she fell asleep, she turned it in her hands, then she polished it with her nightshirt and held it to her face. Daytimes she kept it bundled in her satchel and always with her, insisting to Vinny she wasn't going to waste her film on just anything; she was waiting for inspiration. If Vinny teased, Ruthie simply walked away, and Beatrice would tell Vinny off, asking Ruthie later whether she'd seen anything she wanted to take a picture of yet, and how about the Christmas tree, might that be an idea? Or a picture of Papa, the next time he fell asleep by the fire?

On the last morning, she stood at the bedroom window, staring at the Smart Lawn. She packed for Pilgrim's Lane, then she drifted in and out of the rooms, considering and rejecting: a gilded branch, lain on the lid of the piano; the dressing table in her aunt's bedroom, strewn with jewels and perfume bottles; the view of the meadow from her father's bedroom window; and finally, the left eye of the rocking horse, half covered by its mane.

At about eleven o'clock, Ruthie found Beatrice in the kitchen reading a recipe book. Beatrice said, 'What shall we have for our final lunch, Ruthie-Roo? What would Papa like, do you think?' but Ruthie only stared at the book and wondered, was it too flat for a photograph? Beatrice closed it and asked her again, then a third time, but it was only when her aunt began to chop a carrot that Ruthie's train of thought was interrupted, and she offered to help.

'It's easier if I do it on my own,' Beatrice said. 'Why don't you go for a walk or something? There's a beautiful sky on the meadow,' so Ruthie swung her satchel across her chest and stepped outside.

She was halfway across the courtyard when it happened.

First, there was a mewling from the end stable and she pushed open the door, slowly. A cat stood in the shaft of light, its belly so low it touched the ground. Heavy and round, it mewled more loudly, then it staggered with its own weight and walked away.

Ruthie hovered, wondering about fetching Beatrice, not knowing what to do. Then she pushed the door wider and wedged it with a brick. Her hands were shaking, and she struggled with the buckle on the bag. Discarding the woolly socks, she unravelled the jumper her camera was wrapped in, dropping the jumper on the stable floor and trying to slow her breathing.

The cat had found a corner, still in the shaft of light, and Ruthie knelt apart from her.

When it began, Ruthie's hands stopped trembling. She snapped with her doll's-house camera until she was sure it was over.

The litter was seven in all. Ruthie captured every birth, leaning in as close as she could until she realised it was easier to lie down, and hold herself up on her elbows.

In the afternoon, when it was almost time to go, she knocked on the Lightroom door and handed the film to her father.

'I'm sure they're not very good.'

'Why're you giving them to me then?' he replied, frowning.

When she turned away, she could feel her cheeks burn.

12 TUESDAY

Ruthie hears her sister move about the house, packing for Athens. Later, she hears Eleni in the courtyard, laying the table for supper.

She stays where she is, looking at the things Annie had looked at, when she'd brought her from the water in the afternoon, shutting out thoughts of what Vinny would say if she knew.

'Is that gold?' Annie had said, pointing at the clock on the wall.

'Yes,' Ruthie said. 'Not all the way, though. Just the outer layer.'

She'd left her sitting on the mattress, wrapped in a towel and sipping hot milk, and had gone to look for the Savlon one more time; there were scratches on Annie's neck as well as her arms, and two across the middle of her chest. She came back to find Annie had discarded the towel and put her bikini on again.

'What do you mean?'

'It's called gold leaf. It comes in very thin layers, and you press it on. Sort of like painting but different.'

'Do you do it with your fingers?'

'No, with a special brush.'

'What is it? Is it a model of something?'

'It's a clock.'

'But it's got feathers coming out of it.'

'It's a feather-clock. Haven't you ever seen one before?'

She showed Annie how each of the feathers was fixed at its base to the mechanism and moved with the hour: the stubby white one went the fastest, acting as the seconds, while the two longer ones, dark brown and stripped into quills, indicated the minute and the hour.

Annie looked at it, frowning.

'Do you know how to tell the time?' Ruthie asked.

'Course. I've got my own watch. I left it off for swimming. Your clock's not very clear.'

'Alright,' Ruthie said. She showed Annie how the feathers worked again, then they told the time together.

'Is it the only one you've got?'

'No. Why?'

'It's a bit difficult.'

Ruthie fetched a watch from a drawer. She put it on Annie's wrist. 'How's that?'

Annie held it to her ear and shook it. 'Easier. Is it old?'

'Yes, but not very.'

'Where's it from?'

'Istanbul. It's from the Grand Bazaar at Istanbul.'

'When did you go there?'

'I didn't.'

'So how did you get it?'

'It was my dad's.'

'Did he give it to you?'

'Not exactly. I found it. Runs a bit slow, but otherwise it's fine.'

Annie shook her wrist and the watch dropped to the floor.

It rocked from side to side, then it was still.

In the chapel two days later, Eleni let her torch play on what she'd found there, lying on the altar. Stepping away, she pressed her shawl to her face against the smell.

When she closed the door behind her, the clouds were over the moon or she would have noticed this watch from Istanbul, sitting on the ground in so prominent a position it might just as well have been placed there for someone to find.

Instead, it remained undisturbed until first light, when it was found by a forensics officer and added to a list. By the time it was handed to Vinny, it had been bagged in clear plastic and labelled, and she answered the detective's questions straight away.

'It was my father's,' and, 'He wore it all the time,' then, 'No, I've not seen it since he died, not until today. I never saw my sister with it on. She must have found it in her room,' and 'No, I don't know that for certain. I'm just guessing. She found a lot of things,' and, 'Well, I've no idea why she had it with her. How do you know she did, anyway? Someone else could've – Isn't that your job, to –? Sorry, I didn't mean to suggest – Can I just ask, though? When will I be allowed to take my sister away? To England, I mean. I want to take her home. Do you see?'

Ruthie, picking the watch up from where Annie had dropped it on the lightroom floor, held it to her ear and checked for the rhythm.

'Sorry,' Annie said.

'It's perfectly OK. Anyway, I don't really need it here.'

'Why?'

'I can tell the time by the sun. Roughly, I know where it is for seven, eight. In August, noon's always over there,' she gestured.

'What about seconds? My brother makes me time him for running, with seconds and everything.'

'Don't you know how to count them without it?'

'No.'

'Don't you know your Mississippis?'

'My what?'

'I can't believe nobody's taught you.' She pointed at the gold clock. 'Watch the second hand. That's the small one, the little white feather. Watch it and count with me.' She took Annie on her lap, and whispered in her ear, 'One Mississippi, two Mississippi, three,' and they counted together. Afterwards, Annie counted on her own, then, 'Where did the clock come from?'

'I made it, when I was about your age.'

'On your own?'

'No. With my mum. We took the middle bit from another clock, then we made the pottery bit and I glued the feathers on. She put the gold leaf on the outside, then I gave it to my dad for his birthday, and we put it on the wall together.'

'Then what?'

'Then he took a picture of me standing on the work surface, next to it.'

'When you put it up? Was it a picture of you putting it up?'

'No. I think it was another summer. It's been there ever since, so it could've been any time.'

'Why don't you just ask him?'

'He's not here to ask.'

'Is he Greek, your dad?'

'No. Why do you say that?'

'Because his house is in Greece. So where is he?'

'He was English, not Greek. He just lived here. Sometimes here, sometimes in England. And he's dead, actually, so you may as well stop asking about him. Turn round.'

Ruthie put a hand, lightly, on Annie's shoulder.

'This might sting,' she said, rubbing some Savlon on Annie's neck. She noticed that the child stayed perfectly still. When she tried to rub some on the scratches to her chest, though, Annie shrugged her away, so Ruthie gave her the cream and told her to do it herself.

'Is that your job now?' Annie asked afterwards. 'Do you make clocks?'

'No.'

'What then? Are they yours?' She pointed at the cameras, strung out on a work surface. 'Is that your job?'

'They are mine, yes. But no, it's not. They used to be my dad's and now I've got them. He showed me how to use them when I was little.'

'How did he know?'

'That's what he did. He was a photographer.'

'Gosh. I don't know anyone whose dad's a photographer. My dad's an accountant and my mum's a teacher. When I grow up I'm going to be a helicopter pilot. What's your job, if you're not a photographer?'

'I don't have one right now.'

'So what do you do all day?'

'I swim, mainly.'

Annie looked at her. 'All day?'

'No,' Ruthie smiled. 'I'm joking.'

'What's your name by the way?'

'Ruthie. My name is Ruthie.'

'Do you take pictures?'

'Sometimes.'

'Will you take one now?' the child asked.

'Of what?'

'Of me. Will you take a picture of me?'

'Alright,' Ruthie shrugged. 'If you like.'

That was how it happened, and how Annie came to climb up on one of the work surfaces, the one next to the wall with the gilded feather-clock. She did what she was told and she stood beside the clock: facing Ruthie, eyes to the camera. She held her arms out either side when Ruthie asked, and Ruthie twisted the lens so the scratches on her chest stood out.

When Ruthie pressed the shutter, Annie flinched.

'Is this like the picture your dad took?'

'Hmm?' She was playing with the focus, trying to read the light.

'The picture your dad took of you with the clock. Is this the same as that picture?'

Ruthie paused and took the camera from her face. She didn't answer. Then Annie dropped her arms to her side and said, 'Why're you staring at me?'

'I'm not. I'm looking. That's what you do when you take a photograph.'

'Have we finished? Can I get down?'

'Put your arms back where they were. That's right, bit higher, that's it. Turn your head to one side but keep your eyes dead ahead, towards me. Don't move. One more then I'm done.'

When she pressed it again, Annie jumped down straight away.

'What's that?' she said, pointing at the wall. 'Oh, it's gone. No, look, it's there again. What is it?'

'What?' Ruthie said, lowering the camera from her face.

'There! There!'

Circles of light were shooting across the wall, small and sharp and bright. When they were moving less crazily, Ruthie sat with Annie on the mattress. She pointed up at the glass mobile that hung from the ceiling, explaining how the discs shifted in the breeze and caught the sun.

'They're like shooting stars,' Ruthie said. 'Don't you think? Or planets. That's why I put it there.'

Lifting Annie onto the work surface, she told her to stand with her back against the wall again. 'Now look down.'

The skin of Annie's stomach was patterned with tiny circles. Then she slipped to the floor, and turned to watch the wall again. When the light changed and the shapes disappeared, she went to look at the other wall, opposite the work surfaces.

The whole of the space, from floor to ceiling, was covered in a black-and-white image, imprinted directly on the plaster. What Annie was staring at was a road, deep in snow and late at night. The road swung towards her from around a corner. On its right-hand side was a high wall, twice as tall as a man. Trees grew on top of the wall and hung over the road. On the other side was a verge that was broad and edged by a low wall. Behind that was the beginning of a forest, or a dense wood. The snow on the low wall was untouched and downy. The trees behind it were in darkness, and so were the ones on the high wall opposite: silhouettes against a grey night sky. The trees in the far distance, though, which tracked the line of the road around its corner, shone bright white in the lights of an approaching car.

Its driver had passed in front of the camera's long exposure that night, the headlights searing their traces on the film. A pair of stripes flashed from left to right, two wide arcs suspended in the air, a foot or so above the road. They swept to a halt at the very edge of the picture, exactly halfway up.

The car itself was invisible, but its lights were bright enough to show tyre tracks, with a snow ridge forming in the middle.

Annie shivered.

'Can I touch it?' she said, staring at it. 'Is it a painting? Is it part of the wall?'

'It's a photograph, not a painting,' Ruthie said. 'And yes, you can touch it.'

'But it's painted on the wall. It can't be a photograph.'

'It is.'

'How do you know? Did you take it?'

'My dad took it. I helped him. I wasn't much older than you, so there wasn't a lot I could do. But I was there with him.'

When Ruthie had finished the story of *The Road to Falicon*, Annie took her hand away again and stood back.

'Where's the car? Did you paint over the car?'

'No. That's the whole point. It was taken without a flash so there isn't any light apart from the car's headlights. We were in the middle of nowhere so it was completely dark. That means you can't see the car, but you can see everything its headlights lit up as it drove past, like the snow and the trees and the road.'

'How did it get on the wall?'

'It's a bit complicated.'

'Please,' Annie said, and she put her hand in Ruthie's again, and squeezed it, tight, so that Ruthie, surprised by the sensations that were created in her chest and across her back, just by the touch of a child, was confused.

'Please,' Annie said a second time. She tugged at Ruthie's hand.

'Alright. I'll try. You know I told you that gold leaf is real gold, and you can coat things in it, sort of like a layer of paint but different?'

'Yes.'

'Well. There's a thing called liquid light, which is silver and salt together.'

She told Annie she'd worked at night, and had begun by closing all of the blackout blinds and switching on the ceiling fans. She'd pressed the Velcro panels down, and done up the zips at the bottom. She brought the enlarger from the darkroom and stood it on the opposite side of the room, to line up with the wall's midpoint. When she'd wheeled in an extra fan, to keep the air moving and the temperature steady, she took a large piece of black twill cloth and draped it over the door, fixing it in place with strips of black tape, to keep out even the tiniest splinter of light. Then she covered the work surface with plastic sheeting and turned off the main light, switching on a special light with a coloured bulb instead.

When everything was ready, she stood on a stepladder and painted the wall with the liquid light. It was a sort of a gel, she said.

Because it was almost solid, she'd had to soak the bottle in hot water first, then mix its contents with small amounts of other liquids, one called developer and one called hardener, so it would spread more easily.

When the wall had dried, she slid the negative into its tray in the enlarger. She loaded a filter as well, then she started the timer and pressed a switch on the enlarger so the picture was projected straight onto the wall. It didn't need a lot of light, not as much as an ordinary photograph, but it mattered that the light fell on it for exactly the right amount of time. When she'd turned off the enlarger she took a whole bucket of developer. She stood on the stepladder and sponged the developer all over the wall, working as fast as she could and making sure every part of it was covered.

A little while later, she held up a watering can with a sprinkler top and covered the wall in vinegar. Then she did the same with another liquid, to dissolve away the silver gel. Finally, she cleaned out the watering can and filled it with water and covered the wall again, refilling it until all the other liquids had been rinsed away and her picture was revealed, bigger and sharper than she'd ever imagined possible.

She told Annie she'd gone to the veranda then, to breathe in the fresh air, and wait for the morning, when she would look at the image again, to make sure it was really there.

Ruthie asked Annie if she understood, and Annie said sort of, but why had she done it straight onto the wall anyway, and Ruthie told her the picture had been lost once already. When she'd found it this time, she said, she didn't want to let it out of her sight.

'Will it stay there forever?'

'I don't know about forever. Let's just say it'll be there as long as the wall is there.'

'What's liquid light again?'

'It's the same as the paper you use for making photographs, but it's liquid, so you can paint it on a wall. Does that make sense?'

'Not really. You mean you've turned the wall into paper?'

'Sort of.'

'So could you paint it anywhere? Could you turn anything into paper?'

'I suppose so.'

'Like what?'

'Oh, I don't know. Anything. A stone. Or a brick, or a bit of wood or something. Maybe a sheet. Anything, really. Anything it'll stick to.'

'Could you paint it onto me? Could you turn my tummy into paper?' Annie looked down and rubbed her hand on her skin.

'I don't think that would work so well as a wall.'

'But it worked with the glass circles,' Annie said. 'I had them showing on my tummy.'

'Yes, you did. It's different, though. For a start it would hurt. It's made from chemicals.'

'I thought you said it was silver. My mum's got a silver bracelet and she lets me try it on and it doesn't hurt and –'

'It's not just silver. It's other things too. I can't explain, not exactly. It's silver but it's different.'

Vinny, like Annie, hadn't quite understood.

It was a few months before that Ruthie had woken on the veranda at dawn, and gone to the lightroom to check if it had worked. In the courtyard again, she'd sat on the edge of the fountain, biting her nails and waiting.

'Vinny!' she called as soon as she came out. 'Vinny, come and look!'

'What is it?'

'I found *The Road to Falicon*!' She was smiling, pulling her sister towards the house. 'Come and see. I found the negative and I've been up all night doing it. I want to show you.'

'I'm going for a swim. I mean, that's wonderful, but can't you bring it down to breakfast, show me when I come in?'

'Not exactly.'

'What do you mean, not exactly?'

'I can't.' She let her sister's arm fall. 'Never mind. It doesn't matter. Come up when you want.'

In the afternoon when Vinny saw it, she said, 'It's an awful lot of trouble for one picture, I s'pose. But it's amazing. I'm ever so proud of you, really. And I'm so glad you found it.'

Annie was tugging at her sleeve.

'I have to go. I'll be in trouble. Thank you for my drink,' and Ruthie remembered then, about what had happened in the water, and why they were there, the two of them, sitting in Max's lightroom.

'Wait,' she said. 'I need to give you something.'

She fetched Edward's comb from a drawer. Annie stared at it, then she glanced at Ruthie and her face flushed red.

Ruthie took Annie's hand. She looked at the tips of Annie's fingers, and saw five tiny marks, one on the end of each.

'What was he doing to you?' And, when she didn't reply, she tried to give her the comb. 'What? Tell me.'

'It's a game,' Annie said.

'What kind of a game?'

'It's a game where you make little holes in your fingers and you bleed a bit, if you swing your arm hard enough. It doesn't matter about the comb. I've got to go now.' Then she ran to the door and Ruthie followed.

The night before Ruthie's death, while her sister was in Athens, she took two tins of white paint, and deleted *The Road to Falicon*.

When Vinny arrived back and went up to the Lightroom, wondering where her sister had gone, she saw the new whiteness of the wall immediately. Beyond a sense that the room was changed, somehow, she failed to register the disappearance.

Days later, waking early, she had the idea of studying the snow and the road more closely, in the hope of finding something that might explain what had happened.

Slipping under the police tape, she looked, and saw nothing at all.

She felt the shock as a physical thing, as though someone had punched her in the stomach.

She trailed her fingers over the place where the picture had been, and tried to understand what Ruthie had meant by its painting-over. Then she laid her hands flat on the empty space, and was able at last to cry.

13 A WEEK AT THE VILLA

At Pilgrim's Lane, there was a parcel for Ruthie with a letter inside.

20 January 1974

Ruthie,

Here are your prints, and here's another film. Look at them – carefully! See if you can work out what to do differently. Send the whole roll back without a single shot unfocused, and I'll give you a new one.

M

PS Don't ever talk about your work in the way you did when you gave me these. I've never seen anything like them.

Every week that passed, until the Easter holidays, there was another parcel. Saturday mornings, Beatrice took her to the post office to send a full film back.

When a new film came, she unwrapped it and Beatrice loaded it up. Once, when Ruthie asked her aunt what to photograph that week, Beatrice said, 'How about the girls next door, lovey? I'm sure they wouldn't mind. Or me! I'd absolutely love you to take my picture!'

But Ruthie was too shy to ask the girls next door, and Max, on receiving a film full of images of his sister, was unequivocal: people were more difficult than things, and she should wait till she was older.

On what not to do, he was always as clear as this. Listing things she 'should have known better about', he included 'helpful pointers' for the future. With regard to presentation, he told her she should keep a record and send an index with each film. If she had a sequence of images that made sense as a group or followed what he termed 'a narrative path', then why not call it a series and give it a name?

But he gave no indication as to whether he liked what she'd done, and however many times she read and reread his first letter, she still couldn't be sure if his 'never seen anything like them' meant he'd found the kitten-births acceptable.

At Easter, Beatrice explained she had to take a trip herself, to see an old friend who lived a long way away, so what about Ruthie staying at Pennerton, and why didn't Vinny go on the school trip to Verbier? 'You never know, Vee. You might be a natural!'

When they complained and said, 'We want to see Maman!' she said, 'Of course your maman wants you to visit, but she isn't quite better yet. Don't make a scene, will you?'

In his lightroom, Max placed a hand on Ruthie's head and repeated the rules.

Three of her kitten-births were on the wall beside a line of new pictures. Unsure whether he'd done it to praise her or to shame her, she was too surprised to speak.

She stared at the new images: her headmistress, photographed every day for a week as she walked into assembly. Ruthie had grouped them into a series and called it *Off Sick*, naming each picture for the day it was taken. In all of them the place, the time, the expression on the woman's face and even her gait were identical. There was variation only in the constantly changing style of her dresses, and, in the picture called *Thursday*, the absence of the woman herself.

'It's the timing I like about these,' Max said, flicking each of the pictures with his finger. 'She knew you were taking them?'

'I don't think so,' Ruthie said, reluctant to confess she'd almost lost her camera altogether, when she was spotted by a prefect on the Friday.

'Nice work,' he said. 'Under pressure, too, timing wise. What's pleasing about *Off Sick* is the repetition, obviously. It looks like you're trying to say something. The monotony of authority, that sort of idea. It's the way the woman holds her head. And you'd worked out movement by the last one. You can do movement. Let's face it, though. You were clearly hard pushed to find anything for the rest of the roll. Best not to bother, really, if you're in that position again. Waste of time, mine and yours.'

The lessons continued through Easter week. Early one morning they sat at the edge of the Triangle Meadow with their backs against a tree, doing absolutely nothing. After a half-hour she began to fidget.

'Stay still.' He put his arm around her. 'I'm teaching you to look.'

He told her to describe everything she could see and everything she could hear. While she spoke, he watched her. Afterwards, he said she'd been staring, not looking, and she should just let her eyes go soft and stop trying so hard, and, 'Listen. What was that? There it is again, hear it?' and how had she missed something as obvious as a wood pigeon?

'That, Ruthie, is the difficulty with a terrain that's familiar. It's especially tricky if you know a place as well as we know Pennerton. When you're used to things, they become background noise. Same with what you're looking at. If something's in front of your eyes all the time, you can end up simply not seeing it. That's what I want you to think about this week. Consider it a challenge. It's not just about what you say, Roo. *How* you say it's equally as important. Take the everyday, and shape it. Can you do that? Show me a thing I've seen a million times before and make me believe I haven't.'

She did as she was told, tiptoeing around the house when he was working. Opening wardrobes and rummaging in drawers, she sought out the ordinary and catalogued it.

Because he never asked what she'd shot, she kept it to herself, resolving to develop the prints herself one day, and surprise him.

Once, she was woken in the night by the sound of her door being opened: a click, and silence.

Framed in the light from the corridor was the figure of a man. Then the door closed and it was too dark to see.

A floorboard creaked beside her bed and her cover was being pulled back and she tried to move but her legs and her arms were stuck and the whole of her body was her heartbeat and she couldn't breathe and her skin was burning and freezing at the same time then her bedside lamp was being switched on and it was Max.

'Roo. It's a perfect moon. Come with me.'

She dressed in semi-sleep. Then he lifted her onto him, piggyback, with her pinafore inside out and her socks half up and half down.

When the cold air hit her face she woke up properly. By the time they reached the orchard, her eyes were wide open. She looked where he pointed, but when he asked her to describe what she saw, she couldn't speak.

'We can see everything, can't we, Roo? The moon's so bright it's as if it's the middle of the day. The only difference is that the colour's all gone. The leaves are never green at night, even with a moon like this. This is important, so pay attention, please. Being in the studio's one thing. You can create your own elements. Outside it's another story altogether.' He jerked his head while he spoke, so Ruthie was jostled about. 'A million effects will be thrown at you. They'll change every half-second. You need to know what to choose, and you need to do it quickly. You have to be able to read the light, whatever it does, and you have to make it work the way you want it to. Never settle for less, just because you're outside.'

He stood stock-still and she perched there, blinking at the black-and-white world he'd brought her to. When the owl swept past she felt the rush of air on her face and she held her breath, then he carried her back to bed.

On the train to London, her aunt told Ruthie she wouldn't see her sister: Vinny had gone straight to school from Verbier.

Ruthie was silent, then she started to cry.

'Oh, poppet.' Beatrice took her in her arms. 'Oh, my sweetest little love, I am so sorry. You'll see her again in no time! It's not so very long till half-term, is it?'

'But you said!' Ruthie whispered, both hands over her face. 'You said we'd have a night at Pilgrim's Lane, all the girls together.' And then, when Beatrice confessed that she had been to the Grove that morning and taken Vinny out for breakfast, 'Why didn't you come and get me? I could've come with you. You could've got me really really early and we could've gone out for breakfast all together.'

'I know. I wanted to.'

'So why didn't you?'

'I needed to see Vinny on her own.'

'Why?'

'We had to have a little talk.'

'But why?'

'I can't tell you now. Not on the train.'

Through the window, Ruthie saw flying trees and empty fields with a barn at the edge, or an oast house, rising. She curled up to her aunt and tried to count the days till half-term, keeping time with the rhythm of the train. But then there was the particular softness of Beatrice's body, and the warmth of her breath on her face, and she drifted into dreams of her sister.

At Charing Cross, the conductor had to wake them.

'All clear! All clear, please!'

'Fiddlesticks!' Beatrice said. 'I meant to get off at London Bridge, what an absolute twit!'

'It doesn't matter, Auntie Bea. Let's walk across Trafalgar Square. We haven't done that for ages.'

Beatrice held her handbag under one arm, and Ruthie's holdall in the crook of the other. When her niece stopped to rest at the fountain, she had to call three times before Ruthie came: swinging her camera from side to side, she dragged her feet and wouldn't speak to her aunt. At the house, she tugged Beatrice's sleeve and said, 'Now? Now will you tell me?'

Because the 'little talks' Beatrice had with the girls took place separately, and because the stories she told them weren't quite the same, they would respond differently to her revelation that the friend she'd been to see before Easter was their mother, and that because of the nature of her illness, a visit was out of the question, for the foreseeable future at least.

Earlier that day, Beatrice had held Vinny's hand and explained, quite calmly and slowly, that it was Sophie's mind that was unwell, not her body, so that rather than being able to take any sort of medicine, she could only be watched and cared for by Emile, who had moved her from the house at Rauba-Capeù to a nearby village called Falicon, which was safer and quieter than Nice, and who stayed with her indoors or in the garden, feeding her and washing her and keeping her safe.

'She'd have loved to have had Easter with you, Vee. Of course she would. It's ever so hard for her. The only thing that matters is that she loves you very, very much. Just the same as always.'

They talked, the two of them, about what it all meant, and how it had been over a year since the girls had seen her. Finally, Beatrice said that perhaps Vinny could think of it like this: because Sophie couldn't look after herself, she couldn't look after her daughters.

'Yes,' she said when Vinny asked should she carry on writing to her. 'Of course you should. She hasn't the strength to write back, not quite yet. But she says she will, just as soon as she can. She keeps all your letters. She ties them up in ribbon and puts them in a box Emile gave her, then she ties the box in a ribbon as well, a big yellow ribbon done in a bow. She looks at them every day. It's the first thing she does every morning. Of course you must. Promise you will?' and Vinny promised.

When Vinny said she ought to go to her boarding house, to be on time for registration, Beatrice said, 'Let's not tell Ruthie exactly what I've told you, hey? She's little still, and much littler than you were when you were ten. We'll tell her together, shall we, when she's a bit older? What do you think?' and Vinny made another promise, to hide the details of the tale from her sister.

The distinction between mind and body that Beatrice had drawn for Vinny was entirely absent from the second telling. At Pilgrim's Lane that evening, Beatrice sat with Ruthie in the chair by the window and told her all about the house at Falicon, where Emile had taken Sophie to live. In addition, she said only that Sophie's illness had made her too frail to go further than the courtyard garden, that she needed more sleep than most people, and would have to be properly looked after until she got much better, which might take quite some time.

Ruthie cried, and asked questions. Beatrice answered some of them, then she said it was getting ever so late, and what about the present she'd brought from France – was Ruthie absolutely sure she didn't want to open it?

'Is it really from Maman?' Ruthie had said at supper. 'Did she give it to you to give to me especially?'

'What do you mean?'

'I mean, was it a present or did she just give it to you and you decided to give it to me?'

'It's especially for you, and she gave me one for Vinny as well, which was especially for her. Well, are you going to open it, or save it for when Vee's back?'

Ruthie had stared at the little white box, then turned it in her hands.

'What did Vinny do?'

'You must make your own mind up.'

Later, Ruthie phoned Vinny and asked, had she opened her present? Vinny said, no, of course not, she'd saved it. Ruthie asked, was it in a small white box, and was it tied in a yellow ribbon, which was cut into two little points at each end? Then they agreed to try to guess what was inside, but that they'd wait till Vinny came home again before they opened them.

Ruthie said she liked having a present, but she'd have preferred a visit, or a letter at least, and what did Vinny think?

'It doesn't really matter what I think. She's too poorly to visit and she hasn't got enough strength to write, not quite yet. That's what Auntie Bea said, "Not. Quite. Yet." Which means she will when she can.'

'What does "frail" mean?'

'Same thing as "weak", I think. I'll look it up.'

'Why does she have to stay at home? Is it because she can't walk? Is Maman poorly in her legs? Is that what "frail" is?'

Instead of answering, Vinny asked Ruthie to pass the phone to Beatrice.

Looking for their aunt, Ruthie wondered why Vinny hadn't answered her questions. By the time she found her, she'd decided it was because her sister knew something she didn't, and she hated her for it.

Her dreams that night came in fragments: a stone house that stood right at the top of a small quiet town that was built on a hill and had streets that went up and went down and were difficult for Sophie to walk on; a hilltop house with a garden full of flowers that were pink and had petals that looked like paper and grew beside a lemon tree; her maman's bed with blue silk curtains which fell in a circle around it; a blue silk bedroom right at the top of a stone house which had a courtyard garden; a hilltop courtyard garden with a view that stretched to the sea; Sophie, standing all day beside a lemon tree, picking paper flowers and watching the light on the far-off water; Sophie at a bedroom window, looking down on the courtyard garden; Emile and Sophie framed in an open window, watching for a ship on the horizon, or for a squall racing in with blue silk rain that hung above the water like a curtain or a tent.

When Vinny came home they opened their gifts.

'A leaf!' Ruthie gasped. 'Why did – Maman gave me a leaf! It's dried and it's all curled up in a shape.' She held her box out to Vinny. 'Show me yours, Vee. Show me!'

'What do you mean, a leaf?' Vinny went as if to put her finger in.

'Don't!' Ruthie said. 'It's dried in a special shape. You'll squash it!' She lifted the leaf by its stem. Laying it on the floor, she saw it turn into the shell of a crab, orange-brown and hollow. 'It's a leaf but it's not a leaf. Look, Vee.' Kneeling beside it, she blew, lightly, and the leaf-crab lifted and scuttled. 'Why, Maman?' she whispered. 'Why did you?'

'It's pretty!' Beatrice said. 'Don't you think?'

Ruthie looked at Vinny. 'Is yours a leaf as well?'

'No.' Vinny held the box so Ruthie couldn't see.

'What is it?'

'A snail.'

'Is it moving?'

'No.'

'Is it dead?'

'No, I mean I got a snail shell.'

'Is it gilded?'

'No.'

'Is it painted?'

'No. It's just a shell.'

'Right,' Beatrice said. 'It's gone two o'clock and you haven't even taken off your school uniform, Vee! There's tea and sandwiches before you unpack, and we're on the six o'clock train to Papa's, so down to the kitchen, please. Best leave your presents here, loveys, rather than take them with you. They're ever so precious, aren't they?'

Before the little white boxes were put away, Ruthie fetched her camera and took three photographs: one of each gift separately; and one of them both together.

Max had made supper, but Ruthie went straight to the Long Library and stayed there. When Vinny called, she came in carrying a volume of the dictionary, as a waiter might hold a too-heavy tray. Dropping it on the table, she unsettled Max's glass, then she watched the red circle spread on the white cloth.

He said her name sharply, then he righted the glass and refilled it.

Ruthie opened the dictionary.

'I can't find it, Vee.'

'Eat your soup, please,' Max said.

'This is the volume for F to H,' Ruthie said, 'but it's not in here.' She turned the pages. 'F-R-A-Y-L-E, Vinny. I need you to put it in my notebook.'

Max closed the dictionary. He took Ruthie's spoon and filled it with soup, but when he held it to her mouth, she ignored him. Grabbing her chin, he squeezed her jaw open. She clamped her teeth shut on the spoon, then she reached round him for the dictionary. Her mouth fell open and she said the word 'frail' again, but it was lost in the soup that slid from her lips.

Max stood up. 'Go to your room.'

'I'm hungry!'

'You should have thought of that.'

'Right,' Beatrice said. 'Let's try again, shall we? Elbows off the table please, Roo. How about we all finish eating, then Vinny can look your word up afterwards?'

Ruthie slid forward in her chair. Placing her upper arms flat on the table, she rested her head in her hands.

'Roo,' Beatrice said. 'Ruthie, love. Sit up and –' but when Vinny said, 'Auntie Bea, can you pass the water?' Beatrice looked the other way. Max, who was behind Ruthie, grabbed her hair and pulled it: a sharp tug so her upper body hit the chair and her head jerked up. For a fraction of a second she saw the ceiling. At the same time, her hands clipped her bowl and emptied her soup in her lap.

Her head dropped again and she saw Beatrice, whose attention was still focused on the water jug. In the quarter-second before Ruthie's chin met her chest, she locked eyes with her sister. Fixed in Vinny's bright blue stare, she knew her sister had seen what Max had done.

Vinny held her gaze for no more than a breath.

For Ruthie, though, time stood still, and she was outside time, like the water in the cove at slack tide, going neither to nor fro.

Then, as a pair of swallows who, having paused high up, know when to turn and spiral drop, the sisters let each other go.

Ruthie's chin thudded to her chest so hard she bit her tongue.

Max released his hold on Ruthie's hair.

Beatrice finished pouring the water.

Max's hand lingered on Ruthie's neck. She raised her head. Tasting blood, she said she wasn't hungry any more, and please could she go to her room.

Beatrice looked at her. 'Oh, Roo! What have you done with your soup? Of course you can't go. There's macaroni cheese still! Your father made it especially. Come on, lovey, it's your favourite!'

'I'm not hungry either,' Vinny said. 'I'll go up with Ruthie.'

'It's alright,' Max said.

Ruthie picked up her bowl from the floor and put it in the sink. Then they left, Ruthie in Vinny's footsteps until Vinny reached her hand behind and Ruthie took it.

Later, Beatrice and Max were in the library. Vinny and Ruthie were in their bedroom, but the library door was open, and they heard them. After the shouting there was silence, then the shouting again.

By the time the thing was properly under way, the girls were on the stairs.

First, they heard Beatrice say Ruthie had been up and down like this since the Easter holidays, and even Vinny had been more than usually reserved in her Sunday phone calls. Max said, 'What do you expect? You should have told them you were going to see their mother before, not after. And anyway, why the hell didn't you take them with you?'

In the split second before Beatrice answered, Vinny put her hands over Ruthie's ears, so she missed what came next.

'Because their mother's gone stark raving bloody mad, that's why!'

The library door slammed, and Ruthie pulled Vinny's hands away.

'What? Why, Vee? That's not fair! Why did you –'

There were footsteps in the corridor, and someone running after.

Had the girls gone down and stood in the corridor, keeping just out of sight but craning their necks to catch every word, they might have learned the truth about the trip Beatrice had taken to Falicon, while Vinny was at Verbier and Ruthie with Max.

'I can't believe you're going over that again,' Beatrice said. 'You know she's not well. If you want me to drag up the sordid details, I will, but –'

'Why are you only telling me now?'

'I tried to get hold of you. I couldn't get an answer, so I wrote and said we had to talk and you never called back. Nothing.'

'I was travelling.'

'Nonsense. I needed you, Max, and you ignored me. Then I decided it wouldn't help anyway, telling you.'

'Why?'

'Maybe because I was doing what I've always done, since you were twelve years old and our mother walked out.'

'What? You've always done what?'

'Protected you from the truth. Or do you think I tell you every last thing that happens?'

'This is hardly every last thing. What the hell else have you kept to yourself? What? Has she been in touch? Has she written?'

'To who?'

'To you. To the girls?'

'Look, even if I'd wanted to discuss it, you haven't exactly been available.'

'Cut the bullshit, Bea. It's my wife you're talking about.'

Beatrice spoke more quietly then. She reported Emile's decision to care for Sophie at home, rather than commit her to the psychiatric ward of the hospital at Nice, where the beds were made of iron with a pallet for a mattress, and the patients' clothes washed once a fortnight.

The ward doctor pointed out to Emile that he was old, and would be on his own with her, and that it would be hard for him.

'*Elle est ma fille,*' was his only response, so they let him take her with him.

He'd found ways to lessen the burden: a batch of yellow cotton dresses, one for every day of the week so she could stain them, were sent to a neighbour Mondays and returned clean and dry the same evening. Her shoes were rubber clogs without buckles or straps, and because her hair was kept short, it saved him time, he said, and when he washed it, she was less distressed than she would've been.

When Beatrice had arrived and said, 'Oh, Sophie! What have you done?' Emile said, 'Please. I will explain,' but Sophie took Beatrice by the hand and led her upstairs.

She showed her a pillowcase, tied with a yellow silk ribbon.

'*Trop long,*' she said, putting a finger to her lips and shaking her head. 'For the baby. *C'était trop long pour le bébé Emile.* Do you see, Bea? Do you see?' She pulled the ribbon and turned the pillowcase upside down on the bed, '*Tu vois, Bea? Tu vois?*' then she took Beatrice's hand and placed it on the pile of hair that had fallen, long and red and soft as the day he'd shorn it. '*Doux, Bea. C'est très doux, n'est-ce pas?*'

Emile came from the corridor. He picked up the hair in handfuls, and put it back in the pillowcase.

'*Dîner, ma pitchoune. Dîner avec ta soeur Beatrice, et puis au lit.*'

In the kitchen, Emile fed his daughter. Afterwards, when she attacked him, he took her in his arms, then he said, '*Viens, ma petite tigresse, sois gentile avec ton papa,*' and carried her up to bed.

The last evening of Beatrice's visit, Sophie looked at her and said, '*Je ne vous connais pas. Qui êtes-vous qui dînez avec mon père?*'

'It's me, Soph. It's Beatrice. I am your husband's sister.'

Sophie attacked Beatrice then, pulling at her hair and her cardigan, calling her '*bête*' and '*menteuse*' and '*méchante. Vous êtes une femme méchante.*'

Emile restrained her, then she leaned into him and urinated on the kitchen floor.

'You see how it is?' he said over his shoulder. 'Do you?' and Beatrice fetched a bucket and a mop.

'That's why I didn't take them,' Beatrice said to Max at Pennerton. 'And that's why I never will. Emile had told me things were difficult, but I wanted to see for myself. I wanted to be sure. She'll get some stable periods, of course. How long do you think they'll last? A week, maybe two, before she's no idea who she is again? It's his choice to have her, and to my mind, it's the right one. He is her father, after all. But don't you ever tell me what I should or shouldn't do when it comes to your girls and their mother. It's hard, doing this. Every day I spend with them, I'm guessing. You saw how Ruthie was tonight. I've no idea what's going on in her mind when she's like that. Vinny's different. Tough as old boots, isn't she? Sometimes I get it wrong, though, with both of them. I'm struggling as much as they are.'

'I thought you were angry. That's why I didn't call.'

'I was!' She raised her voice. 'And I had every bloody right to be! Look, I'm your big sister, and I love you. I can understand why you're running away. You're scared, and you're hurt, and you're perfectly aware I'll be here to pick up the pieces when you do. But if you're planning to keep on running, you can bloody stop blaming me for how they behave when you decide to show up.'

'Alright. I said already, I made a mistake. Anything else?'

'Yes, actually. Be careful how far you push the absent father thing. It's not just them I'm thinking of. Do you really want to spend the rest of your life like this? Don't you want to at least try to be happy again?'

'I don't know what that is.'

'What?'

'Happiness. I'm listening to you speak and I have no idea what you mean.'

Beatrice said nothing. Then, putting her hands on his shoulders, 'They're hungry for affection, and it's you they want it from. Look them in the eye. You'll see what I mean. And, Max, there's one other thing.'

'Yes?'

'You might think about giving Emile more than you do. He's as proud as you when it comes to cash, but I know for a fact it would help. Oh, damn,' she said, glancing over her shoulder. 'I always forget there's no kitchen door here. I'm beginning to think your girls do nothing but eavesdrop.'

Ruthie dreamed of Sophie again.

This time, Ruthie was asleep in her mother's blue silk tent-bed, at the top of the house at Falicon. She was woken by the sound of Sophie crying. Finding herself alone, she went to the window. In the light of the moon she could see her mother sitting under the lemon tree. Ruthie ran from the house and went to her. She stroked Sophie's back until she was calmer, then Sophie held her and said, 'Thank you, *ma pitchoune. Merci ma petite pitchoune*,' and Ruthie felt Sophie's tears on her own face. Then Sophie started to speak and to sing at the same time. When her voice rose up, like bubbles through water, the sound passed straight into Ruthie and she became her mother's voice, and they were one person not two and the sound was beautiful.

She was in the kitchen with Vinny the following morning, drying the cutlery, when the dream re-emerged.

She reached the part where she'd run from the house and was stroking Sophie's back. She picked up a spoon, and the sounds in the dream grew louder. She was watching Vinny run more hot water into the bowl, but at the same time she could feel her mother's arms around her and she could hear her voice rise up like bubbles through water, and it passed right out of Sophie and into Ruthie, as though the sound was coming from inside Ruthie, then Vinny looked at her, and said, 'Why are you making that noise? Are you alright?' and the dream stopped.

In the afternoon, when it started again and Vinny told her to be quiet, Ruthie left the house. At the Triangle Meadow she walked the lime tree border, knowing no one could hear her there. Coming in for supper, she was surprised to find that even though the dream had stopped, the sound went on inside her head.

On the stairs, Sophie tapped her daughter on the shoulder and told her, quite clearly, she wanted to join her family for dinner. When Ruthie ignored her, she was insistent, entreating and beseeching so that when Ruthie got to the hall she could hear her reproach not as a solo but a chorus. By the time she was in the kitchen corridor there were hundreds of voices, not one, and the sound was lodging in Ruthie's chest and in the cavities of her skull and the voices were singing from those spaces, until she said, 'Alright, alright,' and they all fell silent.

Beatrice told her to lay the table. Ruthie did as Sophie asked and set an extra place. In answer to her mother's next request, she brought over a chair from beside the stove. Nobody said anything about her doing this; neither Max nor Vinny nor Beatrice. Nor did they comment during the meal, when they'd helped themselves and Ruthie pushed the dishes of food in Sophie's direction so they formed a ring around the empty plate.

Max waited until the girls had gone, then he pushed the extra chair to the wall with a little too much force so it scraped on the floor and Ruthie, halfway up, heard it and paused.

'It's ridiculous, Bea,' her father shouted. 'You'll have to talk to her.' Then he threw the unused cutlery in the drawer and banged it shut.

In the clatter and the slam of it, Ruthie made out her mother's 'I love you, Roo', and called it back to her. When Vinny, watching from the landing, said, 'Who are you talking to?' Ruthie looked at her, then turned away.

At the end of June, Vinny went to Hamburg for a week at a languages summer school.

Max drove Ruthie to the villa on her own.

Before the ferry to Patras, they spent an afternoon in Brindisi. He photographed the sardine trawlers unloading, and bought her a sundress from a boutique on the promenade. At dinner, he argued with the owner of the restaurant about the bill, and Ruthie looked away while they fought. Afterwards at the police station he said they couldn't detain him: his daughter had no one else.

When he was sober, they took the next boat going. He told her to sit with him in the bar: if a squall blew up, it would be safer.

The first beach after Patras he drove onto the sand. He stood while she changed then he took a photo of her wearing the dress: back to the camera, straps off her shoulders, feet in the water, hair tied up and falling on her neck.

They were a whole day travelling. At the villa, he carried her bags and she stayed in the car until he came out and said, 'What's the matter? Why are you crying?'

'I want Vinny. I want my sister.'

'Come on, it's late. If you go straight to sleep I'll swim you to the island first thing.'

It was a week before Vinny came with Beatrice. Apart from Eleni, they were alone.

One evening after supper he stayed on the Olive-Tree Bench. Eleni cleared the things from the courtyard and he said thank you, he would stop reading now and sit for a while and yes, she could put out the candles if she liked.

When Eleni had gone, there was only the moonlight.

Ruthie, who had watched from her bedroom window, called out. 'Goodnight, Papa.'

'Come down, Ruthie-Roo. Come and say goodnight properly.'

She went and sat with him. She was aware of the meltémi on their faces, out of the north-east, and the scent of wild thyme. Then she wasn't aware of anything.

While it went on, neither of them spoke.

Afterwards, he put his arm around her and kept it there, so she couldn't move.

Then she said, 'Let me go,' and he did.

In her bedroom she stood at her window. He stayed where he was, with the breeze playing in his hair, and she got into bed.

An hour later she is woken by a noise.

At first she thinks she's imagined it, and turns in her bed to go back to sleep, but then she hears it again, and tiptoes to the window.

The clouds are across the moon and the courtyard is in darkness. There are voices but they are quiet. Then there's the noise that had woken her: a thud, and another, and the voices are rising to a series of shouts and the kitchen door is flung open and it bangs against the wall and two people appear and she thinks one of them is her father and one of them is Eleni. She can't be sure but they are in their shapes: the one tall and broad, the other tiny and slender.

They seem to be holding on to each other so Ruthie thinks they are dancing but when the smaller figure stumbles, the taller figure lunges and the clouds part and the moon floods the courtyard and it is her father and he is holding Eleni down and Ruthie is running from the room and along the corridor and through the kitchen and into the courtyard but when she reaches it there is no one.

A noise comes from beyond the fountain. She drops to all fours and crawls along the Pergola.

When she sees them, she stops.

The clouds have closed again but she can just make out her father. He is kneeling on top of Eleni, who is lying on her front. He is holding her hands behind her back with one hand, and pinning her face to the ground with the other.

Ruthie stands up. She wants to speak but her heart is beating too fast. Without saying a word, she is turning back when two things happen at once: her father releases his hold on Eleni, and Ruthie lets out all her breath.

'Who's there?' Max says. 'Ruthie?' He stands and turns about, then again. 'Is that you?'

He hasn't seen her, so she steps behind a vine. Eleni stands up as well. Lifting her head, she catches sight of Ruthie, who is half hidden. As they hold one another's gaze, Max stumbles across the courtyard in the other direction and Eleni shakes her head at Ruthie. Then she brings her finger to her lips and gestures towards the kitchen door.

When Max stumbles further away, out towards the trees on the promontory, Ruthie runs. Taking the corner of the Pergola too fast she's flat on the ground and scraping her knees, then she rights herself and runs again and she's inside and she's on the stairs and she's in her room and her heart is beating too fast for her to breathe and Sophie is there.

'No, Maman,' Ruthie whispers, climbing into bed and holding a finger to her lips. 'I can't. Not tonight. I have to be very quiet. Tomorrow. I will tell you everything tomorrow.'

Then she turns to face the other way, shutting out the pain from where she has fallen, and sleeps.

In the morning, she finds pieces of grit buried in her knees. The blood, which has congealed, is stuck to her sheet. She pulls off the sheet, and the skin tears.

'Quickly then,' Eleni says in the kitchen, 'before he comes in from his swim.' She sits Ruthie up on the kitchen table and stretches out her legs. Sponging them first with hot water, she tells her it will sting but they have to, or the cuts will never heal, not in the August heat. No swimming today or the next, she says, and it will be alright.

'When did you do this?' Eleni asks then, so that Ruthie is confused.

'What do you mean?'

'The cuts are deep. How did it happen?'

'Last night,' she says to Eleni, who has bruises under both her eyes, like purple paint daubed on her skin. 'Last night in the court-yard, when you told me to go in. I ran so fast I tripped –'

But Eleni, who is pouring iodine onto cotton wool, says, 'I don't know what you are talking about. I wasn't in the courtyard.'

'I saw you with Papa.'

'Your father was asleep,' Eleni says. 'So was I, and so were you. You can't have got these just by tripping over in the courtyard. Look at this!' she says, teasing out another piece of grit. 'You must have fallen in the grove and forgotten, or slipped on the rocks by the water's edge.'

She looks up at Ruthie, who is staring at two more bruises she's noticed on Eleni's wrists, like red-black bracelets. Because Eleni doesn't say anything about them, neither does Ruthie.

She is leaving, when Eleni says her name.

'Yes?' she answers.

'Don't ever tell anyone what you saw. You were sleepwalking, or dreaming. Do you understand?'

Eleni is by the door to her apartment.

When Ruthie nods, she goes in.

Ruthie stares at the closed door, then she goes to the cove.

Her father is swimming. She watches his arms rise and fall, then he is beyond the island and she can't see him.

Before Vinny arrived with Beatrice, there were nights when, not yet in her room, she heard him in the house. He was shouting her name and he was moving quickly and there was nothing to be done.

Once, she almost outran him.

In the book-lined room on the first floor, while she was waiting for

Eleni to call her to bed, a shutter swung open and the breeze caught her nightdress. She saw how it took the fabric and made it dance away from her, back to her and away. She was dancing with it and moving across the room towards the door when she heard him crashing about in his lightroom and remembered she had been in there when he was swimming, and had taken the cap from his telescope.

Because she was dancing quite fast she carried on through the door and along the corridor and down the stairs. She was dancing across the courtyard faster than the air and without meaning to she danced through the bars of the gate and he was slower than her and when he stopped to open it she was slipping and flying and then she was just flying.

Low in the olive trees more like an owl than a child.

Or a sprite or a liquid thing in her slip.

A flash of white disappearing through the grove then the sound of a man, running.

She crouches behind the agave, arms disjointed, a giant spider.

Hiding behind a tree, arms held high above her head, leaves sprout from her hands, and roots shoot from her feet into the earth.

She's a blade of grass, then, lying flat on the ground in front of the trough of giant rosemary bushes, so slender as to be a part of the dust.

Half running and half skipping, she traces patterns around the grove, as though she is a child who is playing, then she follows the path to the west, hurtling the steps to the beach where she slides into the water and squats, a turtle or a fat salamander.

Back to the grove and round it and through it, she slams up against the boundary wall and tries to scale it.

Beating her swallowtail wings she crashes down, tearing scratches in the skin of her chest and her arms. She slips back through the bars into the courtyard, and crouches with her breath heaving.

He is on the other side of the wall. He runs first one way, then, more slowly, the other. His hands brush the bars of the gate and she sees his fingers clearly. He says her name and she steps away.

Glancing behind her, she sees a woman, standing by the fountain. She thinks it is Eleni, but then the figure moves back into the shadows and disappears altogether, and Max is opening the gate, and it is just her, on her own with her father.

Daytimes she kept her distance.

Coming back to the villa once, she stood in the grove. Hands held as a visor, she squinted at the veranda for any movement but the way the sun fell meant there was no sightline.

On the veranda again, she looked into the grove to the place where she'd stood. She picked out a tree it wasn't possible to see behind, then she walked back and forth on the veranda until she was sure this tree would hide a person of her height, and that it would do so from any of the veranda's vantage points. Later, she found the tree and stood by it.

When Vinny and Beatrice arrived, Max reported that Ruthie had slipped on the rocks at the water's edge more than once, so Vinny should be careful not to do the same. Her little sister had become a tomboy in her absence, he said, and sometimes ran too fast in the grove and fell, or cut herself jumping from a boulder in the Viros Gorge.

Vinny had scratched her head non-stop since their flight had landed, and was ready to try anything. When Eleni said she knew a cure, Vinny said, 'What? Just tell me,' and Beatrice said, 'Oh, lovey, if only

it had started before we left London, I could have gone to the chemist. It might just as well have happened at the Grove. Don't be daft.
It's nothing especially to do with the children at the language school.
It happens to everyone when they're little. Ruthie'll have them next
term! I had them! Max had them! We've all had them. Don't scratch,
though, or you'll get scabs.'

Their aunt was less sanguine in the morning, when she came
down and saw what Eleni had meant by a cure. Her coffee cup
smashed on the courtyard floor and Max swept up the pieces.

Ruthie had sat apart at first, meaning just to watch.

Vinny and Eleni were just ahead of her, right on the edge of the
cliff above the cove. Max had placed a chair there, saying they may as
well compose the shot; it wasn't something that would happen every
summer.

Just before it began, Vinny asked Ruthie to come to her. Would
she hold a mirror, she said, so that she could see for herself? So that
Eleni wouldn't make a mistake?

Ruthie ran in to get one. Then she stood in front of her sister, bringing it close and clenching both fists to keep it steady until Vinny said,
or whispered, 'Hold my hand, Roo. Will you please hold my hand.'

If she ever thought of that summer, she'd remember only the sound
of the razor meeting skin; the way the sun caught Vinny's curls as
they fell, and how the breeze took the weight of them, like gold leaf
or wild-flower seeds, scattering.

Beatrice stayed a little longer than planned. When she left, she said
they just had to phone and she'd come straight back, but it would be
more fun for everyone if they could manage on their own.

The next day, Max did the same to Ruthie, so the sisters would look alike.

Waking in the night, Ruthie stared at Vinny's cut-straw head on the pillow next to her and thought she had a brother for a sister, then she went back to sleep. When Vinny shook her in the morning and said, 'You look like a boy,' Ruthie said, 'So do you,' and they ran down the steps to the water.

In the weeks that came after, Max called them 'my lads', and they ran between the coves like urchins or Ariels.

He took photographs of Ruthie, standing on the work surface in the Lightroom, next to the gilded feather-clock.

Arms held out, she did what she was told: making sure the scratches on her chest and her arms were clearly visible; tilting her head slightly to one side; keeping her gaze centre-on.

'Don't move. Put your arms back where they were. Eyes up, please, towards me. Towards me, I said.'

Once, she looked and saw Eleni, watching from the corridor.

14 TUESDAY

'Sorry,' Vinny says. 'I know I'm not supposed to come up unannounced. I just wanted to say goodnight. In case you're still asleep in the morning, when we leave.'

'You're going for a day, Vee. A day and a night.'

'I know! But I'll miss you! Here, give me a kiss.'

Ruthie gets up from the mattress, and holds her mouth to Vinny's cheek.

'You'll only be cross if I wake you,' Vinny says, 'so it's up to you to come down and say goodbye. Alright?'

'Alright.'

'Goodnight. I love you.'

Ruthie wishes she'd said 'I love you too.'

She will spend the rest of the night wishing that.

She knows she should have gone to see Vinny when she'd arrived back from town, and asked to share a meal with her.

She should have asked her if *Chalk Circle* had gone OK in the end, and whether it was done and sent off, and Vinny would have told her all about how she'd translated the last scene, and said that she still wasn't happy with it but it'd just have to do.

Then Ruthie would have told her that she's worried about her going to Athens, and would rather she was staying.

She might have told her about seeing Max at the top of the steps, and Vinny might have said not to be silly, she'd imagined it, and they might even have laughed about it.

Then she could have told her about Annie, and about how she'd brought the child from the sea and taken her into the villa. If Vinny had been patient, and kind, she'd have told her as well that the reason she was so late back from town was because she had followed the girl and her family up the gorge, and that something about this child has troubled her, and she doesn't know what, exactly.

Then, if Vinny still wasn't angry, she would have described the images that have begun to play inside her head, like pictures spun through a zoetrope, or like tiny cine-films played fast-forward, one after the other and back-to-back.

Some of the films are perfectly ordinary. Just a glimpse of their mother at the sink at Pennerton, for example, washing up a pan after a day of apple-cooking. Then Sophie turns to say something about cinnamon, but Ruthie can't hear her and says, 'What, Maman? What did you say?'

Or their father, running in from the Triangle Meadow with sweat on his forehead saying, 'Soph! You have to come outside and see this! Now! It's the most amazing sunset and I don't care what you're doing, you have to see it!'

Then the film rewinds and there is Max, running in again a split second later and saying, 'Soph! You have to come outside and see this! Now! It's the most amazing sunset and I don't care what you're doing, you have to see it!'

When it happens again, Sophie is in the yard at Pennerton and she has put a basket of laundry on the ground and Ruthie is there with Vinny. Their mother is standing on a ladder and is undoing the length of rope that is looped against the stable wall. She is collecting another rope from inside the stable door, and holding it up to show them. 'Look,' she says. 'These are two coils of rope that I am holding.' Then she is giving the peg bag to Ruthie, and asking Vinny to help with the ladder, and when Ruthie looks at her Maman, she is placing a rope around her neck then she is taking it off and placing it there again.

Then Max runs into the yard with sweat on his forehead and says it's the most amazing sunset, it's the most amazing sunset, it's the most amazing sunset, it's the most amazing sunset, and Ruthie wants to stop it but she can't, and it goes round maybe twenty times before another one starts, the one that is beginning to be played more frequently than the others:

She is watching herself, with Max.

She is a child and they are holding hands and they are swimming from the cove at night, and they are in the water and out of it, and in again and out of it, and then they are on the beach and he is holding her hand and saying, 'Look! Can you see it?' and the film stops, and she looks to see what he is pointing at and she thinks it is Eleni who is standing there but the clouds are over the moon and there is Sophie again, turning from the sink and looking at Ruthie and laughing and saying something that Ruthie can't hear, and Ruthie is saying, 'What, Maman? What did you say?' but before Sophie has answered there is Max again, running in from the Triangle Meadow with sweat on his forehead and taking the rope from Sophie's neck, and putting it back.

Then it is just him on his own, on the cove at night, then she is there beside him and they are in the water and swimming right out, then they swim in and Eleni is waiting on the cove and the moon is shining brightly enough for Ruthie to see that there are bruises under both her eyes and purple bracelets on her wrists, then Eleni looks at Ruthie and speaks.

'When did you do this?'

Ruthie wishes she could tell Vinny that the films are making her tired, and confused, and that they are there all the time, whatever else she is doing, and she doesn't know how to stop them.

But because she can't work out a way to say these things, and because her sister will already have been asleep for hours and has such a long way to drive in the morning, Ruthie gets up from the mattress and goes to the darkroom instead. She looks at the negatives of Annie, standing on the work surface next to the feather-clock. She chooses one, and loads the strip in the tray. When she's decided on a filter, she locks it all into place. She stands in the warmth of the safelight's red, inhaling the sharp scents she'd known as a child in her father's darkroom.

Doing as she was told.

Keeping quiet.

Not touching anything unless he asked her to.

Making and discarding and remaking her picture of Annie, she thinks back to earlier, in the morning, when she'd sat outside the taverna, with her coffee.

She remembers seeing the children, playing a game in front of the supermarket. Their parents had come out, and their father put some things in their backpacks: fruit, and biscuits, and extra little bottles of water, and their mother reached forwards and tried to rub suncream on Edward's cheeks.

She can recall there being a small argument, and the mother handing the suncream to the father, who started to put some on Annie.

She is also quite sure that, shortly after this, they had moved off towards the old town, and that as soon as they were out of sight, she'd thrown some coins on the table and crossed the road.

At this point, though, her memory falters, and she is confused about what happened next.

She'd reached the halfway point in the road when she'd swung her head the other way, meaning to check for cars. Her gaze had come to rest on the empty space where the children had been playing, and she saw her father there.

The girl who was with him was nine or ten years old.

'I don't want to, Papa.'

She saw the child's mouth move, and heard her speak to Max. At the same time, she heard herself say the words in stereo, looking up at him.

'I don't want to go on a walk. It's not fair. I want to wait until Vinny's here, with Auntie Bea.'

She saw him hand the girl a water bottle, then she saw him kneel down to tie her shoelace. He tied the knot too tight, and she felt the pain in her own foot. She saw her ten-year-old mouth move, and heard herself tell him he was hurting her. She put her hand on top of his head to make him stop and she felt his soft, thick hair and the warmth of his head against her palm.

There was a movement to the left, just in her peripheral vision. A moped took the corner too fast, and she yelled, 'Papa! Papa!'

It swerved and hooted and her father spun round and she spun round with him and the memory was interrupted and she was just herself, as an adult, watching the driver's helmet as he sped away. Hooting his horn, he looked back at her, and shook his fist.

She turned for Max, but there was no one.

In front of the supermarket, she knelt on the ground, patting her hands in the dust.

When she stood she was clasping a small metal comb. She felt its teeth and the sharp little points pierced her skin.

She brought her fingers to her mouth. Tasting blood, she stared into space.

Where the road should have been, there was only a whiteness. When her vision had returned she'd walked on, following in Annie's footsteps.

Ruthie and Max had gone the same way once. Cutting through the gorge and up into the hills, they had climbed so high there were birds beneath them, and she was frightened.

At the Old Town, the gorge was no different from the Paillon at Nice: a broad white strip, sweeping from the hills and on through the town to the sea. Walking there now, Ruthie could see the boy, Edward, in the ramparts of a tower with his father. She hung back and waited. When the family had regrouped and moved on, she tracked them; turning aside if they looked for the view of the sea; or dropping to fasten her sandals, or to pretend to pick some thyme.

They did as she expected at Agios Nikolaos, and left the path to see the church. She went on, slipping into a half-jog. They'd be twenty minutes at least, she calculated, consulting their map, and drinking water from their little bottles. Still she ran, wanting to be out of sight when they came to the point where the path dropped to meet the gorge and offered a choice: either a long and steady climb up the riverbed itself, clambering over boulders and picking out a route to where the track ran down from Tseria, the tiny town perched almost on a cliff face; or a quick traverse of the riverbed, to join the path that rose sharply from its other side and snaked cross-country via Pedino, to approach Tseria from its other flank.

Ruthie chose the latter, and watched from the trees above.

Eventually, the four of them stood in the riverbed. They looked at the map and up at the mountains, then they did as she'd anticipated and began to make their way, boulder by boulder.

She saw the four little figures move like miniatures. She walked on, keeping Annie always in sight. It was early, still, and she knew they would reach the head of the gorge by lunchtime.

Near Pedino, the land became flat and she lost them. At Tseria, though, she was almost in the sky and could see the whole of the gorge.

She waited an hour, then they appeared, like ants on a gravel path. When they reached the head of the gorge they were stationary, then they turned, pointing and taking photographs, climbing on boulders and down.

The narrow track that Ruthie stood on was a straight diagonal. Cut into the cliff, it fell sharply to where the family was.

On the same track with Max, she had lagged behind.

He'd taken her elbow and she was half running, half being dragged, then he doubled his pace and she complained so he let her go, but suddenly, and she reeled back, slipping right off the edge. In that split second, he turned and caught her with both hands and she'd hung in the air with the straight wall of rock in front of her face and nothing beneath her.

He had tightened his grip but he'd made her wait.

In the half-minute that passed before he hauled her up, she had tried to find a foothold.

This morning, at the same place exactly, her heart raced and her breath came quickly. Tripping on a loose stone and righting herself, she heard him shout her name.

'Don't,' Vinny had said to her the following week, when Ruthie told her what had happened, and made herself cry just by talking about it. 'He'll hear you.'

Ruthie couldn't stop, though, so Vinny told her to bite the inside of her cheeks.

Now, jogging down from Tseria, she did the same again.

She looked down and could see the boy, crouching on a boulder. When his sister clambered on, he pushed her off and a scream rose up. The sound bounced from the rocks like the cry of an eagle.

'Please, Papa,' she had yelled as Max had held her. 'Please.'

Now, Ruthie sat down and put her head in her hands.

At the bottom of the path, she stopped to catch her breath, and was surprised by the position of the sun.

In the gorge, she looked to the left, and to the right. Then she stood as still as she could, and listened.

The family had gone, and she was alone.

15 ALL OF ME

The first of Sophie's letters was only a note. Beatrice read it, and resealed it. Ruthie came home from school, and Beatrice gave it to her to open, saying, 'I think it might be from Maman! The postmark's Falicon!'

I think of you every single day and I am getting better! I really, really am and I will come back soon, I promise, and we will be just like we were, all of us together!

'Can I telephone Vee?' Ruthie said.
'Yes. After tea, though.'
'Should we tell Papa?'
'He's a jolly long way away.'
'Where?'
'Zaire, lovey.'
'Where's Zaire?'
'Africa.'
'Why is he there?'

'It's the *Rumble in the Jungle*! Everyone's talking about it. He's taking pictures for *The Times*. Here, look. He must have wired this one straight back. It's rather good, don't you think?'

Ruthie read the headline, then she stared at the photograph.

'Can we send him a telegram?'

'It's awfully expensive.'

'But it's a letter from Maman! We have to tell him!'

'Maybe next time, lovey. Come on. Let's have tea.'

The second letter arrived a month later, on a Saturday morning. When Beatrice got to breakfast, Ruthie was already there. Her cheeks were flushed and her breath was coming quickly.

'Let me see, lovey,' Beatrice said, holding out her hand. 'If you find another one, why not give it to me and I'll save it for Vinny to open? Then you can take it in turns, hey?'

> *Today I was strong enough to swim at Villefranche. Do you*
> *remember, when you were little and we lay on the beach*
> *and looked at the sky, then we ran through the rain? Do you?*
> *Tomorrow I will swim again and next week I may even go on*
> *my own. It is colder now and Pépé says I shouldn't but the*
> *water's not so cold, not really. I love you, my little ones. I love*
> *you IloveyouIloveyouIlove. At night I dream of you both.*

They read it again, together, then Ruthie said, 'We can send a telegram to Papa this time. He's only in Norway, which isn't as far as Zaire. I checked in your –'

'In my what?'

'Your atlas! I found the letter on the doormat and I looked in your diary and it said "*M to Norway*" and –'

'Listen, darling.' She sat Ruthie down at the kitchen table, and held her hands. 'Maman and Papa aren't friends any more, are they? So I don't think we will, hey? Why not go and get the atlas and show me where Papa is? Oh, love, don't cry, don't. Here, let me hold you, please let me.'

When the third letter came, in the spring of the following year, Beatrice was quick enough. Half finished, it was in pencil rather than pen, and the script fell from the page or trailed, faltering before its end.

I cannot. I cannot. I cann   ot. I can   not.

You mustnot mustnotmustnot ask me to because I.
        I can't write.   I want to say all the moments of real happiness in my life. In my
I cannot write.
You have been incredibly good.

She waited until Ruthie was in bed, then she readdressed it to Emile, enclosing one of her own: was he taking her to hospital again, at least for a while? And please have a care: she'd asked the postman to look out for envelopes from France, but the girls were growing up now. Ruthie was eleven years old, and there was nothing unusual in her opening her own post.

He replied by return: it had been weeks without any sign, so he'd thought she was well enough. He would be more careful, and was sorry for Beatrice's trouble.

Emile continued to write as he'd always done, once a month and every month.

Addressed to both girls together, their beginnings and endings were invariable: 'Your maman asks me to tell you she loves you very much and misses you,' and, 'Please give my greetings to your aunt, and I wish you both well with your studies.'

There were specifics.

He'd taken her to Nice, for ice cream at the Place Rossetti: he had chosen strawberry; she had had blackcurrant sorbet. They'd stood at the window of Zoppi the shoemaker, like they used to when she was little, and she'd shown him the ones she liked.

She'd had a very good day the previous week, and had helped on the neighbours' farm. In the stables where you played, *mes chéries*, do you remember? She'd brushed down the mare, and had laid out all the ropes and recoiled them. If she continued getting stronger, it would become a regular thing.

He'd bought her a bright yellow dress.

Once, he wrote that he'd painted her toenails a deep, dark red, since that was the colour she'd chosen.

Ruthie read his letters and reread them, keeping a list of the images he described. Over time, there were enough for her to piece them together into a series of wholes, as though he'd sent photographs, which meant that when her mother's letters stopped coming altogether, she could open her notebook and see her.

Sometimes, Sophie asked Ruthie questions, and she answered her.

If Beatrice heard Ruthie around the house, and asked her who she was talking to, her niece brushed her off.

'No one!' Ruthie said, 'I never said anything!' Or sometimes, 'Myself, Auntie Bea. I was talking to myself. Like you do when you're stuck on the crossword.'

One night, Ruthie went into Beatrice's room.

'I can't sleep, Auntie Bea. Auntie Bea, I can't –'

She shook her, but Beatrice didn't move. Climbing into the bed, she felt the soft warmth of Beatrice's back. She wrapped her arms around her, then she closed her eyes, slowing her breath until it fell in with her aunt's.

When she woke she was in her own bed, and her aunt was in the chair by the window. Beatrice said, 'Who were you talking to, Roo?' and Ruthie tiptoed across the room. Beatrice held Ruthie into her, and kissed the top of her head. 'I'd like you to answer me, lovey. Will you do that for me? Can you?'

Sitting in the chair by the window, they watched the trees on the Heath, which moved with the wind, like tall ships at sea.

Once Ruthie started it came out easily: how sometimes she wished her maman would leave her alone. At the villa, Vinny had accused her of sleeptalking but she wasn't, she was telling Maman about her day, because Maman wanted to know absolutely every single thing, and would never let Ruthie sleep until she'd told her.

'Wait, wait, wait, lovey. You're going too fast for me. Wait a minute.'

More slowly then, Ruthie said it was worst of all at Pennerton. Papa was always cross with her, and he never said Maman's name, so it was like she didn't exist and she never had, even though she actually used to live there, and now there weren't even any photographs of her anywhere in the whole of the house and Ruthie knew because she'd looked. Maman talked to her all the time and she never stopped even when she asked her to. Sometimes it was just as bad at the villa, when Maman followed her everywhere, and Ruthie couldn't tell anyone because no one would believe her.

It wasn't so much of a problem at Pilgrim's Lane. There were Sophie's letters, and Emile's, and sometimes Auntie Bea said Maman's name, Ruthie explained, so it was like she was a real person. On a day when Auntie Bea said her name, Sophie hardly talked to her at all, and she could go to sleep properly.

After this conversation, the two of them would look at photographs of Sophie, and they might play one of the records she'd made with the company at Sadler's Wells. If Ruthie cried, Beatrice held her and said she missed Maman too, of course she did: Sophie had become her sister, those days at Pennerton.

Eventually, they took the record player to Ruthie's bedroom. They spent an afternoon together, and Ruthie learned how to lower the needle and lift it up.

Sophie's voice became quieter in Ruthie's mind. In time she hardly heard it, or only as an echo, and was easier about going to Pennerton, where it was once so much louder than anywhere else.

By her thirteenth birthday, she was quite accepting of the idea that it was where they spent their Christmas and Easter holidays, and some of their half-terms.

Of the two of them it always took Ruthie longer to settle, but eventually she followed her sister's lead: going with Max to Headcorn and back; helping with his parcels if Peter was busy; holding a bucket in the orchard, taking the apples from him and placing them in.

She complained to her aunt, though: she was a teenager too, now, didn't Papa realise? He talked to Vinny like a grown-up, and he paid her more attention. Why did they spend their whole time shut away in the library, and why wouldn't Vinny tell her what they talked about?

Beatrice said she had no idea, and not to make a fuss, so Ruthie found it out herself, standing at the library door and hearing them discuss how soon after Vinny's seventeenth birthday she'd learn to drive, and would the lessons be in London or Kent; should she go back to the summer school in Hamburg or did she want to try something different; whether Max could find her a holiday placement at the Foreign Office, before she went to university.

Vinny laughed, and Max said, 'Why turn your nose up? You could travel the world!' When she asked what was wrong with staying at home, or at least in one country, he contested her alternative.

'A teacher? Vee! Whoever heard of anything so boring?'

'What about a translator? Mrs McCullin at school said –'

'A what? Get a bit of glamour in your life! Just think who you could be with all these languages.'

There was some merit in Ruthie's complaint that Max paid her less attention than he did Vinny, but as her aunt pointed out, their correspondence went on: Ruthie sending films, Max returning prints and a commentary.

While she was punctual with her part of it, shooting a roll a week, he was, at best, sporadic. If he skipped a turn altogether, there were half-hearted apologies. She smiled into the telephone: 'It doesn't matter. Really it doesn't,' waiting until he'd said goodbye before she cried.

When nothing came to Pilgrim's Lane for the whole of March, Beatrice showed her his shot of the Sex Pistols signing a record contract in front of Buckingham Palace. Ruthie said, yes, alright, she knew he was busy, and yes, alright, it was pretty cool, but not that cool. So what if he'd taken their photograph? And so what if it was on the front page of *The Times*? It didn't mean he was going to start listening to their records.

She was patient, but when April was barren as well she was disbelieving: checking under the hall table in case they'd fallen; going to the post office on Rosslyn Hill to ask was there something for Ruthie Hollingbourne, and had he forgotten a stamp and did she need to pay to collect it?

Eventually, Beatrice offered to take her films to a place in town which she said was 'right next to the club and no trouble. Really, lovey.'

With the third set of prints, Beatrice brought back a flyer.

Ruthie wrote to Vinny that there were only a few people in the Camera Club and they were teenagers, like her.

'Are they nice?' Vinny asked when she phoned, but Ruthie said she'd no idea, she was only really there for the darkroom. The tutor was alright, she said, and it lasted all day on a Saturday. The others were all boys, which was fine: she knew what she was doing, so she could ignore them.

Because she was part of the Camera Club without really being part of it, nobody minded if there was a weekend at Pennerton and she missed it, or Beatrice took her out early, for an afternoon lecture at the Royal Academy. Or when, occasionally, the two of them packed their cases and went to Rome for the Sistine Chapel, or Barcelona for Picasso's *Las Meninas*.

'It's not just about photography,' Beatrice said to Max. 'She needs to know there are other ways of looking at things. She's a teenager now. She should be learning about the world. Anyway, it's none of your business how I spend Rupert's money. It's a bit of fun, and it's precisely the sort of thing he'd have wanted me to do with it.'

Giving up altogether on Max's parcels, Ruthie kept her hurt to herself. With this burying of her feelings came a ready forgetfulness, so that if he offered her a lesson at Pennerton, she said yes.

In that little red-lit space where they worked rather than talked, it hardly mattered that there was none of the ease she saw between him and her sister, none of the back-and-forth of ideas or imagining of the future.

His conversation rarely strayed beyond instructions, or predictions of what would happen if he switched something or masked something. Sometimes, though, he spoke more openly, so that she was able to report in her letters to Vinny that the reason he never wore a tie was because he hated wasting time with a proper knot, and that, given the choice, he preferred his kippers jugged rather than grilled. Or that he'd bought his first record in 1949 from a man called Vincent on the rue de la Huchette, and was introduced to jazz by a woman called Melanie, and once, that he'd done his national service at a military hospital in Sussex, as a photographer's assistant.

'*Pictures of burns,*' she wrote. '*Burns so awful you wouldn't believe it. He actually showed me some prints. Faces half-melted. No eyes. Half a mouth gone. That's what he did all day, taking pictures of those poor blown-to-pieces men. Everyone who came in, everyone who went out. Did you know that was how he started off? Can you imagine?*'

At May half-term, he took her to the courtyard and said, how about an outside lesson?

'Look at the sky,' he whispered. 'It's perfect. The woods, I think. The light's just right for it.'

She wondered about breakfast but didn't say, then she made for the kitchen garden. He told her to stop; they were taking a different route.

'Don't assume anything. Just do exactly as I ask.'

She followed him down the Long Avenue and onto the road, turning right and tracing the boundary wall. He said the direction of the breeze would have given the game away if they'd entered the woods from the Triangle Meadow.

'This way, it'll be an actual test.'

'Of what?'

'Of whether you can read the light.'

They'd walked for twenty minutes when they came to the place where the wall dipped slightly. Above it was a tree with a branch hanging low and she followed him, swinging onto the wall and jumping down the other side.

She stood and brushed herself off. He put his hands on her shoulders and turned her so she was facing away, then he pulled her body into his and held his arms across her chest.

'Don't look at the path. Keep your eyes up. You go first. Here, like this. Lean back against me. I want you to see if you can pinpoint the place where the sky changes colour, and I want you to tell me the exact moment you see it happening.'

They moved as a hobbled animal. His hips were steering, his abdomen was pressed against her spine. Her instinct was to look at the path, but when her chin dropped, he pulled her hair at the back half gently.

'Look up, I said. Trust me. Walk as I walk. And keep your eyes on the sky. I'll guide you. Just look up and walk.'

When the scent hit her, it was sudden and sweet and it filled her face and her lungs. She stopped short, thinking he must have felt the breeze changing direction, and would realise she was cheating, but still she said it anyway.

'This is the place, Papa. Just here, up ahead.' She pointed through the trees and claimed to see the faintest difference. 'Lilac,' she said. 'It's changed colour, it's not grey or white or blue any more.'

'Yes! Not just the sky, though. It's everything. The air, the trees. Look around you now. Look!'

He let go of her hair. Her head fell forward and there were blue-bells everywhere, laid like a rug to the edges of the wood.

They collected armfuls, walking on into the morning. At the house, they placed them in all the rooms and stood the rest in a small metal bucket on the hall table: a block of purple wedged into tin.

'Where did you go?' Vinny called from the library. 'What did you do?'

'Never you mind!' Max called back, and Ruthie kept silent. 'Have you come home to revise, or to chat? Head down, please. Time for another hour before lunch, I should think.'

'But where've you been?'

'In the woods!'

'Doing what?'

'Nothing especially interesting. Ask your sister later,' but he looked at Ruthie, and put his finger to his lips.

In the darkroom that afternoon, she reached to the topmost shelf for a cylinder.

'What's this, Papa?' she said, pulling out a leather purse.

'What's what?' Max said.

'Doesn't matter.'

She stood at the sink, keeping her eyes on the water as it crept towards its mark.

Through the meniscus there was Max, split into three. When she tilted the cylinder his three parts united, and she spooned the crystals in.

'What's what?' he said again.

'That,' she said. Nodding towards the purse, she emptied the cylinder into another, and placed them both in a stand. 'Is it yours?'

'No, it's not.'

'Whose, then?'

'Sophie's.'

There was a jolt in Ruthie's stomach. She reached for the purse again and weighed it in her hand. 'No it isn't.'

Max was at the enlarger. Then the switch clicked and they were in the safelight, and he counted under his breath. Once the paper was in the stop, he looked at Ruthie. 'Put the purse back. And hurry up with that hardener, would you? Everything will be cold if you –'

'It isn't Maman's.' She switched on the main light and saw the image turn to black in its tray. 'I've never seen it before. She wouldn't have –'

'Ruthie,' he said, lifting out the ruined print, 'you don't understand.' At the sink, his arm touched hers and she jumped. 'Jesus! There's no need to be so bloody dramatic. It's not Mum's, you're right. But it is Sophie's. Sorry. I should've told you.'

Ruthie gazed at the cylinder, watching for the colour to settle to sky blue. When her father spoke, she only half heard.

'Sophie is a friend. She was here last week and must've left it.' The solution was smoky now and he sounded muffled, as though he was speaking from another room. Then finally it was lilac, and she knew it would stay that way. 'I'm sorry, Roo. I didn't mean to confuse you.'

In the kitchen, Vinny's work was spread across the table. Beatrice was halfway through a crossword, so neither of them heard her come in and she had to say it twice, or try to.

'Papa's got a –'

'A what?' Beatrice said. 'Papa's got a what?'

The discussion as to whether to tell their mother about Max's girlfriend was over as soon as it began.

'We could put it in a letter, Vee, next time we write to Emile.'

'Why?' Vinny said.

'Then he could tell Maman.'

'Even if we wrote to Emile he probably wouldn't tell her, and even if he did she wouldn't understand. Anyway, it's probably just a fling.'

Ruthie persisted, and Vinny said, 'Well, if you think you know so much, why not go and see her in hospital and tell her yourself?'

'She's not in hospital. She's in Emile's house at Falicon.'

'See, you don't even know where she is.'

'How would I? Why is she in hospital? Nobody tells me anything. Not any single thing!'

Beatrice spoke to Ruthie.

'Let's have a proper talk, shall we? How about a stroll on the meadow?'

While they walked, she tried to tell Ruthie about the nature of her mother's illness, and Ruthie tried to understand.

When the second-Sophie began staying over, the sisters made it clear they'd no intention of being friendly, nor were they interested in her opinions, or her jokes, or her solicitousness as to their well-being. They were perfectly well provided for in the sphere of maternal affection, having their aunt for that sort of thing.

'It's not that we don't like you,' Ruthie said one morning, when the second-Sophie came to breakfast earlier than usual and asked Vinny what she was reading, and did Ruthie need a hand with the crossword?

'How could we?' Ruthie carried on. 'We don't even know you, do we, Vee?'

Vinny shook her head, then without looking up from her book, said, 'Yes. Whatever, yes.'

'And I'm not sure either of us can be bothered to get to know you enough to find out. Whether we do like you, I mean. We lack the application, you see. Can I say that, Vee? Is that a word, "application"? Am I using it right?'

'Using it correctly. Not using it right.'

'Well, am I?'

'Yes, you are. It is a word, and yes, you are using it correctly. We lack the application.'

Ruthie turned back to the second-Sophie. 'There you have it,' she said, smiling. 'So you needn't waste your time being nice.'

Beatrice observed to Max that if this hadn't been enough on its own, it must at least have been a factor in the new Sophie's departure, adding that if he'd been a little more careful over how he'd told the girls, they'd perhaps have made her more welcome.

'Well, what did you expect?' he said. 'They'd greet her with open arms? They'll get used to the idea of there being someone, further down the line.'

A year later, Vinny won a scholarship to Cambridge. She spent her gap year in Göttingen, au pair to a professor's daughter.

Ruthie read her sister's letters as soon as they arrived, then she read them once more on the way to Little House, so the girls next door said there was no need to show off; they already knew Vinny was in Germany. She read them again in afternoon lessons, when she couldn't help herself and held the envelope under the desk, her eyes darting to the teacher.

Her final reading was in summary rather than in full, out loud while Beatrice made supper.

'She ate pig's-knuckle dumplings with the Buschboms! In a restaurant called – Oh, I can't say it. In a restaurant called something, next to the Mar-ee-en-ker-cher. Which means St Mary's Church. And the man she sat next to ate three of them. He put his hand on her knee when the chef brought the pudding which was a cake called Mo—something. It's poppy-seed cake and it's very sweet and a bit crunchy, and the seeds are really tiny so you can hardly see them. Oh, and the man who ate three dumplings is English, not German. He's working for Professor Buschbom but only until Christmas then he's going back to England. Vinny says he's going to be a professor himself one day. And he said Vinny's German is alright but could be better. And she didn't mind about him touching her knee because he's not much older than her. And she thought he was only doing it to be friendly. And he stopped when she asked him to. Auntie Bea, what does a pig's knuckle taste like?'

'Fatty, I suspect. Shall we ask the butcher to do us one? Here, Roo, let me read it. I want to know everything about this man who ate three dumplings. What's his name, and how old is he, and does Vinny say he's nice, or should I write to Professor Buschbom this instant?'

There was only one letter that she didn't read out, telling Beatrice instead that it had fallen from her pocket on the way to school, before she'd had a chance to open it.

31 October 1979

Darling Roo,

I know I've upset you by leaving, and I'm sorry you've been worrying about me – you mustn't, really you mustn't.

I miss you too, of course I do, but Göttingen was something I just had to do.

I'm not like you – I won't slip through life being beautiful and getting away with stuff just because of how I look, and just because I'm a bit exciting and a bit creative.

I'm neither of those things. I'm just plain old, boring old, sensible old Vinny. I know that's how you think of me, or at least, that's not fair – I mean I know it's how Dad thinks of me. And he's right, I suppose. I've inherited a carbon copy of his face near enough. Or his eyes and his nose anyway, which means I look like an eagle from side-on and God knows what from the front. I'm too tall and too fat and too clever and too English and I want to know what it's like not to be any of those things. I want to know what it's like to be someone else. When I speak another language I AM someone else, do you see? I say things I'd NEVER say in English. I think I might even end up DOING things I'd never do at home, too.

I'm not awkward at the Buschboms. No one knows me, so no one expects me to be awkward, which means I don't have to BE awkward.

Dieter and his wife, Ines, say if I pretend to be German, then everyone will think I am. They say I have to get used to swearing in German, and I have to start telling jokes. And they say I shouldn't be self-conscious or I'll never make any progress.

So I'm experimenting. It backfires, though. Dieter told me last week I've been saying to Ines night after night that her suppers are 'not bad, adequate, could be improved on', when I thought I was telling her they were 'completely delicious'. So basic! I feel like a complete twit. She's making Streuselkuchen at the weekend, so I've learned 'It's exquisitely delicious' and checked it with Dieter.

He's got an in-translation plays project coming up at the university, so I'm helping him with that. It's just a scene here or there, but it's so much fun, and he's actually using some of my lines.

I like it. German, I mean. I know exactly where I am with it. You can make a word by joining other words together. Like sticklebricks, Anke says. In fact, it's more like a whole building made of sticklebricks. Things fit, and they do what you expect them to. It's sort of ugly, but it's beautiful as well, and there are lovely words like 'heartfelt', and 'heartsore', and 'heartsick'.

Anke is completely adorable and hardly needs any looking after. All I have to do is walk her home from school, and sit with her while she does her homework. Sometimes they put her to bed themselves, and sometimes I do, and she's so lovely it's no problem if they ask me to.

I love you very much, you know that, don't you? You can't imagine how much I miss you. I think about you every day, and I feel awful for having told you not to visit but I need this time to be me. Not 'Ruthie Hollingbourne's sister', or 'Max Hollingbourne's daughter'. Does that make sense? Can you understand? Please don't be hurt, and please don't be cross. I can't believe I'm writing like this! You sounded so upset in your last letter, that's all, so I wanted to explain.

Write again soon, will you? And don't show this to Bea.

V xxxxxxxx

*PS I forgot to say on the phone yesterday, 6 Across was
'Temple Fortune', or did you work it out already?*

*PPS In answer to your question, the man who ate the
pig's knuckles is called Julian, and I've no idea how old he is
(maybe 25, or 26?) or what his middle name is. Do you know,
though, the most amazing thing? He's at the college I'm going
to at Cambridge! He's only here for a term because he's Dieter's research assistant, then he's going back to finish his PhD.
And yes, I do like him, and no of course I haven't kissed him –
I've only met him twice, and Dieter and Ines were there!*

Vinny never wrote in the same way again.

Ruthie never told her how surprised she was by her outpouring,
nor how much she'd cried when she'd read it.

With her sister so far away, Ruthie lasted just a term at Little House.

Because Max was travelling, the white-hot anger of his immediate reaction came later, in the form of an airmail letter written in
red ink and posted in Tunis. When she read it, he'd already been and
gone, but still she felt his rage as a physical thing: in the dents scored
in the onion-paper tissue of the hotel stationery; in the lines under
phrases such as 'very serious' or 'frankly, pathetic'; and in the words
he'd capitalised: 'CHILDISH' and 'DISAPPOINTING.'

Arriving in Hampstead straight from the airport, Max had
announced that he'd 'get it out of her whatever it took'. But when he
paused on the bottom step, Beatrice told him, 'I've asked her every
day, so don't waste your breath. The police have asked her, the headmistress has asked her. For goodness' sake, Vinny's telephoned a
hundred times, and she still won't say anything.'

Because Ruthie had done it quickly, no one had seen her go. Her empty
desk was explained by a girl who reported her heading for the nurse's

room with her hands to her tummy, as everyone ran to their first lesson. By mid-morning, the period-pains story had gained the status of fact, going unchecked until lunchtime when the nurse said, 'No, I'm sure I haven't seen Ruthie Hollingbourne,' and the search began in earnest.

Nor, Beatrice said, was there much chance of discovering when, exactly, she'd settled down to sleep on the bench in Regent's Park where she was found the following morning, clutching an empty Martini bottle. The silver cigarette case, lying on the ground beside her with its lid snapped from its hinges, was Beatrice's, but as for the four crisp twenty pound notes which were found with it, Beatrice couldn't comment.

'She seems to have caught bronchitis, but as far as we can tell that's the worst of it. She's alright, isn't that what matters? That she's here, not frozen half to death in a flower bed, or lying in a ditch with her throat slit? Well, isn't it?'

'I was simply observing that –'

'Christ, it's a bit late for observations. Give her a break. Why not try to be nice, even?'

'What was it you said to me once, when she showed up at Pennerton with a stack of home detentions? "Go easy on her"? "A lot of hot air at Little House"? Bit off the mark there.'

'Are you blaming me? How dare you? If you ever –' then she stopped dead, brushing away tears.

'Steady,' he said. She was shaking. 'Steady, Bea.' He held her. 'Sorry. I'm sorry. Of course I'm not. Thank you for taking care of her. And of course I'll be nice. We'll just have a bit of a chat, if you can see your way to allowing that.'

The letter from the headmistress said that it was *'terribly hard'* to write like this to anyone, but *'doubly so'* to have to do so to Beatrice.

Whilst we believe Little House to be excellently placed to provide a level of pastoral care and support above and beyond

*what might be expected from most schools, it would seem
Ruthie doesn't quite fit in, one way or another.*

*In the appropriate setting, and surrounded by the right
sort of people, I think it entirely possible she'd be able to fulfil
her very evident potential.*

*A crammer, or another sort of place altogether (a secre-
tarial college, for example), might be the best course. If you
could see your way to arranging it, we're quite confident that
things will resolve themselves in her best interests.*

Ruthie's bronchitis was treated and cleared within a fortnight.
Then she was simply laggard, sleeping in till lunch and spending
all day in her pyjamas. Refusing the meals Beatrice offered, she
asked instead for milk and biscuits. In the evenings she went up
first, clutching a mug of cocoa and saying, 'Don't wake me in the
morning.'

At Christmas, Peter sent chestnuts for roasting, which made
Ruthie smile for a half-minute. She smiled again when she opened
Vinny's parcel: a box of *Lebkuchen* made by Ines and wrapped in
layers of tissue by Anke, labelled with a childish script. Ruthie shared
the little cakes with Beatrice, but she saved Vinny's letter to read
later, on her own.

The last of the packages was postmarked Cannes, and contained
five fresh rolls of film. When she'd read Max's note, she took the
chestnuts Peter had given her, and stood by the fire. Her aunt passed
the skillet, and Ruthie knelt before the grate. Afterwards, the scent
filled the room. Ruthie gathered the skins, which were burnt and
crisp. She scattered them on the fire, and when the flames were high,
she put the films on top.

Beatrice was at the door, holding a tray. In one movement, she
dropped it and crossed the room, falling to her knees.

'Jesus, Auntie Bea,' Ruthie said, putting a hand on Beatrice's arm.
'Calm down! Ten to one he'll forget he ever sent them.'

They cleared the broken tray and sat together. When the fire had settled to embers Ruthie said goodnight, then she went up, leaving Max's note where it had fallen.

Chin up, old girl. Tell me what you make of these: 3 fast, 2 slow. Shoot something I haven't seen before, and I'll send back the prints faster than the speed of light, I promise. I've opened you an account at SilverPrint for when you're up and about. It's at Elephant & Castle, though, so get Bea to go with you.

Anything you need for Camera Club, put it on the tab. They know who I am (I've been going there for years). Ray's the chap you want to talk to. Get him to show you some of that slow paper I told you about. Actually try anything by Kosmos, not just the slow stuff (they're in Letchworth, I think, so he can order it in). He'll get hold of the Vitegas De-Luxe if you ask him nicely. Try the smooth, in a warm tone. There's not a lot left, but if it's out there, Ray'll find it. Catch him on a week-day if you can. He's always in a better mood on weekdays.

I've told him to expect you.

Oh, and by the way, 16's still on the young side for an account. They've only given it the nod because it's me, so make the most of it.

Ruthie stayed in bed for the rest of the week.

Beatrice's doctor came, and suggested Beatrice leave the two of them to talk.

He wrote the next morning, advising that Ruthie take a break for 'two months, minimum, probably more like three'. Her weight would at some stage be troubling, but only if there was no improvement in the coming month. School, Dr Petersen said, was out of the question: her mind would be fragile for some time.

Ruthie settled into a new phase at Pilgrim's Lane. She made the top floor her own. She borrowed pot plants from the conservatory, and unwrapped a pair of Sophie's gildings to put on the windowsill: a blackbird's skull, and a stiffened foot from a larger bird. She collected all the throws she could find and draped them from shelves or nailed them to the walls. When she brought home an incense burner from the charity shop on Rosslyn Hill, Beatrice said, 'Well, alright then. If you really have to,' but she drew the line at visitors: Ruthie could have as many as she liked in the sitting room, or the kitchen, but would she at least pretend she was behaving with some kind of propriety, and do her best not to take them to her room.

In those first months of her recuperation, she walked with her aunt on the Heath. Going further afield, Beatrice insisted on taxis.

'Just until you've got your strength up, Roo. Then you can try the Underground again.'

With Beatrice's approval, Ruthie went back to the Camera Club, and she wrote to her father that she'd been to Silverprint. She'd said hello to Ray, just as Max had told her to, and when he realised she was Max's daughter, he'd agreed to track down some Vitegas De-Luxe after all.

In answer to her father's next letter, asking how she was spending the rest of his allowance, she sent a two-line note that she was, 'getting on with my life', and would be sure to let him know if anything remotely interesting happened.

One morning when Ruthie was leaving to spend the day on the steps of the British Museum, taking pictures of its visitors, she'd paused in the downstairs kitchen. There was a note on the table from her aunt. Next to it was an envelope postmarked Germany.

She read Vinny's letter to Beatrice, and flicked through the photos: Vinny and Julian on a tandem, a picnic hamper strapped on the rack at the back ('*He's over from Cambridge every other weekend. He says it's for the work he's doing with Dieter, but I know it's for me, really, which is sweet, isn't it?*'); with Anke, the pair of them doing handstands against the wall of the Buschbom family's house ('*Can you believe it? A handstand! Anke taught me and it's quite easy, actually.*'); with Dieter at his desk, heads bent over a manuscript ('*I did it! A whole 3-Act play! Just the bare bones but he'll use it as his "Literal" – that's when you prepare a straight translation for someone else to take on and make it dramatic, or literary, or whatever, so it works as a play, not just a word-for-word translation.*'); then last of all, Vinny and Julian hand in hand, with Anke sitting on Julian's shoulders, laughing with her mouth wide open ('*It's like being a little family, Bea. A completely normal family.*').

This Göttingen-Vinny was slender. Her hair, rather than being clipped back, fell in loose curls around her face. The person her sister had become wore dresses and smiled at the camera, and Ruthie no longer recognised her.

Wiping away tears, she took up her aunt's note.

Darling Roo,

I know you'll want to go out today but don't, will you? I'll be back by ten and there's something I need you to help me with.

B xxxxx

PS Listen out for the door – there's a tiny chance Peter might show up before me.

Reading the note a second time, Ruthie frowned.

Then the bell rang, and she took the stairs two at a time. At the door, she was about to say 'Hello, Peter!' and 'Why didn't you tell me you were coming?' and 'By the way, what's going on?' and 'Oh my goodness, is this the first time you've ever even been to Pilgrim's Lane?' but then he handed her a cloth sack filled with what looked like wood.

'Apple trays? You've brought the apple-tray drawers from Pennerton! But we don't have any trees. And we don't have a shed to put them in. Why are you –'

'You'll see,' he said. He untied the ribbon of his glasses and retied it, then he smiled at her, the broad smile she remembered, so she felt a warmth spread through her chest and her tummy. 'Actually, love, we're on a meter. Let's just get it all in.'

Ruthie wasn't quite right: Peter had been to Pilgrim's Lane once before, on a Saturday morning when Ruthie was at the Camera Club.

Beatrice had shown him the upstairs bathroom, and when he'd taken his measurements, they'd sat at the kitchen table making lists.

He sent his drawings within the week. At Silverprint, Beatrice said she would like an account of her own, and Max wasn't to hear a word of it. When she saw Ray hesitate, she asked if she should take her custom elsewhere. Then he entered her in the ledger and they sat for an hour, the two of them, reviewing and revising the plans.

On the day of the construction of Ruthie's darkroom, two men came in a van from Silverprint.

They did their best but the enlarger became stuck, not quite at the top. Peter and Ruthie stood three steps down and stretched their arms to its base. While they shoved, hard, the men pulled from above and, in one motion the machine was on the landing, taking some paint and plaster with it.

When the men had gone, Beatrice told Ruthie and Peter that a repaint was the last of their worries: she was more concerned about the ventilation.

'You'll just have to remember to open the door every now and again, Roo. I still think we could have found a way to fit an extractor without letting the light in.'

'It doesn't matter,' Ruthie said. 'It's not worth it.'

'I don't know what Max would say about not having one, that's all.'

'Yes you do. You know exactly what he'd say.' She kissed her aunt. 'Forget it. I'll open the door in between pictures, like you said. It's amazing,' she said, turning the enlarger's dials first one way, then back. 'An actual enlarger. In my bathroom. How much did it cost? How did you know it'd fit? I mean, what if it hadn't?'

Then Beatrice handed Ruthie a brand-new boiler suit, telling her she couldn't very well paint walls in her ordinary clothes, and while she was at it, she ought to tie her hair up.

They painted the room coal-black, and Peter carried in the wooden door he'd brought from the stables at Pennerton, to serve as a work surface. Attaching a chain at either end, and hinges down the length of one side, he screwed hooks to the wall and fitted it above the bath.

'Have a try,' he said, putting Ruthie's hands to it and levering it up to the wall and down.

Ruthie laughed, and said it was perfect, all of it, and she didn't know how to thank them.

Beatrice said not to make a fuss. All she asked was that they swear a vow of silence together, the three of them. And if Ruthie started putting too many extras on her Silverprint account Max would know something was up, so for anything out of the ordinary, she was to use the account that had been opened in the name of Mrs Rupert Finch-Brookes, to which Ruthie was joint signatory.

Once Peter had gone, Ruthie put the stepladder to the wall. They perched together, with the window flung open and their hands on the sill. It was dusk and they listened to wild songs of blackbirds, carried on the breeze.

Afterwards, Beatrice held a square of black plastic to the windowpane, and Ruthie taped it up.

Within a week she'd as good as moved in, eating enough at breakfast to last her the day, or so she said to Beatrice. She brought the
record player through from her bedroom and balanced it on a piece
of board laid across the toilet seat. The landing floor throbbed with
the sounds of Dexys Midnight Runners, and of Ruthie singing along.

If she emerged in the early evening, and if Beatrice asked for
a hand with the crossword, she'd stop, half dazed, but only for a
minute.

Once, she came to breakfast early, dressed in her boiler suit, hat and
fingerless gloves, with one of Beatrice's coats on top. Beatrice was
sitting at the table.

'Can I use this coat?'

'Of course you can.'

'It might get a bit—'

'Have it! It's far too 1950s for me. Use it, use it, please. You look
quite the Parisienne artiste! You do realise it's only May? What on
earth'll you do in the winter?'

'Scarves, I imagine. Scarves and another hat. I'll be used to it by
then. Anyhow, don't go on. I like being all wrapped up. It's hardly
cold up there, I'm just not moving around much. Also, I wanted to
tell you –'

'What? Do you need something else? Can I give your back a rub?
You must get so stiff, hunched over those trays. I'll ask Peter if he can
raise the drop-down door a bit. It can't be doing you any good –'

'Stop fussing!' She stood by her aunt's chair and smiled. 'I just
wanted to tell you I'm happier than I've ever been. Ever in my whole
life, I mean. You've given me something amazing.' She put her arms
around her, and kissed the top of her head. 'Bea, you're getting
awfully small!'

'I'm sitting down, you twit.'

'No, I mean you feel little. When I hug you. You're still so flipping gorgeous, movie-star gorgeous. You know, everyone at school always used to ask me, is your auntie a model? Did I ever tell you that? You're getting super-skinny, though. Bea, why did you never have kids? I mean with someone else, after Rupert died.'

'Don't be nosy.'

'Sorry. You'd be such an amazing mum. Would be. Are. I mean, you're such an amazing auntie. Sorry, I'm not being nosy, I just—'

'If you really want to know, for a long time afterwards, I had the idea I should find someone just like him, and because I knew I couldn't, that I shouldn't even try. Then I woke up one day and realised it was too late. I might have worked it out sooner, I s'pose, that it wasn't about that. But other things happened.'

'You got saddled with us, you mean?'

'That's not what I said.'

'It's true, though. How old were you, when Maman went away and we came to you? Was that why it was too late?'

'Ruthie, sweetheart. I wouldn't have had it any other way.'

'How old are you now?'

'Never you mind! I'm eight years older than your father. Work it out yourself and stop being so cheeky, or I'll have my coat back. It does look a bit peculiar. Rather defeats the object of the boiler suit, doesn't it, wearing a posh coat on top?'

'You said you didn't mind! Here,' she said. 'Have it.'

'Don't be daft. I'm teasing.'

'I only came down to say thank you. Thank you and I love you.'

The darkroom christening was Beatrice's idea. 'A launch party,' she said. 'Think of it like that. A launch party for your very first darkroom!'

They began their celebration at midnight. By 2 a.m., Beatrice had seen all of Ruthie's prints and watched her make some more. The two of them finished a bottle of champagne and a packet of crackers, and half of the bottle of dark rum Beatrice had brought from the pantry.

'Are you sure you won't have some pop instead?' she'd said, coming up the stairs with the rum. 'I've got some lovely dandelion and burdock, you and Vee used to adore that. Oh, never mind, but don't blame me in the morning!'

Then Beatrice asked if she could have a go at a photo, and Ruthie said, 'Why not? It's an absolutely brilliant idea!'

The breakthrough came at 3 a.m., when Beatrice struck a match and Ruthie said, 'Bea! How could you?'

'What?' Beatrice said, inhaling. 'What've I done? Did I finish the rum, was that the last of it? Or aren't I allowed to smoke? Golly, you sound just like Max! Really, you're becoming quite a dictator – Oh damn, sorry! It was the match, wasn't it? I completely forgot! What? Will it really have spoilt it? It was only a tiny, tiny flame! Hang on, can you just turn the music down just a little? I can't – What's so funny? Why're you laughing? Are you alright, Roo? Stop, stop it! You'll choke if you – You're really worrying me now. Stop!'

When she'd got her breath, Ruthie apologised, saying she'd had no sleep for a week, it was almost tomorrow, she'd never mixed her drinks before, and she was feeling 'pretty strange'. Beatrice said she wasn't feeling so good herself, and they should go to bed immediately.

'But it's amazing!' Ruthie said, when the print was in the stop. 'Auntie Bea! I think you've actually solarised my picture. You've solarised my picture without even trying!'

The print Ruthie gave her aunt in the morning was scratched and sepia, the whole thing marked and rubbed and torn in places.

For a moment, staring at this image of herself and Rupert on their wedding day, Beatrice said nothing at all.

'Do you like it?' Ruthie whispered eventually.

'Yes,' Beatrice said. 'I do.'

Max's first visit to the bathroom-darkroom was, so he claimed, unpremeditated: he just happened to be driving past the house on his way back from Yorkshire, where he'd taken Ted Hughes's portrait on the banks of the River Calder.

Beatrice told Ruthie she'd no idea he'd gone upstairs, and if he'd had the decency to ask she'd have stopped him. She was looking for a letter he wanted, one that had surfaced at the time of their father's probate. It concerned a boundary dispute between their father and the neighbouring landowner; Max was thinking ahead in case he ever came to sell off the meadow. He'd gone through his papers and couldn't see it; had she been sent a copy, and if so could he have it?

While she wasn't for one minute suggesting he'd tricked her into it, it just so happened that it was when she was digging around in her filing cabinet, with her study door closed, that he'd gone up and made his discovery.

She'd interrupted him emptying the shelves above the washbasin. All but one of the plastic bottles were on the floor, and he'd found a cloth to wipe them.

'I can't –' he was saying to himself, grabbing the last one and pushing up his glasses, 'I can't even see what it is. She hasn't labelled a single bloody one of them. Christ alive –'

Then he looked at Beatrice and let his glasses fall.

'Is this cooking oil?' he said. Holding the bottle up to the light, he read the label, then he sniffed the contents. 'What the hell's she using oil for?'

'It's an old bottle. She's recycling. Can I just ask, actually, what you're doing in here?'

'Having a coronary arrest, or something like one. What's going on? What is this place? How long –'

She began to explain but Max was shouting.

'Converted! Is that what you call it? I'd say it still looks remarkably like a bathroom! Christ, it's bloody July, Bea. The tarmac's melting outside! It must be pushing ninety in here with the window shut. What's all that sheeting taped over it? And what the hell are these?' He reached to the shelf for a plastic box, which fell to the floor. 'Tea bags!' he said, removing the sodden parcels from his shoes. 'Bloody hell. Used tea bags?'

'It's not what you think. If you will—'

'Whose damn fool idea was it to lean the wipe board on the bloody enlarger? I've only been in here five minutes and my shoes are soaked through. And the chemistry? When did she last use the chemistry?'

'Yesterday. This morning, maybe. I don't know.'

'It's filthy.' He picked up one of the trays. 'And it stinks.'

'If she's doing a long session she reuses it. Max, I really don't see it's any of your business. She'll be back this afternoon and she won't be happy to find you nosing willy-nilly through her things.'

'I'm not. I'm trying to work out how to make the place a bit safer. I've got time to do it now, before I go. It'll take me half an hour, tops.' But then he picked something else up and said, 'What the hell is she doing with a bowl of lemons? Do you have any idea how dangerous it is, mixing drinks in the same room as—'

'Don't be ridiculous. Of course she's not mixing drinks. She uses them for her photos. She's amazing, the things she thinks of. You need to stop—'

'Amazing? Idiotic, you mean.'

'Jesus! Who are you to judge? You can't just show up and barge in like this. It's just not on. She's had a bloody difficult time since Christmas—'

'Self-inflicted! Completely self-inflicted!'

'If all you're interested in is taking to pieces what I've tried to do, you can bloody well sod off back to Pennerton. We're coping pretty well, Ruthie and me, but—'

'Ruthie and I.'

'Oh, fuck off. If you'd spent less of your life caring about being precise, you might not have messed it up quite so spectacularly. We're muddling along, alright? She's OK, and so is her sister, which is more than a bit surprising, considering.'

'Considering what?'

'That you abandoned them? Do you have any idea what it was like for them, when they were little? Stuck here with me, when they wanted to be with you? I could see it in their faces, every single day, how miserable they were. And bored, a lot of the time.'

'All children are bored! That's what childhood is!'

'No, I mean bored of me. Bored of missing you, bored of missing their mother. That's a different kind of boredom. It's flat, it's dull, and it's horrible to watch. Then there are these crazy bursts of happiness and excitement and back to the same old dull, flat sadness. Do you know, when they first moved here, I used to cry, almost every day? I could feel how much they were struggling, and I hated it. I'd shut myself in the pantry so they wouldn't see, and I'd put my head against the wall and weep, just with the frustration. And the sadness of it all! I'd had enough of it to deal with already, before they came along. I've soaked up all their pain and I've cared for them and loved them, but sometimes I've absolutely hated it. And Ruthie! God knows the number of times I've nursed her back to bloody normality. They're tough, your girls. Vinny more so, but Ruthie too. She manages. However much you've hurt her, she manages.'

'Hurt her how? What's she been telling you?'

'How? Do you even have to ask? I saw it for myself, the way you were when they were little. Why do you think I put my own life on hold so readily, if it wasn't because I could tell how badly they needed someone? Anyone. Your behaviour today, though – if she comes back and finds you up here she'll be really upset. It's her private space, Max. Her workspace.'

'Work! It's a bloody mess!'

'It's not "mess". It's creativity. She's experimenting, all the time.'

'Nonsense. It's just bloody slapdash!'

'Fine, go ahead and make all your photos clean and precise and neat and lifeless. Get your reviewers going wild over your straight lines and your empty spaces. But that's not what her work's about. Life's messy, Max. You should know.'

'I'm not talking about life, I'm talking about work. I just couldn't work in here.'

'Well, you're not her, are you? She's a different person from you. Will you never understand that? Why try to change her? All this –' she gestured at the room, and the tea bags and the lemons – 'is part of who she is. Tidy everything up, knock every last thing out of her, what would be left? It'd be like taking a brush to Vinny's hair and trying to make it straight. You were just the same when they were little. Losing your temper every time they dropped a cup, or spilt something, or painted over the edges. That's what kids do, but you couldn't handle it, could you? Well, she's growing up now, and I'm just trying to let her be herself. I'm trying to let her live. She creates beautiful pictures, and she tells me she's happy. It makes things make sense, she says, doing all this. It's her thing, so why try and stop it?'

'Fine. Say what you like about creativity. But this,' he picked up a sachet of crystals, stashed in a half-open tin, 'tells me everything I need to know. She's making her stuff from scratch. Get a whiff of that in your tea and you're done for. End of story. I should—'

'You should go. I'll say it one more time. It's her space, not yours. She told me she knows what she's doing and I trust her.'

'It's just not safe. I'll need a pair of rubber gloves, long ones. Couple of sponges, or make that three. And do you happen to have such a thing as an old toothbrush?'

When Ruthie came home to find a darkroom she no longer recognised, she asked had Beatrice had the cleaners in, or why was it so
bloody pristine, all of a sudden, and she'd never seen it so shiny, was
that a new coat of paint?

'He insisted,' Beatrice told her. 'What could I do?'

Down on his knees, with his jacket on a chair and his sleeves
rolled up, he'd put the trays in the bath and scrubbed them. When
they were dry, he tackled the walls and the skirting boards, once with
a sponge, then again with the toothbrush. Mopping the floor and
mopping it again, he became apoplectic when he noticed the bucket
on top of the boiler, catching drips from the leak in the ceiling, and
when Beatrice answered, no, there was no actual extractor, as such,
but you could get a hell of a draught by opening and closing the door
every now and again, he was speechless, and she left him to it.

Coming up, two hours later, she saw him before he saw her.

'How the bloody hell does she do the drying-off?' he said to himself, looking at each of the walls, then the ceiling, then the walls
again. 'Oh,' he said, then he smiled. 'Of course.'

He reached forward to pull open one of the apple-tray drawers, brought by Peter from Pennerton. He took out a print, then he
pushed his glasses onto his forehead. Staring at it, he became completely still.

Beatrice said nothing. Eventually, when he continued to stare at
the picture, she coughed, and said, 'Time to go, I think.'

Max didn't look at her. He put the print back in the drawer. When
he went to open another, Beatrice banged it shut.

'You said you wanted to clean the place up, not rifle through her
work. How would you react, if she did the same to you?'

'Alright,' Max said, 'alright,' then he swore and sucked his finger.

In the kitchen, Beatrice removed the splinter.

'Christ!' he said, flinching. 'She's sixteen years old. She should know better. I've put in a call to Silverprint. They're sending through a stack of long gloves, and a proper pair of goggles, and they'll do a repeat order for the chemistry. It's not always a bad thing, being conventional. Half of being an artist is very, very boring. It's about process, and technique. Order in the studio and order in the darkroom means order in your prints. If she doesn't take herself seriously, no one else is going to. Photography isn't some haphazard easy-going affair. It's precise. It's difficult. Respect your work, respect your workplace, and people will respect what you produce. The sooner she gets that into her head, the better. I saw the prints in the drying racks. She's got something quite extraordinary. Has done from the off. I'd never seen anything like it, the stuff she produced when I gave her that tiny camera. What was she then, nine, ten? But that's only part of it. Being creative doesn't have to mean being slapdash, and it doesn't have to involve breaking every single rule imaginable. You'll do more for her by helping her to understand that than by letting her do what she wants.'

'Have you quite finished?'

'If I've made myself understood, then yes. Don't worry. I'll see myself out.'

At the end of September, Beatrice and Ruthie collected Vinny from Göttingen and took her to Cambridge.

Over supper that evening, when it was just the two of them and Ruthie made no mention of Vinny's absence, Beatrice announced she had a plan: instead of a crammer and O levels, how about a diploma in photography, at a college of art and design run by a man Beatrice knew from her club?

The course director had to talk to Beatrice more than once about Ruthie's habit of changing subjects halfway through, but by the summer of 1981, Ruthie surprised even herself by having half completed enough of them to qualify for a place in the final show. The invitation to exhibit, she explained to Beatrice, meant there was only this last hurdle between her and her diploma.

Vinny sent a congratulations card. She hoped Ruthie wouldn't think it premature, but she assumed the show was a formality. She and Jules would have loved to be there, but it was crunch time for both of them with work. They'd think of her, and wanted to hear all about it, and she must keep a copy of the programme.

Beatrice didn't ask what she'd chosen to exhibit, nor did she disturb her when, night after night, she stayed in the darkroom. If they met in the corridor, Beatrice looked at her in a way that told Ruthie she could smell the chemistry on her, and was trying hard not to say.

She asked her aunt up only once. She was calling the series *All of Me*, she said, and had already picked four of the five. Now, though, she was tired and couldn't see for looking. Max had agreed to come first thing in the morning, so she'd have time to incorporate his suggestions and do reprints if he thought them necessary, but she needed Beatrice to help her decide which should be the last one.

'I think he'll like them,' she said to Beatrice. 'I'm almost sure he will.'

Laid out on the drop-down door were seven prints.

Ruthie pulled on her cigarette. Letting it hang from her lips, she rolled one for her aunt. 'Bea?' Beatrice was staring at the prints, though, and didn't take it. 'Alright then, don't. Here.' She reached over and tucked it behind her aunt's ear. 'Keep it for later. These four are definites, so two of these three have to go. Bea? Are you alright?'

Beatrice had pushed her glasses up. She asked Ruthie to take her Walkman off, at least, if she wanted to have a proper conversation. When she spoke again her voice was hushed.

'When did you take them?'

'I can't remember. It was a Pennerton holiday. One of the long ones, I s'pose.'

'Did he tell you to do it?'

'Not exactly. Maybe, or, wait – I can't remember. Don't you like them?'

'I just think they're a bit –'

'A bit what?'

'Let me put it this way. *I* know they're Max's things. And *you* do. But –'

'But what?'

'Well, other people might find them a bit, I don't know, mundane, maybe.'

'Bea! I didn't ask you for your opinion on the concept! I just need to work out which to jettison! Honestly. I'm trying to say something about a person, that's all. Dad said –'

'Dad said what?'

'It doesn't really matter what you choose to shoot. It's arbitrary. You don't have to be interesting all the time, he said. Just make it real. There was this thing he always went on about, this parrot. He said you could have a – How did it go? You could have a shot of a parrot flying through a house for absolutely no reason, without trying to make a statement, and it could end up mattering more than any other photo you take for the whole of the rest of your life. Or a knife, on a kitchen table. You could just have a knife on a tabletop, with nothing else in the shot, and for one person it'd be one thing and for another person it'd be another thing altogether and a knife is never just a knife and – Oh, Bea. Don't turn critic. Just help me.'

They did away with Max's shirts at the off.

'Maybe if the collars were frayed, even,' Beatrice said. 'But this is just a row of shirts in a wardrobe. Perfectly ironed, perfectly boring shirts.'

Beatrice lit the cigarette Ruthie had given her, then she looked at the next photo.

'Oh, I see. It's this way up.'

The inside of a cabinet drawer had been shot from above; a coiled leather belt sat beside an open box with a pair of gold cufflinks, lolling apart on a velvet base. There was a tiny torch as well, and last of all, at the very back of the drawer, a stack of bright silk handkerchiefs, piled alternately as squares or diagonals so as to show a part of each.

'That's more like it. Look,' Beatrice said, flicking her ash in the bucket, 'you can even see the monogram! It's jolly good, Roo.'

They chose his walking jacket in the end. Slung on the back of the kitchen door, it hung above his wellingtons. Ruthie had caught the light so as to suggest the figure of a man inside the jacket, both legs plumb in his boots.

'Oh, how spooky!' Beatrice said. 'That's ever so clever. Bit odd, but ever so clever.'

'Thanks. Make some tea, will you? I've got to get more tobacco, and there's tons to do before Dad gets here. I'll have to redo the contrasts in almost all of them. I want him to like them. I really, really want him to like them.'

Later, at the kitchen table, Ruthie told her aunt she didn't want her to come.

'Of course I'm coming!'

'It'll be up for days, you can see it any time.'

'But why not tomorrow night?'

'I just don't want you there for the opening. I'm nervous, OK? I told Dad he couldn't come either but he's not free anyway.'

'Where's he off to?'

'Dorset. He's leaving straight after he's seen me. Elisabeth Frink in her studio. Some new thing she's doing. It's a *Vogue* shoot and they set it up ages ago blah blah blah. It's fine. It's all fine, and I'll be fine on my own, but if you two are there I'll go to pieces. The whole thing's scored out of a hundred and there are these people walking around having these judging conversations and giving some kind of commentary and I –'

'Remember Chardin!'

'What?'

'You know, the talk we went to last week! Don't you remember?'

'No.'

'Do you ever listen to a word those people say? You needn't keep coming if you don't want to. Anyhow, that's what Rebecca West told us. Whenever she reads some daft review in the paper, you know, saying this is good and this is bad and – Critics, Roo. I'm talking about critics. Well, if you'd taken any notice, you'd remember that the great Chardin, who was made president of the Beaux Arts and had to give a speech, and to everyone's astonishment –'

'Bea! I can't believe you're giving me a bloody lecture! Now!'

'I'm not, lovey! I'm just telling you. He said there's far too much criticism going on, and people shouldn't give painters a hard time, because it's – What did he say? It's a marvellous feat to paint even a bad painting! So take no notice of anyone, whoever they say they are! That seemed to be the gist of it. For goodness' sake. If you really won't let me come, there's a dinner at the club I can go to. What about a temporary dye, though? Just for tomorrow? We could pop down to Bruton Place in a cab right now, I'm sure José would do something ever so quick, make you look a bit more normal.'

Ruthie had changed her hair again. Cut close to her head and an all-over blonde that was whiter than before, it was short enough for Beatrice to have told her she looked like a boy, and would have to put on some weight and wear something other than skintight jeans for anyone to know she wasn't.

When Ruthie refused her offer, Beatrice asked, 'Who are you trying to be now – is it someone I should recognise?'

'Just myself,' Ruthie said. 'I was going to be Siouxsie Sioux but then I cut the rest off and whited it out anyway, so it's no one, just me. This is who I am, now.'

In the morning, not long after Max arrived, there was an argument.

Ruthie wouldn't tell her aunt what he'd said, and he left before Beatrice could ask him. She offered Ruthie a hand with taking the prints over to college, but she said she was fine on her own.

'So? How did it go?' Beatrice asked that night.

She'd come in from her dinner and found Ruthie at the kitchen table. 'I want to know absolutely everything! Oh, love. You do look down. Was it awful? Were you terribly nervous?' And, when Ruthie stared at the wall without so much as acknowledging her, 'You knew you would be, so you mustn't be too disappointed if it wasn't what you wanted. These things never are, and it was the first one you've ever done, so – Didn't you change, lovey? You're wearing the same clothes you were in when I left. Mightn't that have helped, smartening yourself up a bit, and taking out some of your earrings? Roo? Are you alright?'

Ruthie left the room. Halfway up the stairs she sat down and Beatrice sat beside her. When she said she'd missed the show altogether, and please could she go to sleep now, she was very, very tired, Beatrice took her up and helped her into bed. Then she sat in Ruthie's armchair, looking out at the trees on the Heath.

16 TUESDAY INTO WEDNESDAY

Ruthie stands in the darkroom, thinking of her sister and how she will miss her. She half considers going down to wake her, despite the time.

Instead, she turns again to her picture of Annie. She sets the timer for another test strip, meaning to start with eight stops this time, and take it up to twelve. After that, she thinks, she'll play around with the filters.

She's an hour in when she hears it.

The click of a lighter, right behind her.

There's no flare, though, so at first she thinks she's imagined it.

But then there's her voice.

'Ciggy?'

Ruthie doesn't move.

'Why're you up so late, Roo?'

She wants to answer but she can't. There's a long exhalation and, 'Come on, let's have a smoke and you can tell me all about it.'

Only then does Ruthie turn to look into the shadows, trying to make her out. When she can't see anyone, she speaks, hoping to provoke some movement.

'Not one of yours, Bea. You know I hate those things. Anyway, I'm busy, can't you see?'

'Why not let me do you one? You carry on and I'll roll you one of yours.' Ruthie takes the tobacco from her skirt pocket, and afterwards the papers. She holds them out, in the direction of the voice. 'Come on, Roo, tell me. Why so late, hey? Why not get a bit of sleep, have another go tomorrow? Early start, early finish, and you can put your feet up and relax. Hmm, lovey?'

She's handing Ruthie the cigarette then, or, rather, Ruthie's holding one of Beatrice's finest: poorly rolled and overfilled so it sags in the middle where there's a gap in the tobacco. Tendrils spill from both ends, catching on Ruthie's lip so she takes the cigarette and twists off the strands in the darkness, hoping Beatrice won't see and be offended, which of course she does, and is, immediately.

'Well, if you will turn your nose up at a proper one, what d'you expect? Here, at least let me light it for you.'

There's another click. This time there's a tiny flare, and Beatrice is holding up the lighter and saying, 'Whatever you do, don't tell Max we've been smoking in his darkroom.' She can see her aunt's face then, just the bottom half, lit up and smiling. In the split second before the flame dies, she comes into focus and Ruthie sees her lips, a blood-red stripe, and her teeth, glowing as she smiles. 'Really, Roo, don't. He'll have our guts for garters!'

'Auntie Bea, it's my darkroom now,' Ruthie says, but the flame dies and the face disappears. She tries to inhale in sync with Beatrice, but on their exhales, her aunt carries on for much longer. Ruthie's confused and thinks again she's imagining it, but then Beatrice asks a question.

'By the way, what're you using as an ashtray?'

'Really, it doesn't matter. Max isn't here any more. Use the floor if you like,' and, when Beatrice doesn't reply, 'Oh, alright then. I'll get you something. Hang on.'

Ruthie takes the tongs and moves the print along. When it's safely in the fix, she turns on the main light and is surprised to find herself alone. There's a little pile of ash on the floor where Beatrice was standing, though.

She shivers, shrugging her shoulders and going back to her work. When the print is washed and hanging, she looks and sees Beatrice's lighter has left its mark. There is a faint glow around Annie's head, where the flame was picked up by the chemicals. But she can't be sure, and for the rest of the night she works quietly, listening for a cough or the shuffle of feet, or the rustle of a toffee being opened.

At last, when she hears what she thinks might be a sigh, she sacrifices the print in its tray and switches on the light.

'Bea? Auntie Bea? I'll stop in a minute, I promise. I just have to redo this one, then I'll stop. I'm nearly there, honestly. Then we'll have a cup of tea and put our feet up, like you said, you and me together.'

There's no answer, so she switches off the light and goes on with her work.

In the photograph, Annie's hair is cropped so short, she looks like a boy. She is standing on Max's work surface next to the feather-clock, with her back against the wall, and her arms held out.

When the final version is hanging up to dry, Ruthie goes to her mattress and tries to sleep.

At five in the morning the films begin again.

She watches them for an hour, then she drifts off, making them stop by thinking of Annie: hoping she'll come again the next day; hoping at the same time that she won't.

At 6.30 a.m., a cockerel crows.

The noise wakes Ruthie, who has been listening at some unconscious level for Vinny's car starting, which, after the cockcrow and a wood pigeon and the water in the cove, is exactly what she hears.

'Damn.'

She's running then, or flying.

Up from her mattress, the stairs to the first floor in three leaps, back up them in four to pull on her dress then down again, steadying herself on the landing but only for a second – 'They'll wait! They will, they'll wait for you!' – spinning through the kitchen out past the fountain and round to the yard, but the car's moving off through the grove and she runs properly and waves at the rear window – 'Vinny! Wait! I wanted to say goodbye! I wanted to say –' but there is the number plate and the exhaust, and a cloud of red dust. Then she runs harder and shouts, 'Vinny! Please!' but the dust is rising and the track is empty then, 'Christ, Vee, you could've –' and still she's running and her right foot catches on a stone and she's arching in the air and twisting her torso to stop herself falling but she's on the ground, moving, scraping, bumping to a halt.

Her hand is twisted under her ribcage. Her leg is pulled up and under her, somehow, but she doesn't feel anything so she's standing and tries to run again, but she can't, so she walks instead. Her right wrist hangs limp and her right arm is numb, and so are parts of her right leg.

The road when she reaches it is empty. She kneels on the verge and holds herself, rocking back and forth and licking blood from her knuckles – 'They can't have seen me. They would have stopped.'

When she walks back to the villa she's crying – 'It's only a day. Or a day and a half. It's only a day and a half.'

In her childhood once, when Ruthie swam into the cove, and ran through the grove, Eleni took a splinter from the softest part of her foot. She brought a pair of tweezers and pierced the skin, in between the heel and the ball. She said she was digging for a pine needle, or a chip of bark, but they'd found a piece of a shell instead, scalloped and pretty. Then Sophie bathed the gouged-out hollow with salt water and blew on it until it dried, so that Ruthie's foot was tickled and she was laughing instead of crying. Sophie tickled Ruthie's feet properly, and Vinny and Eleni joined in and tickled her under the arms, and Ruthie was laughing and gasping for air. Then Max called down from his lightroom, 'Quiet, please, quiet, whoever it is with all that noise. I'm working!'

Eleni fetched some iodine, and Ruthie liked her orange skin and didn't mind the stinging.

This morning in the courtyard, Ruthie stands in the fountain and lets the water wash the blood from her knees, and from the front of her calf and her knuckles and her arm. Sitting on the edge, she picks pieces of grit from her elbow. When she's eased out slivers of stone from the thin skin of her kneecap, her elbow starts to sting and she sees that a wasp has settled in the bright red blood. She watches it, then she realises she isn't aware of the stinging any more, though it continues with its probing until she brushes it away.

It's still too early to swim, and in any case, she wants to wait for the bleeding to stop. In the darkroom, she unclips the picture of Annie from the drying line and looks at it, looks away, looks at it again for longer the second time.

'There isn't a single photographer who can judge their own work,' he told her. 'If you haven't got anyone to do it for you, look away, and look back. Pretend you've never seen it before. Pretend someone else took it. And don't ever allow yourself to like it. That's not what you're doing it for. If you like it, that means there's something wrong. That's when you know it's time to discard.'

Ruthie hears his voice so clearly she glances for him. There's no one, though, so she takes a pair of scissors and cuts the print into pieces, then she puts the pieces in a pile by the door.

The previous night it had seemed complete. She'd made it and remade it and was satisfied. The composition is what she'd intended: a child stands on the work surface next to the feather-clock with her back against the wall. Her head is tilted slightly to one side, but her gaze is centre-on, and her arms are held out with her hands palms-front. The scratches on her chest and the inside of her arms are clearly visible as dark lines against her body.

This morning, these little stripes scraped into the skin are too faint. Looking a third time she sees a white dot, the size of a pinprick, just to the left of Annie's head. Wondering how she could possibly have missed it, she sees as well that she's misjudged the pooling of the darks and the sharpness of the brights. The balance of the piece is out of kilter: there's no life, no movement, nothing elegant in the exchange between light and dark, only a blocky ugly hard-edged absolute wrongness.

She will start again with a higher grade of paper; something softer, with fibres that are fatter and will hold the light differently. This will mean working harder for her image, coaxing it out with tricks, and feints and pleadings. First, though, she patches the pinprick.

Reading the negative more closely, and seeing how flat it is, she decides to use a stronger filter. She'll need to go back to the beginning and do another test strip, or several. She'll flick her hand over the too-dark patches where the scratches should be better defined. Then, when the image is out of the fixer, she'll wash it for longer.

'Why bother,' Max said to her once at Pilgrim's Lane, studying her prints, 'if that's the best you can do?'

He'd agreed to come straight off. She was excited, she'd told him on the phone. She had her final show and wanted him to see her submissions, before anyone. 'Only if you'll be in London for something else anyway, Dad. If you are, would you come? Would you really? It won't take long, I promise.' There would be time then, she said, to do whatever he recommended. She'd still have a day and a night.

He studied them, one by one, then he dropped them on the floor.

'When you start to exhibit, everything stands or falls on a single image. You're only as good as your last photograph. There's a contract, Roo, between you and your work. When you've committed to a show, it's binding. Look at it this way. It's too late to back out now. If you do what I've told you –' he kicked her prints, lightly, so they moved across the floor – 'the first two are just about retrievable.'

Buttoning his coat, he moved towards the door.

'Got to go, Ruthie-Roo.' He looked at his watch. 'You've passed the point of no return. There's still time, if you get to work now. Remember. At this stage of your career, everything stands or falls.'

When he'd gone, she cut the prints up, then she skipped her final show altogether.

He was right of course. She'd seen what he meant instantly, though before he'd arrived they'd seemed different. Brighter, and sharper. Individually and as a series they made sense to her, each of them telling a story. Later, standing close enough to smell his skin, she heard him explain why every single one was expendable.

'You're wasting your time,' he said at the last, turning just for a second, so their eyes met. 'And mine, Ruthie-Roo. And mine. You've stolen my time and given me nothing back. Don't ask me here again, will you? Not until you're ready.'

'Ready how?'

'Think about it.' He switched off the light and left the room.

'But what do you mean?' she said, going after him. 'Ready for what?'

'I mean –' he turned, his hand already on the banister – 'don't ask me back until you're happy with your work.'

'I'll never be.'

'Not happy, then. Forget happy. When you're ready for your work to be judged. Don't ask me again until you're ready to be judged.'

This morning at the villa she moves quickly. As she lowers the new paper into the first tray, she thinks of a way. Before the image has even appeared, she takes it out, turning to expose another. This time it won't lie flat so she lifts it and bends it, running her fingers along one side then the other, teasing and smoothing. Checking for the sheen she hesitates; it's harder to detect on the grade she's gone for. Still it won't lie flat, so she cuts tiny pieces of tape and secures it to the enlarger's base before she flicks the switch and counts with the timer: 'One, Mississippi, two.'

Pressing it into the developer, she feels the weight of the liquid. Miscalculating the resistance, she presses harder and lifts the tray, but she moves too fast and it drops and flips back and the fluid is everywhere.

Her heart runs and jumps: a snare drum played by a soldier on parade but louder and harder, and everything becomes white and she can't hear, can't feel, can't find her hands any more.

When she can see again, it's too late.

The girl in the tray is a dark mass of black.

She rinses the print and dries it, then she cuts it into pieces and puts them in the pile with the others.

She takes them all from the floor and carries them to the courtyard, and puts them on the Olive-Tree Bench.

She finds matches in the kitchen and a tin can in the shed, then she goes back to the courtyard. She unscrews the can and pours the contents on. She strikes the match, and the pieces burn faster than she expects.

When she comes back out of the house, someone has cleared up the ashes, and put the can and the matches away. An hour has passed, she thinks.

The white kitten sits on the path to the chapel.

'Hello again.' She stoops to touch it. 'Can't cuddle you today, I'm covered in scratches already. Scoot!'

It looks up at her and she shakes her head, half smiling. She steps around it and over it, until it turns and walks just in front, brushing against her legs.

The next time the kitten rolls in the red earth, she takes her chance and backtracks, making for the road. The breeze from the sea has come in early: it's only 9 a.m. and she feels it push against her, like someone trying to make her do something she doesn't want to. Wishing the noise would stop, she ducks under a branch. When she looks up, its leaves are silver-green feathers, pointing at the sky. Though the noise of the breeze is louder than before, they are completely still. She raises her hand to her face, feeling for some movement in the air.

Nothing.

The noise continues as she walks on towards the road, and still nothing moves: the grasses everywhere are flat on the ground and the tiny olives hang limp in the trees.

There is a laugh she recognises, carried on the breeze. She stops to listen but it fades. When it comes again she knows it is Beatrice but she knows it can't be. Then she thinks it's Vinny come back, but she doesn't hear the laugh again and there is only the meltémi, and nothing moves.

At the point where the path rises to the road, she turns to face the sea. On the headland opposite, a white haze is a stripe above the water. It spreads up the headland. When she looks down to the water it disappears. Then she turns to the path and there is Max, walking so fast he's almost jogging.

He's younger than he was the day before. His stick is gone and his hair is sandy and thick. He's broad and strong, and not at all stooped. Because he doesn't seem to have noticed her yet, she steps behind a tree. He turns and calls out, over his shoulder. She can't hear what he's saying, though, and her heart has separated from her body and is beating too fast. She can't feel her hands or her feet, and she is thinking about how it is as though they're not there any more, when she hears another voice coming from behind Max, a voice she recognises.

Max continues walking, then she sees there is a child following him, a girl of maybe eight or nine years old. The girl is stumbling to keep up, and when she comes closer, Ruthie sees it is herself.

She watches the child walk past, a foot or so away. Stepping from behind the tree, she wants to ask her to stop, and to speak with her, but Max is saying, 'Hurry up, Roo,' and the child is running.

The breeze is louder than before. Ruthie follows, but the path is empty.

She crosses the whole of the grove, and doesn't find them.

For Ruthie, having come back to the grove after such a long time away, Max is everywhere: in every branch of every tree and every tiny stone in the cove. His appearance on the steps the previous day, after she'd said goodbye to Annie, had been somehow expected, as though it had already happened before it happened.

The other sightings, though, when she had seen herself with him, were stranger.

She has reached the stone houses when she hears the laugh again, carried on the breeze. She crouches on the ground to listen harder, her eyes shut tight: sometimes she hears Beatrice, sometimes Vinny, and sometimes there are voices she knows but doesn't recognise.

When she opens her eyes, there are people appearing, or parts of them: a leg, first, emerging from between two branches, only to be hidden by the trunk of a tree. Then an arm and a torso and the legs again, walking faster than before, and coming straight towards her.

A moment later, she understands: it is the family coming home from town. As their bodies re-form, Ruthie slips behind the nearest tree; unable to think of an explanation, she is too embarrassed to reveal herself.

The mother and father go in. Annie and Edward sit on the terrace, not talking. Then Edward walks down the steps and round to the side of the house. He picks up the hose and turns on the water. Placing a thumb half over the end he sprays a jet into the air. Annie leaves the terrace and watches Edward hold the hose, low above the ground. He sprays the water horizontally. She jumps over the jet of water, then back again, and Ruthie understands it's a game they've played before.

Annie takes a turn with the hose. They're laughing, and she sprays the jet higher above the ground. Edward jumps over it and back again. He's fooling around and making shapes with his body and pulling faces. When Annie sees the kitten come towards her, she drops the hose, which hits the ground and rises. Edward catches it and sprays a jet into the sky. Annie picks up the kitten and holds it to her chest. She dances with it, a waltz then a two-step dance, swinging her hips and skipping.

Edward doesn't look. Instead, he plays with the water.

When Annie is called in, Edward takes the hose in one hand and lifts the kitten with the other. He holds the kitten against himself with that arm, grasping its forelegs so it can't move. Then he brings his thumb up and sticks it in the kitten's mouth. The kitten is biting him, but he forces its mouth open just enough to bring up the hose with his other hand and shove it in. The kitten struggles. Edward uses both hands to clamp the animal's mouth shut around the hose. He's pulling his own head back, and he stares at the little almond-yellow eyes which are bulging, and the little white legs which are scrabbling, and the little white stomach which is distending rapidly as the hose pipe pumps it full.

Edward smiles. The kitten's legs are still scrabbling and its stomach is distending further. Then the legs aren't moving any more, because they are splayed out stiff. There is a skein of faeces from the kitten's backside, and Edward stands with the new creature he's made: part kitten, part balloon, this grotesque inversion hangs from his hands which are locked to its head, so as to force its mouth more tightly shut around the hose.

Finally, the kitten's stomach is full and the pressure of the water is too much, and Annie is running from the terrace, screaming Edward's name. She lunges at his legs, and because he is taken by surprise, knocks him sideways. The kitten hits the ground and actually bounces in the air. It hits the ground again and it is clawing itself forward, and shuddering and mewling. There is water everywhere, and Annie is scratching Edward's face and screaming. Edward is lying back, playing with his sister's head like a lion with a cub, but then he has her underneath him and is punching her arm slowly: once, and a second and a third time, and he is saying does it hurt, does it hurt, Annie?

Annie stops scratching.

The kitten is hunched over, spewing out lumps of something on the ground, then Edward and Annie are rolling in the red earth again.

Ruthie, watching, isn't able to move.

She tries to but she can't feel her hands and her feet, nor can she work out where they are in relation to her body.

Then Annie screams again, and the mother runs from the house. Annie is on top of Edward.

She is scratching at his face and screaming, then the mother is pulling Annie away and Edward is still smiling but then his mother says something to him and instead he is shouting.

'She did it!'

'I did not!' and Annie hurls herself at him again, but her mother pulls her back and slaps her.

The kitten is beside them on the red earth. It is lying down and is entirely still.

The father comes out of the house and the mother says, 'It was both of them,' and Edward says, 'It was not, it was her. I stopped her.'

The kitten twitches. Annie sits beside it. 'You are moving. You are moving.'

The kitten twitches again and Annie is crying and lifting the kitten into her arms and it is sick on her chest. It is juddering in her arms and its eyes are wide open but they are rolled right back in their sockets and the mother says, 'Put it down, Annie. Put it down and go inside.'

The father grabs Edward's arm. He takes him away from the house and they stand under the fig tree and he slaps Edward, square on the face.

Edward kneels on the ground with his head in his hands, and the father kneels beside him. He strokes his son's head and Edward shrugs him off.

Annie and her mother are with the kitten. It gets up, unsteadily, then it is sick. It shakes itself and walks away, and its gait is awkward: in between each step it jumps slightly and staggers, falling and righting itself, falling and righting. Then it stops and is sick again, and there is a steady fast rhythm to its puking.

In a minute, though, it puts its tail in the air and trots rather than walks.

Annie folds her arms and stamps her feet. The mother tells her to turn off the hose, then they are together by the terrace steps, and

Ruthie hears the mother say, 'Alright. I believe you. We'll wait and see what your father thinks.'

The father and Edward come back from the fig tree.

The four of them go inside the house.

Ruthie waits. Ten minutes, fifteen, then they all come out.

The car moves away through the grove. When she's sure they're not coming back, she steps from the tree and goes onto the terrace.

Annie's book is folded on the table, a pencil holding her place. Ruthie opens it and sees the same crossword. After the '*r*' that was there in the first box for *4 Across: Broken; dirty; after a loss of fortune (6 letters)*, she sees the '*u*' she'd added the previous day. Annie has drawn a circle around the '*u*' and written a line of question marks at the side of the puzzle, ten or more in a bold hard hand, so the page is scored and dented. Beneath the question marks, and in an altogether fainter script, there are the names 'Edward?' and 'Mum?' with another two question marks.

Ruthie takes the pencil and adds an 'i' in the third box, after the 'u'. She crosses out the 'Edward?' and the 'Mum?' and she writes her own name, with a note.

It was me, Annie. I saw what happened with the kitten. Come to the courtyard. I'll wait for you.

In the courtyard, a chair has been turned over. The tea lights are blown from under the Pergola and are scattered on the ground. The swallows, high above the villa, are thrown about like scraps of leather, each tied to a string. Flung and pulled back, they look more like bats than birds, as though day is made night.

At half past five in the afternoon, the wind drops and Annie appears at the gate. Ruthie goes to unfasten it, but Annie is small enough to slip through the bars, and suddenly she's there in the courtyard. Her face is clear of any expression, her eyes like slate. She is pale, and the light shines through her ears and the stubs of her hair. For a moment, Ruthie thinks she is imagining her. When they sit together on the fountain's edge, Ruthie sees that she is trembling.

'Do they know you're here?'

'No.' Then she cries, and Ruthie reaches out her hand.

Afterwards, Annie tells her that Edward and her father have gone to the old town again. Her mother has a headache and is resting in the house.

Because of what happened, she tells Ruthie, and here she begins to cry again, her father and her brother will go to the circus at Stoupa without her.

'But why?'

'Because Edward said I tried to hurt the kitten.'

'And they believed him?'

'Mum said she knows it wasn't me, but Dad's angry and he always believes Edward.' She sniffed.

'Do you want to blow your nose?'

'I don't have anything.'

'Here, use this.' Ruthie holds up the hem of her skirt.

'No, I can't.'

'Come on, it's fine. It'll be washed anyway.'

So Annie does, then she wipes her eyes as well. She sighs, one long sigh, then she rests her head on Ruthie's arm.

'When are they going to the circus?'

'Tomorrow.'

'Well, I've been to that circus and it's not so good.' Annie doesn't say anything. 'Really, Annie, it's not very good.'

'But it was Edward who did it, not me. It isn't fair. I want to go.'

'Of course you do. I'm just saying, it's not up to much anyway. Are they all going?'

'No. Dad and Edward are going, and Mum and me are staying here.'

'Mum and I,' Ruthie says.

'OK. Mum and I. Mum and I are staying here.'

'Well, that's not so bad then, is it?' She ruffles Annie's stubbly head. 'Is it better now?'

'What?'

'The cut.' She parts the hair on Annie's scalp and sees it, a little mess of a scar that's healed already and is only a dent in the scalp, as though someone has pressed something down on it for too long.

'How do you know about my cut?'

'Never mind. I just know.' She kisses the top of Annie's head. 'Were you upset about having your hair cut off?'

Annie doesn't answer.

'You'll get used to it. I like mine short. Dries quicker, after swimming, and you don't need to brush it.' Annie stares at Ruthie's hair, then Ruthie says, 'I think I've got a picture of the circus. There must be one upstairs somewhere. Shall we go and look for it?'

'Dunno.'

'What would you rather do? How long's your mum having her rest for?'

'I'm allowed to play for one hour. Mum said I can run around in the grove and play and she won't tell Dad. She'll say I was in my room. But I need to wake her up when it says half past six on the kitchen clock. She said I shouldn't go far from the house, and I should keep checking the time. She won't know, will she? When she has a headache, she takes a tablet and it makes her sleepy – Ruthie?'

'Yes?'

'Can we go swimming?'

'What about your mum?'

'I told you, she's taken a tablet.'

'Alright. Run and put your costume on, and I'll find some towels. If you're only allowed an hour we'd better get on.'

When Annie comes back, she makes for the path to the second cove, but Ruthie says, 'My beach not yours, don't you think?'

On the way to the cove the kitten is lying on a step, like a white glove forgotten from a party.

'Is it alright now?' Annie says. She touches it and it gazes up, then it licks its paws and closes its eyes.

'Looks it, doesn't it? Hello, little one.' The kitten jumps up. 'There's no point following us, you won't like the water.' It weaves between their legs and against them.

'That's not its name,' Annie says.

'What's not?'

'Little one. You just called it "little one".'

'What's its name then?'

'I don't know, but you wouldn't call a kitten "little one". Are you sure it's alright?' She is touching its ears and letting it lick her hand.

Ruthie crouches, lifting the white kitten into her arms and draping it on her shoulder.

'Let's make sure, shall we? Let's take it with us.'

'What happened to your elbow? And your knee?'

'I fell over.'

'How?'

'I tripped. I was running and I tripped.'

'Does it hurt?'

'No, not really. Actually, not at all.'

At the cove, Ruthie unbuttons her dress, and the kitten slinks away. Annie turns to follow, but it cuts back and runs up the steps.

'It's fine, Annie. Look at it, it wouldn't be running if it wasn't. Anyway, I thought you said you wanted to swim.'

Annie turns. 'I'm coming!'

In the water, Annie says, 'Why don't you have a swimming costume?'

'I do.'

'So why aren't you wearing it?'

'It's nicer without. You can go faster, and you feel like a fish not a person. Do you mind?'

'No,' and she kicks and splutters and says wait for me, and they're moving across the cove.

They're in the water for almost an hour. Sometimes they swim side by side, and sometimes Annie clings to Ruthie's back and kicks her legs a little. Then they're both swimming, out to the edge of the cove and back. Ruthie swims breaststroke and Annie a kind of doggy-paddle, steady and slow. When she asks Ruthie to show her how to do what she calls 'proper swimming', Ruthie takes her back in again, closer to the shore.

Placing both hands under Annie's tummy, she holds her up so the child can move her arms when Ruthie tells her to, and roll her head to breathe, 'One, two, three, four, breathe! One, two, three,' and so on.

Then Annie's doing all of this at once, and kicking at the same time. She's almost doing it properly, and is about to try on her own, but then she turns her head to breathe and chokes on a lungful of water.

Ruthie holds her and takes her in.

They lie flat on their backs on the cove. Annie tells Ruthie she's tired, and maybe they should put their clothes on again, and can they go inside for a hot drink. But when she says, what's the time, and Ruthie tells it by the sun, Annie jumps up and rushes for the steps.

'No, no,' Ruthie says. 'I was guessing. You've got a little while. Slow down, and say goodbye properly.'

When Annie has pulled on her sundress, she says, 'Thank you for teaching me to swim front crawl.' Ruthie, buttoning her dress, says, 'Well, you've got a little way to go yet, don't try it on your own, will you?' and Annie says, 'Of course not.'

'Shall we have another go tomorrow?'

'Yes,' Annie says. 'When Dad and Edward go to the circus, and I have to stay behind. If Mum goes inside for a rest then I will.'

They sit on a rock, right beside the water.

'Do you think she will?'

'Will what?'

'Do you think your mum will go inside for her sleep?'

'Yes. When she gets a headache like this, it lasts days. The tablets make her tired and she's always resting.'

'Well, let's make a proper plan. What else shall we do?'

'What do you mean?'

'I mean what else do you want to do, as well as swim?'

'I don't know.'

'Think of something!'

'Like what?'

'Anything you like!'

'Can we see the photograph?'

'The circus photograph? Yes. I'll look for it tonight, then I'll –'

'No, not the circus one. The one of me. The photograph you took. Did you make it?'

'Yes, but it didn't work.'

'What do you mean?'

'I got it wrong and had to start again and it still came out wrong.'

'Can I see it anyway?'

'No. I'll try again. I promise. I'll try again tonight and I'll show you tomorrow. If it still doesn't work, then I'll show you the one of the circus.'

'OK. But mainly I want to see the one of me.'

'Come to the courtyard. Same time as today, half past five. If I'm not there, you'll find me down here.'

'What if I can't find you and I have to go straight back?'

'Then leave me a note.'

'OK!' Annie says, jumping down. 'I'll put it here, under this rock! Right at the back, so it's dry! Promise you'll leave one too, if you can't come?'

'Alright,' Ruthie says. 'I promise.'

'We'll bury them, so no one else can find them. Shall we? Shall we bury them?'

'Yes, Annie, if you like. We can bury them. They can be our secret notes, and we can bury them in a secret hiding place. Time to go now, though. Time to go home.'

In the courtyard they say goodbye. Annie is caught in the sun and glows in it. For a moment, she becomes transparent, then she slips between the iron bars and runs through the grove.

When the white of the child's sundress has stopped appearing and disappearing, Ruthie steps away from the gate.

After Ruthie's death, Vinny was confronted with the catalogue of injuries that were found on her body, and was disbelieving.

The first time was by lamplight in the chapel, with Eleni.

At the mortuary, her sister was pulled from a cabinet and Vinny was asked, formally, to identify her.

She heard a list read out at the inquest, when it was explained that while some of Ruthie's injuries were sustained over the two-day period leading up to her death, others, which were more severe, took place incrementally, and over the few hours that had passed immediately prior to her losing consciousness.

At Pilgrim's Lane, there was a day when the post was early and the coroner's report arrived unexpectedly. Seeing the descriptions of Ruthie's wounds set down in writing, Vinny was, once more, distressed, and said to Julian, 'She just wouldn't have done these things to herself. She was gentle. My sister was small, and kind, and gentle. So she couldn't have, do you see?'

17 AUNT BEATRICE

At the top of Parliament Hill, Beatrice and Ruthie watched a boy fly a kite.

'It's easy enough for you to do without even thinking, and it's a lovely gallery. You'll be out and about and you'll be with people. I know them and they're all perfectly nice. The pay's tiny, of course, but I'm hardly about to ask you for rent. You'll have to smarten up a bit, grow your hair out, you know. Not so many studs in your ears. Honestly, it'll take you out of yourself and into the world, and I've a feeling that's exactly what you need. And I'm sorry, lovey, but I'll have to tell Max what happened with your show. Vee doesn't want to fib, and you know she'll be talking to him.'

Vinny did her best to calm him, and then to persuade him to have Ruthie at the villa that summer.

'Just let her. What else is she going to do? Bea's taking off to Antibes with her new man, and you know how busy I am.'

'Fine, fine. Beats me why she wants to, though, if I'm apparently such a monster I can't give her a piece of professional advice without bringing on a wholesale breakdown.'

That summer there was an American girlfriend, whom Max had met at Cannes. Her name was Alice and, as Ruthie would report, she worked for the APA and wore 'an actual Alice band!' Ruthie offered Vinny 6–1 odds the woman would be gone in a fortnight: she was older than his usual, and slightly uglier. Beatrice was in for twenty pounds; did Vinny want to match it? In another letter she asked, please would Vinny reconsider and come, even for a week? *'The bastard's banned me from his darkroom, of course. Worse: I can hear him and Alice fucking all night long, whichever room I sleep in, so it's a bit grim, really.'*

Her hair grew to its former length and back to its natural colour. She put on some weight and started at Downey's, in a job she described to Vinny as requiring very little of her on reception, and not a lot more at soirées or salons or opening nights, in return for some small change and four weeks' annual holiday. When she asked could she take it all at once and spend August at her father's villa, she was told, 'Of course, Ruth. Your aunt Beatrice has already explained.'

Although Alice-from-Cannes would be ousted (the following year by Natalie-from-Zurich, then by others, who were each of them younger than their predecessor), Beatrice's romance continued, and she spent the late summers in Antibes. Vinny was either in Cambridge with Jules, working, or at the Buschboms' summer house in the Bavarian Alps.

Invariably, then, Ruthie flew to Greece on her own.

She knew that without the women who fell in love with her father, it would just have been the two of them with only Eleni for company. So she both objected to his girlfriends and didn't.

If she was woken in the morning by an argument, she minded

only a little. On the veranda, she'd wait until she saw Max on the path to the cove, then she'd go to his room and watch the girlfriend pack. Realising she was to have him to herself again, she'd mind even less.

'The problem with my girlfriends,' Max said once, after such a parting, 'is that none of them can swim properly.' He undid his shorts and left them by the fountain, pulling on his trunks. 'Come on, little lady.'

Ruthie fetched her bikini. At the cove, he sat on the pebbles and watched her swim across the bay. To make him laugh, she switched to the choppy little four-beat crawl she'd used when she was small, and he was teaching her.

If he joined her, she returned to her grown-up stroke and he matched it. Pausing at Meropi Island, they rested on the steps of the ruined chapel then they raced each other in. Turning back just short of the cove, they tracked the coast south with a slower, lazier crawl; pulling in at a strip of sand and talking for a while, swimming out, pulling in at another.

It was almost dusk when they embarked on the long swim home. She dropped her speed altogether, moving with a limpid stroke and hoping Max wouldn't notice. She wasn't really tired; she just didn't want the day to end. Almost as though he knew what she was doing, he said, 'Hop on, Roo, for old times' sake.' He flung back the words without breaking his stroke, so the water hung in drops above his mouth.

Climbing onto his back, she felt his body move and she clung to his shoulders. Not as tightly as she'd done when she was a child; more of a kind of balancing of her weight against his, so she was suspended just above him. She allowed herself to lower her body onto his, the length of it, and she kissed the top of his head and there was nothing strange to her in any of this: he was her father, and she loved him.

The June that Vinny phoned about her prize for her degree, Ruthie proposed they all meet at the villa for a 'Graduation Feast' on the cove. Vinny said no, so Max flew to London and gave a dinner for her at a Soho restaurant. He said he had to be in town anyway; an after-party was being thrown for the premiere of the new Bond film. The Prince of Wales and Princess Diana would be there, with Roger Moore, and he was shooting it for *Vogue*.

Ruthie telephoned her aunt. 'It's a bit OTT, don't you think, given how tight he is the rest of the time? Why won't Vinny and Jules go out there? Why?'

Still, things stayed the same and Vinny kept her distance. If she wasn't working she was travelling.

'Time's passing!' she told Ruthie. 'Jules says we've got to see India, before we're stuck at home, surrounded by kids.'

'They've got ages before that,' Ruthie grumbled, and Beatrice had to tell her not to. When Vinny and Jules tried, the babies didn't come, and because Vinny didn't talk about it, Ruthie didn't ask.

Once, Ruthie phoned Vinny and got Julian instead. They talked a little, then he tried to steer the conversation away from the villa and she said, 'What's with all this keeping Vinny to yourself?'

'Hang on!' Julian said. 'How about living your own life, instead of trying to butt in on your sister's? Actually, yeah. While I've got you, can I suggest you find a more interesting job, or even a boyfriend? I mean an actual job, and what about an actual boyfriend, not just one of your one-night stands?'

'Shut up.'

'Well, come on, Roo, why not?'

'Don't ever call me that,' Ruthie shouted, 'Don't you ever.'

He gave the phone to Vinny.

'Who does he think he is, calling me "Roo"?' she cut in. 'He's not even in our family!'

'I'm not having this conversation.'

'Why?'

'Because I'm your sister and I love you and I don't want to argue.'

Ilías walked up from town to help Julian carry the table. As Eleni brought the first dishes down, Vinny lit the candles.

There would be a celebration feast on the cove after all, in honour of Vinny's engagement.

In the kitchen, Ruthie put some music on, and just as Vinny came in and said, maybe something a bit more mellow, they heard Beatrice's taxi. She'd emailed to say she would come alone, her Antibes romance having faltered, and they went out to greet her.

If Max had told them his girlfriend was on the same flight, Ruthie might have held the door a moment longer. As it was, she closed it as soon as Beatrice was out, catching the ankle of the woman that came after, and delaying things while Eleni got a plaster.

When Ruthie saw the woman's face, she behaved as though there was nothing out of the ordinary. During dinner, though, she stood by the water's edge and beckoned Vinny over.

'Can you believe it!' she whispered. 'You realise she's from way back? Do you recognise her? It's Alice-from-Cannes! Look at her. She's so much older than I remember! Relatively speaking, I mean. It was ages ago now, but still. I reckon there's a chance she was born in the same decade as Dad! Do you think?'

Later, when they went up to the courtyard for dessert, and Alice said for the third time, no, really, her ankle was fine, nothing a stiff drink wouldn't fix, Ruthie whispered to Vinny again.

'It's coming back to me now. Properly, I mean.'

'And?'

'She was the only nice one. Do you remember, ages and ages ago?

I wrote and told you. There was that summer she was there first, and she was— She actually made an effort, I mean. She did stuff, you know?'

'No. I don't.'

'It's so idiotic but this one thing really stuck in my mind. If she went to the supermarket she always asked what I wanted to eat. I mean, it was that one simple thing! And she actually remembered. I'd open the fridge and there would be a pile of American ham. Or choc-olate biscuits, just because I'd asked for them. I never ate the stuff but she carried on, whatever I wanted, you know? Jesus, there was this one time she bought all this strawberry milkshake, which I absolutely loathed. Tons of it, so Eleni had to drink it, or bin it. And there was this other thing she did. This tiny, little thing, but it really –'

'She'll know we're talking about her if you keep staring. Hurry up, tell me!'

'Alright! It's just this. She let me sit in the front with Max when we drove anywhere, that's it. I know, I know, it's nothing. It sounds really stupid but I remember it so clearly. If the three of us went any-where, she sat in the back and let me sit up front. She was always watching Max in his rear-view, you know? I didn't mind them look-ing at each other. I was just glad she let me sit with him.'

Despite Ruthie's best efforts, she was drunk by the time Eleni brought coffee, and when Max made his speech, she cried.

Later, Julian found her in the kitchen. With his hands on his hips, he said, did she always have to make a scene, and who'd told her she could choose the music, and since when was Depeche Mode an appropriate choice for an engagement party?

He switched off the tape, and ran his fingers through his hair. In the silence, Ruthie stared him down.

'She could have told me you were engaged,' she said. 'Do you have any idea what that felt like, finding out from Max?'

'Christ! Don't be so bloody melodramatic.'

'It's alright, Jules.' Vinny was at the door. 'Go, we'll be fine.' She told Ruthie to stop crying, then she changed the tape, and they embraced.

In London a month later, Ruthie wrote a letter.

She apologised for having spoilt things. Did Vinny not realise how much she missed her, though? It was hard that night, Alice-from-Cannes showing up and draping herself all over Max. And it was even harder to look up halfway through his speech to see Vinny kiss Julian on the cheek, and to realise she was losing her for good.

On the final page she announced, almost as an afterthought, that she had some news of her own.

You must tell Julian, I've taken his advice. Not only have I found a new job, but I've got an actual boyfriend! Or at least I think I have. I mean I've definitely got a new job and I think I've almost definitely got a boyfriend, and not just a one-night stand.

The job's at this totally fantastic gallery in Camden, which is SO much cooler than Pimlico. I'm basically PA for the artist-owner, which is just a brilliant thing to be doing.

As for the boyfriend situation, I'll keep you posted!

It's him of course, the artist-owner whose name is yet to be revealed . . . Jury's still out on the honourableness of his intentions but I think I might have fallen in love for the first time ever (with my new boss, which isn't exactly ideal, but don't go on about it and nothing's definite anyway . . .).

You haven't written for ages. I wish you would. Or better than writing, come and see me and Bea at the weekend. I'll know by then, about the boyfriend side of things.

Ruthie Xxxxxxx
(Not Roo! It seems I'm finally becoming a grown-up.)

Vinny took her sister to the Paradise curry house on South End Road.

Was it true, she said, that Ruthie was in love? And when would she be able to meet him? Jules was coming the next day, so they could have a double date if Ruthie wanted.

Yes, Ruthie said, it was true. But when Vinny asked should she book somewhere for tomorrow evening, Ruthie shook her head.

'Why not?'

'There's a little obstacle to the whole dating thing. Will be for a while, I think.'

'Like what? He doesn't want to meet your sister? What?'

'Oh, nothing like that!'

'What, then?'

When Ruthie told her, Vinny put her hands to her face.

'She's not so much older than you, actually,' Ruthie said. 'She's called Jacqueline,' then she looked away. 'Oh for God's sake, don't cry. There's nothing to cry about.'

Nick had been married for five and a half years, Ruthie said. He was pretty sure he'd be finishing it sooner rather than later, at which point he would be Ruthie's, 'for the absolute taking'.

She put her hand on Vinny's arm. 'No one has a straightforward start in a relationship, and the people who tell you they do are lying.'

'Nonsense! Falling in love should be easy. It doesn't have to be complicated. And it doesn't have to hurt people.'

'Right. It just isn't easy so far, that's all. And it'll be a while before it is.'

'You've only known him a week. You can still just walk away now, instead of messing up your life. And hers, for goodness' sake!'

'Hers? What's Tacky-Jacky got to do with it? Look, Vee. You'll just have to meet him. He's lovely. You'll understand the instant you see him.'

'Please. I can see where this is headed and I don't want it to get there. You do love me, don't you? I'd like you to make me a promise.'

'OK, OK. Stop looking like you're about to cry again. Whatever I have to say, I'll say it. Yes, I love you, and yes, I promise.'

Vinny held Ruthie's hand and spoke slowly. Neither stopping nor pausing for long enough to be interrupted, she carried on for a half-hour.

Ruthie cried, but only a little, and afterwards she smiled. Vinny should be happy for her, she said. It would be complicated for a while, then it wouldn't be. If Vinny really wanted her to, she'd agree to her deal: if Nick was still with Jacqueline in six months' time, she'd draw a line and move on.

Later, replaying what Vinny had said, it was another voice Ruthie heard: the low, soft voice that Sophie had used when the two of them argued and were upset, and she'd say, 'How about "The Song to the Moon"?' and hold them while she sang it, and whatever had come between them would be forgotten.

For eighteen months, Nick would be Ruthie's boss. For almost as long, though with varying degrees of constancy on both sides, he was her lover. He'd no more leave his wife than Vinny would condone the situation. Nor was Vinny able to settle on a description of what he did, though most of her friends had heard of him. If they hadn't seen his work they'd read about it, and were aware that the 'R. Hollingbourne' he cited in all his credits was Vinny's little sister. For anyone else who asked, Vinny settled on a version that mentioned the Turner Prize and had Ruthie preparing his materials.

If one of his shows was covered in the press, Vinny said with an almost breezy confidence that yes, it was her little sister who'd arranged it all, and hired the caterers and the band, and yes, she'd done the publicity and the guest list as well. Whenever he had a sale, she'd show people the catalogue and say she was proud of Ruthie for preparing it: he'd never have asked her unless she really, really understood what he was trying to do in his work, and the job her sister had landed was a pretty big deal, really; or at least, it was a good enough place to start.

When it came to the nature of their relationship, though, she was sketchy.

'Oh no,' she claimed in the early days, 'of course it's nothing like that; he's married, with kids!'

Later, she'd aver it was only Ruthie he worked with on all of his projects, and yes, that had been the case since she'd been his assistant on *The Family of Woman*, which everyone had talked about when it transferred to MOMA: four human skeletons, two women and two girls, covered in gold leaf and seated at a dining table, eating a meal entirely fashioned from carved-up lumps of coal.

If Julian told her to be more circumspect in her answers, she'd say what was the point? – people in the know would draw their own conclusions, and anyone else could enquire of other sources.

In the months before Vinny's deadline, Ruthie would try to explain.

'He asks very little of me.'

'Roo! He asks for everything! And you give it to him!'

'Only when I want to. And he can't complain if I say no. We're not officially together, so he can't exactly break up with me, can he?'

'But you told me he loves you!'

'He does.'

'If a man loves my little sister he should shout it from the rooftops!'

'Well, he can't!'

'So find someone who can! If all it is is a torrid little love affair, what does he give you, really?'

'We fuck, that's what. We fuck whenever I want to and it's great. And if I want it from someone else, then he has to put up with it. Call it what you like. I don't care if you think it's torrid. We live outside a moral compass, Nick and me.'

'Nick and I. For God's sake, you're in his moral bloody compass, aren't you? Or at least you're in his wife's moral compass, that's for sure. Don't you mind having to share him? Don't you even mind a little bit?'

'Jacqueline is very definitely Nick's problem, not mine. And no, I'm fine with sharing. She's there to listen to all his boring problems. I just get him for the fun stuff.'

'But it's a game. It's make-believe.'

'What's wrong with make-believe? It happens to suit me.'

'And does it suit Jacqueline, do you think?'

'Look. However many times you ask me that question, my answer will stay the same. She's not my concern. I imagine they've reached some kind of agreement, don't you? I'm not stupid enough to think I'm the first of his assistants he's slept with. And if she hasn't worked it out yet, then she's too idiotic for words and doesn't deserve my sympathy. Or yours for that matter. So why not run back to good old Julian and your PhD, and forget about me and my make-believe?'

Vinny's deadline would arrive faster than either of them anticipated. And because of what happened in the meantime, when it did, Nick would be the last thing on their minds.

'You have to tell them something else.'

'She was their mother. They have a right –'

'Christ, I'm not questioning their rights as her daughters. I'm suggesting you exercise yours, as their father. I'm in complete agreement it's got to come from you. But why the specifics?'

'I'll be careful. I'll sit them down and I'll –'

'Can you imagine what it'll do them?'

'What, then? You want me to lie? They're adults!'

'I'm not asking you to lie. I – I don't know. Just tell them something else.'

That was all Ruthie heard. She'd been in the hall at Pilgrim's Lane, about to knock on Beatrice's study door and say, 'I'm going for some stamps, do you need anything?' Aware that her aunt was with someone, she'd paused for long enough to catch this fragment. Later, she'd wonder why she hadn't stayed to hear more, or barged in.

On the way to the post office she stopped and was sick on the pavement, having realised her mother was dead.

Over supper, Max told only part of the story. Watching her father lie, Ruthie had a sense he was simply reciting lines, sustaining the act he'd begun when she'd come back and found him in the hall.

'Darling,' he'd said, folding her in his arms, 'I should've told you I was coming. I'm sorry. It must be a surprise.'

'Doesn't matter.' She'd shrugged him off. 'Why are you here?'

She'd given him this chance, assuming he'd tell her something, at least. He'd sidestepped, though: discussing arrangements for dinner; saying Vinny was driving from Cambridge and the traffic would be terrible.

'Vinny? Why's she coming? And where's Bea?'

Again, he'd dodged her. Caught in the trap of wanting and not wanting to hear him say it, she'd been scared, and struggled through the conversation. When she'd realised he really wasn't going to tell her anything, she'd been angry and played with him: pretending to vagueness about timing; deflecting his questions about what to cook.

'Why not a restaurant?'

'Because I said so.'

When he'd fallen back on this phrase he'd favoured in her childhood, she'd spoken in a hard, cold voice.

'Actually, silly old me. I've just remembered. There's a party Nick wants us to go to.'

'Ruthie. We need to have a talk.' He'd looked away while he spoke. 'Your aunt's gone out. She'll be back to cook for us. Vinny and I will be here for seven, and I'd like you to join us.'

'Fine,' she'd said, biting the insides of her cheeks until she tasted blood. 'Fine.'

In her room, she'd looked in all the cupboards. She'd found a small white box, tied with a yellow ribbon, and she'd read the note Beatrice had written on the lid: *'April 1974. Maman's Leaf-Present, for Ruthie.'* Taking out the dried leaf, she'd placed it on her dressing table. Putting her face next to it, she'd blown it across the surface so it scuttled like a crab. When it was still, she'd lain her hand on top and crushed it. She'd put the box in the bin and blown the leaf-dust away, then she'd climbed into bed.

At a quarter past seven, Beatrice knocked on her door. 'Roo, darling? Are you coming down? They're here, lovey. It's just you we're waiting –'

'Alright,' she called. 'Alright.'

In the kitchen, her aunt was at the stove.

When Vinny looked at Ruthie, Ruthie could see she'd been told something. Not the whole of it, though, so that when Max said the words, her sister choked, and couldn't get her breath.

Ruthie, watching Beatrice rub Vinny's back, registered nothing by way of emotion.

When Vinny was breathing normally, Ruthie turned to her aunt.

'How?'

'What, lovey?' Beatrice was at the stove again, wiping her eyes with a tea towel.

'How did she die?'

Beatrice glanced at Max, who answered for her: 'She had an acc—'

'Really,' Ruthie cut in. 'An accident?' She turned to her sister. 'Vinny? Did you hear that? Our mother had –' Then, without taking her eyes off Vinny, 'What kind of an accident, Auntie Bea?'

Nobody spoke, until Ruthie said, 'What do you think, Vee? What kind of an accident do you think our mother had?'

Vinny shuddered.

'Dad?' Ruthie said. Her voice was tight, and she spoke viciously. 'Perhaps you can enlighten us? Your elder daughter seems to be in some distress.'

Beatrice said, 'I think you should go, Ruthie.' She was leaning over Vinny with her arms around her, and the expression on her face was entirely new to Ruthie.

Leaving the kitchen, Ruthie met her father's gaze. Something in its coldness told her she was right: her mother had killed herself. More than that, it told her he was aware that she knew, and he would say nothing about it.

The funeral was at Falicon. Sophie's body was taken to the crematorium at Nice, in the English Quarter.

Afterwards, Emile, whose only child had hanged herself from a beam in the neighbour's stable, collected her ashes. Ruthie asked to go with him but he said no; he'd rather she stayed at the house with her family.

Vinny was more insistent, but her offer was refused as well: '*Merci, ma pitchoune. Mais je vous demande de me laisser seule avec ma fille.*'

It was dark when he got to the Cap Ferrat.

On the rocks at the end of the peninsula, he switched off his torch. The beam of the lighthouse played on the water. Parsing the signal once, then again, he scattered his daughter to the sea.

The fountain at Pennerton had frozen hard.

Max and Vinny opened up the rooms. Throwing back the shutters, they pulled dust sheets from the furniture. Ruthie came after and collected the sheets, then she took them to the attic.

Coming from the top floor, she heard them talking.

'I can't believe you blew your top at Peter like that.'

'The least he could've done was get the place ready.'

'How was he to know we'd come straight back?'

'That's not the point.'

'Well, I think you should apologise. He's only ever been good to us. And he loved her, in his way. Surely you could see that? Why do you think he just stood there and let you shout at him?'

At the doorway, Ruthie watched her father collapse to the floor, like a coat slipping from its hanger.

Vinny caught him as he landed. 'Here – Papa. I know, I know. You're hurting. Please. Let me hold you.'

He made a long, low sound, and his body shook. They knelt together, and when he was quiet, Vinny half sighed, half spoke.

'My poor papa. My poor, poor papa.'

On the stairs, Beatrice was on her way to her bedroom for a rest, and Ruthie told her what she'd seen.

'Just a half-hour then,' her aunt said.

Beatrice slept through supper, though.

Max had refused to eat, tapping his fork on the table and saying, what the hell did Beatrice think she was doing, opting out at a time like this? Then he took his anger out on Ruthie, who had let slip she'd given up a residency in Berlin.

She brushed off his complaint, saying it was nothing special, nor was it any of his business. All he'd done was make a few phone calls on her behalf; she'd submitted a portfolio, the same as everyone else, and could submit it again next year. Right now, she had her work in London.

'Work?' He half snarled, half smiled. 'Is that how you describe what you do with Nicholas Travers? That jumped-up little pimp who calls himself an artist? For Christ's sake –' he raised his voice – 'phone and say you've changed your mind. Tell them something. Your mother's death, anything. Tell them you weren't thinking straight.'

'What did you just say? Not your pathetic little jibe at Nick. I mean, what did you just say about Mum? About her death?'

'Nothing.'

'Yes you did. You said I should use it as an excuse. You said I should lie about it.'

'No, I just said –'

'Shall we talk about that? Shall we talk about lying about Mum's death? How did you say she died? Why not tell us again? You were remarkably unforthcoming on the detail.'

'Roo,' Vinny said. 'Stop.'

Shortly before midnight, Beatrice found them in the kitchen, and things were calmer.

'Maybe Dad's right,' Vinny said. 'Maybe you should rethink Berlin.'

'Finally!' Max said. 'Someone seeing sense.'

'What's this about Berlin?' Beatrice said.

Max was at the table, Ruthie against the wall. When Max asked what Nick's wife thought about her staying in London, she laughed and said, since she'd learned everything she knew about morals from her father, would he please shut up about her love life.

Max picked up his plate and threw it.

She ducked, hands to her head, but it smashed against the wall and a shard hit her face.

Holding both hands to her cheekbone, she left the room. Max shouted after her that it was one thing having an artist's tart for a daughter, but quite another to see her giving up on her own talent just to stretch the bastard's canvases.

'Come back here and apologise.'

'For what?' She was at the door again, shouting. 'Apologise for what?' Blood ran from her cheek and onto the collar of her shirt. 'Shall we talk about apologising, Max? Shall we talk about why you never have, not once your whole fucking life, and why you fucking well ought to start?'

'Get out of my sight, Ruth.'

'Ruth? Did you just call me Ruth?'

Vinny held out a tea towel.

Max turned, and Ruthie went.

In the silence, Vinny cleared the pieces of the plate. She fetched the mop, but Beatrice took it.

'Go after your sister.'

Beatrice went up later. Vinny was on her sister's bed, holding a cloth to Ruthie's face.

'Where's Dad?' Vinny said. 'Is he alright?'

'Of course not.'

'What did he say?'

Beatrice took the cloth and squeezed it in the bowl, and the water darkened.

She told them he'd said nothing coherent about Sophie, but that when it had come to Ruthie, he'd been 'unequivocal'.

'And he'll stick to it, I'm afraid. I know my brother. This is what he'll do, Roo, and this is how I think you should respond.'

The envelope that appeared under Ruthie's bedroom door at 3 a.m. was addressed '*To Ruthie, my Sometime Daughter*'.

On the choice she was given, the letter was intransigent: her father, or her lover.

The decision was entirely hers: either she break off contact with Nick, immediately and permanently, or Max would never see her again.

Shortly after dawn, she walked through the kitchen garden. A frost had fallen and she slipped, once, and righted herself. At Peter's cottage she banged on the door. Stepping from one foot to the other and blowing on her hands, she asked him to take her to Headcorn.

'When, love?' He was still in his pyjamas. 'Is lunchtime alright?'

'No. I want to be on the first train. Sorry, I realise you're still half asleep, but it's a bit of an emergency.'

On the way, she asked him to give Max a message.

'Of course. Why are you leaving so early, though? Why not stay for breakfast at least, let Vinny drive you back?'

She didn't answer.

'Alright, well, I can see you're upset. Everyone does these things differently.'

'What things?'

'Grieving. I mean, of course, I understand you want to be in London. I suppose it would be a detour as well, for Vinny.' And then, to her silence, 'What shall I tell him?'

'Hmmm?'

'You said you had a message for your dad.'

'Oh, yes. Tell him I chose Nick.'

'What else?'

'Nothing.'

'Really? Are you sure he'll understand?'

'Really. And yes, he'll know exactly what I mean.'

A year after the funeral, Max married Alice-from-Cannes.

The 'Second marriage of Maxwell Hollingbourne, photographer' was reported as 'quiet': apart from Alice's sister, the guest list comprised Beatrice, Vinny and Julian.

The ceremony was at the register office in Chelsea, where Alice had a flat, and Max was 'furious' with Beatrice for missing it.

'Nice of you to show up,' he said when she arrived at the restaurant, just off the King's Road. 'What happened to your hair? You look like you're on day release from a – And what's that on your cheek? Are you alright, Bea? Is it face cream, or what? There, on the end of your –'

Beatrice pushed him away, saying she was ever so sorry, something had come up. She'd wanted to change, but had thought it more important just to get there.

Alice told Max not to be rude, then she told Beatrice she looked 'totally divine, honey'. There wasn't a dress code; Max was only teasing. Heels were so yesterday, anyway, and of course she should wear a cardigan if she wanted: it was February, for goodness' sake! More importantly, what did she want to eat?

The talk was of the honeymoon he'd arranged on the Cap Ferrat, with views from the villa onto the beach at Villefranche. Max didn't complain when Julian, who had lost weight and was wearing a new suit, flicked back his hair and flirted with Alice. Even Beatrice relaxed, so that when Vinny said, 'Let's share a pudding, Auntie Bea,' she said, 'Yes, why not then?'

By the end of the afternoon no one had drunk too much, nor had anyone mentioned the empty place, set in case Ruthie changed her mind.

A month passed before Beatrice phoned and asked Vinny to meet her for tea at her club.

First, they spoke about how sad it was that Pennerton was all shut up.

'But he's not going to sell it, surely. How could he?' Vinny said. 'It was our home, all of us. Was that what you asked me here to talk about? And if so, why isn't Ruthie here? Pennerton's as much to do with her as it is with me.'

'No. There's something else. I need you to make me a promise.'

'What? What, Bea? What's the matter?' and when Vinny pressed again, Beatrice said that she was no longer comfortable being Ruthie's only guardian. 'I don't mean literally, or legally, or whatever. I mean, Ruthie needs looking after more than most people.'

'What do you mean, most people?'

'She goes into her shell for days. She won't wash her hair and she mopes about coughing. Half the time I think she's putting it on, but it does sound awful. Sometimes it's weeks, not days. She hardly says a word!'

'She's always been like that. We both know it.'

'It's different now. I need to ask you this one thing. If there's ever a time I can't look after her, then you must promise to take over.'

She said it again, and, when Vinny protested, a third time. Only at the last, when Vinny said, 'I've spent my whole life looking after her!' and, 'You're not asking anything of me I don't already do. Why should I promise?' did Beatrice say, 'Alright then, I suppose I shall have to tell you.'

At 10 a.m. on the morning of the wedding, she'd said goodbye to Ruthie in the basement kitchen.

There had been some tension in the preceding week: the invitation disappeared from Beatrice's dressing table, but when she cleaned the fireplace and found a tiny corner of card behind the grate, one edge gilded and the other singed, Ruthie denied it. That day and the next she skipped work, appearing in the kitchen at intervals and making comments about Alice so that Beatrice told her, 'If you've nothing nice to say, don't say it.'

Beatrice tried only once to suggest a rapprochement, something along the lines of wasn't a wedding the perfect opportunity, but she received short shrift and dropped it.

When, on the day itself, Ruthie asked was it alright if Nick came over for lunch, Beatrice said, 'Of course, why not? Just leave the kitchen tidy if you're cooking. I'll be gone in a min, so I won't be under your feet.'

'Bea, it's only half past nine! The wedding's not till twelve!'

'Oh, I know. I'm popping to the club first then I'll go straight from there.'

'When will you be home?'

'Oh, not for hours and hours. There's the ceremony, then the lunch. You know what Americans are like, Alice will want us to go on somewhere. I imagine it'll be all day. Yes, let's say that. You can have the place to yourselves until this evening.'

At a quarter past eleven, she was in the club library when a call came through from Nick. They spoke only briefly, and when another call came a second later, to say her cab had arrived for the wedding, she said there had been a change of plan, and she had to get to Hampstead as quickly as possible.

At Pilgrim's Lane, the front door was ajar. Nick was in the hall, his hands in his pockets. He said straight away that whatever happened, his wife mustn't find out.

'No press,' he said. 'Can't get mixed up in something like this. I told Ruthie it was over weeks ago. She kept saying to wait. "Wait until after my dad's wedding, Nicky." Said she didn't want to deal with a break-up on top of Max getting married.'

He started up the stairs while he talked. Like a child, he put both feet together and waited on each step, jumping to the next between sentences.

'So I come round today, thinking we'd just talk it through, say goodbye, you know?' He jumped to the next step. 'Like grown-ups.' He paused. 'I'm not about to fire her. She can stay on at the studio, don't get me wrong. She's good at what she does.' He jumped up again. Then, at the middle landing, 'I'll fix her up with something else, though, if she'd rather.'

'Oh for God's sake.' Beatrice pushed past him. 'Shut up.'

On the top floor, he said, 'No, not in her bedroom,' and pulled Beatrice back.

'Where, then?'

He put his foot to the door of the darkroom that once was, and pushed it gently.

Everything in the room, up to waist height and no further, had been painted bright white.

The whole of that little space, which was formerly black from floor to ceiling, was transformed into another world.

The floor, once black linoleum, was white.

The sides of the bathtub, formerly black metal, were white as well.

The bare bulb that swung from the ceiling was muted by the white of the paint that covered it.

Each of the walls was slathered in messy-white brushstrokes, exactly up to waist height and no further. The cut-off was precise, as though drawn with a ruler. Above this invisible line the walls had been left black, but there was the curious detail of the windowpane, set high up in the wall. This small square of glass was coated in paint as well, so that there was no natural light as such, but only the faint sun that filtered in.

And then there was Ruthie.

Squatting on the floor in the middle of her one-time bathroom-darkroom, she looked up at her aunt and frowned.

'Hello, Bea.'

She was holding a paintbrush in one hand. Her arm was in the air, slightly, and the paint was running from the brush and down her forearm. She was dressed in a kind of half-slip, which stopped just below her waist. White paint was slathered on her skin, to the tops of her legs and over, so her pubic hair was thick with it. The insides of her thighs were daubed with white as well, and so was her neck. It was smeared in patches on her face, and there were streaks of white through the dark red of her hair.

A strap fell from her shoulder and she replaced it.

'Sorry, Auntie Bea. If I'd known you were coming, I'd have cleaned myself up a bit.' She smiled. 'Would you like to help me?'

Beatrice took the brush and knelt beside her. Wrapping both arms around her, she half pulled, half lifted her up. 'Give me a bloody hand, would you?' Only then did Nick step forward, taking Ruthie's legs so they carried her between them.

'But I haven't finished,' Ruthie said. 'I've hardly even started!' She spoke in a child's voice.

In her bedroom, they laid her on the bed. She started to cry, and she said in her own voice, 'I hate you, Nicholas Travers. I hate every last thing about you. I don't hate you, Bea. You're so nice. You're always so, so— But you, Nicholas-jumped-up-fuck-anyone-who-moves-Travers. I really hate you, and I hate your stupid fucking wife and your stupid fucking daughter and your stupid fucking son. I hate Max and I hate Alice and I wish you were all dead and I never want to see you again.'

She rolled over and buried her face in her pillow, showing them her bare bottom and part of her lower back.

'Oh Jesus,' Nick said, stepping away. 'She's pissing herself. She's actually pissing on the bed.'

'I think you ought to go,' Beatrice said, pulling a sheet over her niece's body. 'See yourself out.' She followed him to the landing and called, softly, 'And, Nick. Don't come back, will you? Even if she asks you to.'

Beatrice's doctor arrived, and she whispered to him in the hall, should she have telephoned an ambulance? He said no. He would give Ruthie a sedative and stay with her until she was settled. When she was up to it, he'd book her in with someone he knew at the Royal Free Hospital. She'd see him every day at first, then they could review things.

'Go to your brother's wedding. She'll be asleep in no time.'

Beatrice stripped Ruthie's bed and put the sheets in the machine. Then she made it up with clean ones and said goodbye to her niece. In her own room, she threw her wedding clothes in the bin and put on the first thing she could find, leaving the house and hailing a cab for a tiny restaurant, near to the Chelsea Register Office.

Vinny cut in to her story then, and breathed the promise she'd been asked for, telling Beatrice she was sorry she'd ever questioned her.

When Beatrice had her fall a fortnight later, it seemed at first she'd done no lasting damage.

Ruthie arrived at the hospital to find her crying with laughter, and partway through a tale of how a Jack Russell terrier had run amok on Trafalgar Square.

Vinny filled her in on what she'd missed, saying their aunt had come from the National Gallery and, being in no particular hurry, had lingered by the fountain.

The woman next to her had been holding the terrier, which was a puppy still, letting it dip its feet in the water. Then, just as Beatrice asked her how old it was, the terrier leapt from the woman's arms in a single movement, snatching away its lead and tearing into the pigeons like a half-crazed thing, snapping and barking until it snapped so hard that a bird fell sideways and lay with one wing flapping, until it rolled onto its front, and there was no movement.

'It was the shock, I think, more than anything,' Beatrice said, describing how the woman had stood with her mouth half open, and her hand on Beatrice's arm. 'What shall I do?' she'd asked. 'What on earth shall I do now?'

'Well, I couldn't just sit there, could I?' Beatrice explained to her nieces. By this stage, the terrier's attention had been caught by a crowd of schoolchildren whose ankles it was nipping. 'He must have known I was after him,' she carried on. 'I swear I actually touched the tip of his ear with my fingers.'

'Why did you get involved?' Vinny asked. 'It was nothing to do with you.'

'Who else was there? Honestly, it was awful. That poor woman, just staring!'

'Just waiting for someone else to pick up the pieces, you mean!'

Beatrice said that, as a matter of fact, she'd quite enjoyed having a proper run around, but that, just as she was on the point of giving up, and had cut back in a last-ditch attempt to block the terrier's path, she'd run head first into a policeman.

'It wasn't head first, though. It was head backwards, if you can imagine. And he was awfully short, that was the thing. So his helmet made contact with my head in absolutely the tenderest place. Look!' she said, lifting up her hair. 'I've had stitches and everything!'

At Pilgrim's Lane, after Vinny had made dinner and Ruthie had cleared it away, Beatrice told Vinny there was no need to stay. She had Ruthie for company, and Vinny should get home to Julian.

'Yes,' Ruthie said. 'Go, go, go!'

Opening the front door, she made Vinny laugh about how Bea had no idea of the strength of the painkillers the hospital had given her.

'She'll sleep like a log. I'll give you a call in the morning, let you know how she is.'

An hour or so after Vinny left, the secondary effects of their aunt's collision caused a swelling in her brain that would kill her.

Max came immediately to London and issued a writ for negligence. But when the hospital handed over the defence, his solicitor told him to drop it, saying he should grieve for his sister at home, rather than spend money doing it in a courtroom.

At the funeral, Vinny placed flowers on the coffin from Ruthie, who stayed away because of Max.

Six months later, Alice-from-Cannes filed for divorce.

'No,' she said when Vinny phoned. 'As a matter of fact, that isn't the reason. I mean, yes, there's a girl, but when isn't there? Setting aside the fact this one's older than the last one and should've known better.'

'Oh, Alice.'

'Oh nothing. It's Max we're talking about here. I had my eyes wide open when I married him. But no, she's not the reason. You want to know what finished it for me?'

'What?'

'I just didn't think he should've used the flat at Chelsea, that's all.'

'I'm so sorry.'

'As it happens, so am I. I'll say this about your father. He sure knows how to hurt. Fine, so he was all cut up about your aunt, says he'd lost direction, wasn't thinking straight, was trying to reconnect with the world, needed someone, I wasn't there. He says a lot of things. But, you know, if he'd even tried to hide it, I could've – Even just a little bit! What did anyone ever do to him? That's what I'm left wondering. What did anyone ever do to him to make him like this?'

Beatrice named only Ruthie and Vinny in her will.

Sophie's death had given her daughters no fortune; she'd left the little she owned to her father, and when he'd died, a year later, it passed to the church at Falicon.

Their aunt, though, bequeathed the sisters equal shares in the house at Pilgrim's Lane. In addition, they were to derive incomes as lifetime beneficiaries under the trust Beatrice had set up on Vinny's birth and amended three years later when Ruthie was born. Established with those of Rupert's holdings she'd never drawn on, its stated purpose was 'to give life and a future to his legacy'.

Their inheritance freed and crippled them.

Because Vinny was 27, she received her income immediately. She wrote to Max that she was dropping her PhD.

Academia suits Jules far better than it does me. I'd rather focus on my translation work without having to think about

research. I've an idea of trying novels as well as plays, what
do you think? And it'd mean I wouldn't be tied to the library,
so I could bring a load of work to the villa, and spend some
time with you.

Ruthie, who was only twenty-four, would have to wait a year to draw from the trust. It was her intention to get back into photography, she told Vinny. When the time came, she'd be able to let her gallery work go, and find a collective to sign up with. Something experimental, she said. Something new.

They agreed between themselves that until Ruthie sorted herself out and decided where to live, Vinny would stay on in the flat that came with Julian's college post. She'd leave her equity in Pilgrim's Lane without requiring a return. In exchange, Ruthie gave over a quarter of her share of the cash sum from Beatrice which, together with an amount in kind from Julian's parents, Vinny put towards a weekend cottage at Grantchester.

With Vinny's help, Max wrote to Ruthie. Though his letters were direct in their appeals, they went unanswered: there was a softness to his tone she didn't recognise, and she assumed it likely he'd sat at his desk like a schoolboy, taking dictation from her sister.

Vinny's own attempts in the years that followed were gentle, but persistent.

He was old, she wrote, and missed his younger daughter.

He's strong, but not as strong. Like an athlete past his best.
He still swims every day, but he's been caught in a swell at the
island twice now, so he stays closer into shore. He says he'd
rather you were here to swim with him, so he could follow
your stroke.
Do you know the absolute saddest thing? He told me he

doesn't hear the cicadas any more. His general hearing's fine,
but it's the top notes of things he misses. The birds, and the
cicadas.

In the mornings he stands on the promontory and I can
see him out there, staring at the water like a child, and I know
he's thinking about you.

When the gallery on Albemarle Street where Max's work was first
shown announced a retrospective, Vinny wrote to Ruthie that he'd
be there for the opening.

Do you remember going, when we were little? He had those
amazing parties. Beatrice took us once, in a cab with Sophie,
and we were all dressed up and you were so excited you cried.

I shall have to get him to brush up a bit. His skin is as
dark as a saddle, and he won't have his hair cut, even by
Eleni, so it's this great shock of white.

It's been years, Roo. Why not surprise him at Albemarle
Street? It'd mean the world to him, you can't imagine! Isn't it
time to have a try, at least?

Ruthie read the previews for *Max Hollingbourne: A Life Reflected.*

Several pieces spoke of the harsh isolation of his landscapes, and
speculated as to why those assignments appealed to him: weeks on
end alone in empty country, when in London he'd been known for
his 'easy sociability'.

His resolute preference for black and white was picked up on, and
his 'suspicion' of colour photography cited in the context of a stated
aim to maintain as close an allegiance with reality as was possible.
'A colour image,' he was quoted as saying, 'can be manipulated, even
fabricated, in ways that the same shot captured in two-tone cannot.'

The *Observer* heralded the 'raw, rough storytelling' of his portraits which, it said, were 'relentless' in their seeking out of the depths his subjects tried to hide. For *The Times*, in the same vein, 'Headhunter Hollingbourne's' portraiture was characterised by 'a cold honesty, where the mask is set aside from the start, and truth held higher than beauty'.

This latter tendency, the *Telegraph* observed, supported his claim to the label of 'artist', rather than 'photojournalist', and might have been behind the 'deep fissure' in his output which occurred in '87, on the death of his first wife, an event he'd never spoken of publicly. 'Though years after the couple's separation,' the article continued, 'the impact of the loss was enough to bring about a wholesale change of direction. After a period of producing nothing at all, Hollingbourne's output became entirely unpeopled. Its tone was one of aching melancholy, taking for its spine a series of images captured on the small area of land that surrounded his home in Kent, where he and his wife had lived together with their two young daughters, before their separation in the early seventies. In addition, there was a sequence of images taken at the villa he had built in southern Greece, in 1965, where the family had made a summer home, and where he now lives alone, after a brief second marriage ended in divorce.'

Alongside almost every article, Ruthie saw a picture of a man she didn't recognise.

Only one of the previews carried another portrait: a child, half in shadow, half in light, her gaze dead on and expressionless. The child's hair was tied up, with a strand falling loose, and Ruthie stared back, wondering. When she saw the caption, *RH at Pennerton, 1972*, she looked again at her eight-year-old self. She could find no memory of the shoot, and stayed away from the show.

Ruthie fell into a habit of leaving Vinny's letters unopened in the hall. But then it was spring, and there was one with a message on the outside.

> *Get yourself a nice cup of strong, sweet tea before you open*
> *this. When you do, (and you really do have to), make sure*
> *you're sitting down, somewhere comfortable. XXXXX*

She walked to Pryors Field with the letter still in its envelope. Holding it between two fingers, and allowing the wind to tease it, she'd reached the copper beech on South Meadow when she opened it, which meant that when all the breath went out of her, she could at least lean against the trunk.

2 April 1993

Darling Roo,

Without wanting to be overly dramatic, I hope you've followed my instructions! If you don't know what I'm talking about, look at the back of the envelope, and put the kettle on.

Done it? Good, now take a deep breath.

Max is selling Pennerton.

There. I've written it. I hope you're not too upset.

I was. Even though I knew it was coming – I mean, I suppose we all did, didn't we?

Please, please call if you are. I wanted to tell you on the phone but you never pick up any more.

In fact he got a buyer straight off, so it'll be going through by the end of June. He discovered he could get a lot more for a vacant plot, so this is the bit that might shock you, if the rest hasn't already: it's being pulled down, Roo. The whole thing. Does that matter to you? I mean, I really don't know if it will matter to you. It mattered to me terribly, and I cried for days until Jules told me to grow up and get some real problems. But it did feel like a real problem, for a bit. It was our home, wasn't it? It was our home when we were together, with Maman and Bea and Max and Peter? All of us, I mean, when we were little and everything was normal. We were happy then, weren't we?

So here's the other thing: Max and I are going to visit, one last time. We've put in Wednesday 5 May, and I can't see any reason why that would change. We'll spend a day there, check in on Peter, make sure he's alright with the whole thing. And we'll say goodbye to the place, properly.

Max is looking at a flat in town, around Wigmore Street again. Just something small for the winter. He says it's too cold at the villa – it's never as bad as here, obviously, but he says December through to March is a bit of a drag.

When he's found somewhere, he'll put the rest in trust. He's thinking of us really. Us and his future heirs, he said, though that's not looking likely, is it, unless you do the honours?

I still don't want to talk about it, Roo, but I'm not having much luck on that front. Hurts like hell, that's all there is to say. I suppose I somehow always assumed I'd be a mother. In the way that, I don't know, in the way you assume the sky will be blue a certain number of days of the year, and it'll rain roughly so much in May, and roughly so much in June, give or take a few millimetres, and that after December it'll be January.

Anyhow, I went to Pennerton last week, just to have a bit of time there on my own. I called and called to see if you'd come but you didn't answer. I thought we could go together, you know? Do some reminiscing, just the two of us.

I had a wander, in the woods and the kitchen garden. Peter was out when I got there, but it felt like nothing had

changed. It felt like home, I mean, despite all this time.
Nowhere else has ever come close for me.

The irises were pushing up in the beds. Do you remember
them? Peter sent me some photos a while back. There's one
of you next to the Bullsheads, those dark purple ones, you
know the ones that are almost black and have those furry
bits on the petals where they unfurl and flap over? So, in this
picture you're three years old, maybe four? You're wearing
this sweet little dress which you're clutching at like you think
it's about to fall off, and you've got your other hand to your
mouth, and there's this HUGE iris – it's a good six inches
taller than you, with this ENORMOUS head that's almost
as big as yours!

Will you come with us in May? I'll drive us down, so you
can leave it right to the last minute to decide – just phone
and we'll pick you up. It'd mean so much to Max, if we went
all of us together. And it'd mean so much to me.

Whatever you do, go. I think it'll be good for you. And I
know for a fact Bea would have wanted you to.

Take care, Roo, and call if you're upset, won't you? Actu-
ally, call anyway, even if you're not upset! And please let's
meet up soon – I'm longing to see you.

V XXXXXX

The demolition was brought forward, and Ruthie was too late.

She arrived in the evening, and got off the train one stop early, meaning to go to the house by the woods. It wasn't until the Triangle Meadow, strolling through crow flowers and summer snowflakes, that she had an idea something was wrong.

She stopped beneath the oak. Its leaves were moving, and they made the sound of the sea. A branch creaked, like a ship at harbour.

Ahead of her there was the green of the orchard hedge, flecked with white. There was the low wooden gate, and the tips of the apple trees, new and babyish.

Above them and beyond, though, where the eaves of the house should have reached to the sky, there was absolutely nothing.

She struggled with the orchard gate, then she stood on the Smart Lawn and the empty space hit her as though she had walked into something much bigger than herself.

She breathed, slowly, and turned to the right. The line of cherry trees was there, but the wall to the kitchen garden had disappeared. There was a movement. Quietly and carefully, she walked across the lawn. Peering round the first tree, she saw a single vegetable bed, newly planted up. Wigwams of canes had been placed in a line, with sweet peas climbing. She scanned the line twice, but there was no one, just a spade thrust into the earth and a robin, playing about it.

Beside the spade was a chair. A coat was slung over it, which she recognised as one that her father had given to Peter, a long time ago. Looking further, she saw that the greenhouse and the cottage were gone. In their place was a tiny caravan. Next to it, she could see a pile of logs, and a little bonfire with its embers burning.

The light was fading, and she brought her hands to her neck, feeling a chill.

When she knocked on the door of the caravan, nobody came.

Walking back through the garden, she took the coat from the chair and wrapped herself in it. She passed under the cherry trees, and let the leaves touch her face so the dew ran down her cheeks. Standing on the lawn at the point where the slope to the library used to start, she saw where the earth changed colour, and she could see the shape of the house.

In her memory, it had been enormous. Now, though, the space

marked out on the ground seemed tiny to her, as if a child had drawn a picture.

She trod its bounds like a tightrope walker, and counted her steps aloud.

When she'd walked it a second time, rebuilding its walls and looking in its windows, she went to the front door.

A nightingale called: a wild song, answered by its mate.

She breathed in the dusk, then she lifted her hands and laid them on the wood. She pushed the ghost-door open, and called out softly, 'I'm here, everyone. I've come home.'

18 WEDNESDAY

In the Greek summers of their childhood it rained only rarely. First, the girls would find millipedes, crawling into the villa. Fat and black, the creatures were followed by spiders, one as big as Ruthie's hand, or so she said when she called from the window, 'It's coming! The storm's coming!'

When the heat broke and the sky darkened, the courtyard filled with drops as big as coins. The drops bounced and rose up and the swallows played in them, swinging crazy into the villa's eaves.

Once, Max heard Ruthie's warning and waited by the fountain with his face to the sky. When it began he took Eleni and he waltzed with her in the rain. Then she stood under the Pergola and he took Sophie instead. They danced faster until her hair was a bronze-and-copper sheet, wet and slick down her back.

The girls, watching, were drowning in this rain and Sophie said, 'Max! I can't, not like this, I can't!' Their parents moved more slowly then. Their mother's dress was clinging to her body, and Max kissed the water from her mouth and her eyes.

Vinny turned and ran. Ruthie ran after her and they watched the rain shift on the sides of the island, like a blind pulled down.

This evening, Ruthie stands on the edge of the promontory. She smells the rain before it comes in. Then she can feel it on her shoulders and her back but it's invisible against the sea and she's confused, until she looks to the island and it's moving in sheets on the cliffs.

She lets it fall on her face, then she wanders through the meadow. The tall grass is limp in the rain, and she takes the steps to the sea.

On the cove, two turtle doves glide from the opposite headland. They pass above her, then they sweep into the trees.

There's a kingfisher, big as a blackbird thrown from the sky. It is heavy and low and dark blue, and Ruthie turns to say, 'Look, Papa! Look, it's a kingfisher!'

He isn't there, so she watches it touch the water and flip into the shadows of the cliffs, then she waits at the sea's edge.

The waves roll in and a line of storm clouds stands on the far horizon. Rising like an English sky in autumn, they sail to the east and leave the cove untouched.

After they've gone, the sky is massive. There are smaller clouds which are silhouettes, with dark pink through the blue. When the breeze comes up again it's out of the north-east, and Ruthie can feel it: on her face as she climbs the steps; on her back as she reaches the courtyard and sits on the fountain wall.

The heat from the stone soaks into her thighs and her calves and her hands. The breeze is gentle on her face and in her hair. Birds become bats, wheeling in the semi-dark.

Then Max is there, sitting right beside her.

She is calm, and waits for him to speak.

'Why are you here all alone, Roo?'

He puts out his hand but she moves away.

'Swim to the island, just you and me?'

'Why?'

'Because I'm your father, and I love you.'

She stays silent.

'And because I've missed you all this time.'

'You hurt me, Papa. You hurt me so much.' When she says it, he lets his hand drop.

'What?' He's standing now and frowning. 'What did I do?'

'You know. You were there.'

Neither of them speak. He's smiling again. Laying his stick on the fountain wall, he draws his hands through his hair, and scratches the back of his head. He stretches, yawning like a cat so she can see his tongue and his teeth, then he shrugs his shoulders.

'Come on,' he says. 'The waves are up, but it's nothing we can't deal with. If we go right this minute, there's time before Eleni calls us for supper.'

She doesn't answer. When he walks to the edge of the courtyard, he's slow, and his stick makes a sound like a mallet on a block. 'If we go now, I mean,' he calls over his shoulder. 'If we hurry.'

She stands up. 'I don't want to.'

He is at the path, one hand held out. She walks towards him and he goes a little further, keeping his hand out for her to take it.

'Race you,' then he's walking faster.

'I don't want to,' she says again, then she watches him. His head is bobbing through the trees, until she can't see him any more, and there is only the sound of his stick.

'Goodbye, Papa,' she says. 'Goodbye.'

She sits for an hour. There is the water in the cove, like a rake pulled over gravel, and there are the cicadas streaming.

She is bitten by an insect. She slaps her neck, then her arm, then her neck again.

A door bangs, somewhere in the villa.

'Vinny?' she calls, wondering. But when she goes inside, there's no one.

In the night, the sounds Ruthie hears are all awry.

At first there is the wind, louder than she's ever heard it, but when she looks from the veranda the trees are motionless.

A dog barks: one short, loud bark, repeated at regular intervals.

She walks the circuit of the veranda but she can't tell where it's coming from. After trying for a half-hour to place the source, she goes to the Lightroom. It's a harsher sound there, and she watches the feather-clock: ten minutes to the second between one bark and the next, then the ticking of the clock, and the wind, for another ten precisely.

At 2.30 a.m. the cicadas stop. A minute later the cockerel crows: four hours early and a half-crow only so the phrase fails to find its full height. The notes of a second attempt sound lower still, and a third is aborted at its start.

After, the silence is absolute.

Halfway down the stairs she puts her hands over her ears and away again, confused. On the veranda, in this absence of noise, she sees the trees in the grove are blown about by a storm. She cups her hands over her ears again and away, but still there's no noise. At precisely that moment the olive tree closest to the villa lifts into the air where it hangs for a half-minute before separating, slowly, into pieces. Reconstituting itself in slow motion, it sinks back whole to the ground. One by one the trees rise up in this way. Some of them, having come apart, stay like that and drift before disappearing altogether; others become whole again and sink back down.

Then Ruthie can make out nothing at all.

When she can see again, a sensation passes from the back of her head down her neck and over the whole of her body, as though someone is pouring water from above, but slowly. When it reaches her feet she becomes aware that every part of her has gone completely numb. She pinches her face and her arms, but she doesn't feel anything. The numbness is more like pins and needles, as though she has tucked her feet under herself and sat on them for too long, so that when she stands she will stumble. This time, though, it is the whole of her, not just her feet.

The trees are still now, and she's watching them. Then all at once, her vision is obscured by a series of moving images played fastforward, right in the middle of her mind.

Max, at the top of the steps from the cove, looking down at her.

Beside her in the water keeping their strokes in time. His face rolling left as hers rolls right so they breathe in together, their mouths wide open.

Julian in the courtyard. He is drawing a map. 'I'll take you up in the morning, if you like. Show you where.

'I'll take you up in the morning, if you like. Show you where.'

Max, standing with her on the cove at night, holding her hand. 'Look! There is a shooting star, can you see it? Look, there!' but she is too late. 'Look, can you see it? Look, can you see it? Look, can you –'

Eleni is on the cove with them and he is pointing at her and she looks at Ruthie.

'I don't know what you are talking about. I wasn't in the courtyard.'

Max, turning from his desk at Pennerton, a camera to his face and the sound of the shutter closing.

Julian in the courtyard, pointing at the map he's drawn. 'Here.' And Eleni, 'Yes, that is where we scattered them.'

Sophie, in the yard at Pennerton, passing Ruthie the peg bag and standing on a ladder to take a coil of rope from the stable wall, which she places around her own neck.

Max, on the first evening near Falicon. 'We've made good time and we can do what we like, just you and me together. What'll it be?'

'Just you and me together, what'll it be.
  Just you and me together, what'll it be.
  Just you and me together, what'll it be.'

Max, looking up from the Olive-Tree Bench.

'Come down, Ruthie-Roo. Come and say goodnight properly.'

The meltémi on their faces, out of the north-east.

'Goodnight, Papa.'

Eleni in the kitchen. She is pouring iodine onto cotton wool and there are purple bracelets on her wrists.
'When did you do this?'

Ruthie leaves the veranda and goes downstairs to the shed.

'When did you do this?'

She is still numb, and when she reaches to the top shelf for a tin of white paint and a paintbrush, sweat runs from a point between her shoulder blades.

In the Lightroom, she levers open the tin. Then she climbs on the work surface and stands in front of *The Road to Falicon*.

'Goodnight, Papa.'

When that tin is empty, she fetches another.

19 THURSDAY

Ruthie had risen in the early morning. Before the sun was on the grove she'd carried one thing then another to the chapel. Working steadily, she crossed them each from the list she'd written in the night when, turning in her half-sleep, she'd woken from a dream.

The dream, although fleeting, answered a question which had troubled her since her first conversation with Annie, when the child stood on the work surface with circles of light playing on her tummy. Or it provided a solution to a problem, rather, and did so in the form of a plan.

Because it was a relief to know what to do, having been so confused, instead of questioning her dream or probing its logic, she simply got up and wrote her list. When she'd calculated timings and quantities and temperatures, she fell back to sleep, more deeply than before.

If Eleni had been there, and they were on better terms, she would have sat with her on the Olive-Tree Bench. Eleni would have listened for as long as it took, and told her what she made of her dream. As it was, it went uninterpreted, and when she woke again at five, feeling so calm she no longer felt anything at all, she sat at the work surface and began to write a letter.

'Promise you'll leave me one too, if you can't come,' Annie had said.

'Alright,' Ruthie had replied. 'I promise.'

Dear Annie, the letter began.

You're reading this, so you'll know I'm not there. Don't be disappointed. I haven't abandoned you, we're just going to do something different, that's all, instead of swimming. If you were here I'd say, 'Listen Very Carefully,' but you're not, so you'll have to Read Very Carefully *instead.*

I've come up with a plan. It's a Very Exciting *plan, and I know you'll absolutely love it, but I'm going to need your help.*

It won't work without you so make sure you do exactly what I say. It's not complicated, and I've made you a list so you can't go wrong. Just work your way through the list and it'll all be fine. Can you do that? There are only a few steps, and you're more than up to it, I know you are.

I won't tell you what it's all about because I want it to be a surprise. You do your bit and I'll do mine then you'll find out what it is tomorrow.

Are you Reading Very Carefully? *Then I'll begin!*

1.   Go up the steps to the villa (don't worry, there's no one else there today, they're getting back from Athens tonight). Cut through the courtyard and out onto the path, the way we went yesterday. Turn right, and follow the path until you find the little white chapel.

2.   When you get there, look on the ground outside the door. I'm going to put my watch there for you to find, the one from the Grand Bazaar in Istanbul that you tried on in my room. (It's sort of like a treasure-hunt, isn't it!) The most important thing at this point is that you Mustn't Come In, *and you* Mustn't Open the Door. *That bit's* Very Important Indeed. *I'll be inside the chapel, so you can shout hello if you like but* Don't Come In!

3.   *Look at the door and you will see a square of black masking tape right in the middle of it, with a corner folded over. Put your hand up and make sure you can reach it, but* Leave It Where It Is! *It should be the right height, but you might have to stand on your tiptoes just a little bit.*

4.   *When you know you can reach the tape, pick up the watch and check the time. It should be about 5.45 when you arrive, or at least I think it will be, once you've been to the cove and found this and read it. So just have a little walk around and keep an eye on the minute hand. When it gets to 5.55, then get ready. Here's what you have to do next. Count the minutes down, and then, when it's 6 p.m.* EXACTLY – *by the way, this bit's easy (it's all easy, isn't it, really?) but it's also* Very Very Important *you get it right so here goes* –

The rest of the letter was straightforward. When she'd checked it through three or four times, rubbing out anything unclear and making her handwriting as legible as possible, she went to the cove.

'We'll bury them, so no one else can find them,' Annie had said, crouching on the pebbles. 'Shall we? Shall we bury them?'

'Yes, Annie, if you like,' Ruthie had replied. 'They can be our secret notes, and we can bury them in a secret hiding place.'

She did exactly as they'd agreed, knowing that Annie, being a careful sort of a child, would get there on time and wait on the rock until she was sure Ruthie wasn't coming, before jumping down to look, not leaving until she found Ruthie's letter.

When Ruthie had dug a shallow pit on the rock's dry side, and covered the letter so that just a tiny tip of its corner was showing, she went back up to the villa.

In the Lightroom, she collected her equipment.

There were the ice trays to be filled and stacked in the freezer in the darkroom, to be ready for just before midday, when she'd ferry them over and come back for the last two canisters. First, though, she took a sponge from Vinny's bathroom, the biggest she could find, rinsing it and wringing it and leaving it in the sun. While it dried, she brought buckets from Eleni's cupboard, and cleaned a second paintbrush. From the darkroom store she fetched acetate and a cotton cloth and a stiff wire brush, and from the shed, a tin of varnish. Last of all there was developer and stop and fixer, in plastic bottles of varying sizes. She lined them all up and checked them from her list, carrying them to the chapel and checking them off a second time.

In the darkroom again, she made the liquid light from scratch. Time was tight, so she chose the simplest formula in her book: as well as using only three ingredients, the emulsion could be prepared in under an hour.

She was slower, though: the recipe was new to her, and her work was held up by the adjustments she had to make on account of the August heat.

Once the gelatin had swollen, she put the solution in a water jacket. She took the temperature throughout, and watched for the bromide to dissolve. When the second solution, of silver nitrate and water, had reached forty degrees, she added it to the first, measuring it out in tiny quantities. If the bottom of the meniscus passed the 5 ml mark by accident, she emptied the test tube and started again. Stirring continuously, she fought the urge to drop it all in at once and, later, resisted the temptation to do away with the filtering; even though the funnel was fiddly; even though she hated the way the cotton wool stuck to her fingers; even though she wanted just to be there, seeing her plan unfold.

There was a precision in her movements that acted almost as a drug: the more care she took, the calmer she felt.

'Focus is everything.'

She heard her father's voice from inside her head, as though she was speaking the words herself.

'It's a contract between you and your work, Ruthie-Roo, and whether you like it or not, it's binding.'

She closed her eyes, and opened them.

'You're a photographer, or you claim to be.'

She added a teaspoonful of developer to loosen the emulsion, stirring it in with a small glass rod.

'Look at it this way. It stands or it falls,' she said in chorus with him, turning to wash her hands. 'Everything stands or falls on this.'

When she'd filtered it for the last time, she decanted it and made the second batch. Once both canisters were full, she carried the ice and the water to the chapel. Then she came back and checked that the caps on the canisters were screwed on tight, and put her checklist in her pocket.

It was midday when she left the villa, and the sun was directly above her.

Ruthie knew the risks would be better described as unavoidable probabilities. She turned them over on her walk. Because she was concentrating hard, and the canisters were heavy, she moved awkwardly, so that anyone watching might have thought she was afraid of falling in a hole, or stepping on a snake. There was nobody, though: Annie's family would be either swimming or in town, and Vinny and Eleni wouldn't be home until late. No one else would cut through the grove at that time of day: the sun was so bright and the air so hot, it felt like something solid on Ruthie's skin and shimmered in front of her, distorting things.

For instructions on applying the emulsion to her chosen surface, the closest equivalent she'd been able to find in her book were those it prescribed for leather. There were additional steps she could take to improve the chances of it working: already in the chapel was the acetate for cleaning; the wire brush for abrading; and the varnish to apply as a layer beneath the emulsion, for better adhesion.

By the time she reached the chapel door, she'd considered the whole exercise three, or even four times. At that stage, if she tried to think seriously about what might happen, and how she would feel if it did, her thoughts became rapid and unstructured. When her mind spiralled, she simplified things by focusing instead on the potential success or otherwise of the process she was about to attempt.

Laying a hand against the warmth of the door, she felt a sudden clarity: she was too far in to stop, and in any case, she'd written to Annie that she'd do it, and didn't want to let her down.

In the very early morning she'd missed a call from Vinny. She found the message on the machine when she came back from the chapel the first time. After Vinny had talked about the hospital, and confessed to having forgotten the travel-sickness pills, which meant they'd had to stop three times on the way, she said they'd shared a room at Eleni's cousin's house and Eleni had snored the whole night through. If Ruthie wanted a chat, she should make sure she was in for around eleven-ish, when Vinny would pull over and try again.

Feeling a sudden urge to talk to her sister and tell her her plan, Ruthie considered being there for that second call.

She went as far as picturing herself standing by the phone and picking up the receiver when it rang, and telling her sister that her mind had become a ship's sail at sea, and that the sail was made of a thin blue silk that was stitched with paper flowers, and that Annie had taken a knife and climbed her ship's mast and cut this sail in two, so that the wind was passing right through it in a squall, and that her plan, when she had written it down, was both needle and thread, and each of its parts a stitch.

To Ruthie, all this made perfect sense.

But then she imagined what Vinny would say, and she decided not to tell her after all.

The very last thing Ruthie did before she stepped into the chapel was to remove a roll of thick black tape from her satchel. Standing outside with the sun on her back, she cut off a square and secured it over the hole in the middle of the door. Making sure the hole itself was completely covered, she peeled away the bottom corner and folded it back on itself, forming a little flap so the square could be ripped off easily, even by a child.

Inside, her final preparations were directed at what she'd come to see as the central challenge: from a certain point on she'd be working in total darkness and, to be ready in time for Annie, she'd be doing so at speed.

She struck a match and held it to the oil lamp. On the shelf beside it was the bottle of acetate and the wire brush, along with the tin of varnish and a paintbrush. She moved them aside and held up a square of black twill cloth to the window, fixing it in place with the tape; then she placed more tape around the edges of the door.

At the altar, she lifted down the candlestick and folded away the cloth. She put both the canisters on the stone surface, one at either end. She took a second paintbrush and the sponge from her satchel, and laid them on the right-hand side of the altar. Then she stood back, adjusting their positions, checking and rechecking the items from her list. Moving backwards to the chapel door then to the altar again, she whispered the steps that she took, 'One-two-three-four.'

With her eyes closed, she felt her way by holding her arms in front of her. When she'd stood and checked the things on the altar one more time, she placed her hands on its surface and jumped and twisted round so that she was sitting on top, facing the chapel door. She shut her eyes and felt for the canisters and the paintbrush, opening her eyes and moving the canisters closer, or further away, then closing her eyes and feeling for them again.

She slipped to the ground and stood back away from the altar. Turning, she looked around the whole of the chapel.

She'd brought every bucket she could find: a couple from the shed and two from the kitchen, and two more from the yard behind the villa. Next to them were a series of plastic bottles, in varying sizes, that she'd carried from her darkroom. The bottles of developer were packed in bags of half-melted ice, which dripped onto the floor when she lifted them. She decanted the developer into the buckets, then she did the same with the contents of the other bottles and stood the buckets in a line against the wall to the right of the altar, in the following order: developer, stop, fixer, then three of iced water, though the ice in the water buckets was melting as well.

When she'd checked once more that everything was in position, she took the negative from her satchel.

Earlier, she'd painted a little of the emulsion on the darkroom wall, then she'd run back to the chapel to measure the size of the hole in the door, and the distance from the door to the altar. Bearing in mind the strength and the speed of the emulsion, and the adjustments she'd made to the mix, she'd estimated that the photo would need a minute and a half.

She'd wanted to bring the exposure time down to sixty seconds, assuming it would be easier for a child to count, so she'd chosen the negative with the greatest contrast: Annie in her bikini, standing up on Max's work surface against the darker of the walls. Her head was tilted slightly towards the feather-clock that hung there, and the scratches on her skin stood out clearly. Her gaze centre-on, she stared at the camera.

Ruthie put the negative up to the hole in the door, with its shiny side facing through the hole and out, directly onto the square she'd fixed there. Lining it up so the image was within the hole's diameter, she attached it with two small pieces of tape, one on either side. She'd wavered over the idea of a lens, slipping one from the enlarger that morning and turning it in her hand. Having measured the distance again, she'd decided there was no need: she knew the size of the circle that shone on Christ's face at sundown, when the light passed through that tiny hole, and she was sure of the chapel's dimensions. Whether the process worked or not, a lens would make no difference either way.

Ruthie's plan, as presented to her in her dream, went something like this.

Annie, according to the instructions in the letter, would arrive and stand on the other side of the door, where she would find Ruthie's watch on the ground. When it showed 6 p.m., the sun would have fallen to precisely the point where its strongest beams would hit the hole dead on. At exactly that moment, Annie, standing on her tip-toes, would pull the square of tape from the hole and follow Ruthie's instructions to 'Stand Well Back!! – and Count Very Carefully!!!'

And so, as the little girl began to count, a perfect circle of the brightest light would shine directly through the negative, and the process would begin: the sun and the tiny hole together the enlarger, the chapel the darkroom, and Ruthie herself the surface, sitting naked on the altar and covered in liquid light, ready to be made into a photograph.

Following the second hand of the watch once around its face, Annie would stay focused for the whole sixty seconds by reciting her Mississippis.

(*'Can you do that, do you think? You're going to be a photographer's assistant now, you know that, don't you? It's a big responsibility! Exactly 60 seconds. No longer and no shorter. It really matters that you concentrate. Do the Mississippis like I taught you, and you'll be absolutely fine!'*)

When she got to, 'fifty-nine-Mississippi, sixty', the child would reach up to replace the tape square, pressing it down as hard as she could so the hole was completely covered. With the chapel returned to darkness, the next stage of the process could begin.

For now, stepping away from the door, Ruthie undid her dress and let it fall to the floor. At the shelf with the oil lamp, she soaked the cotton cloth with acetate. Starting from her clavicle and working down, she wiped herself clean. The liquid was warm and stung only a little, but when she scrubbed herself with the wire brush, every stroke made her wince and she snagged her left nipple, tearing her skin. She used a downward movement then, turning the brush to abrade the hollow between her tiny breasts, slowing when she reached her hip bones rising, like tree stumps, buried in her skin.

After this the varnish went on easily. The scent was sharp, and when it was dry but still slightly sticky, she blew out the lamp.

She turned, and stepped into total darkness.

Moving slowly across the chapel floor, toe-to-heel, toe-to-heel, she counted her steps out loud. She laid both hands on the surface of the altar and jumped up, twisting round as she landed so that she was facing the door with her naked back towards Christ's face.

Spreading her legs so she was more balanced, she felt the coldness of the stone on the underside of her thighs and her bottom. She reached out her hands to the edges of the altar and brought them back, moving her palms span by span until she was sure she was at the midpoint, so that the sun would follow a course through the negative and fall directly on her torso.

Ruthie thought of Vinny then.

They are together, and they are at Pennerton. They are very young and they are running barefoot through the gooseberry bushes. Then Max is there and he is telling them to put their wellingtons on and the lining cloth scratches her calves. They pull off their boots and run across the Smart Lawn and Little Peter brushes past her so she trips and rights herself. They play on the grass. Later, Max lifts them onto the stone slab by the sink and inspects their feet and declares them too dirty for the stair carpet and he is scrubbing their skin with a wire brush and she can feel the cool of the stone slab through her knickers and the water is steaming and Ruthie is in the chapel again, and a grown-up Vinny is with her.

'It's amazing, Roo!' Vinny says. 'It's an awful lot of trouble for one picture, I s'pose. But it's amazing. I'm ever so proud of you.'

'Thanks,' Ruthie said, but her voice echoed, and Vinny was gone.

Beyond the application of the emulsion, the sequence of events was to continue as follows.

After Annie had replaced the tape, they would call their goodbyes through the door.

(*When you've put it back on, leave my watch on the floor and shout goodbye and go back to your mum. And I know you'll want to, but you* Absolutely Must Not Come In! *It's* Really Important *the door stays shut until I've finished'*.)

It was Ruthie's intention, next, to stand down from the altar and pat about for Vinny's bath sponge. She would turn to her right and step towards the wall, feeling in the dark for the first of the buckets. Kneeling, she would sponge the developer onto her torso, neat, so that the picture of the child would emerge in a second reversal.

She'd decided to stand up for the stop-bath; it seemed simpler to pick up the bucket and pour it. She'd do the same with the fixer, then when the formaldehyde in it had dissolved all the gelatin, and the silver nitrate was stripped from her skin, she would at last be able to relight the oil lamp. Moving more freely then, she'd tip the buckets of water over her, one, two, three, and wash the chemicals from her body.

When the warmth of the chapel had dried her, she would clean up as best she could. Then, leaving the door open to let the floor dry, she'd take everything back to the villa, where she'd turn out the light and lie face up on her mattress before Vinny and Eleni came home.

In the morning, before either of them was up, she would go to the cove and wait. She wanted to get there before Annie, so that when the child ran down the steps, the first thing she would see would be the results of their collaboration.

(*'You'll be able to call yourself an artist then, Annie. It'll be your first ever show!'*)

The chapel had much to recommend it as the perfect darkroom for her experiment. On the other hand, there were a number of things that made it the last place to go on an August afternoon in the Peloponnese, with the chemicals she was using, poured out into a row of open buckets.

In the end, Ruthie went no further than applying the liquid light.

It was an hour or more drying, and by the time it had she was already dead.

It's the preparations she made for what would happen after that suggest she had no sense of what she was doing.

> 5.   *When you're sure the square of tape is stuck back on properly, run home and forget about it all until tomorrow. Then, first thing in the morning, come back to the cove and I'll show you. You'll be amazed, I promise! Come as early as you can. I'll be waiting!*

This instruction to Annie to meet her must have meant she believed she'd survive her own experiment. And because such a belief could only have been held by someone incapable of rational thought, she must have been so herself.

Under normal circumstances she would have understood, for example, what would be the effect of taking her paintbrush from the altar with one hand, and then with the other, reaching out for the first of the canisters and, holding it to a point just beneath her clavicle, tipping it against herself, gently.

The heat had clogged the liquid light just a little, and at first attempt it was sluggish, like gravy that's been left for a day. Then it flowed and she kept the paintbrush moving, so the rivulets of white were distributed evenly over her breasts and the whole of her chest and her stomach, sweeping just clear of her pubic hair and coating the tops of her thighs before being caught again and brushed back up, ensuring a thicker surface onto which the image could be projected.

Had she been thinking straight, she'd have known that sitting there in that heat, cleaned and abraded and coated in silver and salt, would have been enough, even without the fumes that rose from the buckets beneath her. On top of the action of the emulsion on her already broken skin, she'd have realised that the processing of the print, with the sponging and pouring-on of chemicals, would inevitably have caused her further injury: there would be some burning (more than mere sensation), and as well as the consequent scarring, it was probable there would be a piercing of both the outer and the inner epidermis, followed by a leaching of chemicals directly into her bloodstream. She'd also have understood that the concentration levels were sufficient, at the least, to disrupt the proper functioning of her digestive and nervous systems, and at the most, to kill her.

While her primary concerns were as to the success or otherwise of the process (would the liquid light adhere, or, when she flooded it with chemicals, would it rise and separate, taking the image with it?), it's inconceivable that these risks weren't among the ones she turned over on her way to the chapel, only to set them aside in favour of a clarity of mind.

What is less certain is whether, in coming up with her plan, she'd given any thought to the effect of taping over the hole in the door, which, as well as acting as the chapel's sole light source, provided its only ventilation, the window having been shut tight, and fixed around the edges with thick black tape.

In the beginning there was the acetate and the vinegar, then there was the formaldehyde and the ammonium rising from the buckets. She'd become high almost straight away, and wasn't afraid when she felt the back of her throat begin to burn; the euphoria masked the pain a little, as it intensified.

The first few minutes after taping over the door had felt no worse than the sensations brought on by cleaning a bathroom, if the window is closed and the bleach is sprayed on neat. The initial sharpness in her nostrils, and the way her eyes watered, reminded her of being in the darkroom with her father, when she was very young.

She was made happy by the memory, and felt no resistance to what she was beginning to experience. When she'd coated herself in liquid light, and was waiting for it to dry, she wasn't at all scared by the searing inside her chest, nor by the blistering of her skin as the heat rose, and the fumes, unable to find the slightest crack to escape through, combined to a cocktail in her lungs and in the cavities of her skull.

At about half past three, drawing her hand across her stomach and over her chest to check if the emulsion was drying, she entered the last minutes of consciousness.

Almost at the end, the pain became an embrace, as though someone was holding her, having first wrapped her in a blanket of broken glass. And because this pain acted as a release, somehow, from another pain she'd lived with as long as she could remember, she felt lighter in her mind and glad for it.

In the moment before the schism in her brain that stopped her neurons firing, there was a click, and the door to the chapel opened.

She raised her head and saw a man there, blocking out the light.

When he took his first step towards her, Ruthie recognised her father.

'Why did you stay away, Roo?'

She tried to reach out, but there wasn't the strength in her arms.

'I've missed you,' he said, taking another step. 'Why did you wait so long?'

'I thought of you,' she said. 'All this time, I thought of you.'

She tried again to reach out, but he was already turning, and she could see him only as a silhouette.

She stayed as she was, breathing in the hot, quiet darkness. She noticed, without noticing, that her temperature was rising still, and her skin was burning on the inside. Even her eyeballs felt hot: a kind of thudding pulsing heat she could hear as well as feel.

Drowsy now, she let her chin drop to her chest. Her jaw hung slack and her mouth filled with blood and bile, which slipped between her teeth and onto her lower lip. She half tried to wipe away the emulsion that had run onto her thighs, dabbing at her belly and her pubic hair until her arm came to rest on the altar.

Then she closed her eyes and waited, listening for a child's hand, knocking on the door.

Ruthie had never so much as imagined the possibility that Annie, granted a last-minute reprieve, might be taken to the circus with her brother.

Nor, then, could she have envisaged how, as the last of the evening sun left the cove and her letter was caught in the lap of a wave, her words would be lifted from the page: unfound, unread, unattended to by anyone.

A few hours after Ruthie's death, Annie's mother called from inside that dinner was nearly ready.

Annie jumped in her chair, remembering.

There still might be time, she thought, to slip away and run through the grove to the courtyard and say to Ruthie, 'I'm sorry! I'm sorry I didn't come but they said I could go to the circus after all. It was amazing! Everything in it was amazing,' and, 'Did you go swimming?' and, 'Did you try to make my photograph again? Did it work this time? I can't look at it now, though. I have to go straight back because my mum said dinner's nearly ready and they'll notice I'm not there.'

But then her father and Edward were play-fighting in the dust, and she watched them. When they fetched a ball, she stood beside the fig tree for piggy in the middle, and forgot about Ruthie altogether. By the time her mother called, 'It's ready! Who's going to help me carry it out?' she'd gone back to her crossword and was buried in it.

Edward and Michael went in to get the food. At that exact moment Annie found an 'n', and an 'e', and a 'd'. Slipping from her chair, she took her crossword in to show her family.

Halfway through dinner, she decided she would take it to Ruthie in the morning. She'd let her see that she'd finished it, then she'd tell her about the circus. She'd say she hadn't realised people could jump so high or dance so fast, or fly through the air on a trapeze, nor had she ever seen a tiger, not running loose like that, right in front of your eyes.

The family was booked on the first flight from Kalamata. They drove from the grove before the cockcrow, and Annie hardly thought of Ruthie. Half asleep and half awake, her mind was homeward-bound and focused on what to do first: unpack her things or run next door to see her best friend. When she looked from the rear window and caught a glimpse of the villa, she wondered, fleetingly, about asking her father to stop the car so she could go in to say goodbye, but then she thought better of it, not knowing how to explain.

At about 10 p.m., Vinny and Eleni parked behind the villa. Eleni went ahead to put a lamp in the courtyard. Vinny unpacked the car, coming after with their things. She found Eleni by the fountain looking up at Ruthie's room.

Inside, Eleni prepared some supper, while Vinny stood at the stairs and called softly, 'Ruthie, are you awake? Roo, sweetheart, we're home.'

'Louder. She won't hear you.'

'I don't want to wake her. If she's already asleep.'

'She never goes to bed this early. She'll still be up, you know she will.'

'Where, though?' Vinny said. 'Where is she?'

The villa was all in darkness. Vinny went from room to room, opening and closing the doors, switching on the lights and off again.

Coming to the kitchen, she found Eleni at the table, with the food laid out.

Vinny said she'd rather wait: she'd left messages that morning, telling Ruthie when they'd be home. It would be better, she said, if the three of them ate together, since that was what she'd promised.

Eleni said that with the moon so bright, Ruthie had probably gone for a swim, and might be out for ages. Or she was somewhere in the grove, and hadn't heard the car. Either way, she would understand if they started without her: it was late, and they had travelled a long way.

When Vinny insisted, Eleni took off her apron and said she would light her candle for Panagiotis: if she left it much longer, he would think she had abandoned him. Vinny should change, she said, or have a rest. Ruthie would be there by the time Eleni came back, and they could do as Vinny wanted.

'Vee-Vee, please. You mustn't be like this. Your sister is a grown-up.'

'I know,' Vinny said. 'I'm sorry.'

When Eleni had gone, Vinny took a torch and jogged down the steps to the villa's cove. She waited, craning her neck to watch for any movement in the water. Then the clouds rolled across the moon, and she shivered and went in.

On the path to the chapel, Eleni glanced for the moon. When she saw the clouds come in, darker and thicker than they should have been, she had a sense of something untoward. It was only the tiniest flicker of an idea, and it went as soon as it came. She looked at the path, noticing the way her torch played on the stones. When her tummy grumbled she picked up her pace, thinking of the supper that was waiting on the side.

A half-minute later, an owl swooped from a tree, close enough for her to see its eyes. As she missed her footing and stumbled, a chill spread across her back and she knew something was wrong.

At the chapel door she reached up, meaning to place her finger in the hole at its centre.

Tonight, her childish gesture was rejected.

Raising her torch and seeing a small piece of tape had been fixed over the hole, she felt her heart stop. She opened the door and stood back, overwhelmed by the fumes that hit her.

Later, she let the torch play on Ruthie's body.

She'd fallen to one side as she died. Slumped on the altar, her torso was coated in a mixture of emulsion and vomit. The liquid light had set hard and bruises showed through; dark stains on her midriff. Her mouth was open and her tongue hung out, black and hard and shrunken. Blood was caked on her chin and underneath her eyes, and it was drying in patches around her ears.

Turning from the altar, Eleni heard the door to the chapel swing shut. When she held up the torch to find the handle, her eye was caught instead by the negative, taped over the hole.

Holding the small square up, and shining her torch directly at it, Eleni half shut her eyes in an attempt to see more clearly.

There was nothing, though. Just a piece of plastic that was shinier on one side than the other. Puzzled, she lowered her torch. In the same motion, still holding up the negative, she turned, meaning to blow out the oil lamp.

With the light behind it now, the image revealed itself. She held her breath and looked at it, bringing it closer to the lamp and squinting.

A child with close-cropped hair stood on the work surface in Max's lightroom.

She was wearing a bikini and standing with her back against the wall.

Her body was black, and the wall behind was white. There were white holes for eyes, and white lines on her chest and her arms that stood out clearly.

Her head was tilted to one side, but her gaze was centre-on so her ghost-eyes stared at the camera.

Looking closer still, Eleni saw the gilded feather-clock that had hung there since Ruthie's childhood, and assumed Max to have been the photographer. Not recognising Annie, nor knowing anything of her meetings with Ruthie, she mistook the child for Ruthie as she had been in her girlhood, and was reminded of certain events which had taken place at the villa one summer, a long time ago.

For the whole of the time that had passed since then, she'd forbidden herself to think of them. Tonight, though, she looked at the girl on the work surface, and a sequence of silent images flashed through her mind.

Some of them were scenes which had occurred in the courtyard, or in the Lightroom, and which she'd either witnessed for herself, or been participant in. Others were reported to her by Ruthie, so that Eleni had explained them away as bad dreams, or as accidents: Ruthie must have been stung by a jellyfish, or had hurt herself on the rocks by the water's edge. Or perhaps she'd fallen, having run too fast in the grove.

When the sequence had played right through, Eleni slipped the negative in her pocket. Then she blew out the oil lamp and left, closing the chapel door behind her.

Before long, the old woman would go to the villa and find Vinny. First, though, she stepped through a gate in the boundary wall and picked her way through the trees. At the water's edge, she knelt and took a small box of matches from her pocket. Striking one, she held the negative to the flame and watched it burn, so that no one would see what she had seen.

While Eleni knelt by the water, Vinny climbed the stairs to the villa's top floor.

Pausing midway, she was aware of a sudden movement beside her face. The air shifted, as though someone had walked past her. She reached out, but there was no one.

In the Lightroom, the glass mobile was moving about in the breeze. Vinny reached up to hold one of the glass discs, to stop it turning.

She stood for a moment, with her hand above her head, until the breeze dropped and she let it fall.

She walked around the room then, not knowing what she was looking for.

She'd seen the empty wall as she came in, and had noticed the absence of *The Road to Falicon* only subconsciously. She had a sense that there was something different about the room, and it occurred to her that someone else had been there just before her, someone other than Ruthie.

Picking up clothes from the floor and folding them, she dismissed the notion as absurd, then she saw a photography book, open and face down on Ruthie's pillow. Beside it was a tiny piece of paper, so scribbled over with tiny script and so covered with crossings-out and ticks and exclamation marks that Vinny could read none of it. Turning it over, there was a list of chemicals that was clearer, and next to them, what looked to be a series of measurements, which meant nothing to her.

She sat on the mattress. The sheets looked to have been left on for weeks. There was a patina that was hard in places, like a part of a linoleum floor that's been walked on more than any other.

'It's something I can do, at least, while I'm waiting,' she said out loud.

She brought clean sheets and stripped the bed.

'Something nice for you to come back to.'

Her hands were trembling and she struggled.

'Why you won't let Eleni come up here and clean, I can't imagine. I'm not going to make a habit of it, mind, so don't go getting any ideas.'

When she tried to take off the second pillowcase, she couldn't.

'I'm doing this one thing for you, Ruthie-Roo, then I'm going to the cove to call you in once and for all, whether you like it or not!' She tugged at the pillow. 'If I can't find you in the water then I suppose I'll just have to trawl round the grove with a bloody torch. Eleni's probably right. You're bound to be out there somewhere.'

Tugging harder, she felt something catch on the inside, something neither pillow nor case. She sat down to pull it out, and when she saw that it was a photograph, she was still.

Black and white and A4-sized, it was an image of Sophie she'd never seen before.

She was lying in bed at Pennerton. Her daughters were cradled in her arms. They were both of them very little, and fast asleep. Vinny looked to be no more than four, and Ruthie was still a baby. Sophie's head rested lightly on Ruthie's, and her eyes looked straight at the camera.

A memory surfaced then.

Of her little sister, Ruthie, nestling her face against their mother's and breathing with her. Wanting to join in, Vinny climbs into the bed and burrows right into her mother, who holds Vinny with her free arm and turns her face away from Ruthie so that Ruthie wriggles on the pillow and, as Vinny stretches across to kiss her, buries her face in their mother's hair.

Her mother, half in sleep, says, 'I love you.'

Her father leans in, and there's the sound of the shutter closing.

The memory starts to fade before it's formed. In a half-minute, Eleni will stand behind her and say, 'Vinny. Vee, I have something to tell you,' and it will disappear altogether.

For now, standing and looking, Vinny will glance at Max's inscription: *My Girls, at Pennerton, July 1965.*

There is Eleni's footstep on the stair, and Vinny looks again at her mother, looking back at her. Sleepy eyed and half-smiling, Sophie's mouth is open. She is forming a word, or laughing, and Vinny is trying to work out which.

Then Eleni speaks, and everything goes.

20 AN EPILOGUE

Max Hollingbourne (1929–2002), *The Road to Falicon*, 1973.
Gelatin silver print. Victoria and Albert Museum, London. Gift of
Lavinia Hollingbourne, in memory of her sister, Ruth.

ACKNOWLEDGEMENTS

The Road to Falicon (p. 373) was taken by Florence Dollé in the south of France in April 2007. As well as giving her permission for that photograph to appear and be credited to Max, Florence gave me a series of darkroom lessons, and showed me Nice and Villefranche. I'm grateful to her for those things, and for reading drafts and redrawing my map-on-an-envelope.

I would like to thank Darian Leader for his suggestions as the story came together, and for telling me it made sense to Ruthie. I was given lots of help with *Silver and Salt* by several people. Thank you to Sarah Addenbrooke, Caroline Anderson, Melaina Barnes, Matthew Brotherton, Dee Byrne, Mara Carlyle, Tiffany Charrington, Chris Choa, David Cosway, Fotini and Eleni Dimitreas, Andrew Dobbin, Susan Dowell, Pamela Dymott, Keith Dymott, Adam Foulds, Terry Glover, Tracy Hargreaves, Sarah Irvin, Catherine Johnson, Charis Karagianni, Svetlana Kropp, Andy Swee Aun Lim, Paul Magrath, Simon Marshall, Rachael McGill, Maile Meloy, Nick Mercer, Natalie Meyjes, Mark Millward, Anna and Fotis Paliatseas, Angela Peyton,

Charles Peyton, Rebecca Peyton, Tim Pozzi, Susanne Rook, Roli Ross, Merijn Royaards, Simon Scardifield, Kate Summerscale, Iain Sutherland, Sally Tudor, Michael Whitworth, Pete Wickstead, Robert Worley, Brendan Wright, and Nathasha Xavier.

To my amazing editors, Beth Coates at Jonathan Cape and John Glusman at W. W. Norton, and to my wonderful agent, Anna Webber at United Agents, I give heartfelt thanks.

At Jonathan Cape and Vintage, I'm grateful to Katherine Fry, Victoria Murray-Browne, Matt Broughton, Lily Richards, Greg Clowes, Neil Bradford, Nick Skidmore, and Sally Sargeant. At United Agents, I'm grateful to Seren Adams. At W. W. Norton, I would like to thank Alexa Pugh, Eleen Cheung, Lynn Buckley, Louise Mattarelliano, Lydia Brents, Elizabeth Riley, Rebecca Homiski, Nancy Palmquist, and Amy Medeiros.

Neither the Hollingbourne villa at Kardamyli, nor Pennerton House at Pennerton, nor Auntie Bea's house at Pilgrim's Lane, exists. For Ruthie and Vinny's olive grove, I drew on Patrick Leigh Fermor's essay 'Sash Windows Opening on the Foam' from *Words of Mercury* (John Murray, 2004), and his book *Mani, Travels in the Southern Peloponnese* (John Murray, 1958), as well as George Hassanakos's *Meet the Mani in 300 Pictures,* Charlotte Higgins's *It's All Greek to Me* (Short Books, 2008) and Carola Scupham's translation of Kadio Kolymva's *The Upper Side of the World* (Armos Publications, 2013). I'm indebted to the Ponireas family for their warm hospitality. Photographer Costas Zissis kindly showed me the work of Dimitris A. Harissiadis, at the Rizarios Exhibition Centre at Monodendri, Zagoria, in 2015. Harissiadis's print *Portrait, 1938* is incorporated within the book's British cover, and for that I'm grateful to Georgia Imsiridou and Aliki Tsirgialou at the Benaki Museum. For the English parts of the novel, and for Max's career, I relied on the staff of the British Library, and am particularly thankful to Victor Bristoll and the reference staff of the newsroom at St Pancras. Julie Melrose at the Local History Centre of Islington Heritage Services helped me with background to the 1959 staging of *Rusalka* at Sadler's Wells. Matthew Brotherton kindly allowed me to draw from his grandmother's journals, written in Kent while Europe went to war. Ruthie's summer snowflakes are from Georgina F. Jackson's *Shropshire Word-book* (Trübner & Co, 1879), and Max's 'pigeon on a windowsill' anecdote comes from Yasmine Alwan's 'My Friend Said' (*NOON*, 2005). The last words of the book are taken from Sharon Olds' poem 'Everything,' in her collection *One Secret Thing* (Jonathan Cape, 2009).

For home and hearth and fruitful conversation while I was writing, thank you to Angela, Rebecca, Charlie and Terry at Hope House; to my French family at Luchon, Morgan, Artémis, and Carine; and to Andrew at Clun.

Thank you, Tim, for everything, and especially for Frisbee at sunset.